D0042102

The Better Angels of Our Nature

★ *A Novel* ★ WITHDRAWN

S. C. GYLANDERS

CONTRA COSTA COUNTY LIBRARY

RANDOM HOUSE

NEW YORK

3 1901 04072 2938

This is a work of historical fiction. Apart from the well-known actual people, events, and locales that figure in the narrative, all names, characters, places, and incidents are the products of the author's imagination or are used fictitiously. Any resemblance to current events or locales, or to living persons, is entirely coincidental.

Copyright © 2006 by S. C. Gylanders

All rights reserved.

Published in the United States by Random House, an imprint of The Random House Publishing Group, a division of Random House, Inc., New York.

RANDOM HOUSE and colophon are registered trademarks of Random House, Inc.

Library of Congress Cataloging-in-Publication Data
Gylanders, S. C.
The better angels of our nature / S. C. Gylanders.
p.   cm.
ISBN-10: 1-4000-6514-3
ISBN-13: 978-1-4000-6514-1
1. Sherman, William T. (William Tecumseh), 1820–1891—Fiction.   2. United States—History—Civil War, 1861–1865—Fiction.
I. Title.
PR6107.Y58B48 2006
823'.92—dc22

Printed in the United States of America on acid-free paper
www.atrandom.com

2 4 6 8 9 7 5 3 1

First U.S. Edition

This book is dedicated to:

My husband, Jed, a one-man support group, who untiringly and patiently chauffeured me around every Sherman and relevant Civil War site in the U.S.A.

You drove the enemy from the field, kept the tent over our heads and the hardtack on our table. If not for you, I would never have completed the journey. You are the great love of my life.

In your hands, my dissatisfied fellow-countrymen, and not in mine, is the momentous issue of civil war. The Government will not assail you. You can have no conflict without being yourselves the aggressors. You have no oath registered in heaven to destroy the Government, while I shall have the most solemn one to "preserve, protect, and defend it."

I am loath to close. We are not enemies, but friends. We must not be enemies. Though passion may have strained it must not break our bonds of affection. The mystic chords of memory, stretching from every battlefield and patriot grave to every living heart and hearthstone all over this broad land, will yet swell the chorus of the Union, when again touched, as surely they will be, by the better angels of our nature.

—ABRAHAM LINCOLN, *First Inaugural Address*, MARCH 1861

The legitimate object of war is a more perfect peace.

—GENERAL WILLIAM TECUMSEH SHERMAN, JULY 20, 1865

Contents

★ ★ ★ ★

The Better Angels of Our Nature

1

"I could a tale unfold . . ."

★ ★ ★ ★

Have you seen Sherman? It is necessary to see him in order to realize the Norse make up of the man—the hauteur, noble, yet demo-
cratic. . . . Try to picture Sherman—seamy, sinewy, in style—a bit
of stern open air made up in the image of a man.

—WALT WHITMAN, "Of the Corps and Generals,"
Walt Whitman's Civil War, 1881

To the blue-clad men who'd spent the past three days pouring off the
transports at Pittsburg Landing, and trudging inland to pitch their tents
around a small log church called Shiloh Meeting House that chilly
spring of 1862, it must have seemed inconceivable that civil war had
gripped their promising young nation for almost a year.

The months had slipped by and with them their innocence. Next
month would see the first anniversary of Beauregard's firing on Fort
Sumter and here *they* were bivouacked on the west side of the Tennessee
more miles than they cared to think about from their homes and loved
ones in the North.

Maybe it would soon be over. After the ignominious defeat of First
Bull Run, the Federals had tasted some recent success. The U.S.S. *Mon-*

itor had battled the *Merrimack* to a standoff in Norfolk, Virginia. General Buell's army had flushed the Rebs out of Kentucky and then taken Nashville. General Burnside had captured Roanoke Island, General Curtis had defeated Earl Van Dorn at Pea Ridge, and General Pope was about to invade the uninspiringly named Island No. 10, in the swamps of the Missouri. As for Sam Grant, his victories at forts Henry and Donelson were being hailed as "the turning point."

The only fly in the Federal ointment right now was George McClellan. That very week Abe Lincoln himself had told the newspapers, "Mr. Joseph E. Johnston is falling back in Virginia and General McClellan is after him," but these men knew the army in the east wasn't after *anyone*. It was going around in circles, like its leader.

They may have lost much of their innocence, but they still had hope. Maybe the war could be won right here in the West, where there were some good men *and* some good commanders.

William Tecumseh Sherman was not a handsome man. Yet his features—the sharp, arching nose; the firm, set mouth; the coarse, cinnamon-colored beard; and red hair—were striking in the extreme. The six-foot, rail-thin general with the almost feminine narrowness that belied a muscular build was a man blessed, or perhaps cursed, with a peculiar nervous energy that knew no cessation. Every action, every gesture, every thought and word bespoke intellect and vigor. Careless of dress, shiny brass buttons and gold bullion held no attraction for this man. His shabby field officer's coat was stained with ash; his boots were caked in mud and his hat, without cord or badge, was of the wool slouch variety, commonly referred to as shapeless, since it lived up to, or rather down to, its name. From under the narrow brim the Ohioan's most striking feature, eyes of an indeterminate color, fixed the world with the intensity of a bird of prey.

By suppertime the rain had finally stopped, though a threat of more hung in the damp air above the bare hills, and the ground beneath many an army blanket was hard with frost. Nevertheless, rain or no rain Sherman would take his nightly stroll.

As he walked, he reflected with satisfaction upon this good high ground, with plenty of room for drilling and exercise. It was an excellent site for the Federals to camp when its main objective was Corinth, Mississippi, and the Rebel force gathering there only twenty miles away. Once captured, this railroad town would leave Memphis naked, and open the Mississippi for hundreds of miles. Sherman knew all this, since with characteristic thoroughness, he had made a personal reconnaissance of the area.

By now, the division commander with the distracted look in his eye and a half-smoked "segar" protruding from the left side of his mouth was a familiar sight to his soldiers. They would call out to him as he passed. A disembodied growl and an inclining of the large head would, invariably, greet a friendly "Evenin', Gen'al." Not that Sherman was distant or cold; on the contrary, any honest soldier would find in him the easiest of men to approach for a fair hearing. It was simply that such an active mind as his was constantly occupied, constantly engaged in thought, never at peace, never in repose. His was a truly tense soul.

This night as he walked in the direction of the distant picket lines on the Hamburg-Purdey road his ever-racing thoughts were interrupted not by the greetings of his men, or the strains of a familiar song, but by a muffled rustling in the bushes. Drawing his sidearm, he strode unafraid over the tangle of fallen timber, holding the branches aside with his free arm and demanding, red-faced, "Make yourself known. Speak up, or I'll shoot."

There, kneeling on the wet earth with bowed red head, was a small figure, a will-o'-the-wisp in the oversized uniform of an infantryman.

Sherman took a step closer. "Who are you? What are you doing here? Have you fallen out of the sky?" He grasped the boy by the chin and raised his head. "Answer me."

The boy stared at him, eyes wide with an undisguised devotion that for a second left the usually articulate man lost for words. He said, "Are you hurt? You should not be out here alone. The enemy have cavalry and pickets scattered all around."

"*You're* out here alone, sir," the boy now said boldly.

"That's different. I know the dangers; you evidently do not, why else would you be wandering around in the dark?"

The young soldier, who was beginning to feel very cold, could not restrain a shiver. He was wearing only a blouse, the sleeves of which hung down over his fingers, and there were but two buttons holding it together across his narrow chest. Sherman peered closely at his cheeks, smooth and freckled, cheeks that had never seen a razor. Why, he was nothing more than a child, with a wide, full mouth and a strong chin, punctuated by a deep cleft. His pants, of such ample proportions they could have accommodated a sack of potatoes without straining a seam, were held up with a length of coarse rope.

Sherman's breath, a potent mix of whiskey and cigar smoke, appeared to make the young soldier dizzy, for he momentarily closed his eyes and seemed to sway.

"Get yourself back to your camp," Sherman ordered, "and into your blanket before you freeze to death or the enemy carries you off. Go on!"

As he turned, the young soldier sprang up before him: "Sir—may I go with you?"

"With *me*? Certainly not. What regiment are you with, my boy?"

"None, sir, I came here to serve you." The enormous eyes, like the stained-glass blue of a cathedral, round and shiny as military buttons, watched him with an intensity that might have been disconcerting to a lesser mortal. However, the gaze was without guile, and he had as pleasing a countenance as the general had seen for many a year.

Sherman laughed his sudden snatching laughter, laughter that was somehow shocking, coming as it did from such a grim and dignified personage. The sound itself was an identical twin of his hoarse, basso voice, guttural and rasping, starting deep within his chest, and building up with every gasp of air sucked into his lungs until it burst forth possessed of all the force, energy, and enthusiasm that characterized every aspect of the man. "You came here to serve me, ah?" he asked gruffly, giving the boy a kind of cuff, but only gently, around the ear.

"Yes sir."

"Where is your equipment?" Sherman asked, and tugged at the boy's collar. "Your musket? A soldier should never be without his musket. What would you do if the Rebels attacked?"

"I have no musket, sir, I have no equipment."

"Did your quartermaster sergeant not issue you with any?" Sherman made a noise of disgust, but the young soldier could not say if it was directed at him or at the quartermaster sergeant. Before he could reply, the Ohioan had marched off with the brisk order, "Follow me."

Five minutes later, when this particular quartermaster sergeant was rudely aroused from his bleary-eyed beauty sleep, he burst from his tent, a mad bull cursing all God's creatures, but most specifically the man who had so thoughtlessly disturbed him. Then he recognized his commander and fell instead to apologizing with the same energy he had invested in his cursing. Sherman brushed him aside to demand brusquely, "Sergeant Wiley, issue this boy with blanket, sack jacket, knapsack, and all accruements."

"Yes sir, first thing in the morning, sir."

"No, Sergeant, not first thing in the morning. *Now!*"

"Certainly, sir, right away, sir." The sergeant looked at the young soldier with eyes that warned swift and savage reprisals when they were alone.

To the young soldier the general said, "In the morning see the ordnance officer in your company, ask him to issue you with musket and ammunition—sixty rounds of minié cartridges—percussion caps. They go in a box on your belt, which this sergeant will give you."

"Yes sir, thank you, sir." The young boy shivered as he spoke.

"Find yourself somewhere warm to sleep, beside a fire, but not too close. I have known men sleep too close to a fire, fall asleep and burn themselves. Isn't that so, Sergeant?"

"Whatever you say, Gen'al." The sergeant, nursing a punishing hangover, wished both commander and boy would be consumed by fire, and the flames of hell themselves would not have sufficed.

"Make the acquaintance of some older men," Sherman advised. "They'll teach you what you need to know to survive. Keep your musket by you, and stay around camp at night unless you are on picket duty. Then there's safety in numbers," he added emphatically, wreaths of smoke enveloping his large red head as he gave the young soldier's cheek a gentle slap.

"Sir, will you wait for me!" the boy called hopefully, but the commander was already gone, swallowed up by the darkness. He looked up at the sergeant's cruel red face and could not help uttering a howl of pain as his ear was twisted viciously.

"Wake me in the middle of the night, will yer? Scabby little son of a bitch—we'll see 'bout that—I'll make yer sorry yer mother ever suckled yer. I'll break that scrawny back of yers."

When the boy caught up with the general, he found him before the dying embers of a campfire, kicking at the smoldering ashes with the tip of his boot, while his mind seemed to be elsewhere, perhaps on the battle to come. As the boy approached clanking and clanging, the Ohioan turned abruptly. "What in the devil—!"

"I was trying to stay with you, sir, but I don't think I can go another step—" Bent-shouldered, the boy looked up pleadingly at the commander from under the brim of a brand-new Hardy hat complete with gold-bullion cord, a hat that only the bend of his ears and the thickness of his curls prevented from falling over his eyes. He was laden down with what the general had called "accruements." They hung from every part of his body and clothing. Much, it was true, useful to a soldier in the field—tin cups, tin plates, a coffee pot the size of a small bucket, skillet, drum canteen, sewing kit, eating utensils, belt and ball pouch, cartridge box and sling. On his back was a knapsack; slung across the top was a woolen blanket roll and a rubber-lined blanket and inside was a large cake of evil-smelling soap, a wedge of chewing tobacco, and two pairs of hard woolen socks knitted by some elderly matron of Maine. The quartermaster sergeant had been true to his word. Oh, yes, much that was necessary, but also much that wasn't, such as a pair of spiked riding spurs and a pair of enlisted man's shoulder scales!

"Well, my boy, now you *look* like a soldier in the field," Sherman declared before he tossed his cigar stub into the fire and walked on.

Actually, the boy, laden down as he was, looked less like a soldier in the field and more like a beast of burden. "Sir—" He struggled after the general, clattering and banging like a portable galley, breathing noisily as if his lungs would burst. "Sir—will you . . . teach me to be a good soldier?"

Sherman stopped again and turned around. He would have lost his patience had the soldier not been buried under this mountain of equipment. However, it was difficult to be angry with someone when all you could see of him were two big round eyes. Besides, there was something else, the boy's coloring reminded him of his own son, Willy, just seven years old and already taking a keen interest in his father's military career. The thought might certainly have occurred to the general that if Willy were in a war far from home, might not the father pray that another commander take the time to teach *his* son some basic rules of survival? "Five minutes," he said suddenly, "and what you do not understand the first time of explaining I shall not repeat."

"*Yes sir!*" the young soldier agreed enthusiastically, managing a broad grin despite the pain between his shoulder blades. Had he not been on his last legs he would have broken into a run to catch up with the rapidly disappearing Ohioan. But he moved as fast as he could, struggling manfully with every step, the tin plate and large coffee pot banging remorselessly against his bony knees. Nevertheless, he soon fell behind as he drifted into a group of men concentrating on a game of chuck-a-luck in the light of their campfire.

"Cut that goddamn hullabaloo!" one of them bellowed as he passed. "Kain't hear maself think."

"Damn your eyes!" shouted a second soldier, while a third tossed a brogan that struck the boy squarely in the tin plate hanging from his sack jacket. "Nex' tayme'll be a bullet, yer goddamn shit-house rat!"

"Why you dirty bag-a-bones country boy, stop that goddamn noise!" came an order from one of the tents.

"Lord a'mighty, it's the whole goddamned Reb army!"

"I guess that's one way a scarin' Johnny Reb" was a wry comment.

"I reckon they can hear yer all the way to Richmond, boy. Ain't yer got no place to bed down? Yer lookin' ter git yerself hog-tied."

A third man stuck out his leg and this portable cook's galley went crashing headlong to the ground amid a cacophony of tin cup, plate, and coffee pot.

"Haw, haw, haw!" came the chorus of laughter.

Just when the boy was beginning to think he had lost the commander in the maze of canvas streets, every tent identical, from out of the darkness was heard the hoarse command, "I'm over here, and for pity's sake, cease your noise, you will rouse the entire camp!"

Over the entrance of the large wall tent, fluttering occasionally in the cold night air, was the headquarters designation flag: Fifth Division, Army of the Tennessee. Beside this tent was another, smaller wall tent, where the commander himself was bivouacked. The headquarters guard, all but asleep on their feet, jumped to attention at Sherman's approach and the sentinels marching back and forth moved with renewed vigor, stifling a yawn. The youthful lieutenant of the guard merely stared in astonishment.

"Leave your equipment neatly stacked on the ground outside," Sherman ordered.

"Yes sir—thank you, sir—" The boy-soldier made a groaning sound and finally, gratefully, collapsed under the weight.

Anyone not completely fixated by the sight of the boy upended on his back like a helpless turtle wobbling upon his shell, legs kicking air, might have spotted the momentary smile that lit the commander's stern features as he rushed to free the trapped boy from the straps of the knapsack that were cutting into his narrow shoulders. When the officer of the guard, blond fuzz on pale cheeks passing for a man's beard, continued to look on in speechless astonishment, Sherman was fierce.

"Damn you, Lieutenant, don't just stand there, lend a hand, sir, lend a hand!"

"Yes sir." The transfixed lieutenant came instantly to life, doing what he could to disentangle boy from blankets, knapsacks, straps, and cartridge boxes. He then watched in curiosity tinged with envy as the young soldier followed the general into his tent.

"Have you had your supper?" Sherman wanted to know.

The young soldier hesitated.

"Well?" said the general sharply. "When was the last time you ate? Was it so long ago you can't recall?" Sherman puffed at his cigar and laughed. "Well, it's no wonder you can't carry an infantryman's load!"

The young soldier sat on a cracker box before the folding table and ate the chicken and sweet corn that the general had ordered his cook,

Horatio, to dig out of the stores. Although prodded into wakefulness from what might have been a sweet dream of freedom, the talkative old Negro, with tufts of white hair on the back of his head like cotton balls, displayed none of the resentment of the quartermaster sergeant, but simply shuffled back to his blanket with the young soldier's hearty thanks still ringing in his ears. Now the boy tasted the thick dark liquid in the cup and wrinkled up his rather shapeless child's nose.

"I never imagined it would taste so bitter," he said.

"*Imagined?* Have you never tasted coffee before?"

"No sir, never—" the boy replied, his mouth full of chicken and sweet corn.

"Well, don't take too much sugar in your coffee. You'll get dysentery."

Sherman was lighting a fresh cigar. Again, his mind was elsewhere. His bony, thickly veined hand had grabbed up a letter from the table and his deep-set, piercing eyes were now traveling wildly across the pages as the nails of his other hand made a scratching sound across his coarse beard. He stood up suddenly and started to march the short distance between table and tent flap and back again, puffing away noisily at his cigar, rubbing his beard the wrong way and murmuring to himself in a manner that made the boy guess that the contents of the letter irritated him. This man was easily irritated, prone to excitations, temper swings, and prompt changes of mood that could raise him as high as the heavens and cast him down to the depths of despair. The boy drew in a deep breath, inhaling cigar smoke and whiskey, the smell of sweat, stale and manly, and the aroma of physical and moral courage that hung in the air and clung to the general's crumpled uniform.

When the boy opened his eyes, the Ohioan had stopped pacing and was watching *him*.

The boy cleared his throat. "Please, sir, may I ask what it is I am eating?"

"Why, it's chicken! Have you never eaten chicken before either? No coffee *and* no chicken? You haven't lived." The Ohioan was laughing at him.

"I think it very fine."

"I'm sure Horatio would be gratified."

" 'There are more things in heaven and earth, Horatio, than are dreamt of in your philosophy.' "

"What? What did you say?" After having briefly resumed his marching, he now stopped again and fixed the boy with those glittering eyes. "*You* know *Hamlet*? Well, knowing it is one thing, understanding it, that, my boy, is another thing."

"I think I would understand it far more if I saw it performed on a stage."

Evidently, Sherman approved this reply, since he made a noise that sounded like approval.

"Here, here, how can you hold your knife and fork that way—?" He grabbed up the boy's hands one after the other and turned back the sleeves with a roughness that belied the compassion behind the gesture.

"Thank you, sir." The boy looked up at him gratefully.

"Watching you laden down with all that equipment just now reminded me of the recruits I saw in Washington when I was there in June last year. Their uniforms were as various as the states and cities from which they came. Their arms were also of every pattern and caliber and they too were so loaded down with coats, haversacks, knapsacks, tents, baggage, and cooking utensils that it took from twenty-five to fifty wagons to move the camp of a regiment from one place to another." Sherman puffed and reflected. "Some of the camps had their own bakeries and cooking establishments that would have done credit to Delmonico's!" He was still laughing that strange hiccupping laughter as he sat on a camp chair on the other side of the small table, his frock coat hanging open by the side of his narrow thighs, cigar ash falling onto his already dusty vest. His old-fashioned "sideboard"-collar shirt was ringed in grime and his dickey bow had gone awry, hanging limply, as though it had given up any effort to look military. "Where do you come from, my boy?"

"Far from here, sir."

"We all come far from here. Where does your mother live?"

"I have no mother, sir, only a Father in heaven."

The boy stared at the general and the general, who had lost his own father at nine and his mother when still a young man, thought he understood.

"An orphan. Well, there are worse things."

"Such as politicians and newspapermen?" the boy suggested, knowing the general's loathing for both professions.

"Quite so," the general confirmed, smoking his cigar and laughing again. "Where were you educated?"

"I hope, sir, to learn about soldiering from you."

"We'll see, we'll see."

"Sir, I am an excellent reader, and can read to you at night when you are too weary even to hold a book. I can read to you from all your favorite writers, Robert Burns, Sir Walter Scott, Mr. Dickens. I can even read to you from your book of Shakespeare, sir, if you wish it."

"How do you *know* my favorite writers?" The general looked at his footlocker stacked high with books. "Ah—very observant. A good soldier must be observant."

"I'll rise before dawn and bring you coffee. I only want to serve you, sir."

"You can serve me best by serving your *country*."

"I want to ride into battle beside you, sir." For emphasis, as though it were a saber, not a bent eating utensil, the boy waved the fork in the air and a piece of chicken that had been hanging there precariously finally dropped into his lap. The boy retrieved it hastily and returned it to his tin plate.

"To ride into battle beside a general you must first be an officer. Have you ever fired a gun?"

"No sir, but I'm a very fast learner. Anything you teach me I will retain forever."

" 'An excellent reader' and a 'fast learner' are you? You don't lack for confidence, that's a fact." The commander seemed to make up his mind about something, since he got abruptly to his feet and, calling over his shoulder, "Wait here," left the tent.

The young soldier looked around the interior, so plain, so practical, the absolute barest of necessities, cot, campstools, small folding table, the battered wooden footlocker with his name stenciled on the lid, and the books. Well-thumbed copies of Robert Burns's collected poems, Shakespeare's *Coriolanus* and *Hamlet*, and on the table, Scott's *Rob Roy*, from which several paper markers protruded. Beside that an inkwell, a pen, and some sheets of paper, covered with his bold, assertive hand, a candleholder with the stub of a candle, the flame fluttering in a draft, by which the young soldier read several lines of the unfinished letter:

> Dearest Ellen—Let what occur you may rest assured that the devotion and affection you have exhibited in the past winter has endeared you more than ever, and that if it should so happen that I can regain my position and self respect and should Peace ever be restored I will labor hard for you and our children.

"Now we'll see just how fast you learn!" Sherman burst in, a musket in one hand, a cartridge box in the other.

"The first question is, do you know which end out of which to shoot?"

The boy grinned, screwed up his freckled nose. "Oh yes, sir."

"Then we are indeed on the way to making you a soldier. Now listen well, for your very life may depend upon it. This is a Springfield model 1861 rifled and sighted musket, which takes a .58-caliber minié ball. Do you know what a minié ball is? The men call them 'minnie' balls. Invented by Claude Minié, a Frenchman, the ball and musket, or shoulder arm, is deadly at any range up to five hundred yards. Are you listening carefully—for there will be no time for revision."

The boy repeated all he had heard so far, not at all like a parrot, so much so that his excitable, enthusiastic instructor said, "Splendid, splendid," and clapped him on his narrow back.

Without preliminaries the general swept up papers and pen, threw them onto the cot and laid cartridge, percussion cap, bullet, ramrod, on the table, identifying them one by one, as the young soldier repeated each name. He took the boy through the procedure for loading the musket. He showed him how to tear the cartridge at the corner of his mouth, pour the powder into the barrel, and ram a bullet down on top of it.

"Then," Sherman gravely instructed, "it is necessary, *absolutely* necessary, to put a percussion cap under the hammer. Unless you do this, you can pull the trigger until kingdom come without discharging your piece."

As Sherman spoke, the young soldier's gaze moved back and forth from the gun to the man's grim features. At forty-two, his dark red hair was already in retreat from the domed brow and his gaunt cheeks bore the early ravages of past failures and present anxieties. It was a face of such strength and character that the boy thought it like a canvas upon which fate would etch every moment of passion and pain that was to come, finally turning it into a flesh-and-blood monument to integrity, courage, and patriotism. The boy thought that into that suffering face every man, woman, and child in America would one day be able to gaze and know the pain of a nation at war with itself.

"At the command 'load' you will stand your rifle upright between your feet, the muzzle end in your left hand held eight inches from your body, at the same time moving the right hand to your cartridge box on your belt. There"—he indicated just about where the boy would locate it—"at 'handle cartridge' you will bring the paper-wrapped powder and bullet from the box and place the powder into the muzzle, like so, and the minié ball into the bore. Are you following every movement?" he demanded sharply, showing the boy the ball.

The boy said he was, an alert look in his eye confirming that truth.

"Then draw the rammer, which will send the bullet down the bore to sit on the powder charge. Replace the rammer and prime!" The general brought the weapon up and extended it outward from his spare frame with his left hand while with his right he pulled back the hammer to the half-cock position, explaining all as he proceeded. Then he reached into the cap pouch, removed a cap and placed it onto the nipple. "Now comes the moment of truth—*Shoulder!*" he cried loudly, took the appropriate foot stance and brought the rifle up to a vertical position at his right side, his right hand on the lock, his thumb pulling the hammer back to full cock. "*Aim!*" Up went the rifle to his right shoulder, his cheek to the butt so that he could sight between the opened *V* at the rear and over the muzzle. His finger hovered against the trigger and his hoarse voice bellowed "*Fire!*"

It was at this very moment that the tent flap was thrown aside and a well-built individual appeared, brandishing an army Colt .44, followed in close order by as many of the headquarters guard and their muskets that could squeeze into the tent. Bringing up the rear was the bemused Lieutenant Lewis.

"What in blue blazes—Gen'al—?" The tall, imposing-looking man with the pistol halted in his tracks as the commander of the Fifth Division stood there pointing a rifle at him.

Immediately Sherman brought the piece carefully to his side.

"Gall darn it, Gen'al, I thought you were being dragged outa here by Rebs."

This officer was wearing a large brown felt hat with a wide brim and a high crown of the type cowpokes wore to shield them from rain and sun. He looked as though he had just arrived from a cattle drive, only instead of leather chaps and a dust coat, he was wearing Union blue and the shoulder straps of a captain. Under the hat, his strong features had been burned permanently brown.

"Relax, Captain Jackson, there's no one here but me and this raw recruit, whom I am instructing on the loading and discharging of a firearm. We're enjoying ourselves enormously, aren't we, my boy?"

The boy, who was now standing rigidly to attention, smiled saucily at the captain and saluted. "Yes sir, *enormously*."

The officer nodded. He had known the commander too long to be surprised or alarmed by any eccentric behavior, or his fits of anxiety and rage. But it didn't stop the captain from staring suspiciously at the boy out of small, deep-set gray eyes buried beneath thick gray brows. "Darn it, Gen'al," said he tearing off that large hat, "I thought you were bein' hauled outa here by Rebs." The man had a deep, manly voice; both this and his demeanor gave the impression of someone accustomed to being obeyed without the need to raise his voice or his hand.

"Yes, yes." Sherman placed a placating hand on the taller man's arm. "So you said, Andy, so you said, sir." He turned to the headquarters guard: "Good night, gentlemen, and thank you for your vigilance."

As Sherman let the tent flap down, the lasting vision in the boy's brain was of six open-mouthed enlisted men and one incredulous lieutenant.

"Well—just so long as yer okay, Gen'al—" said Captain Jackson, still looking distrustfully at the boy out of those gray, wrinkled eyes. He tugged on his thick Western mustache, a truly impressive affair, iron-gray like his brows and his eyes and his thick collar-length hair.

"Jesse Davis," the boy said, introducing himself, though he hadn't been asked.

"Boy?" Although it seemed impossible to Jesse Davis, one small gray eye got even smaller as the captain inclined that impressive head. "Did you say *Jeff* Davis?"

"No sir." The boy laughed. "*Jesse* Davis, sir."

"*Private* Davis?" Jackson wanted to know.

The boy did something strange then. He glanced at his sleeve, devoid of any rank, as if, it seemed to Jackson, he needed to check, and said, "Yes sir, *Private* Davis."

The Hoosier then mumbled something that sounded like "Awell—" He slipped his Colt back into its worn leather holster and said good night to the general. He shot a final warning glance at the boy that made it crystal clear he wasn't going far and could be back, pistol drawn, should this *Jesse* Davis, who didn't seem to know if he was a private, turn out to be a young Rebel bushwhacker.

"Come along, Private, now it's your turn, *load and fire!*" Sherman said excitedly.

The boy now took the general through the entire exercise, repeating word for word the exact instructions, and doing it in a bright and lively manner that showed he had understood the reason for every action and had not merely learned the procedure by rote. Even then, the Ohioan could not be silent but had to interpose excitedly every few minutes with a wave of the cigar, as though he thought, or perhaps hoped, the boy needed a refresher. How long was it since he had had a room filled with eager young faces hungry for instruction? *Too damn long.*

"Splendid! Splendid! You are a fine student. You will make corporal in no time, no time at all."

"Do you really think so, sir?"

"No question, no question. You will rise swiftly through the ranks. I myself will keep an eye on your progress."

"*Thank you*, sir." The boy spoke and saluted so seriously that Sherman laughed his hoarse, crackling laughter that was so much a match to his snapping, croaky speech that the boy marveled and started to laugh himself, uncertainly, nervously.

"Never mind, never mind," said Sherman patting the boy on the shoulder. "I'm not laughing at you, my boy. Your enthusiasm is admirable, admirable, though a good soldier needs more than enthusiasm to survive. It's the knowledge of little details of camp life that keeps men alive. I've always believed that distributing the raw recruits, like you, among the older men, the veterans of even one battle, those already familiar with the rigors of camp life and campaigning, will give the youngsters a better chance of survival. You can learn from your older, more experienced comrades the mechanics of drill, the care and use of arms, and all the necessary scraps of information it would otherwise take months to pick up, and in the meantime it would be too late for the raw recruit, he'd be dead. For instance, there's a habit you might care to adopt when you go into battle. Take a piece of paper, write your name, company and regiment, and the address of your family, someone you wish to have notified should you be wounded or killed, then pin it to your coat so that the surgeon will be able to identify you."

The boy thought for a moment and then said, "Sir, since I have no family, would it be acceptable for me to write *your* name on the paper?"

Sherman stared at the boy. The youth had a black mark at the corner of his full mouth where he had torn open the cartridge as instructed. The commander turned away, made a great fuss of finding something in his footlocker, was bent over it with his back to the boy for a full minute before he turned again and said in a voice both emotional and overbrisk,

"Read this, it will help you master drill and bayonet exercise."

The well-worn, blue soft-cover book was entitled *Patten's Infantry Tactics*, published in 1861. On the cover, the boy noted, was a personal endorsement by George McClellan. Knowing *that* general's unimpressive reputation thus far in the conflict, the boy wondered if this was in the book's favor or not. Though McClellan was indeed highly thought-of for making that unruly mob of independent-minded citizens called the Potomac Army into real soldiers, he didn't appear very eager to march them off to fight anyone.

"Thank you very much, sir, I'll take good care of the book and return it to you."

"I know you will. I know you will. Yes, read it and I'll loan you another. Wait!" Again, he was gone.

The boy didn't know whether to laugh or cry, so overjoyed was he to have made such a good impression on the general his first night in camp. Now he had only to work as hard as he could, be a good soldier, and his path to Sherman's side would be a smooth one.

"Here." Sherman threw aside the tent flaps and handed the young soldier a brown paper bag of the type used by sutlers.

The boy peered inside. There was a piece of baked bread and a hunk of hard cheese, together with a big rosy-red apple. From his pocket Sherman took a large square biscuit.

"Have you tried this? Hardtack. Very nutritious." He banged it on the table and coughed, clearing his throat. "Never mind." He tossed the biscuit onto his cot. "If you're going to become a good soldier, you need to get some flesh on those ribs." He poked the boy in those same ribs with one bony finger. "Now go on, get out, get out, I have letters to write."

"Thank you, sir, thank you for everything." The young soldier hesitated, desperately searching his mind for a way to prevent his expulsion from the warm tent and enthralling company.

"Sir, will you promise to think about what I said? I'd make you the finest servant you could—"

"Out!" Without further ado, Sherman manhandled the boy backward through the opening, sending him into the chilly night to fend once more for himself.

"Gen'al?" Captain Jackson queried, observing his commander's still-pensive, almost tortured expression as he came into the tent moments later. "Everythin' okay, sir?"

Sherman puffed at his cigar, gazed up at his aide-de-camp with moist eyes and explained,

"I found that boy out near the Hamburg-Purdy Road. He had nothing but the uniform on his back. Some corrupt quartermaster sergeant lining his own pockets, no doubt. I advised him to pin his name on his coat before a battle. You've advised other recruits to do the same. He said he had no family, asked me if he might put *my* name on the paper,"

"Darn it—" said the sentimental captain, all suspicion gone, at least for the present.

Sherman sat back in his chair, his experience with the boy leading him to another in his past. "I heard today through captured prisoners that my old friends Braxton Bragg and Beauregard are out there—and all my Louisiana boys, the cadets of the academy, whom I must fight when the time comes. I remembered the fresh-faced youngsters I had drilled and instructed in infantry tactics at Benton barracks and then sent off to General Grant at Fort Donelson. I wonder how many of them are still alive, how many of them have benefited from the instruction I tried to drum into their young heads."

"I reckon there's many a boy still alive today and will be at the end of this war who'll owe their survival to you, Gen'al."

"I wish I could believe that—" Sherman said, walking to the tent flap and staring up at the sky lit by the reflection of myriad bivouac fires. "I wish I could believe that—" After a moment he said, "That boy's earnest manner, his eagerness to learn, reminded me of Willy. I saw him plain as day, lying in a ditch somewhere, his guts spilled and a paper pinned to his bloodstained jacket, the words 'Next of kin: Brigadier General William T. Sherman' scribbled in his childish hand." He turned back to his aide. "Too close to home, Andy, too close to home, sir." He sighed, squeezed the corners of his eyes. "You are fortunate, sir, you have only daughters—how many mothers' sons must I advise to pin a next-of-kin to their uniform before this madness is over?"

The very best we know how

★ ★ ★ ★

I hear the bugle sound the calls
For Reveille and for *Drill*,
For Water, Stable, and Tattoo,
For Taps and all was still.
I hear it call the *Sick-Call* grim,
And see the men in line,
With faces wry as they drink down
Their Whiskey and quinine.

—Anonymous Civil War soldier, quoted in John D. Billings,
Hardtack and Coffee; or, The Unwritten Story of Army Life

As Jesse Davis tried to come fully to himself, he found that he was shivering uncontrollably and could hardly feel his feet. His blanket was gone and the ground beneath him was wet.

An unfamiliar sound had awoken him, the company bugler sounding reveille, summoning soldiers to roll call.

He sat up with a start and made a panic-stricken grab at his knapsack, hugging it to his narrow chest. Fortunately, he had used it as a pillow, for whoever had taken his blanket could not have robbed him of the knapsack without waking him, or knocking him senseless. He plunged his hand inside; the precious book that General Sherman had loaned him was still there. The food also. He would not go hungry even if he froze to death. The collection of utensils, plate, cup, knife and fork, bucket-sized coffeepot, in fact everything given to him by the hung-over quartermaster, was gone, even the spurs. Only the infantryman's shoulder scales remained to mock him. At least he still had his sack coat, appropriately named, since it was two sizes too large and indeed hung like a sack on his thin frame.

He gazed around him with feverish eyes. It was a mistake to have slept so far away from the center of the camps. Despite his general's good advice, he had settled down on the edge of the camp rather than risking the ire of the men already slumbering. He hugged the knapsack closer to him, and puckered up his full mouth determinedly. One only learned by bitter experience.

He started in the direction of the tent city. The enlisted men lived in wedge tents, or "A" tents, because they looked like the letter *A*. They lined the fields as far as the densely wooded areas beyond, and outside each tent were stands of muskets, within easy reach, should there be a surprise attack during breakfast or while they slept.

At the head of each row of five tents were the officers' tents. Ten to fifteen feet separated the companies, allowing room for the men to wash and cook. The quartermaster tent where the general had taken him the previous night was located somewhere to the rear. He could just glimpse in the distance the log house, which gave this camp its name and where the people of the area did their Sunday-morning worship.

He stood there watching as the men reluctantly threw off their warm blankets and, like him, shivered in the early-morning dampness that penetrated their bones. Men in various stages of undress, yawning, coughing, cursing, groaning, or washing, or not, in the last instance, as they struggled to prepare themselves for the day ahead, and, more urgently, for assembly, where they would answer, only half-awake, to their names.

In a little while, the smell of food cooking wafted across, accompanied by the rhythmic clinking and grinding noise that meant coffee would soon be on the boil.

Directly ahead was a row of larger wall tents, from one of these, the most prominent, flew a yellow flag. The boy watched a soldier in an infantryman's blouse, the stripes of a corporal on his sleeve, crouching in front of a fire, a skillet in his hand. On the skillet were fatty strips of bacon. He stood there staring at the soldier frying the bacon, enjoying the sizzling sound, almost lulled by it, and the aroma of the coffee.

The corporal looked up, stared a moment and then grinned at him, dark gums where his teeth should have been. The boy blinked uncertainly. A second soldier emerged from the large white tent, an enormous man, broad-shouldered and tall with a magnificent lustrous black beard that grew to the third button on his jacket, his large head crowned by a thick head of black, wavy hair.

"What's the matter, boy, yer hungry?" asked the first soldier, holding out the skillet as he might have offered a crumb on the palm of his hand to a nervous bird hovering near the table.

"Yes sir."

"Then git yerself over here. I ain't yer mama."

The boy glanced from the corporal to the other man, whose sleeve displayed the stripes of a sergeant, beneath a sew-on badge that the boy did not recognize, and held even tighter to his knapsack.

"The boy is afraid," said the sergeant, who had the very slightest of accents that was not American. "Don't be afraid of us."

"He's scared fer sure—" said the corporal. "He's jest a young'un too."

"If you are hungry," said the sergeant, "come, eat breakfast with us, we have plenty."

The corporal went cautiously toward the youngster, who backed away. He had lost too much during the night to risk the theft of the book.

"Gently," counseled the sergeant. "He is very nervous."

"Kin see that, kaint ah? Nervous as a jackrabbit, aright," agreed the corporal. "Come on, boy," he said, going toward him, bent over as though he was getting ready to pounce, "we ain't gonna hurt yer none."

The young soldier moved forward toward the fire and the food. He trusted the sergeant, if not the toothless corporal. All around him now the camps were coming to life, somewhere was even the melancholy sound of a harmonica, and many of the men who moved around between the tents, lighting campfires and filling coffeepots, wore bandages, had an arm in a sling or hobbled on a crutch, as if they had been wounded. He looked into the large white tent from where the sergeant had emerged and saw a row of cots on both sides where men lay or sat.

There was sweat on the boy's face, on his upper lip and on his brow. He rubbed it away with the back of his hand. The sergeant came to meet him; quickening his pace, guessing that the boy was weak, and he lifted him effortlessly in his strong arms as the boy held tight to the knapsack, held with the last ounce of strength left in his arms. The sergeant called for a blanket as the boy closed his eyes.

When he opened his eyes again, perhaps only a few minutes later, he was wrapped in a blanket and sitting near the fire, the knapsack still held against his chest. The sergeant was holding a tin cup to his lips and urging him to drink the warm liquid.

"Drink slowly, child, very slowly." He laid a hand on the boy's damp brow, a remarkably gentle hand, considering the sergeant was a giant of a man with hands to match. "There is no fever." He spoke with the authority of one who knows from experience.

"Thank . . . thank you . . . sir . . ." the boy stammered. "I wasn't afraid, sir—"

"No, just cold, and hungry, I think." The sergeant's full red lips parted in a reassuring smile.

"Does he wanna eat sumpthin'?" asked the corporal, coming into view at the left corner of the boy's sight as he dangled a slice of bacon dripping grease onto the earth. He peered into the young soldier's pale, generously freckled face. "Bacon grease and oatmeal. Good fer what ails yer."

"Just the drink . . . thank you, sir . . ." the boy said, cupping his hands around the tin cup that the sergeant was still patiently holding for him. "Coffee?"

"Tea," said the sergeant, "better for your stomach." He drew the blanket closer around the boy's narrow shoulders and inquired, "How is that?"

"Warm, sir, thank you."

"I am Sergeant Jacob De Groot, and your name is . . . ?"

"Jesse Davis. Pleased to meet you, sir." The boy extracted his right hand from the folds of the blanket and offered it to the sergeant, who grasped it tightly. His rich laughter warmed the boy almost as much as the tea and the blanket. To the corporal he said, "Pleased to meet you too, sir."

"Sir, is it? Well, least he's po-lite." The corporal poked the boy in the ribs like a housewife checking for meat on a hen before parting with any money. "Though seems to me if'in he's what they're enlistin' these days we ain't never gonna whip those Rebs, not in a month a Sundays. That there boy don't look strong 'nough to lift a musket. A whole darn regimint a boys like him ain't worth spit."

"Not only can I *lift* a musket, sir, I can load and fire one," said Jesse Davis. "General Sherman *himself* taught me how!"

"Pfufff! Now yer don't have to go makin' up no stories jest to prove a point."

"General Sherman advised me to find veteran soldiers who would show me what I needed to know to survive. You look like a veteran soldier, sir."

"Well, now, ain't that jest like old Gen. Sherman, always handin' out good advice to anyone who'll listen." To the sergeant he said, "Boy's soft in the head."

"I don't believe he is," said the sergeant with an esoteric smile, "and if so—all the more reason for us to take care of him."

"Barble talk." The corporal was disdainful as he first scratched at and then removed a "grayback" from his armpit, squashed it between forefinger and thumb and deposited the corpse in the fire. He coughed up a ball of phlegm that he shot at a large black beetle that was crawling across the ground in front of his feet and missed by a mile. He flattened it instead with the heel of one of his enormous brogans.

The boy sat on a tree stump and ate two strips of bacon and some beans while he watched the great activity at this hospital camp of the Seventieth Ohio, Fourth Brigade, commanded by Colonel Buckland. He watched as the men went about their important business, serving breakfast to the wounded and sick inside the tents, while two men the corporal identified as doctors did their daily rounds, moving from cot to cot examining and then discussing the patients.

While the boy watched and ate, still wrapped in the blanket like an Indian squaw, the corporal, whose name was Cornelius Grimes, and who, between cooking for the patients and generally making himself useful, talked. He seemed to like to talk more than anything, mostly about those he served with.

". . . the Dutchman, Sergeant De Groot? He's okay, I guess, fer a Barble reader. Reads the Barble like it was—" He blinked his lidless eyes rapidly as he thought about it. "—Well, like it was a Barble, I guess," he concluded and burst into a wet laughter that sprayed the boy with spittle. "Queer thing, though, he reads the Barble but he don't go to church," he continued quizzically, scratching his few gray hairs. "I been 'round 'im two months or more and I ain't ever seen 'im go ter church. If'in he's so taken with the Barble why don't he go ter church like other ree-li-jus folk, that's what I wanna know."

Army food was another of his favorite themes.

"Hardtack." He crumbled the large dense cracker into the bacon grease the boy had left on his plate. "Ain't no mystery. Shortenin' and flour. Only mystery is how a man can stay alive on these things. Boys call 'em wormcastles on account a the weevols and maggits livin' in thar." On his plate was now a wholly indigestible mess, which the old soldier proceeded to eat with undisguised relish, a starving man tucking into the greatest banquet ever set before a king. "Ain't no point wastin' good bac'n grease. If'in yer break up yer hard bread into yer coffee an see those weevils a swimmin' around on the surface yer just skim 'em off this away." He showed the boy. "An' they don't leave no taste, well, hardly any. That's a-why most boys is shy a drinkin' thar coffee in tha dark. No tellin' what yer might swallow!" He laughed his crazy cackling laughter, giving the boy his second showering of the morning, and then shoveled the mess into his toothless mouth. "If'in yer can't eat 'em, yer just hurl it at Johnny Reb." He produced a clay pipe with a stem as long as his arm and nearly as thin. He looked across at the tent where two doctors were engaged in animated debate. Actually, the younger of the two was animated; the older man was merely listening with set, arrogant features. "Them sawbones know nuthin', they's jest guessin' most a the time. If they cures us they takes the cred-ite, if they kills us they go blaming God a'mighty. What you got in that knapsack yer keep aholdin'?" Cornelius fixed the boy with his red-rimmed eyes buried in so many sun-baked wrinkles it was impossible to see where the sockets began and the wrinkles ended.

"Bread and cheese and an apple," said the boy, "given to me by General Sherman. I would consider it an honor to share them with you at suppertime." Jesse brought the food from his knapsack and the wily old corporal stared at the *real* baked bread with the dark brown crusty edges and soft, white interior. "I don't expect to be around here for too long."

"Why's that, boy, where yer plannin' on goin', Richmond?" Cornelius dug something out of his bulbous, pockmarked nose.

"No sir, but I expect to become one of General Sherman's servants."

"Is that a fact? Well, yer expicktitions is gonna be disappointed. Gen'als don't need servints, they git dumb-arsed niggers to fetch an carry and such like, and them orderlies git the best jobs, like ridin' round the country deliverin' messages no one, least of all other gen'als, wants ter hear, and secondly what makes yer reckon the gen'al even knows yer alive?"

"I told you, sir, it was General Sherman who gave me the cheese and the bread and the apple."

"Well, I'll say one thin'." Cornelius scratched his crotch. "Yer sure didn't magic them vittles outa thin air. Yer stole 'em some place and I giss ole Gen Sherman's mess is as good a place as any."

The large hospital wall tent at the rear of the regiment was bursting with incapacitated soldiers fighting off the effects of the severe diarrhea and dysentery decimating the ranks of the Tennessee Army. In one cot a young infantryman called Davy Hubble lay stretched out, pale and thin, without, it seemed, the strength to raise himself and greet his own brother when he visited. He laid aside the dime novel he was reading to sink under his blanket, moaning loudly.

"You look a whole lot better, Davy," said Amos Hubble.

"We was jest sayin' he looks real peek-ed," piped up Cornelius, appearing from nowhere to take Davy's last jelly off the sheet and pop it in his own mouth. He glanced around him. "I wouldn't wont none a these surgeons working on me, leastways not if I was alive. The hospital ain't no place for sick folks, not 'less they plan on gettin' sicker."

"I'm dyin'," Davy said.

"Well, yer sure don't look like yer dyin'," Amos insisted.

"I'm dyin', I tell yer, I got me an awful pain right 'bout here." He gingerly touched his abdomen. "I reckon I won't last out the night, Amos."

"Have you told Doc Cartwright?"

"Won't do no good," said Cornelius, shaking his knotty head.

"Ohhwha . . . ohhwhaaa . . ." groaned Davy, but rallied long enough, as the boy approached, to tell his brother, "That there's Jess Davis, bin real karn'd ter me, Brother, gettin' things and such like."

"Good morning, sir," said the boy, who had been running errands in exchange for the kindness shown him by the sergeant.

"Boy's waitin' fer hiss pre-motion. He's gonna be Gen. Billy Sherman's aide-*dee*-camp," Cornelius told them with all the gravity he felt this announcement warranted and much of the contempt.

"That *right*?" asked Davy, so impressed he forgot to moan or hold his stomach.

But the boy wasn't listening. Cornelius had kept him so busy this was the first time he'd actually stopped to gaze around the twenty-three cots with barely a space to pass between them, and a narrow aisle down the center, where men lay motionless, staring up with glazed eyes at the canvas ceiling or tossing fitfully under stained, sweat-soaked blankets. Even though the tent flaps were tied back and a fresh breeze stirred the leaves on the trees outside, the unmistakable, overpowering smell of excrement and stale urine pervaded the air.

The boy watched as an orderly sauntered past with a full, uncovered bedpan, the contents already attracting a whole company of eager, buzzing flies. Across the aisle, a soldier was hanging out of his cot and retching into a bucket held for him by the sergeant.

"Ain't a preety sight," Amos said. "Ole Cornelius there, he ain't far short a the mark. Yer might suspect some a these doctors was sent here by Jeff Davis hisself jest to make us Yankees suffer. The men line up for sick call every morning and Doc Fitzjohn, he's the regimental surgeon, hands out these pills, big as hazelnuts they are, called blue mass. If'in yer clever, boy, you'll just toss 'em in the bushes."

"Is that Dr. Fitzjohn?" the boy asked, pointing to a young man in a soiled white apron, bending over a cot, examining a patient.

"Nah, that's Doc Cartwright, regimental *assistant* surgeon. He takes his orders from Fitzjohn. Doc Cartwright is o-kay. He cures more 'an he kills, which ain't no mean task in this army. Got a real bad bark, though it's a deal worse than his bite. He takes a might gettin' used ter, he ain't got what city folks call 'bedside manner.' "

The boy watched as Dr. Cartwright carefully checked the patient's pulse and then gently palpated his abdomen. The poor soldier let out a soft moan, as though he lacked even the energy to articulate his pain. He was pale, almost ghostly in appearance, hollow-eyed, his wasted body sunken into the shallow mattress on which he lay. If not for a brief movement of his skeletal hand, it might have seemed that he was already dead. Cartwright snatched up the record card from the foot of the patient's cot and made a few quick notes. He administered a dose of medication and helped the mortally sick soldier take a sip of water. As the doctor turned away, the soldier lifted his hand a few inches off the cot, reaching out to touch his savior. The doctor merely nodded. The soldier's need to touch him seemed to make the doctor angry. Though perhaps it wasn't so much the touch as the unspoken question in the patient's eyes.

The doctor pushed the small, round eyeglasses up his manly nose, and expelled his breath in a rasping sigh, his anger restrained. It was hardly the poor soldier's fault that he would soon be another statistic; he smiled, gave him a more reassuring nod and moved on to the soldier who had been vomiting. He sat on the edge of the cot and wiped the boy's mouth, placed a cold cloth on his forehead, spoke joshingly to him.

"You been sneaking out to the sutler's wagon again, Guthrie? I thought I told you to lay off the oysters and champagne?"

The boy shifted his gaze to the three strong-looking orderlies standing leisurely at the entrance with apparently nothing more urgent to do than smoke their evil-smelling stogies.

"That *there's* Doc Fitzjohn now." Amos nodded toward the entrance and the change in his manner, from admiration to dread, spoke volumes.

Fitzjohn was certainly a hard-looking man, tall and very thin, clean-shaven, with high, sharp cheekbones and colorless eyes that would have unnerved the bravest of veterans in his care. His uniform was spotless, brushed, pressed, like a store-window dummy, his black hair slicked back. He had a straight slit of a mouth that remained frozen in a kind of arrogant sorrow. He might have been a very prosperous undertaker who had prepared too many corpses, breathed too much embalming fluid, and attended too many interments.

"If'in yer ever find yerself occupyin' one er these cots, get yerself fixed by Doc Cartwright, not Doc Fitzjohn."

Cornelius returned at that moment and Amos said, "I was just tellin' the boy here that if'in he gets sick or wounded he oughta get hisself fixed by Doc Cartwright."

"That's a fact. Fitzjohn jest don't listen," agreed the older man. "Afore yer can say what ails yer hiss handin' out them big blue pills like they was bits a candy on the Fourth a July. I seen him a hundred times since I been here."

"And I ain't seen him smile a once," said Amos. "Not a once." His expression changed to amiable as the younger surgeon came toward them. "Howdy, Doc."

"There's not a damn thing wrong with your brother. Take him back to camp with you. The diarrhea's cleared up."

"I know that, Doc. But Davy's homesick. He misses his ma; she always took good care a him. He's the baby. This is the first time he's ever been 'way from home. Why, he even got scared when Ma sent him ter town ter get Pa outa the saloon on a Seterdy night." He laughed and Cornelius laughed. Cartwright was unmoved. He'd heard it all before. It didn't make it less true, of course, just less effective on a surgeon who'd served since Bull Run.

"I don't want him lying here like a sack of rotting vegetables." He turned to the subject of the discussion, who, since the surgeon's sudden appearance, was lying prostrate again, holding his stomach and issuing forth a low, monotonous moan. "We need the cot." In order to demonstrate this truth, Cartwright tried to pull back the blanket, but Davy held on to it for dear life. "You gotta take some nourishment, and I ain't got the time or the inclination to spoon-feed you. If you need a good excuse to get out of doing your duty, I can give you a dose of strychnine, painful but effective. In two minutes you'll be laid out stiffer than a—"

"Whoa—" interrupted Davy, his sly gaze moving from Cartwright to his brother and back again.

The boy studied the doctor as he spoke. His uniform looked as if it had been on his back since old Edmund Ruffin fired the first shot on Fort Sumter. He wore no shoulder straps, his boots were caked in mud, and his pants were shapeless. He was dark-skinned, which exaggerated the four-day stubble on his firm chin. His thick, untidy hair was quite black, Irish black, and grew way past the collar of his grubby shirt, while a straight, impervious fringe hung rakishly over his brow.

He was younger than one might first suppose; in his late twenties, despite the gray in his hair and the premature lines about his brow and mouth, bitter lines, and dark shadows beneath the eyes. Those eyes, brown in color, gazed out from behind small round spectacles with a sardonic amusement, as if he'd known for years something the rest of the world was only just beginning to find out. All this gave the surgeon's face more character than mere handsomeness would have done; in fact, his very youthfulness was tarnished and worn, like the single remaining button on his shabby frock coat.

"A fresh sacrificial lamb, huh?" he said to the boy in his usual mocking tone. "What cradle did our benevolent government pluck *you* from?"

"Good morning, sir," the boy said respectfully, and saluted. "I'm older than I look."

"And, I hope, *wiser*," was the surgeon's wry observation.

"Boy's slow-witted," explained Cornelius.

The surgeon pushed his spectacles negligently up his nose. "Ain't we all, Corporal, ain't we all. Why else would we be here slaughtering each other, if our wits weren't slow?" He turned back to Davy Hubble. "Well, what's it gonna be, strychnine or beef broth? Decide now, damn it, I'm not wasting any more time on malingerers." He reached down and made a sudden grab at the blanket, which came away to reveal the bottle of whiskey Davy had been concealing. The boy moaned, but this time it was genuine. Cartwright turned to Amos and said with more sympathy, perhaps recognizing a fellow imbiber, "Get him to eat something. I *know* he doesn't want to go back to his regiment. He's been listening to rumors. He's scared to death and I don't blame him. I'm also scared and I also want to go home to my mama but the army insists I stay here. If he doesn't want the Prince of Darkness to fill him full of blue mass he'd better stop drinking that stuff and start eating. We've got a tent full of genuinely sick men. If he ain't sitting up and taking nourishment by supper I'll have him marched out of here and shot, then all his worries will be over, *permanently*. Understood?" He thrust the bottle at Amos's chest and walked away.

The strange patch on Sergeant De Groot's sleeve was called a caduceus, and meant that the Dutchman was permanently attached to the medical department as Dr. Cartwright's personal steward.

"Steward's the next best thing to a doc," the talkative Cornelius told him, as they wound cloth for bandages and dressings. "If'in they kain't find a doc they git a steward. Steward gits the key to the medicine chest. They got alcohol in there." He grinned and a black hole appeared in the lower half of his face. "That don't make no never mind, not to the Dutchman. I never seen him take a drop, nor look at no woman neither, not that we seen any decent ones 'round here. He jest reads that Barble. Ain't that a caution? Works all the hours the Lord sends an' when he gits time he reads that Barble an' keeps hisself ter hisself."

"Sir." The boy spoke to Sergeant De Groot as he came out of the operating tent. "I'm sorry to bother you, sir, will you give me some more work to do?"

The steward's sad brown eyes focused on the boy's freckled face. With his powerful body, black hair falling in a mane around what could be seen of his ruddy cheeks under the thick black beard, it was impossible to guess the Dutchman's age.

"Your company sergeant will be looking for you. He will think you have deserted."

The boy said nothing, just held the Dutchman's steady gaze. Then the Dutchman nodded his gigantic head slowly, as if he understood something the boy had silently imparted to him. "You will need somewhere to sleep, the nights are cold. You will share my tent for now; Cornelius has habits bad for a young boy to see. I will take care of you."

"Thank you, sir," the boy said in the steward's own tongue.

"You speak *Dutch*?" The steward's eyes filled with tears. "How is that possible?"

"Anything is possible, sir," said the boy, "if you believe."

Alone in his tent, the tall, thin, slightly hunched figure removed his frock coat and turned in time to see a movement in the shadows. "Who's there?"

"Me, sir. Private Jesse Davis. I turned back your blanket, sir."

Sherman glanced at his cot. He had never seen it look so neat, so inviting. Irritably he said, "We are not at Willard's and I dislike fawning sycophants." The Ohioan suddenly narrowed his eyes. "I've seen you before," he said slowly, reflectively.

"The other evening, sir, when you—"

"No, no, no! I mean before that. I know I've seen you before."

"Eight years ago. Early April, in the year 1853, sir, you were on voyage for what is now San Francisco, to take up your position as director of the banking establishment of Turner, Lucas." Sherman drew his slender red brows into a quizzical frown. "You were shipwrecked, *twice*," continued the boy. "The first ship ran aground north of San Francisco, then the schooner which rescued you capsized in the bay."

"How in damnation do you know *that*?" Sherman was staring at him. "I asked you a question, Private, now *answer* me."

"After the first shipwreck you had a companion, a boy—"

"Yes, yes, about sixteen, your *brother*?"

"No, sir, not my brother."

"Then?"

The boy's smile was sudden and rueful.

"That's impossible," Sherman said, wiping the boy and the thought out of existence with one gesture of his arm. "He would have been in his twenties now, if he had lived, but he drowned—I was becoming entangled in the ship's rigging—the boy jumped in and assisted me. I didn't see what happened to him. I assumed he had lost his own life in trying to help me." Sherman drew the back of his hand across his brow, which had grown beads of sweat. "I tried to find out who he was, I wanted to tell his family, perhaps he was the sole support of a widowed mother. I did not want my continued misfortune to be the cause of her poverty, but the ship's passenger manifest listed no such person. I questioned the master, as many of his crew as I could, none remembered seeing him, either working his passage or as a passenger. I concluded that he had been a stowaway." He stared harder at the boy. "Unless you are a ghost, and I warn you now, I do not believe in spectral visions, unearthly phantoms, or any such nonsense, you will get back to your company where you belong."

The boy followed him to the small folding table, upon which the flame of the candle flickered precariously in the slight draft and said earnestly with emotion, "I belong with you, sir. Please let me stay here. I'll black your boots and fetch you hot coffee in the mornings when it's so cold the breath freezes on your lips and I'll clean your horse's bridle until you can see your face in the brass. You could, sir, imagine me your plebe and use me as such. I would be your most obedient servant and there will come a time, sir, when you will ask yourself how you ever managed without me."

"If you are not the most audacious— I don't *need* anyone to black my boots or fetch my coffee. I am surrounded by orderlies enough to sink the *Merrimack*, and if I was so inclined I could have more nigger servants than the biggest chief in all Africa."

"None would be more loyal and dedicated than I, sir, I swear it."

"I told you last night, do your duty in battle. That will be sufficient loyalty and dedication for any commander. Now get out of here. I have more letters to write."

"You always have letters to write. You write too much by the dim light of the candle and smoke too many cigars. That is the reason for your headaches, sir."

"Why, you are outrageous—how dare you talk to me in such intimate terms? Damn your impudence—if I did not truly believe you were slow-witted, I would have you arrested. Now get out of here and stop pestering me. What are you doing now?"

"You advised me to find somewhere warm to sleep, sir. In a corner of your tent is very warm."

The commander's red-bearded jaw fell open.

"If you need anything in the night, a light for your cigar, or a drink from your canteen, I would fetch it immediately."

Sherman jammed the cigar into the corner of his mouth. Then with both hands free, he grabbed hold of the young soldier by the collar of his coat and the seat of his pants and propelled him toward the exit, that hoarse voice issuing a dire warning as he did so. "If I find you hiding in here again, soldier, I'll have you put in front of a firing squad. Do you understand?"

"Sir—" The boy struggled as he was evicted from the tent. "I could not help but notice, you have so many books. Would you loan me one that I might improve my slow wits and make myself more worthy to serve you?"

3

Dare to do our duty

★ ★ ★ ★

That was the first sound in the song of love!
Scarce more than silence is, and yet a sound.
Hands of invisible spirits touch the strings
Of that mysterious instrument, the soul,
And play the prelude of our fate. We hear
The voice prophetic, and are not alone.

—Henry Wadsworth Longfellow,
The Spanish Student, act 1, scene 3

As the day declined into afternoon, and the air, which had been at intervals clear enough to allow the French coast to be seen, became again charged with mist and vapour, Mr. Lorry's thoughts seemed to cloud too. When it was dark, and he sat before the coffee-room fire . . .

"What's a coffee room, Jess?" the soldier asked with a frown.

The boy laid down the book he had been reading to a small group of patients well enough to leave their cots and said, "I imagine it's a special room where wealthy men like Mr. Lorry can drink their coffee and warm themselves at the fire."

"I reckon yer can have a room to do almost everythin' if'in yer rich," said a young sergeant with his arm in a sling.

"I reckon," agreed Jesse, only half-listening.

Across the ward, Dr. Cartwright and Dr. Fitzjohn were engaged in yet another heated argument. "Take a look at the boy's leg," the younger man was saying as they stood beside a cot. The sheet was pulled back to reveal a large ulcer, slightly purulent at the base, but clearly showing pink healthy tissue around the edges.

"I have already looked, three times, Doctor." Fitzjohn spoke quietly, in a grave monotone, like a man in a funeral parlor stiffly comforting the bereaved. "The leg is gangrenous, sir."

"No, no, no." Cartwright made a sweeping motion with his hand. "That's just it, you looked *last week*, last week you might have seen *a hint* of gangrene, but not now, now the wound is healing. In a couple of weeks this soldier will be walking around as good as you or me, maybe better," he added with his twisted smile. "Take a look now, not for my sake, to hell with what you think of me, but for the boy, will you do that, Fitzjohn?"

"Dr. Cartwright, I would appreciate it, sir, if you were to calm down and take a grip on yourself."

"And if I don't, what will you do, have me court-martialed?"

"No, sir, but I will make a formal request of the chief medical officer that you be examined for traces of insanity." Fitzjohn spoke like a man who had been considering this option for some time. He turned on his heel and walked away.

"Maybe I am insane, maybe we're all goddamn insane!" Cartwright shouted, following him down the aisle. "Look around you, Fitzjohn, does any of this look like the work of a sane people? *You're* crazy, I'm crazy, *Old Abe* is crazy. *Jeff Davis* is crazy! But I'm not gonna let you cut off that leg, do you hear me, Fitzjohn? You're a damn fool—and one of these days so help me God I'll put you out of your misery—" His voice tapered off as he suddenly became aware of his cheering audience—the patients whose well-being he was so energetically defending. "—And when they lock me up I'll say I did it because you killed more of our boys than the Rebels ever did." He concluded in a more subdued voice, removing his spectacles.

A soldier in a nearby cot who heard him called out, "Hey, Doc, wanna lend ma pistol so yer can shoot that old coot?"

"*What?*" Cartwright blinked at him.

This soldier produced a rusted navy Colt from under his pillow, which he stroked lovingly. "Took it from the same lousy stinkin' Reb who done this to ma leg. I kept it close by when I hear'ed you an that old buzzard debatin' whether I was gonna lose this'an." He tapped the leg with the pistol.

"Give me that gun." Cartwright walked toward him, his hand outstretched. "No damn guns in here. No damn guns in my hospital, you understand?"

"Ah, Doc, don't yer know'ed ah'm on yer side." The soldier held the gun to his chest.

"I said *give me the gun, goddamn it!*"

Reluctantly the soldier handed it over. Cartwright slipped it into the pocket of his apron.

"Yer know sumpin', Doc, yer got one hell of a mean disposition for a sawbones," said the soldier who'd just lost his prized possession, laughing heartily.

"I'd have me a special room to keep ma hound dogs."

Jesse brought his eyes back to Davy Hubble, who was fully dressed, lying on his cot staring up at the canvas ceiling and grinning. "I wouldn't have no coffee room. I'd have me a room special fer ma old hound dawgs and then Ma wouldna keep gettin' at me so when they shite on her new-scrubbed floor."

"Read some more, Jess," said the sergeant with the sling in the next cot.

Jesse lifted the book and continued to read, " '. . . When it was dark, and he sat before the coffee-room fire, awaiting his dinner as he had awaited his breakfast—' "

"That fella ain't got nuthin' t'do but wait on his vittles from morn' 'til night." This observation came from a corporal of artillery recovering from a bout of dysentery.

"Hey, Doc—"

Cartwright had joined their small reading group.

"Doc, I ate ma breakfast." Davy showed the surgeon the empty bowl that had contained rice pudding. "Jess here fed me, jest like ma old ma used to do when we were young'uns."

"That's the spirit, soldier," he said in a tired voice, his mouth making the shape of a brief smile. It was barely midday; he had been on duty all night but had no inclination to leave. He wouldn't sleep anyhow, he would dream of the gothic Fitzjohn hovering overhead with an amputating saw between his teeth. "What you doing in here?" he asked Jesse. "Ain't you supposed to be drilling or marching?"

"You said Davy needed encouragement to eat, sir."

"Did I? I don't remember saying that. It doesn't sound like the kind of thing I would say, leastways not when I'm sober. Go on reading, don't let me interrupt you. You read very well."

"Thank you, sir. 'A bottle of good claret after dinner—' "

"Yessiree." Cornelius's shrill high-pitched giggle drowned out the next words as he came limping down the aisle. A broken leg at fourteen had left him with a permanent disability, which got more, or less, pronounced with his mood. "That thar Mr. Lahrey don't think 'bout nuthin' else but eatin' and drinkin'. I wish ter hell I was that Mr. Lahrey and no mistake."

Cartwright gave a snort of laughter. "Somehow it always comes down to their stomachs in the end. What's the book?"

"*A Tale of Two Cities*, by the English novelist Mr. Dickens."

"Gen'al Sherman borrowed it to him," Davy informed the surgeon. "Jess here is a close personal friend a the gen'al. Ain't that so, Jess?"

"Not exactly." The boy got to his feet. "I'll come around at suppertime, Davy."

"Hey, Jess, if'in yer gonna read to me some more will yer ask the gen'al if he's got one a them dime novels with cowboys and Indians and a whole heap a outlaws?"

"I'll try," the boy said, "but I don't think General Sherman will have—" He saw the purposely skeptical look on Cartwright's face as the surgeon stood there, his arms crossed over his blood-and-pus-stained apron, his dark brows raised over his eyeglasses. "I'll ask him, Davy." He left the surgeon by Davy's bed and crossed to the other side of the tent, where he hoped he might find a more appreciative audience for Mr. Dickens's inimitable prose.

This morning the consumptive corporal Franz Gerhard, between spitting gobs of blood into a filthy rag and staring bleakly at a photo of his brother, told Jesse, "You haff for me plenty paper? I got lot to say, ja?" She had promised to write a letter for him.

Jesse brought out three sheets and waited, pencil poised expectantly.

"Brother dear mine, I am through the greatest adventure of my life living. I therefore ain't got time to you to write. Gerhard your brother affectionately."

From a few feet away Jesse heard Cartwright laugh. He said, "That'll stir up the folks back home."

Jesse fared no better at the cot of Private Alonzo Pickands, who dictated his letter: "Today they drilled. They drilled yesterday and well probably drill tomorrow. They drill alla time in this here army. I guess drillins' better 'en fighten' 'cos yer kaint die from drillin' lest yer drill so much yer coll-apse. I kaint do neither I got me a in-flammed foot. But when the foot ain't in-flammed no more I guess I gotta drill and fight too."

"Innocents ripe for the slaughter," the surgeon muttered as he passed.

"Wouldn't you like to say something about the scenery and the weather, Alonzo?" the boy coaxed.

"Sure, that's a good idea. We got plenty of scenery here, all of it preetty and plenty of weather, all of it warm."

Jesse took the liberty of adding,

The trees are all in bloom, pink petals cover the branches of the peach trees, and the people living around here say it's one of the hottest springs they can recall. At night the temperature drops, so we still need to light camp fires.

"Nice touch." The surgeon stopped to read over the boy's shoulder. "I'll have to get you to write my letters. What do you charge?"

"Charge?"

"Your rates. You mean you do all this letter writing gratis?" The surgeon laughed suddenly. "No, no, no, you've got it all wrong. No one does *anything* for nothing. You ask, say five cents per letter and when you've earned enough you use it to buy the assistant surgeon a bottle of whiskey. That's how it works."

Five minutes later Cartwright stood watching as the boy poured some water on a piece of cloth and placed it to the parched lips of Sergeant Drum, so sick with dysentery that the once-hulking teamster was now a fleshless skeleton lying beneath the soiled bedsheet. Then from across the tent came the sounds of a patient shouting in agony. But the boy did not flinch, did not even lift his head from his task, but continued to bathe the unconscious sergeant's feverish cheeks, his clammy brow, and his throat, where the Adam's apple now stuck out like a growth.

"Where did you learn that?" the surgeon finally asked. The boy intrigued him.

"From Sergeant De Groot, sir."

Cartwright nodded, then said, "Why are you hanging around in here anyway? No one hangs around in here unless they have to. This is an army, you know, you can't go anyplace you please or do what you please, at least that's what they tell me."

"Sir, will that soldier keep his leg?"

"Damn right. In a few days His Satanic Majesty will find someone else to torment—he just likes to put me firmly back in my place every now and again, lest I get the inflated notion that I'm a *real* doctor." He peeled off the boy's kepi from where it was perched precariously on the shock of red curls, stared at his freckled face, and demanded suddenly, "Just how old *are* you?"

"Sir?"

"It's a simple question, Private, I asked your age."

The boy seemed to be thinking for a moment and then he answered, "Well, sir, it's not really that simple," and smiled in that way he had, kind of rueful and apologetic.

"Fetch me the bedpan, boy," called out the soldier in the next cot, poking him hard in the back with his crutch, "and be right quick about it if you don't want no accident."

Cartwright moved aside for the boy to pass. Suddenly there came a short high-pitched squeaking sound from Sergeant Drum. The soldier had stopped breathing and was turning blue.

In a second, the surgeon was bending over the prostrate man and forcing his finger down his throat. "Who the *hell* fed this man salted pork?" he shouted as he brought an undigested lump of hard meat from the struggling soldier. Drum was fighting to catch his breath, choking to death. "Get my surgical kit—there—off the table—now!" he ordered Jesse, flinging his arm toward the table by the entrance. As soon as the boy returned, Cartwright went to work. He took up a blunt rubber tube and briskly snipped off the end with a dressing scissors. Then he used a scalpel to make a slender incision in the man's throat through which he carefully inserted the rubber tube.

The boy, standing there, gasped in amazement as he heard the soldier breathing *through* the tube. "Come on, Sergeant, that's it, breathe for me, you're all right now, you're going to be fine, but you have to breathe. Come on, you'll be home in a couple of weeks, and all this will seem like some terrible nightmare, come on, Sergeant—you've got to try, damn it—"

Jesse watched the surgeon rub the man's hands, stroke his brow, massage the once-strong shoulders where the muscles had atrophied, leaving the gray flesh to hang limply from the bone. In a matter of seconds the sergeant had responded, surely as much to the doctor's encouraging words as to his unorthodox medical procedure. He was no longer struggling for breath, but beginning to breathe more easily, his color returning to normal, or what was normal for the man's pitiful condition. His eyes had flickered open and he was holding tight to Cartwright's hand.

Unbid, the boy placed a padding of lint against the bleeding wound. The surgeon looked at the boy's awed, intelligent face. It was a hell of a long time since he had encountered a private soldier who cared more for a dying man's comfort than the size of his boots, so he took the trouble to explain. "It's a urinary catheter, very versatile, can be utilized as a tracheotomy tube if one isn't available—" He seemed about to say more, but then spotted someone over the boy's shoulder. "Make him comfortable, I'll be back in a minute."

Cartwright ran between the tightly packed cots and grabbed hold of the orderly, who was trying to make a quick getaway. "*You* gave him the salt pork after I told you not to—"

"I thought I was doin' the right thing, Doc, he said as how he was hungry—and he ate it, didn't he?" wailed the misbegotten orderly, trying to wriggle out of the doctor's clutches.

"I ought to choke the life right out of you—you lousy little cretin."

"Please, Doctor—let him go, sir, let him go." Sergeant De Groot spoke these placating words. He eased the surgeon's hands from the orderly's coat, telling the still-struggling soldier, "Go back to your regiment; you are no use to us. We don't want you here. Go away."

"Let me shoot him!" Cartwright was shouting; he still had the rusty Colt in his apron pocket and now shook it aloft. "Just one good shot! I'll aim low, I swear, I'll just *cripple* the little bastard."

The orderly fled as if his clothes were on fire.

"Okay, okay." Cartwright turned to his steward. "I'm calm as a cadaver." He went back to Sergeant Drum's cot and asked the astonished boy, "Do you want a transfer to the medical department? We have a sudden opening for an orderly."

Jacob De Groot was Dutch by birth but "American by inclination and patriotism," he told Jesse proudly. Twelve years old when his parents came to America, this soft-spoken giant from Minnesota showed Jesse how to accomplish many chores that were needed around the hospital. Easy ones at first—how to empty a bucket so that the urine did not stain his uniform, how to rub lemon juice into his hands to kill the smell of excrement on his skin, the art of rolling bandages on a winding machine like a small clothes wringer without getting the cloth twisted. Graduating to difficult tasks such as changing a sheet with the patient lying helpless in his own body waste, how to use a field tourniquet, judge the seriousness of a fever, recognize stomach cramps, ague, read the symptoms of diarrhea and dysentery. He wore his hospital steward's insignia with pride, explaining to the boy that its yellow-piped green half-chevrons and caduceus represented the winged staff of a Roman deity called Mercury. Whenever the boy saw the steward, his coat and sky-blue pants were clean and brushed, his shirt freshly laundered, his finger-nails always short and clean, his black hair and beard washed, and he never appeared outside the hospital without his kepi.

Apart from the surgeons, the boy learned, the stewards were the only men permanently attached to the medical department. The orderlies came and went, the only rule being the more ability that they showed as nurses, the more quickly they were reassigned to their old regiments. While the slow and the lazy remained. Every surgeon had a steward appointed to assist him, but Sergeant De Groot wasn't just *any* steward, he was Dr. Cartwright's steward. He assisted at operations, sometimes administering anesthetic when another surgeon wasn't available, and as Cornelius had said, the trusted steward wore the key to the pharmacy chest on a string around his neck, and possessed a practical knowledge of its contents, allowing him to prepare and dispense what the surgeon had prescribed. He pulled teeth too, his great strength a distinct advantage when it came to restraining a victim squirming in agony with a swollen jaw. He was proficient in the application of bandages and dressings, and could, when called upon, apply "cups" and "leeches," though, as he swiftly explained to the boy, he *was* never called upon, for Dr. Cartwright did not approve of their use, for any reason. He was also a good cook, and as far as was humanly possible, kept the young surgeon, whom he very obviously loved, from strangling irresponsible, indolent orderlies, stubborn surgeons, and visiting dignitaries.

Though the other surgeons helped themselves to whiskey from the hospital medical supplies, Dr. Cartwright did not, Jacob stated with fierce pride. Dr. Cartwright liked drink a little too much, it was true, but would sooner have suffered the hell of delirium tremens than touch the patients' alcohol.

During the day, Cartwright had his operating table moved outside, where the light was good. Sergeant De Groot explained to the boy that this was because the surgeon was always anxious about the quality of the light, always demanding that the lamp be brought closer to the wound. The Dutchman suspected it had something to do with a fear that his poor eyesight would let him down. However, his sense of grievance never did, and he aired that without restraint. He abhorred the common practice of old dressings being reused and the government's failure to supply the soldiers with their own dressings, which forced them to bind up their wounds with dirty handkerchiefs or pieces of cloth torn from a sweaty shirt, since they knew no better.

As Jesse moved about the tent, he heard the surgeon lecturing anyone who would listen, including civilian representatives from Washington and their military escorts, uniforms aglitter with brass buttons and gold bullion. Governors and mayors and town clerks who offered a mechanical official smile to the medical staff spoke in platitudes at the sick and injured, while calculating how many more votes this flying visit would gain them during the next election, provided they ever got home, and if they didn't, they had fathers and brothers and uncles who could vote. They never stayed long in the hospital tents, these visitors, but rushed through the tents like a dose of Dr. Fitzjohn's Epsom salts.

Maybe it was the smell, or the sight of a man in the last throes of death, that drove them so quickly into the fresh air and sunshine of the Tennessee spring. Perhaps it was Dr. Cartwright's badgering that plagued them like a particularly infuriating insect that would not be swatted or discouraged.

"Half the surgeons you send us don't even have the dexterity to roll a damn bandage. What we need is men trained exclusively to nurse and attend the needs of the sick and injured. Not idiots, but a corps of medical orderlies—with a little intelligence," he would shout, running after them. "You train men to shoot cannons, steer ships, but ride about on horses. Why don't you train some of them to drive ambulance wagons, wound dressers, food preparers. Is that so crazy?"

Maybe not, but they thought *him* crazy.

Late one evening, as Jesse Davis sat in the hospital tent writing into the pharmacy ledger in his neat, clear script by the light of a candle, Cartwright swung his medical bag onto the table. He seemed always to be around the hospital tents, attending a patient, bent to some operation,

or writing into that notebook he always carried, his free hand distractedly messing up his already untidy hair. Tonight he'd been making house
calls, looking in on soldiers confined to their tents.

"Jacob taught you how to take inventory? Keep the records neat and
tidy, fill out requisition forms in triplicate, list incomings and outgoings
for medicines and supplies. One of these days, this army is going to
choke on its paperwork. I guess you could look at it this way, if you make
it through the war you'll get a good job clerking in some dry goods store.
Provided of course you've still got your arms." He used his pipe stem to
tap the long streams of "medicinals" flowing down the sheet of paper.
*Silver nitrate, iodine, mercury pills, fluid extract of valerian, compound cathar-
tic pills, morphine sulphate, tannic acid*—on and on went the list, more than
fifty in number. "Shall I tell you something, Private, nearly all those so-
called 'therapeutic' drugs are useless, a waste of time and space, not to
mention money. Civilian suppliers make a nice little profit on other people's pain. They sell the government all that goddamn rubbish—worse
than rubbish—you can kill an entire army with only half the ingredients
in that list. You ever heard of the Hippocratic oath? Hypocrites was a
Greek physician, 'The Father of Medicine,' he lived around 400 B.C. and
wrote an oath. 'I will prescribe regimen for the good of my patients
according to my ability and my judgment and never do any harm to anyone.' To this day medical students have to recite that oath when they
graduate." Cartwright snatched the pen from the boy's inky fingers and
scratched, "First of all, do no harm" across the page. "You know what
that means? It means if you can't do any damn good then at least do no
harm." He tossed the pen onto the pristine page, spraying it with ink
spots. "Mercurous chloride and blue mass rots away your insides. Tartar
emetic? Even worse, take enough of it and you'll shit your guts out in a
bloody pile. Who knows what's in half this stuff? Pour them into the
Tennessee, that's what I say and hang the bastards who peddle them. All
we really need is morphine and opium for pain control, chloroform and
ether for anesthetics, and quinine for fevers. And let's not forget those
universal cure-alls, those pathways to oblivion—the stimulants, God
bless 'em—brandy, gin, rum, and my personal favorite, whiskey."

He produced a small flat bottle from his hip pocket, removed the

stopper, swallowed a mouthful, and announced with a grin, "Of inestimable value, to patient *and* surgeon. Most therapeutic. Guaranteed to
restore the balance of bodily fluids and replace black bile with good
humor." He tapped himself on the shoulder. "Doctor, you are a genius,
sir, I feel better already. Just two or three more doses of that invigorating
tonic and I'll be right as a four-dollar bill. See, alcohol sharpens my
senses. Helps me focus and not that I have to explain myself to you, but
just in case you're wondering, I was off duty about three hours ago." He
laughed. "I'm lying. I won't be off duty for another ten years. What do
you think, Private Davis, since you've no doubt discussed this with your
close personal friend General Sherman, is ten years about right for the
duration of this madness?"

The boy wisely refrained from telling him that, only last evening,
while hanging about outside the Ohioan's tent, he had heard the general
express a view that they were facing "a thirty years' war." Instead, he
went back to his work, beginning a new page and carefully copying from
the screwed-up, bloodstained sheets of loose paper Jacob had given him.
Barrels of old linen—20, Bedpans—32, Blankets—106, Crutches—120 pairs,
Splinting/Dressing plaster—10 rolls, stockings, shirts cotton, shirts woolen, bed
ticks, pillows, tin cups—

"Coffins." Cartwright tapped the page belligerently. "Don't forget
the coffins. We can never get enough coffins. Order enough for the
entire army! We'll need 'em all." Cartwright ceased his haranguing and
stared at the boy's full mouth and at that funny-shaped nose, dusted with
freckles that spilled out across his too-smooth cheeks. Something about
the boy, his quiet dignity, his refusal to be drawn into an argument, nee-
dled and irritated him. No one *that* young should be that self-contained,
that self-confident, it was—well, it was unnerving, that's what it was,
and brought out the worst in him. He leaned over the table, purposely
obscuring the list of items that were to be transferred from paper to
ledger.

"I don't know why Jacob's taken such a liking to you. In my opinion
you're too damn clever for a farm boy."

"I never said I was a farm boy."

"No, you never said anything. You just turn up here one day, no com-

pany, no regiment, and old Jacob just accepts you like some long-lost little brother. Cornelius thinks you're a Rebel spy." Cartwright was smiling
that twisted smile.

The boy answered with a tolerant smile of his own as the surgeon
picked up one of his small hands and examined it. "Soft. You're well educated. Maybe you're from some Quaker community? No, you don't talk
all thees and thous—" He opened his medical case and began to check
the contents as he spoke. "The female Quakers make good nurses, they
do what's expected without complaint, not like those dragons from the
Sanitary Commission, always poking their long noses in where they ain't
wanted. I've got nothing against nuns either, you have to respect how
hard they work, but Christ almighty you need 'em to keep a dressing on
a hemorrhaging wound and there they are, down on their bony old
knees, praying. Between purging and purgatory a patient ain't got a goddamn chance."

The boy was looking with interest at the interior of the surgeon's
case.

"It was my father's," Cartwright proudly explained. "He took an
ammunition box, stripped out the interior and lined it with elastic strips,
you know, like a lady's garter belt?—to hold the bottles, instrument cases,
and just about anything else a surgeon would need in the field. You can
strap it to a saddle and the contents won't fall around inside and break."

"Was your father a surgeon, sir?"

"A damn fine surgeon and a damn fine man. I'm just a damn fine surgeon. Not that being a fine man made any difference. When he died this
case was all he had in the world to bequeath to his son and heir."

"I'm sure your father believed that being a fine surgeon had its own
rewards."

"What would you know? And here's some free advice—" Which Jesse
did not get the benefit of since at that moment Lieutenant Nash, another
young surgeon, came into the tent, looked around, and was about to
depart again. Cartwright said, "If you're looking for the patients'
whiskey supply I've locked it away."

Nash's eyes alighted on the well-worn tools of Cartwright's calling.
"Isn't it about time you bought yourself a new set of surgical instru-

ments, *Doctor*?" he inquired with the arrogance of his calling and igno-rance of his youth.

"You shut your mouth. These were good enough for my father, they're good enough for me."

"I would have thought a rusty fork was good enough for you, sir." Nash took a wooden case from his bag, which he opened and placed on the table for the boy to see. There, in perfectly fitting compartments lined with red plush velvet, were well-crafted surgical instruments of shining, burnished steel. As the boy made to finger one Nash barked, "You may look, but don't you dare touch. These are the best set of ampu-tation instruments that money can buy, purchased by my father from Tiemann Surgical Instruments of New York City."

"Now all he has to do is learn how to use them." Cartwright swept his bag off the table and with it went Nash's set of Tiemann instruments.

Nash just managed to catch the case before it landed on the floor and whatever further insults might have been exchanged were halted as two orderlies brought a litter into the dimly lit tent, closely followed by Jacob, who, like his superior, never seemed to rest. On the litter was a young man with flushed cheeks, his eyelids flickering as he murmured softly in delirium. The orderlies, drummer boys on loan from the band, were so small that the young man's arm, fallen from under the blanket, dragged along the ground.

"This officer is sick, Doctor, he needs you."

Cartwright poked the boy in the shoulder. "Follow me."

The surgeon opened his case while Jacob and Jesse removed the offi-cer's frock coat. He was a lieutenant with boyish features, and a head of thick blond hair.

"Ouch," the surgeon said, wincing. Jacob had eased the left arm out of the sleeve. Wrapped carelessly around the arm was a dressing that looked as if it hadn't been changed in weeks. Even from where he stood at the foot of the cot the surgeon could smell, as well as see, the yellow-green pus that had soaked through the layers of cotton cloth. As Jacob stepped aside, Jesse saw a tall, slender officer enter the tent, glance around anxiously, and, spotting Cartwright in his apron, walked toward them.

"Lieutenant Colonel Ransom, Eleventh Illinois," the officer introduced himself as he came close to the cot. "This is Lieutenant Bennett, one of my regimental commanders. He accompanied me to Colonel Buckland's headquarters this evening and suddenly collapsed. How is he, Doctor?"

"I'll tell you when *I* know. In the meantime don't get under my damn feet. Fetch a lantern," the surgeon instructed Jesse, "a good one." When Jesse returned, Cartwright told the officer, "If you get out of the way, the boy can bringer it closer."

Obediently the lieutenant colonel stood back and Jesse took his place beside Cartwright, who was examining the wound. "Throw it out," he said of the foul-smelling dressing he had dropped into the bucket. "Flesh wound. No broken bone. See the entrance and exit wound?" he demanded of Jesse, who nodded. The wounds were but a couple of inches apart, both draining foul-smelling pus. The area was red, swollen, tender, and hot. No wonder the feverish lieutenant had collapsed. Cartwright spoke to the officer patiently awaiting his verdict. "It looks like the ball entered the arm and passed right through. This ain't a fresh wound. How long has he been sick?"

"He was wounded a week ago in a skirmish," the lieutenant colonel said. "He didn't see a surgeon. He had it dressed by a medical orderly. He told me the wound was healing."

"Well, he was lying or blind. I'd guess the orderly rinsed off the arm and wrapped a dressing around it. The ball may have carried a piece of his shirt into the wound, or some dirt or tree bark, if it ricocheted off a tree before hitting him."

"Will he lose the arm, Doctor?"

"Not if I can help it." This was said without the slightest trace of bombast. "I've seen much worse. You'd be surprised how much a wounded man can take, or how far he can drag himself when he has to— I've seen soldiers with half their faces blown away, arms and legs gone, drag themselves to the rear because they know if they stay where they are and wait for help they'll bleed to death. Needs must when the devil drives, isn't that what they say? Well, the devil is doing most the driving in this godforsaken world."

"This world is not godforsaken," said Jesse quietly, almost to himself, soliciting a brief, sad smile from the lieutenant colonel.

"Lantern, closer," said Cartwright, giving the boy a shove with his elbow. "Lantern, closer" was his constant refrain.

Jesse's arm was aching but he did as he was told, using the light just once to sneak a furtive glance at the lieutenant colonel watching anxiously. If asked, he would have said the officer was, in all aspects of feature and physique and dress, the most beautiful man he had ever seen.

Using the sponge and water Jacob held for him, Cartwright washed the wound, rinsing away the pus that had clung to it. He took a good look around the entrance wound, using a pair of forceps and a probe. The young man in the cot moved his head on the pillow and Jesse used his free hand to stroke the moist brow, speaking softly, reassuringly, to him.

"Rest easy, sir, you'll be feeling better very soon."

"Here, Private, let me hold the lantern, your arm is shaking with fatigue," the officer offered, in his soft, well-modulated New England accent.

"Thank you, sir."

"Hold it lower, damn you," Cartwright ordered.

If the lieutenant colonel felt offended at being cussed out by a mere captain, he did not show it, but obeyed in silence, bringing the lantern close to the wound.

Meantime, the surgeon had taken a small pair of scissors and was snipping off the flap of black skin folded into the wound. "There's no pain," he said, feeling around the entrance hole with his index finger, "that was necrotic tissue, *dead* tissue. Okay, that's clean." He turned his attention to the jagged exit wound, the bigger of the two holes. From here, he snipped off more pieces of dead skin, before using his forceps to extract a piece of cloth from an inch or so inside the wound. "Like I said, a piece of the lieutenant's shirt." He showed Ransom the cloth plug before letting it fall to the floor. Next, he rinsed away the remainder of the foul pus that was oozing from the exit wound.

In the next cot, a soldier began to cry in his sleep, calling out for "Charlie," and begging him not to die. This awakened a fever-racked patient across the aisle who began to shout deliriously for water. Somewhere close to the front of the tent a man started coughing, a deep, wet, rattling cough as if he would choke up his lungs. The orderly left him to attend the patient crying out for Charlie, but could not quieten his distress.

"Doc—" he appealed despairingly to Cartwright across the cots. He was willing to dress wounds, bring water, change soiled sheets, and fetch the bedpan, but he had never guessed that his duties would include comforting grown men as their own mothers had once comforted them as children.

"Let Jesse go to him," Jacob said.

"Go on," Cartwright agreed, "before he wakes the whole damn tent."

Jesse eased the troubled soldier slowly back to his pillow, laid his small hand across the wrinkled brow, and spoke reassuringly to him, the way he had spoken to the feverish sergeant. In a few seconds, the man was sleeping peacefully. The boy glanced up to see the lieutenant colonel watching him, admiration in those large eyes set deeply under a prominent brow. He returned to the young lieutenant's cot just in time for Cartwright to give him a lesson in dressing the arm.

"You'll be doing this, Private, so take note. Clean cotton bandage wrapped around a cold-water dressing of compressed lint. Change the dressing twice a day for the next three or four days. As soon as the wound begins to look better, no pus, and the redness subsides, once a day is enough. If the wound starts to look the slightest bit inflamed since the previous dressing change, you let me know immediately." He stood up, wiping his hands on his apron. "We'll get him well again, won't we, Private Davis?" He slapped the boy hard around the head, because instead of listening to the surgeon's words of wisdom he was staring at the lieutenant colonel with awed eyes and parted lips.

"Yes sir," the boy answered quickly, rubbing the sore spot.

"I'll give him a little morphine for the pain, and to make sure he sleeps through the night."

"I am much obliged to you, Doctor." The stern and serious young officer offered his hand.

The surgeon ignored it and jerked his head. "I'll send you the bill."

The lieutenant colonel's sympathetic gaze moved around the tent, resonant with all the sounds of suffering humanity, not to mention the smells. "I know you have other patients who require your skills. As soon as Lieutenant Bennett is well enough I will have him transferred back to my regimental hospital."

"Forget it. You've caught me in my quiet period, we're between battles. After Bull Run you'd have waited months for an appointment."

Ransom nodded his blond head, and then smiled a gentle, indulgent smile. Then gave up. It seemed he had realized any attempt at showing appreciation would be met by a humorous deflection. He watched the surgeon walk off down the aisle, then he looked at Jesse, who said, "With Dr. Cartwright looking after him, sir, the lieutenant will get well very soon." He wiped the beads of sweat from a sick man's neck, brought the blanket to his chin, and laid a cold cloth across his brow. "He couldn't be in better hands."

"Yes, I can see that—" His broad white-toothed smile lit up his entire face, making him look much younger than he had appeared in the dim shadowy light. He was perhaps no more than twenty-six, smooth-skinned and clear-eyed, but his sharp elegant features, severe slicked-back hair relieved only by fashionably long sideburns ending at the base of his jutting jaw, and the upright, military bearing in his immaculate uniform gave the impression of a much older man. A man who knew he was born to command, yet there was about him a touching vulnerability.

"I have some tea for the colonel," Jacob said, joining them. He had a tin cup and a cookie, both of which he offered the astonished colonel. "The cookie was baked by my sister Beatrice; she is the best cookie maker in all of America."

"Well, thank you, Sergeant." Ransom laughed, tasted the contents of the cup, took a bite of cookie. "Delicious, and what fine tea, I never tasted better at any fancy Chicago hotel, nor received better hospitality."

Jacob beamed. "You are very welcome to visit us anytime, sir, but we hope it will be a social call, not because you are in need of our services." He laughed, Ransom laughed, and Jesse nodded enthusiastically.

"What a fine man," said the colonel after the steward's departure.

"Yes sir," the boy said simply. "The sergeant and Dr. Cartwright are the finest of men."

"Indeed. You'll get no argument there." Ransom drank some tea, finished the cookie, and put the cup on the night table. "Please say thank you to the sergeant for me. Would you tell Lieutenant Bennett when he wakes that I'll be back tomorrow to see how he is."

The boy got to his feet and saluted as smartly as he could and the lieutenant colonel brought forth that broad smile again. He mussed the red-gold curls as he had seen the steward do, then he took his hat off the blanket.

"One more thing, is there anything I can do to show my appreciation to the surgeon?"

"Yes sir, whiskey, sir," the boy said unhesitatingly. "Surgeon Cartwright finds whiskey a great comfort. It sharpens his senses, helps him focus."

"What is your name?" the officer said gently.

"Davis, sir, Jesse Davis."

"Corporal Jesse Davis, I shall not forget that name. I must go, thank you again for your attentions to my officer."

"Just *Private* Davis, sir," the boy corrected.

"For now." He smiled that wonderful smile.

"What in hell was all that about?" Cartwright said, approaching Lieutenant Bennett's cot ten minutes later. "Anyone'd thought you'd never seen a goddamn lieutenant colonel before." He was holding his whiskey bottle, only now it was empty. He indicated the young officer sleeping peacefully, probably for the first time in weeks. "Are you going to sit with him all night?"

"Just for a while, sir. I think the lieutenant colonel would appreciate it."

"Oh you do, do you?" the surgeon did a little dance to go with his mocking voice. "Yer, I thought you might be the kind of kid who'd lick up to an officer." He tilted his head back and emptied the very last drop of booze from the bottle onto his tongue, like a child trying to catch raindrops, and with equal frustration.

"He reminds me of a knight in shining armor, noble and brave and dignified. I think he must be a *very* fine man, a very fine soldier," the boy said reflectively.

The surgeon's laughter was thick with disdain. "Is that what *you* want to be, Private, a very fine soldier? Kill people," Cartwright mumbled bitterly.

The boy said nothing.

"I'm not dignified." Cartwright regarded the empty bottle with sorrow. "And you don't think me a very fine soldier, do you?"

"I think you a very fine *surgeon*, sir, and a very compassionate man."

"Forget all that horse shit. What you reading?" He snatched the book off the boy's lap. "More damn Dickens. Stop wasting your time with this rubbish. I'll give you books to read. The *Hand-Book for the Military Surgeon*, by Charles Tripler, *A Manual of Military Surgery*, by Samuel Gross, and in between those we'll start you on journals and periodicals, *The American Medical Times, The Medical and Surgical Reporter.* They should keep you busy." Cartwright was angry. He didn't know why, angry and some other emotion. *Jealousy.* He was jealous of how this boy had reacted to that other officer. He didn't like the admiration so plainly present in the boy's gaze when he looked at the tall, straight-shouldered, and no doubt morally unimpeachable warrior. It was, of course, strictly a professional jealousy, he simply didn't care to see a naturally talented boy waste his respect on a man trained to kill. Far better that he look up to a surgeon, a healer, not a destroyer. It was a professional jealousy. For what else could it possibly be? "I think it's high time I taught you how to set simple fractures, a transverse crack, for instance, bone breaks that don't perforate the skin. I'll show you how to clean up lacerations and close them with adhesive plaster. You should be able to handle many of the minor procedures. I'll make up a list and we'll start right away. We'll kit you out with essential medical items to carry in your knapsack. Put some quinine in there, for all fevers, not just malarial, morphine, a flask of whiskey." He grinned. "A small pocket case of instruments, only the necessary ones. A scalpel, a bullet extractor, forceps, and a pair of scissors, a styptic pen, an eye spud, that's a small metal probe with a sharp point that we use to remove a foreign body from the eye—with shells bursting all over the place, dirt and bits of metal get into a soldier's eyes. Some silk suture and some suture needles. You'll need a tourniquet, some lint compresses, and some rolls of either cotton or muslin for rolled bandage material. Adhesive plaster might come in handy." His lips curled. "Jacob'll tell you to get a Bible to put in your bag. The dying always want a Bible. Don't ask me why. Ask Jacob, he's the expert on all things religious. And oh yer—despite stories you may have heard, we surgeons don't enjoy lopping off vital parts of a soldier's anatomy." Suddenly he grabbed the boy's face by the strong, clefted chin, turned it from side to side and inspected it with narrowed, suspicious eyes. "Do you shave? For a boy you've got mighty smooth skin, did you know that, and small hands." He shook his head as if to shake loose some crazy notion that had invaded it. "Where did you say you enlisted?"

"I didn't say, sir."

"If you wannna keep tight-lipped, that's fine by me. I don't give a goddamn where you come from. You could come from the moon, for all I care. I was just being friendly. Got any money 'til payday?"

No sooner had Jesse brought three crumpled dollar bills and some loose change from his back pocket than the surgeon had snatched them up.

"Jacob's right, you're a good boy. Just stay away from that colonel, he's a bad influence. I know the type. You can't trust a man with such highly polished boots." And just for emphasis he knocked the kepi off the boy's head and kicked it under the table with a bully's satisfied chuckle.

The boy went down on his knees to retrieve it. Cartwright narrowed his eyes. It deserved a good kicking, that small backside in the baggy pants, of that there was no doubt, though for the life of him he could not have said why.

4

A little more than mortal

★ ★ ★ ★

We live amid surfaces, and the true art of life is to skate well on
them.

—RALPH WALDO EMERSON, "Experience," *Essays: Second Series*

The rain that had started midmorning, gone through the afternoon and
into the evening, had finally given way to a cool evening breeze which
carried along with it all the scents and sounds of this early spring night.

The Fifth Division commander, despite having been in the saddle
most of the day, was still on the move, marching up and down in his wet
stockinged feet, a cigar, long since dead, protruding from the left-hand
corner of his mouth, as Captain Jackson came into the tent.

"The boy's still out there, Gen'al, still serenadin' yer," the smiling
aide said in answer to a mute but expressive inquiry on the part of his
commander, who was chewing on his cigar stub the way he did everything, with energy and verve. "Do yer want me to get rid of him,
Gen'al?"

"No." Sherman shook his head. "Let him alone." Andy's smile blos-
somed into a grin. Sherman glared at his aide. "Did I say something
amusing, sir?"

"No, Gen'al, only if yer don't chase him off now, he'll come back every night 'til you do, 'less the gen'al *wants* him to come back?"

Sherman ignored this question. Instead, he took a small package from his locker and thrust it at Jackson's broad chest. "Give him this for his trouble, licorice, a favorite of Willy. Children like it because it turns their teeth black."

Every day, be it in torrential rain, down muddy roads, over swollen creeks, under the heat of the midday sun, in the cold inhospitable hours after midnight, the Ohioan rode out as far as three, often four, miles in every direction on a personal reconnaissance, scouting for hard intelligence concerning enemy strength and positions he could pass along to Grant at Savannah and Halleck in Saint Louis. Diligently, thoroughly, did he question prisoners, deserters, civilians living in the farms and cabins scattered about the area, his analytical mind trying to make sense of their contrary statements, boasts, predictions, lies.

Even as his troops had been disembarking at the Landing, on the evening of March 16, he had been sending out companies from the Fourth Illinois cavalry down the Pittsburg-Corinth Road toward Monterey, urging them to attempt to break up the Memphis and Charleston Railroad.

Although this raid, like the first, had been unsuccessful, he had planned a third, reconnoitering in company with his young friend Lieutenant Colonel James McPherson.

"Andy." The aide paused at the tent flap. "All these people around here," Sherman said, "they're all related to each other through generations of marriage, Jones, Rhea, Seay, Fraley, Duncan, and the rest, did you know that? And they're a naturally closed-mouth bunch. I spoke to old man Fraley two days ago. Rebels told him that we take everything we can lay our hands on." Sherman grimaced around his cigar. "Violate all the pretty girls and leave the old ones for the Negroes."

The father of four beautiful daughters shuddered. "I can't say I ain't thought about what would happen if Rebel raiders got into Indiana," he said.

"Yes, and Fraley really believed it, Andy. I assured him if he stayed at home and minded his own business, I would not permit the soldiers to disturb him. He appeared to take heart, yet when I went to his house today, I found that his wife and children had fled to the woods as though we are savages."

"The only trouble I've heard about, Gen'al, is fence posts ripped out for firewood, and some chickens gone missing from a couple of the farms back a the church. They're the usual troublemakers, the same ones over and over again, a few rotten apples, not fit to be called soldiers, they infect their entire company."

"I don't want my boys ripping out anything, or stealing a single egg. I'll chase them out of the yards myself if I have to." The Ohioan's face got very red as he brought the palm of his hand down on his desk. "I'll punish them severely, make an example of them. If we do not halt these deprivations now they will poison the minds of these people and the whole state will rise up against our army. We will be fighting not only the Rebels in uniform, but also the civilians in whose name Davis and his ilk profess to demand their freedom and rights. These poor farmers want peace, I tell you, but the wealthier classes hate us Yankees with a pure unadulterated hate." Sherman tossed his cigar out of the tent and was already feeling in his pockets for another as he said, "If we do not per-suade the plain ordinary people whose land we sit upon that we mean them no harm, there will be a citizen with a gun behind every tree and bush."

Outside, the collar of his sack jacket pulled up to stop the rain run-ning down his neck, Private Davis had just started singing, "When This Cruel War Is Over."

"Can't be soon enough for me," Captain Jackson said bitterly, going out into the rain to give the singer his licorice.

The officers and enlisted men who now inhabited the beautiful Ten-nessee landscape may well have insisted upon their day of rest, but at the regimental hospitals, on this Sunday morning, it was business as usual.

Since it was said that men appointed to this position in the medical department should be of "honest and upright character and of temperate habits," Sergeant Jacob De Groot was surely the perfect example of a hospital steward. "Drink this." He had poured some tea into a tin cup and handed it to Jesse. "Be careful, it is hot."

"Thank you, sir. You are very kind to me." It was true, the Dutchman's body contained within it the strength of twelve men, yet he was as gentle as a nursing mother. When he and Jesse were alone together they talked in his own language, nothing more readily brought a happy smile to that ruddy face. When not seeking sustenance in the scriptures he sat patiently carving beautiful animals out of rough blocks of wood that he gave to the young Negro boys who hung around the camps looking for food or work.

"You must excuse the doctor if he overwhelms you with his enthusiasm." The surgeon had just given the boy another of his impromptu lectures on how to apply the chloroform, even though Jacob had taken him through the procedure a half-dozen times. "He sees that your natural inclination is to relieve suffering, but *I* think your heart is elsewhere. He is afraid now that we found you the army will make you a cook, or put you in the artillery. From Bull Run to this place I have witnessed the doctor's frustration. I think this anger is like an . . . an engine that keeps him going when he is exhausted, this and the whiskey. Also I have come to see it is a safety valve, to release the steam that would otherwise build up and burst." His long, powerful arms made the shape of an explosion. "Perhaps matters will change when he is promoted, at least in *our* hospital. When you are in command you can say we *will* try something new, we *will* move forward and stop fumbling around in the darkness just because we have been doing it that way for years. How else is progress made?" He drank some tea, and brought a brown-paper package from his knapsack. Inside were his sister's famous cookies, *Dutch* cookies, baked with *real* butter. Jacob placed one in Jesse's lap.

"You promised to tell me how you met Dr. Cartwright," the boy said.

"I did, I did. Just after the Rebels fired on Fort Sumter, I wrote my sister, I go to enlist. In the recruitment office, I signed a paper and told the sergeant, I want to help my adopted country. I have heard that the Union needs men to drive wagons and carry the sick and injured. I am your man, I am strong, I can carry a man under each arm, one over each shoulder." His laughter boomed out. "There must be many places where you can make use of such strength. He said you are a soldier now; we'll make use of you, all right. I tried to explain to every officer I met, I will do whatever you ask of me if it will help save the Union, but I will not kill another of God's children. Still they would not listen. Last July they put a musket into my hands, marched me to the outskirts of Washington City and told me with great excitement I would soon be able to kill other Americans. When the fighting started, I put down my gun and I picked up the injured. A very angry infantry captain with impressive mustaches that fluttered like chicken feathers when he talked asked me why a strong, healthy specimen such as me was running away from the fighting. I explained that I was not running away. I was carrying the wounded from the battlefield, but he would not listen. He said if I *wasn't* a sniveling coward I would stop hiding and fight, and if I *was* a sniveling coward he would see that I paid with my miserable life." Jacob brought his enormous fist down on what remained of the cookies, reducing them to crumbs. "For the birds," he said philosophically. "All God's creatures must eat and Beatrice would not begrudge them her delicious cookies. When the officer saw me again, I was *still* carrying the wounded, so he promised to have me arrested after the battle. He must have had a fine memory that captain for even though there was terrible fighting he did not forget his promise. When he came to the place where the doctor was treating the wounded, he had with him no less than four provost marshals, but the doctor refused to hand me over. If I had not been so afraid that they would shoot me then and there I would have laughed at the sight of the doctor standing up to these four men so that he might protect *me*. But they arrested me anyhow." Jacob sighed. "I was in the stockade for five days while the doctor tried to find out what would become of me. He was very angry and I think he must have threatened to resign if they did not release me. Two months passed before all the papers that had gone back and forth telling about that bad soldier, that cowardly Jacob De Groot, were finally settled and I was transferred to the doctor's regiment. I like a story with a happy ending, don't you?"

"Were you in the stockade all that time, sir?"

"I had a companion." Jacob held up his Bible. "A man is never lonely with the scriptures to keep him company. In here is everything a man or woman needs to live a decent life. Presidents, kings, and despots come and go, their man-made laws and rules change, but the scriptures remain constant. But I do not force any man to read it, all may read and know its truth for themselves, or not, it is their choice, that is American freedom. I simply ask that I be allowed to live my own life by these commandments." He placed an enormous hand on the battered cover of his Bible. He looked suddenly at the boy with a smile. "They think I am strange because I never go to church?" Jacob's smile was tolerant. "Hymn singing is pleasant, men and women raising their voices in praise of our Father, soldiers gathering on a Sunday morning to pray with their comrades is laudable. But after they leave their place of worship until the next time they meet the following Sunday how many keep the Father's commandments? No." Jacob shook his massive head solemnly. "What we do from Sunday to Sunday, *this* is the important thing." He clenched enormous fists, laughed, and shook his head again. "Do they think the Father does not see how badly they have behaved all week and will do so again next week? They ask me, are you Dutch Reform, or Quaker? I say I am me, Jacob De Groot, unique in God's eyes, as are all men and women."

"*God!*" said the surgeon contemptuously, coming up behind the boy and slapping his kepi off his head. As Jesse bent to retrieve it, the surgeon pushed his backside off the tree stump with his own, causing him to land with a thump on the ground. "Don't you two have anything better to talk about?"

"Sit by me, if there is room beside my very large posterior," Jacob said, helping the boy up.

"Pour me a cup of coffee," Cartwright instructed.

The boy obeyed immediately, advising gently, "Be careful, sir, the coffee is hot."

The surgeon took the cup without a word. He removed his spectacles and rested his head in the palms of his hands, his voice rising muffled as he said, "We've been out of certain medicines for weeks. There's only one hospital ship moored at the Landing, *one* for the entire Army of the Tennessee. I heard Grant sent one of the senior surgeons to Saint Louis to request additional transports. *Requesting* ain't good enough. Someone has to go up there and *demand* more transports if we're gonna treat the sick like men, not animals. This general, Halleck, 'Brains' they call him, he's charged 'gross irregularities' in Grant's medical department? *I* laughed for an hour when I heard that one. There are more than gross *irregularities*, there's rank stupidity, and insanity. This Halleck, he demanded to know why the sick were still being sent to Saint Louis when he had ordered they be sent to Cincinnati. Someone oughta ask him, when the hospitals are full at Cincinnati where do we send them then, *Brazil, Africa*, the *moon?*"

Jacob and Jesse exchanged sad smiles. The Dutchman touched the surgeon's thigh reassuringly.

"We can manage, Doctor."

"Yer, we can manage." Cartwright stared into the boy's eyes a second, then at his soft mouth. Something was not quite right about Private Davis, his features were too masculine for a girl and yet too wholesome for a boy, but then some of the youngest soldiers had that kind of face, emanating an innocence that made you think butter wouldn't melt in their mouths. But it didn't stop them wanting to kill Rebels and this one had sorrowful eyes with an expression as old as time itself. No. *Something* was not quite right, but damned if he could put his finger on it, as much as it bothered him. "Has Sergeant De Groot shown you how to use a tourniquet? Did he explain that only those with a first-class honors degree in surgery from Harvard School of Medicine and four years at a big city hospital can be trusted to apply one?"

"Yes, Doctor." Jacob was patience personified. "To both questions."

Cartwright opened his bag and snatched out a strap tourniquet. He applied it to his own arm, pulling tightly. "Why do you think we use a tourniquet, Private?"

"To control the bleeding by compressing the artery against a bone."

"In any case," the surgeon said, "the circular elastic and the middle muscle fiber layer of all arteries contract on injury."

"Yes sir, but Jacob explained to me that the added pressure helps the laceration to close and seal itself with clotting."

"Is *that* what Jacob told you? Maybe Jacob ought to be the surgeon.

Look at this—" Cartwright thrust his blanched arm under the boy's puckish nose. It looked pale and lifeless, the arm of a corpse. "See what's happening?"

The boy frowned his concern and released the tightly wound strap unbidden and the blood began to flow once more. It caused Jacob to sigh with relief.

"A practical lesson beats theory," Cartwright said. He drank some coffee. "These men," he looked at Jesse, "they fry everything. Rice, beans, salt pork, potatoes, *everything*. It doesn't matter a damn how often you tell them, they fry flour and water in bacon grease and they fry their damned beefsteak, then they come to us wondering why they spend the day squatting." He lifted his head and rubbed his burning eyes. "I wish to hell I could get those sick men some fresh fruit. Don't eat *anything fried*, you hear me?" he told the boy. "Cut your meat into cubes and toast it on a stick over the fire. Try to get your hands on some fresh fruit and vegetables. I don't care how you do it, beg, borrow, or steal, and be careful of the water you drink. Stick to coffee or tea. Instead of filling your canteen with water from the stream in the morning, boil it with enough tea to flavor it, that'll keep it from becoming insipid when the sun starts beating down on your head. It's healthy and a damn sight more refreshing on a weary march. It's also the best prevention for dysentery, since you'd have boiled out all the impurities. And don't use the same sinks the other men use, dig your own if you can, get yourself a shovel and dig a fresh hole, dig deep, dig far away from the camp, downwind." The surgeon brought his pipe from his pocket, an ordinary briar, not the flamboyant affair that gave Captain Jackson such pleasure. He poked among the cold ashes of the bowl with a small pocketknife. He peered at Jesse over his rimless glasses, at the thick red-gold unruly curls, at the old-young eyes, stopping to dwell somewhat reflectively on the full soft lips and then move down to his slender white throat. Then he frowned deeply, swallowed, and shook his head. *The devil take him*—he must be more lonely or more tired than he thought because for a second there. . . . "See why we don't demonstrate how to apply a tourniquet?" he demanded to know. "Those imbeciles would leave it tied round a patient's limb until the limb turned black and dropped off. That was only a couple of minutes and yet my arm already felt numb. Can you imagine a limb after twenty-four hours? You can do more damage to a patient with a tourniquet than a . . . a . . ."

"Twelve-pound howitzer?" Jesse suggested helpfully.

Cartwright got to his feet, tugged his battered kepi over his brow, and demanded of the steward, "Got any money?"

"*I* have, sir," Jesse volunteered eagerly. The surgeon already owed him three dollars, but who was keeping count?

"I will get a bottle of whiskey from the sutler's wagon and leave it in your tent," said the Dutchman patiently. "Please, do not take the boy's money."

"If there *is* a heaven, my friend, and you know I vehemently deny its existence, you can be sure of a place on the right hand of God."

"Then we will be together." A broad grin appeared in the center of Jacob's coal-black beard. "All *three of us.*" He gave the boy a hug.

"I've got a recently published pamphlet on miasmic diseases you'll find interesting," Cartwright told the boy. "Some new theories regarding the differences between the effluvia given off by decomposing vegetable matter, mess waste, swamp air, that sort of thing, compared to the effluvia given off by the human and animal excrement lying all over the place."

"Yes sir, thank you," the boy said uncertainly with a frown. "I'm sure I'll enjoy reading it."

"Good. Your friend Lieutenant Bennett was asking about you. No doubt he wants to bore you with stories of the unselfish heroism of his commanding officer."

Lieutenant Bennett's arm was almost healed. This young warrior of the Second Brigade of McClernand's First Division was not the same sickly creature that had been littered in three nights before. "I can't be laid up here if there's to be an almighty fight, I must be in, doing my share," said he, in what was a variation on the same theme uttered since he had been feeling well enough to talk. Moreover, what he talked about mostly as

Jesse changed his dressing was his sweetheart, Lydia Burlingham, and his commanding officer, the Vermont-born Lieutenant Colonel Thomas Edwin Greenfield Ransom, who was at that moment coming down the aisle toward them.

"Sir!" Lieutenant Bennett cried as Jesse returned to his cot with some fresh water.

The boy immediately put down the bowl and saluted very smartly. He had been practicing for just such an opportunity. As the officer returned the salute, his fine, deep-set eyes shining with amused pleasure, the boy saw Dr. Cartwright sitting at the table, pencil in hand, notebook open. He turned to watch, like a sharp-eyed bird perched on a branch.

"Sir," said Bennett, "you remember Private Davis?"

"Of course. How are you, young fellow?"

"I am very well, sir, thank you." The boy felt his cheeks burn and grow red, even more so when Ransom laughed, so pleasurable was the sound. It was a youthful laughter, fresh and clear as a newly struck bell, animating his rather stiff demeanor and softening those chiseled features. The boy and the man held each other's gaze until Lieutenant Bennett broke the strange spell.

"Sir, Dr. Cartwright says I am to be allowed to return to my company tomorrow and may be put back on the duty roster by Tuesday."

"Why that's wonderful news, James, and you have Private Davis to thank."

"Dr. Cartwright made his arm well again, sir, I merely changed the dressing."

"I'm sure the good doctor will have no objection to sharing the praise with you," Ransom said, looking across at the surgeon seated at the table, watching.

Cartwright "Humphed—!" loudly and went back to his prodigious scribbling.

"Lieutenant Bennett told me how you singlehandedly captured a Rebel horseman in Charleston, Missouri," the boy said excitedly, looking up at the tall officer and forgetting to address him as sir. "You shouted we must take the courthouse or bust!"

"I think it such a grand story," said the lieutenant defensively because

Ransom was looking at him in a disapproving way. "Sir, I refuse to apologize for telling it to this admiring boy."

"The Rebel shouted at you in the darkness that he was for '*Jeff Davis!*'—and you barked back"—Jesse raised an imaginary pistol above his head—" '*Then you are the man I'm after!*' Then you shot him dead in the saddle, though not before *he* had shot you in the shoulder. You were wounded again at Fort Donelson. A bullet smashed into your right shoulder. Your coat was ripped by six Rebel bullets and your hat pierced by another. You left the field only for a moment to get your shoulder dressed before you returned once more to take command," the boy concluded breathlessly, his bright blue eyes glistening with admiration.

The Vermonter mussed Jesse's hair and spoke to the officer in the cot. He was laughing as he said, "James, it is my biggest regret that you were with me that night and at Fort Donelson. There were *others* present; if I recall, General Grant was in command."

Bennett laughed. "Sir, you must admit this boy is marvelous, he has remembered every word I told him, line for line."

"Fort Donelson was a savage fight, not one I would care to relive," Ransom said, his smile fading. "The Eleventh lost some good men."

"Evening." Cartwright chose that moment to join them. "Is this for invited members of the Ransom Admiration Society or can anyone attend? We had a fully fledged prayer meeting this morning, you should have been here, they were all prayin' over the recently deceased." He slapped Jesse around the head lightly. "I told this boy, no time to pray for the dead, too many of 'em." To Cartwright's stunned amazement the colonel stepped between him and the boy.

"We are all entitled to have a few words of scripture spoken over us, Doctor, even if they are shared with a dozen other souls in a burial trench. If I fall in this war I hope there will be someone as compassionate as Private Davis to speak a few Christian words over *my* mortal remains, and I must say, sir, I think it unworthy of you to ridicule the boy for caring about the soul of a fellow human being."

Cartwright put away his ironically amused smile and brought out his disdainful one. "I wasn't ridiculing the boy, I was making a point. In the next week there'll be more dead around here than you can shake a stick at. If we stop to mumble scripture over every one of 'em, how we gonna get 'em planted before they start stinking up the place?" As always, he was brutally matter-of-fact.

"I can't believe you would wish us to become the kind of men who view death with no more feeling than the swatting of a troublesome fly?"

"Spare me your pious zeal, Colonel, if I want a sermon I'll see a chaplain."

"I'm sorry, Doctor, if you think I was preaching. But is it pious zeal to maintain and nurture the principles that separate us from the beasts?"

"And just what the hell do you think we do in here all day and all night, Colonel, fiddle while Rome burns?"

"*No sir.*" Ransom drew himself up to his full six feet. "I have only to look at Lieutenant Bennett to know that you are the most dedicated of men. That was the very reason why I said your criticism of this private was unworthy of you. You are one of those who keep these sick and injured men from cursing God and turning their faces to the wall." Silence followed Ransom's impassioned speech. A *V*-shaped blue vein was beating prominently in the center of his otherwise pale brow.

Cartwright blinked. Then he tore the spectacles from his nose and started to clean them on his stained apron with a violence that inevitably dislodged the left lens. He replaced the spectacles and put the lens in his apron pocket. Then he screwed up his left eye out of which Ransom's long, lean body was now somewhat blurred and made a funny sound in the back of his throat. Lieutenant Bennett finally broke the embarrassing silence.

"Sir, some of the men saw Rebel campfires lighting up the sky to the south of us. They say the woods are crawling with Reb cavalry." He looked significantly at Cartwright. "Will I be discharged in time to fight, Doctor?"

"Your lieutenant here is real eager to get back to the killing," Cartwright spat out. "I'll discharge this officer, to go out and get wounded again, to kill or be killed, when I'm goddamn good and ready and not one damn second before." He was really angry now, and when he spoke it was with a sweeping gesture of his trembling hand that took them all in. "If I had my way I'd mark your papers unfit for combat and send you the hell home. If I had my way I'd mark everyone's papers unfit for combat, including my own, and send us *all* the hell home." There was another heavy silence as Cartwright took out his empty pipe, made a whistling sound through the stem, and then chewed on it like it was a piece of Sherman's licorice. Then he nodded abruptly and left.

"Thank you again for attending my officer, Doctor," Ransom called out.

Cartwright waved his hand dismissively and kept right on going.

"I was just giving Old Bob some fresh water," Jesse said as Thomas Ransom arrived at the roped-off area where his horse was tethered alongside others in the corral. The attractive, well-groomed roan was slurping from a wooden bucket.

"He's a good old boy, aren't you, Bob?" He stroked the animal's neck affectionately. Then he looked at the redheaded private with a frown. "How did you know he was *my* horse, come to think of it, how did you know his name?"

"He told me."

Ransom laughed. "He's my horse, all right. Old Bob is my good friend, aren't you, boy?" He used his long fingers to brush the mane. "We've been together since I enlisted and know each other's foibles. We have a very one-sided agreement. If I am seriously wounded in battle he will carry me to safety. Unfortunately I cannot promise to perform the same selfless act for you, can I, old boy?"

Jesse's laughter made the large honey-colored freckles dance across his puckish nose. The Vermonter's expression turned hard, a steely quality in his eyes, as he said fervently, "Bob has always done his part, and more. We must *all* do our part." There was an unmistakable determination in those eyes that looked out at the world in the direct gaze and in the firm set of the slightly raised jaw. A kind of inescapable sense of his own heroic destiny, a destiny he would rush headlong to embrace, even if it brought him face to face with the same fate as his father, who had perished in the Mexican War. "Perhaps one day I shall even be given the opportunity to show the courage and selflessness that animated my father, his strong leadership—" *And his heroic death.* The words hung there, unspoken. "I've no doubt that you too will do your part when the time comes," he added.

"I'm very small," the boy said with regret. "Cornelius calls me runt of the litter."

"You have more than enough character in you to be the kind of man to make your God and your family proud."

Jesse held the bridle as Ransom swung his long, slender body into the saddle. The Vermonter crossed his arms over the pommel and leaned forward. "My mother always told me that the Almighty sends us only as many trials as he believes we are capable of enduring." He looked at the boy looking up at him and smiled hesitantly. "Tell this Cornelius next time he calls you a runt that it requires more than height and broad shoulders to be a good soldier."

"Sir, I'm so sorry about your brother."

Twenty-year-old Eugene Ransom had fought with the Eleventh Illinois at Donelson, been wounded in the arm and captured, Lieutenant Bennett had told him, by a Rebel horseman in the command of a Colonel Forrest. He was in a prison camp in the South, his exact whereabouts unknown.

"Thank you, Private Davis." He briefly touched the boy's shoulder. "Tell me, what reward can I give you for your care of Lieutenant Bennett?"

"I would love to ride your horse, sir." The boy was still looking up at the colonel, who seemed unable to avert his gaze.

For a moment they stared into each other's eyes, the officer frowning his confusion, then with what seemed like a superhuman effort, he broke the spell, laughing nervously as he ran his hands over Old Bob's glossy neck. "Then you may ride Old Bob." He gathered up the reins. "Yes, that can be arranged. Good-bye."

"When, sir, when may I ride Old Bob?" Jesse called out, but the lieutenant colonel had already ridden away.

Jesse walked back to the recovery tent to find the surgeon standing there, blocking the way, his pipe jutting from the corner of his mouth, his hands buried deep in his apron pockets.

"How very touching," he said with that twisted grin. "What the hell's between you and that pompous idiot, anyway?" He raised both eyebrows significantly. "You know what *I* think, don't you? But then it ain't my business. I'm a doctor, not a judge of folk's morals."

"The colonel isn't pompous, sir," the boy said calmly, "and he certainly isn't an idiot."

"Well, I guess it's your business. The pamphlet," he thrust it at the boy's chest, "on miasmic diseases. You'll find the correlation between the presence of marsh miasmas and an increased incidence of malarial fever fascinating. Oh, and as I said before, some very good thoughts regarding the emanations arising from all the excrement found around the camps."

"Thank you, sir."

The surgeon moved slowly aside, just barely enough for the boy to squeeze by, and as he did so, the breath caught hard in the surgeon's throat and something like an electric shock jolted his system. He stared after him, his mouth slightly open in an uncharacteristically dumbfounded pose. Then he swallowed and gasped. "Well, *I'll be . . . goddamned*—" His voice rose to a crescendo of incredulity and then tailed off into silent shock. His pipe drooped. He looked like a man who had at last found the answer to the eternal question.

Pittsburg Landing had been named for Pitts Tucker, long dead, which was just as well, since he'd made a living selling gut-rot liquor to eager river men. These days he'd have found equally enthusiastic patrons among the soldiers, for in the last week the area had mushroomed into an enormous army camp the like of which awed even old warriors, let alone raw recruits.

Every day transports brought up more men from Savannah, twelve miles away, often docking at the narrow landing beneath the bluff, five deep, and the tents now spread as far as the Eastern Corinth and Hamburg-Savannah Roads, under trees covered with light foliage. Forty-five thousand noisy troops, five divisions, were bivouacked across these once-peaceful fields, and any day now, Buell and his Army of the Ohio would be marching southwest along the Central Alabama Railroad, swelling their ranks to eighty-two thousand men.

Soldiers never before drilled in barrack courtyards found themselves drilled and inspected in the middle of peach orchards where the blossoms had already turned to pink and pleasant morning temperatures gave way during the day to the beginnings of an uncomfortable heat. Spring had come early to the Tennessee Valley. The birds sang joyously and a quick eye could spot squirrels or rabbits, even the occasional fleet-footed deer scampering through the lush, abundant woods. Violets dotted the landscape, peeking up between the tall verdant grasses, and while some soldiers openly admired their surroundings others said contemptuously that Tennessee couldn't hold a candle to Iowa, Wisconsin, or Michigan, to Ohio, Indiana, or Illinois. Every soldier thought their own land back home as remarkably similar to wherever they were, only better.

Whatever the truth, these myriad creeks and fast-flowing streams, fields of corn and orchards, once alive only with wild life and farmers now echoed to the harsh clatter of musketry and the gruff, insistent voice of a drill sergeant.

Soldiers not easily impressed by pomp or circumstance, by a high-stepping steed or shiny brass buttons, liked to gossip, especially about the frailties of their officers. The higher the rank, the greater the weakness, as though these poor, ill-educated, strong-minded farm boys took comfort from the knowledge that privilege, wealth, education, or arrogance were no surefire guarantees against crass stupidity and excess. Most officers were drunk, corrupt, overambitious, or just plain useless in their eyes and not worth a dime. Some they liked. Some they even loved. Others they weren't yet sure about. Take Billy Sherman. The stories of his insanity at Kentucky made him suspect, and they never saw him but he looked nervous, fidgety, and kind of wild about the eyes. True, he'd fought bravely at Bull Run, was the last officer to leave the field that shameful day, trying desperately to rally his brigade. He'd won promotion from colonel to brigadier, and even though his superiors now trusted him with an entire division, they weren't at all sure they wanted to be led into battle by a man the newspapers had called "stark raving mad." No one had twisted their arm to enlist. Hell, they wanted to fight, but who could blame them for looking at their officers with a certain degree of trepidation. When battle was finally joined, who could accurately predict what was most likely to get them slaughtered: insanity, drunkenness, or ambition?

At the hospital rumors abounded. Some said the Rebs were no longer in Corinth, but were camped less than half a mile away, at night you could see their bivouac fires glowing in the sky. Others argued that this was a reflection of their own campfires, and there wasn't a Reb for miles, except for stray pickets and the occasional cavalry patrol that skedaddled when they saw blue uniforms. When pickets at Owl Creek went missing, the surgeons said they'd deserted, while the patients, mostly enlisted men who had their reputation to defend, insisted they'd been captured by Reb cavalry. Both groups agreed that Reb sharpshooters were concealed behind every tree waiting to put lead into any Yankee stupid enough to stick his head out.

Jesse Davis listened to the rumors, but was not deterred from taking a trip to the Widow Howell's farm with a gunnysack and a pocket full of poker winnings. He had heard Dr. Cartwright say, "I wish to God I could give the sick men fresh fruit."

5

Every fair and manly trait

★ ★ ★ ★

Women are soft, mild, pitiful and flexible.

—WILLIAM SHAKESPEARE, *Henry VI, Part 1*, scene 4

The Widow Howell had a peach orchard next to her house, but as the old woman told Jesse when the boy came knocking on her door in the pouring rain, offering to buy some peaches,

"Oh Lord, young fella, they ain't near out. Lord, don't *you* know that? They won't be ready 'til near August." And she laughed at Jesse's ignorance.

Nevertheless, Jesse left what she considered a fair price for a sack full of peaches on the doorstep after the still-laughing widow closed the door and climbed the fence into the orchard.

Thirty minutes later, with what would have seemed to anyone a heavy sack over her shoulder, Jesse started back to camp. As he crossed the Corinth Road, he looked for the picket guard on duty when he had passed no more than an hour ago. If the guard had returned to camp, another ought to have taken its place. He had almost decided to investigate when he heard the unmistakable rattle of musket fire in the distance, followed by urgent shouts, more gunfire, and the pounding of hooves. The boy plunged into the dense undergrowth, clutching his precious load, and in a few minutes saw seven blue-clad men and two officers running down the muddy road. One of the officers, a red-faced captain called Shotwell, his efforts at retreat made more strenuous by the dress sword between his short legs, was way out in front of his men, as if in an effort to set a record for cowardly flight in the face of the enemy. A few yards behind, using one hand to gather his men together, like an anxious shepherd whose straying flock is pursued by a pack of wolves, and the other hand to stem the flow of blood from a shoulder wound, Jesse recognized the rugged Lieutenant Washington. Bringing up the rear was the massive bulk of Sergeant Bailey, with young Private Atkinson slung over his shoulder like a sack of meal, dripping blood at every jolt.

Suddenly the crack of a single shot rang out and a look of surprise came over Sergeant Bailey's bearded face. He went down onto his knees and keeled over, his burden slipping off his shoulder into the mud. Another gunshot followed by another in rapid succession and the next to fall was the fleeing captain, taking a Rebel musket ball in the right thigh, and letting out a series of yelps like an animal caught in a trap. Jesse emerged from the bushes and saw Lieutenant Washington gape in astonishment as he ran past him to the two men lying in the mud. A cursory glance at Sergeant Bailey confirmed that he was dead; his red eyes were open, staring up sightlessly at the sky, as blood and brains ran swiftly from a gaping hole in the back of his head. The young private, shot in the face, was lying on his side, struggling with each gasp to catch his breath, making loud, wet, stridorous sounds that could be heard several yards away. When Jesse knelt beside him, it was immediately obvious why. The bullet had carried away part of his jaw, shredding his tongue in the process. The tissues of his mouth and throat had swollen to such a degree that his airway was obstructed. His face had turned ashen and his lips blue. Washington meanwhile had managed to get across the road. He was propped up against a tree not more than a foot away. "How are they?" he called, concerned for his men, though setting his teeth against his own pain.

"The sergeant is dead," Jesse replied, opening the canvas haversack he now carried, which Jacob had filled with all manner of medical necessities. He found the pocket surgical kit, flipped open the tortoiseshell scalpel, felt around the soldier's bloodied neck and found the windpipe, and without so much as a second's hesitation had made a quick horizontal cut.

A horrified Washington screamed out, "What in hell are you doing? You crazy little bastard." He lunged forward and tried to grab the boy's arm but missed and fell back, staring at him from a prone position as though the little soldier was the devil incarnate.

Jesse ignored him, *and* the captain, sprawled out in the center of the muddy wagon road crying that he was bleeding to death, and went on with the urgent task. First, a splattering of blood oozed up through the hole in the private's throat, followed by a slow bubbling. To add further to Washington's horror Jesse put a finger into the hole made with the scalpel and opened the incision wider. Private Atkinson took a huge gasp of air through the hole, one of his hands coming up, clawlike, to grab at Jesse's blouse, whether in gratitude or agony, Washington could not have said. After a few seconds, Private Atkinson's color had improved so significantly that Washington, in a voice of profound awe, said, "God Almighty—"

He got no further as triumphant shouting filled the clearing. In a few seconds, their unhurried pursuers quickly encircled all eight of them, a small unit of butternut troopers led by a handsome captain with shoulder-length blond curls and flowing mustaches. Shotwell propped himself on one elbow and began to shout abuse at the cavalrymen, displaying a now misplaced defiance, since he had already shown his eagerness to desert his men.

"If I can only . . . get to my feet I'll finish you . . . off, do you hear me, you filthy Reb traitors!"

The Rebel captain, unmoved by this display of empty bravado, fell to discussing with his lieutenant what they ought to do with their captives. They were traveling light, on a reconnaissance mission, and evidently did not welcome the burden. Several of them said they should shoot the prisoners and be done with it. Jesse took no heed of this as he rummaged around in his haversack until he found what he was looking for. Like the doctor, he had no tracheotomy tube, but he did have a rubber urinary catheter. He snipped off the end just as he had seen Cartwright do and slipped it through the incision he had made in the soldier's windpipe, fastened a length of bandage around the tube, and then tied it around the boy's neck to hold it in place. Having removed his sack jacket to place under the wounded man's head, he went to Lieutenant Washington, who was now propped up against a tree staring at him.

"What in God's name did you do to him?" The officer's eyes were staring.

"I cleared a passageway so that he can breathe, but he must get to a surgeon." As Jesse reported this, he worked on Washington's shoulder. Finding no exit wound, he told him, "It isn't serious, sir, but the ball's still in there."

He was placing a wad of lint against the wound when Captain Shotwell called out, "You, boy! Help me—I'm bleeding to death. For God's sake, *leave him* and help me—I'm bleeding to death, I tell you."

"Go on, Private, I can tend myself—" Jesse went on swiftly but expertly bandaging Washington's shoulder.

"Private, do you hear me!" the captain screamed. "I order you to attend me—I'll have you shot—goddamn you—"

Washington used his good hand to grip Jesse's slender wrist. In the past few seconds, it had begun to rain again. Blinking rainwater from his eyes, he stared into the boy's face. "Do as I say, Private, take a look at Cap'in Shotwell before he makes me so goddamned ashamed to admit I serve in the same army as him—never mind the same goddamned regiment."

"Tell me, boy," called out one of the Rebel troopers trotting his horse alongside Jesse as he crossed the road to the whining Shotwell. "Does yaw mama know yaw out?"

"I thought you *were* my mama," came Jesse's retort as he bent over Captain Shotwell's bleeding leg. "She has a shawl just like yours."

The blond captain and his men laughed heartily, for their comrade had only that morning found a lady's flower-patterned shawl and was wearing it around his neck. Now he tore it off in disgust and threw it in the mud.

"Yaw oughta learn tow respect yaw elders," said he, waving his pistol in the air menacingly as his horse pranced. "Else yaw gonna git yaw head blowed off." Since he was not much older than the object of his threat, this made his companions laugh even more.

"Ow—is you boys gonna fight over the baby's rattle?" teased one of the troopers, a well-set-up sergeant with a bunch of Indian feathers in his hatband and his right arm strapped to his chest with a wide leather belt.

"Send 'em t'bed without no supper," suggested another.

The young Rebel pointed his pistol at his companions, first one and then another, but the laughter merely increased.

The Rebel captain, who was laughing harder than anyone, leaned over and placed a placating hand on the young trooper's shoulder. "You have to rise above our joshin', Henry. There, look at the Yankee-boy, he takes it like a real good sport and gives as good as he gets."

"*Grab the pistol*—" instructed Captain Shotwell, in an urgent whisper, as Jesse bound up his wound. "—Grab the goddamn pistol, boy, get it to me, I say, while their attention is elsewhere."

"Sir?" Jesse feigned confusion, though it was evident to Washington across the way that the boy knew exactly what Shotwell was suggesting.

"The gun—*my* gun—you half-witted—" He was stretching his hand toward his Colt lying in the mud where he had dropped it. "—*Give me my gun*—"

Jesse glanced up to see the Rebel sergeant watching them, his one good hand on his own pistol, now drawn more than halfway from the leather holster at his side, a snarling smile on his face that was willing, *urging* him to try for the pistol. Jesse kicked the gun out of reach.

"Why you . . . you goddamned cowardly traitor—what the hell are you doing?"

"Savin' yer miserable Yankee life," answered the Rebel captain, slipping his own pistol back into its holster on the horse's saddle. "You may thank this boy, suh, that we don't shoot ya all down like the dogs ya are." He then leaned over and spoke quietly to one of his men, who grinned in agreement and dismounted, coming toward Shotwell with a Bowie knife. Shotwell started to bawl like a baby, until he realized the Rebel was cutting his shoulder straps, not his throat. Next, the Rebel ripped loose the captain's sash and extracted his sword from its sheath. He put the sash through the sword handle and tied it around Jesse's narrow waist, laughing whiskey breath into his face as he did so. Then he tossed the shoulder straps to the floor and walked back to his horse.

"Pick them up and wear them," the Rebel captain told Jesse. "Ya deserve them more than that yellow Yankee dog." He then yelled something at the top of his lungs, something that might have been the Rebel yell, wheeled his horse around, and galloped off, calling out to the wounded captain as he did so, "Remember ma name and my face, suh, Ah am Captain Preston T. Lightborn, of Forrest's Regiment, Tennessee Cavalry, under Colonel Nathan B. Forrest. If we meet again, suh, you will not be given a second chance!"

"Let me know when yaw reach yaw tenth birthday, boy!" called out the young horseman, following his comrades, his horse's hooves churning up mud into Jesse's face and spattering his private's blouse. "I'll send yaw yaw first pair a long pants!" *His* Rebel yell was even louder and more manic than his commander's, as he spurred away after his comrades.

"The boy's a dirty little coward, sir, a dirty little coward. I could have bagged you a half-dozen Reb cavalry to question, sir, instead this sniveling little coward prevented me from reaching my pistol—kicked the damn thing out of my reach—not only a coward, sir—but a traitor—a damn Reb spy—" Captain Shotwell fell back onto the litter and lay still, his eyes closed, his bulbous chest heaving, rain spattering on his blanket.

Silently chewing his cigar stub and making no effort to hide his disdain, Sherman jerked his head at the two orderlies and they trotted off with the wounded officer. One hour ago, Colonel Buckland had raised the alarm when a message arrived from the picket guard that there had been no one around to relieve them when they came on duty. Sherman, out reconnoitering the ground nearby with Lieutenant Colonel McPherson when this incident was reported to him, had decided to investigate in person.

"Sir, can I speak up?" Lieutenant Washington came forward. Jesse had used the string that held up his own trousers to make a sling for the lieutenant's wounded arm and now that worthy officer stood before the division commander's restless horse, blood seeping through his bandage.

"Get to the hospital, Lieutenant, we'll talk later," Sherman instructed.

"No sir, begging your pardon. I couldn't go to the hospital, sir, I couldn't rest easy if I didn't tell what happened. The truth is, sir, the boy saved our hides. If it wasn't for him, we would have ended up prisoners or dead. Cap'in Shotwell is a darn fool, sir. There was already three of us bleeding, Shotwell himself, Atkinson took a ball in the jaw, he was choking to death, you had to see with your own eyes what the boy did, sir, else you would'na believed it possible, and I was nursing this shoulder, when Shotwell tried to go for his gun. If he'd got one of the Rebs or more especially the captain himself, they would have done for the whole damn lot of us. The boy showed courage, sir, a different kinda courage than that darn fool Shotwell could ever understand. He don't care a darn for his men. The boy read the situation. He saw the same thing I saw, sir, that the captain was one of those Southrons who appreciates honor in his foe. Do you know what I mean, sir?"

Sherman nodded slowly and chewed his cigar. He knew precisely what the officer meant—hadn't he lived in the *honorable* South for six years? Captain Jackson at his side tried to read the look on his commander's hawkish features, but the shapeless hat, pulled down low over his brow, and the collar of his oilskin pulled up high against the now hard-driving rain, masked all expression. Instead, the Hoosier exchanged meaningful grimaces with Van Allen, who was also listening intently. True enough, they didn't know the boy that well, but neither the Hoosier nor the New Englander could picture him as a coward, a spy, *or* a traitor, which of course they all knew he wasn't, even that lying son of a bitch Shotwell, covering his own arse.

"He said it right out, sir; he said if the boy hadn't done what he did he woulda shot the whole damn bunch of us without a second's thought. You can't brand the boy a coward, sir, like Captain Shotwell said, he's a good boy, a credit to his folks, to the Union army, and to his commander, and that, sir, is the plain, simple, unadulterated, gall darn truth, so help me God."

"Get your shoulder looked at, Lieutenant Washington," Sherman urged.

"No sir, with respect, not 'til I know the boy won't pay for Captain

Shotwell's tardiness." Washington stood his ground, though his craggy features were contorted with pain.

"You've explained what happened, Lieutenant, and you have my word, sir, that this private will be treated fairly, now take yourself off to the hospital, before you bleed to death."

Lieutenant Washington glanced across at Jesse kneeling on the floor in the rain, gathering up the contents of his haversack. Throughout Shotwell's hysterical accusations as well as during Washington's impassioned defense, the boy had maintained a dignified silence. Even now, the officer was reluctant to leave him to the division commander's mercy.

"Private Davis, come here," Sherman said tersely.

Jesse obeyed, Shotwell's dress sword, still tied around his waist, clanking on the ground as he moved. Jackson and Van Allen gave each other close-mouthed smiles. Beside the division commander, seated upon his large chestnut, was the ever-amiable James McPherson, silently observing the proceedings.

The boy saluted, blinked rainwater, looked from Sherman to Jackson, to Van Allen, to McPherson, whose dark, kindly eyes were twinkling and whose small mouth pursed in anticipation, or was it amusement?

"Why are you wearing an officer's dress sword and sash?" Sherman demanded to know.

"It was the Rebel captain's joke, sir. I believe he wished to make a point."

"And what, Private, was the point he wished to make?"

"I'd rather not say, sir."

Lieutenant Washington, still standing beside the boy, spoke up. "The Reb cap'in's point, sir, was that this boy has more right to those trappin's of an officer than Shotwell, and he was darn right." He touched his shoulder. "Thank you, son," he said in his deep voice, "for everything. I sure am sorry for what I called you. But I ain't never seen anything like I saw you do for Private Atkinson and the Lord is my witness I won't never forget it 'til the day I breathe my last." He would not allow the orderlies to place him on a litter but put his battered hat on his head and started back to camp on foot.

A hysterical voice preceded the arrival of the surgeon who had accompanied Colonel Buckland from his brigade headquarters and who was now running across the road holding up the rubber tubing. "Who inserted *this* into that soldier's throat? Does anyone know who inserted this into that soldier's windpipe? Sir," the surgeon spoke to the general, "I must know who inserted this into the soldier's throat."

"I did, sir," Jesse stated.

"You *did*?" The brigade surgeon stared at him, blinked, and stared at him again, as though the young private was a species of life quite alien to him. "You did, Private?"

"Damn you, Doctor," Sherman said, as his spirited horse pranced restlessly in the rain, reflecting the impatience of his master. "The boy *said* he did. Do you want him to draw you a diagram, sir, take an oath on the Bible?" He shortened the reins and spoke calmly to the animal, stroking its neck. "Easy now . . . easy—"

"He . . . he . . . saved that soldier's life, you see there, sir, he . . . he used this"—he held up the hollow tube higher for the commander's inspection—"to perform a *tracheotomy*—he inserted this into the wind- pipe to help the soldier breathe—I have not heard of such a thing before, sir, nor will my colleagues have heard of such a thing. You see, sir, this is a catheter, a urinary tube, used solely to relieve distension of the bladder. If a patient cannot urinate, we insert this into the—"

Sherman broke in. "Come to the point, sir, come to the blasted point."

Van Allen heard Jackson chuckle.

"Well, sir, according to *Wood's Practice of Medicine*—"

"Damn you and *damn Wood's Practice of Medicine*!" bellowed Sherman. "Lieutenant Colonel McPherson, my staff and I are soaked to the skin, sir, soaked to the skin, and *you* are giving us a lecture on surgery. Did the boy do good or didn't he?"

"He did magnificently, sir."

"Then kindly tell him so and take yourself and your urinary tube back to camp and let me get on with questioning this boy. . . .

"How many of the enemy were in the party that attacked my picket guard, Private?"

Jesse related all he could remember, including the name of the Rebel captain and his regiment, information enough to have Sherman suggest the boy would make a very reliable spy.

"The damn Rebel cavalry are getting saucier by the second," he said, turning to McPherson.

"You recall what the Rebel prisoners you interrogated at Shiloh Church told you, sir, they openly boasted of being part of a grand army that will push us into the Tennessee," McPherson reminded him.

"But can we believe them, Mac? Prisoners will boast of anything to give themselves an importance they do not have. It makes them feel better to contemplate a great victory for their army, even if they are incarcerated and not able to participate." He turned his piercing gaze back on the boy and, stabbing with his cigar stub, demanded, "What were you doing out here anyway, and what's in the sack?"

"Peaches, sir. I picked them at the Widow Howell's farm."

"That ain't the truth, boy," spoke up Captain Jackson, the peacetime farmer. "Everyone knows peaches ain't even out on the trees 'til May, let alone ready to pick ripe."

Sherman was fierce. "I'll ask you again: What have you got in that sack? Have you been stealing chickens from these people? They already think us vandals and barbarians." The commander's face had gone red; his eyes glittered dangerously.

"No sir, I paid the widow a full cent for every two peaches." Jesse held the sack wide open for Captain Jackson to see. He blinked, thrust his head further forward as though to get a better look, and then blinked again, his suspicious eyes getting smaller. "Peaches," he declared suspiciously, as if he now did not trust the evidence of his own eyes. "Well, I'll be darned."

Marcus sniggered at his fellow aide. When he saw the commander look at him sharply, he made a kind of contrite motion of his handsome head, but he could do nothing to conceal the laughter in his dark eyes, which he lowered.

"The peaches are for the men in the hospital," Jesse told Sherman. "Dr. Cartwright said he wished to God he could give them fresh fruit."

"Darn it," Andy said, removing his large hat and holding it aloft by the brim as he scratched his hair with the same hand, a regular balancing act admired by all who witnessed it. "They're peaches a'right and no mistake, nice ones too." He took one out and examined it. It was yellow and large, round, fleshy, and juicy when he bit into it. He grinned at Van Allen.

"You heard the accusations made by Captain Shotwell?" Sherman asked. He was now bored with the subject of the peaches.

"Yes sir."

"Have you nothing to say in your defense? Do you feel that you acted inappropriately?"

"I feel that my actions were entirely appropriate, sir. I knew also that the lieutenant would speak up and tell the truth."

"*How* did you know?"

"How can I doubt the honesty of a man whose name is Washington?"

Sherman, McPherson, and the other members of the headquarters party had ridden off. Only Captain Jackson remained. Gruffly, the aide called out, "Over here, boy." He reached down and gripped the sack, securing it to the pommel of his saddle. "I'll get this back to camp for you."

"Thank you, sir," Jesse said and then started off on foot.

Jackson stared in amazement after the tiny figure in the oversized uniform. Then found his voice. "Hey, soldier, where you goin'? Come on back. This fine strong animal can surely carry me, this sack, and somethin' no bigger 'an a goose egg." Jackson extended his arm. The boy held on as he inserted his foot into the stirrup. "Don't fall off in the mud now, you hear me?" He looked at the boy's arms about his waist. He had wrists no thicker than young twigs. "Tell me sumpthin', were you really gonna carry this sack back to camp under yer own steam?"

"Yes sir."

"Darn it, boy, if I don't believe you."

Over supper that evening the Hoosier and Marcus were discussing that morning's excitement. They both agreed that the boy was no ordinary boy, no farm boy, and well educated, even though, as Jackson reported, the boy hadn't said two words to him all the way back to the hospital. Marcus even suggested that the commander might want to have him transferred to division, since they were always looking for decent copy clerks.

"Left a widowed mother at home ter weep," was Jackson's sentimental view.

"The boy is an orphan. He told me so and I believe him," Sherman informed both men.

Sherman's tone was dry, even for him, as he passed a hand over his stomach and winced. The pickled beef he'd eaten that evening, what the enlisted men called "salt-horse," stank to high heaven and the desiccated vegetables had tasted like cardboard. He smoked six to eight cigars a day and a further four or five during the night. He drank whiskey, ate no lunch, a meager supper, and took only black coffee for breakfast and slept perhaps two hours a night. This lethal combination, mixed with too much nervous energy, had brought on severe headaches and stomach cramps even the strongest of anodynes could not overcome since his turbulent days as commander of the Department of the Cumberland. He was also at this time not immune to the great army curse of diarrhea and looked suddenly discomforted. "Excuse me." He shot up and rushed away.

Horatio chose that inopportune moment to bring forth a tin bowl overflowing with fresh yellow peaches, which he handed around with a proud grin. "Day is a present," he called out after the fleeing commander, "frome dat boy, gen'al, sir, der one yo give dat cheese, bread, an a apple toe der udder night. Yo 'member, gen'al, sir? He dune give me toe fer my own self. Day is real good, gen'al, sir, real good, sweet as honey like they is full ripe. He say toe remind yo they dun settle yo stom'ch real good, they dyn cure what ails yo." He turned his big, red-flecked eyes onto the officers. "Where der gen'al g'on in such a hurry, yo 'spose?"

The next morning Jacob De Groot was in a hurry. For such a large man he could move awful fast when required and he was moving awful fast toward Seth Cartwright's tent, where the surgeon was just reaching for his safety razor, and it wasn't even Sunday.

"You must come quickly; you must come right now!" the Dutchman cried in his native tongue before the surgeon got it out of him in English.

Cartwright drew his suspenders over his naked torso, cussed when the elastic caught his chest hair, grabbed up his medical case, and followed his steward down the mazelike arrangement of tent streets until they reached the clearing before Colonel Buckland's Fourth Brigade headquarters. Then both men stopped in their tracks. It seemed as if the entire brigade, every soldier in the Seventieth, Forty-eighth, and Seventy-second Ohio, had turned out that morning to watch a boy and a horse do battle.

"Oh hell—" Jacob heard the surgeon mutter, and had he been a cussing man he would have concurred.

"Stay with him, boy!"

"That boy sure knows how to handle an 'onouree horse, that boy's from Kentuck and no mistake."

"There was another boy tryin' to ride that no good crazy jug head yesterday mornin', three hours past they were still tryin' to scrape his remains offa the fence rail."

"That little runt ain't got no chance, he's too damn green."

"Hell, it ain't the runt who's green, it's the damn horse. The runt's black and blue." Loud appreciative laughter greeted this observation.

"Gosh darn horse ain't no horse!"

"Goddamn son of a bitch horse!"

"Keep his head up, boy, keep his head up! If yer keep his head up he won't buck thataway!"

"Ain't knowin' which er 'em is more 'onouree, the horse or the boy."

"Hold on to him, soldier!" the excitable Marcus Van Allen was shouting as he waved his hat in the air in a most ungentlemanly fashion. "Hold on with all your strength, young fellow!"

"Hold onta him," echoed his fellow aide, "hold onto him, boy, I tell you he's weakenin', you got him wonderin' now, boy, you got him on the run!"

Thus was the collective advice being offered as the surgeon pushed his way through the noisy crowds to the roped-off corral in time to see the young infantry private go hurtling headfirst through the air, to land face down in the dirt, swallowed up in a swirling cloud of dust, like a chicken in a tornado.

"What the *hell's* going on?" Cartwright stared over at the now-prostrate figure, then at the baying mass of blue pushing against the rope, then at Jackson and then back at the horse, an indisputably handsome, biscuit-colored animal with flowing white mane and tail.

"See for yerself, Doc," Captain Jackson told him, "that boy's game as a two-cent whore."

Jesse Davis, after lying there for a few seconds, just to catch his breath, had picked himself up, brushed himself off, wiped the dust and sweat from his face with the back of his hand, and was approaching the palomino doggedly, for a third time. The horse waited, pawing the ground with his near side hoof as though beating time with the boy's determined march across the corral, his long mane flowing from side to side with every movement of the magnificent head. He waited until the boy had gripped the reins with one hand and the saddle horn with the other and, to a steadily rising crescendo of cheering, allowed the boy to slip his foot into the stirrup. Then the canny animal sidestepped, and sidestepped again, until the boy was hopping on one foot, while trying to extract his other foot from the trap. The uproar of laughter and shouting from a hundred male throats vibrated in Cartwright's ears; he could hardly hear himself think, let alone protest. He stood there in horror, wiping shaving cream from his face with a grubby handkerchief. The horse had become perfectly still, unfazed by the shouting, giving the boy just a second's chance to extricate his foot, to let go of the reins so he could use both hands, before the animal cantered across the corral leaving the boy to topple over backward in a cloud of dust. Neighing loudly, as if with laughter, this ghostly mount watched the boy sitting dazedly on his backside in the dust enjoying to the limit the cruel but delicious game he was playing.

"That animal sure has a mighty fine sense a humor," commented Jackson to Van Allen.

On both sides of the surgeon, sums of money were changing hands, enlisted men and officers were striking bets on how long the boy could stay mounted, how many bones he would break, and how soon it would be before he cracked his skull open like an eggshell.

Cartwright turned to Andy Jackson and shouted atop the noise, "You have to get this stopped, right now!"

"Why would I wanna do that, Doc?" Jackson shouted back. "The boy don't mind, the men are havin' fun, and so far there ain't been one darn complaint from the horse."

"You think this is a joke?"

"Take it easy."

"How can I take it easy when the boy is gonna get his neck broken? Have it stopped—I'm ordering you to have this stopped, right now!"

"Can't hear yer, Doc." Andy cupped the shell of his left ear and winked at Van Allen.

Jesse had risen, albeit shakily, to be greeted by a tumultuous cheer and was once more determinedly approaching the humorous animal, who was eyeing him with a craven mix of admiration, pity, and triumph that seemed to say *Okay, runt, you back for more, I've got more.*

"Listen to me, you don't understand, you have to stop it—Jesse is . . . is . . ."

The aide waited expectantly, grinning from ear to ear, and the surgeon fell silent. "The boy's *what*, Doc?" Before the surgeon could speak, the Hoosier had let rip with another cheer and more advice. "Hold on, boy! You've got him now—hold on I tell yer—hold on there!" Much to Jackson's delight, Jesse had remounted. The officer removed his hat and waved it in the air shouting, "Go get him, boy! You can do it!"

Cartwright grabbed hold of the aide by his arm. "Will you damn well *listen* to me?"

"I'm listenin', Doc, but yer ain't sayin' nuthin'." He shook the surgeon's grip loose.

"Don't you understand, Jesse is . . . Jesse is"—Jackson stared at him—"too small to ride that horse," the surgeon finished lamely.

The aide shoved him aside to shout, "Ride him, cowboy!"

Van Allen looked at the doctor and attempted to show a little more sympathy. "He'll be all right, Doctor, he's a tough little fellow."

"Yer, a tough little fellow," Cartwright agreed, scooping the hair off his brow. "And game as a two-cent whore."

Even as he was speaking, Jesse had leapt into the air for a fourth time, as though there were firecrackers attached to his ankles, and for a fourth time he landed in the dirt, face down, his chest heaving as if it would burst with the effort to gulp breath into his lungs.

"The boy's finished . . . goddamn it . . . he kaint take no more."

"Lord above, hiss gonna try agin."

"He's finished, I tell yer. He ain't never gonna get up."

"He's gonna try agin—that boy won't quit 'til he's dead."

"Someone write his mama."

"Two dollars says the boy don't ever git up no more."

"I'll take some a that—"

"Hey, there's old Gen Sherman hisself come to take a look-see."

"Hey, Gen'al, come to see the fun?"

"Mornin', Gen'al, sir—"

"Let the gen'al through—"

"Hey, let the gen'al pass, you sons a bitches."

"What's going on here?" Sherman demanded to know of Captain Jackson, removing the inevitable smoking cigar from between his teeth. "Colonel Buckland and I could hear the shouting from his tent."

"Gen'al." Jackson saluted and pointed at Jesse still lying on his back in the dirt, narrow chest heaving. "The boy took a bet he could ride the palomino but it looks like he lost."

"It's finished," Cartwright said. "You've all had a good laugh, now it's over."

"Not quite," said Van Allen softly, admiringly, staring across the corral.

"Well, I'll be a—" Jackson never finished his sentence, he cut it short with the loudest "Yee ha!" ever to issue from the lips of a Westerner.

Jesse was stirring to life, first the red head, then the torso.

Horrified, the surgeon shouted, "Jesse, I order you to stop!"

If the boy heard, he paid no heed to the distressed surgeon. He gathered what was left of his dignity and his kepi, hitched up his torn pants, stuck out his chin, and made tracks for the horse. Cartwright tried to climb under the rope, but Andy held him fast.

The surgeon was appalled. "What in hell do you think you're doing? Let me go—"

"Look around you, Doc, this is what you might call a diversion, what you medical boys are always tellin' us we need, to keep up the men's spirits. I ain't seen spirits kept up better'n this since before Bull Run."

"You wanna keep up the men's spirit by breaking the boy's neck?" Cartwright asked Sherman incredulously.

"Do you want it stopped, Gen'al?" Jackson inquired.

Sherman stood there a moment. He had watched the boy rise slowly, painfully, determinedly, to his feet, grab up his kepi and move slowly, painfully, determinedly, to the horse, a tiny, curly-haired ghost covered in gray dust, now almost the same color as the animal he sought to tame. The commander listened to the tremendous cheer that went up and he said, "No, Captain." Just the two words, but his expression spoke volumes.

This time Jesse approached his adversary directly from the front, extending his right hand to the horse's face, talking to him all the while, "Okay, my handsome boy, we both know that when this is all over you and I are going to be good friends. You've had your fun, and so have the men, but we both know I'm going to keep getting up and you're going to keep throwing me off until this body breaks in half or you're just too tired to be bothered, whichever comes first, *but I'm not going to quit.*"

"A week's pay says the little cretin breaks his neck," called out Major Walker.

Several takers came forward, but they would have done better to save their money, for at that moment another almighty cheer rose from the uniformed men packed in around the picket rope. The palomino had allowed the boy to mount up and, for no reason that anyone could think of, was walking calmly and agreeably around the arena, as if competing for the title best-trained animal in the circus. In a few seconds, urged by the boy's knees, the horse had obligingly broken into a trot, tossing his head as he passed close to the rope, thoroughly approving the thunderous applause that met this lap of honor.

"Goddamn little shit!" Walker spat out. "It's a damn trick, I tell you. He knew that horse all along, it's a goddamn trick. They planned the entire thing to dupe us."

"No trick, Captain, the boy knows how to ride, how to earn a horse's trust," Van Allen said. "As any good horseman will tell you, that *is* no trick, sir, *that* is a gift from God. Besides, the animal evidently respects tenacity, as do I, sir." The handsome captain was grinning as though his own son was upon the horse now trotting toward them. "Bravo, Jesse, bravo!" He applauded.

As Jesse and the horse reached the picket rope, they stopped before the division commander. Jesse had the horse move slowly toward the general, facing him. He touched the animal lightly with his knees so that he slightly reared and then the horse and rider made one motion, the horse's head swung down with a bow, and the rider saluted. Then the animal leaned back on his haunches, front legs extended, and executed a kind of slow measured bow, dipping his head in a sweep and then lifting it to nod rapidly in honor of the Ohioan for whom he was performing. Jesse removed what remained of his kepi, swept it across his narrow waist, and bowed his curly red-gold head. Those who had not drifted away to greedily count their winnings or mumble in disgust at their unaccountable rashness stood there with open mouths, and Seth Cartwright stood there right along with them.

General Sherman chewed his cigar and gave the boy a narrow-eyed look as his hoarse voice exploded: "You *again*! Whenever there is trouble or excitement in this regiment why in *hell* do I find *you* at the center of it?"

Jesse grinned.

"What did I tell you, sir?" Captain Walker followed the division commander as he walked away. "You cannot persuade me that any vagabond alive can ride such a spirited animal after so brief an acquaintance. It is, sir, impossible, it is, sir, some kind of witchcraft, black magic—the boy has put some kind of spell on the horse."

"You're a sore loser, Cap'in Walker," Jackson told him.

Sergeant O'Connor and a second teamster had placed a rope around the horse's neck.

"What are you doing?" Jesse cried out, dismounting, "He's mine! Captain Walker said I may keep him."

"Away wid yer, yer little cuss." O'Connor gave him a swipe around the head. "Horses is for officers' use, not the likes a you, still wet behind der ears."

"But no officer can ride him, sir," insisted Jesse, hanging onto the horse's neck, "no one else can ride him but me, you said yourself, Sergeant, no one else but me has ever stayed on his back."

"Get away from here, I say, afore I cut yer liver up for the beast's breakfast!" O'Connor produced a knife whose ten-inch blade gleamed in the April sunlight and seemed to settle the question of the horse's ownership, at least for the present.

"We'll ask General Sherman," Jesse said and ran off to find him.

"Jesse!" Cartwright called, exasperated, for he had only just made his way from the throng of jostling men to reach the boy, and now the boy was off again. The surgeon followed, his medical case slung over his shoulder, banging against his back.

Jesse had not only reached the commander, but had overtaken him and was blocking his path. Sherman had no option but to stop. He looked at the boy standing there before him, sweat streaming down his red, grimy face; a face cut, bruised, and bleeding. One sleeve of his shirt was hanging away from the shoulder; the other was in shreds, the peak of his kepi, which was practically all that remained, clutched tightly in his hands.

Behind him, he heard Captain Jackson say, "Gall darn brass-neck a the boy."

"You will have to pay for that uniform" was Sherman's only comment.

"Yes sir. Forgive me, sir, but I undertook a wager with Captain Walker." The boy tried to catch his breath, but nonetheless spoke assertively, boldly holding Sherman's glowering stare. Beside him, Walker went pale as the boy pointed an accusing finger. "*This officer* declared, sir, in the presence of at least a dozen witnesses, that if I were but to remain on Quicksand's back long enough to walk him around the corral, I could keep him as my own. Sir, will *you* now witness that I not only remained in the saddle but also trotted the horse, yet Sergeant O'Connor refuses to give me what is rightfully mine."

"Sergeant O'Connor is correct, he cannot give you what does not belong to him but to the United States Army, and you, Private Davis, are too saucy by half, sir, too saucy by half!" Sherman shoved the cigar into the corner of his mouth and growled in Walker's direction. "Did you tell this boy he could keep the horse if he fulfilled the challenge?" Beneath his shapeless slouch hat, his eyes had narrowed almost to slits.

"I may have intimated something of the kind, sir," Walker mumbled evasively.

"Captain Walker, I ask again, sir, *did you tell the boy the horse was his if he fulfilled the challenge?*" Since there was no mistaking the anger in Sherman's voice, Walker nodded slowly. "You, sir, are a knave. I know this boy, and despite his presumptuous, saucy manner, his gall-darn brass-neck, as my aide so succinctly puts it, he deserves far better treatment."

"May I then keep the horse, sir?" Jesse asked excitedly, wiping away the sweat in his eyes with what remained of his sleeve.

"No, you may not; the horse is useless for a soldier. Any officer will tell you a horse of his distinctive coloring and highly strung character will get his rider picked off by a Rebel sharpshooter immediately after riding onto the field."

"True," Walker said philosophically.

"Shut *up!*" Sherman barked.

"But, sir, have I not earned the right to keep the animal? I did, after all, win the wager."

"I do not approve of wagers, Private, whether they be sporting challenges or gambling."

Jesse lowered his gaze, his lower lip quivering, not with tears but bitter disappointment.

The general gripped the boy's face by his chin and tilted it upward. A wince of pain temporarily contorted the handsome features. A telltale purple shadow as large as an apple was beginning to emerge just where the division commander's bony fingers were gripping, a deep cut ran horizontal to his right brow, and a patch of blood had crusted up around his left nostril.

Cartwright at last managed to push his way through the thinning crowd as Sherman was saying, "The injuries on your face will no doubt pale into insignificance compared to what Dr. Cartwright will find when he takes down your drawers."

Everyone laughed, everyone but the doctor, who groaned as if the humiliation were all his own.

Sherman looked at him, at the shaving soap running down his face with the sweat. "Take this boy to your hospital and tend his hurts."

"Sir, does this mean I cannot keep the horse?" Jesse demanded to know, digging in his heels as Cartwright tried to drag him away.

"I thought I had just finished telling you. In the infantry only officers ride horses. Are *you* an officer?"

"No sir." The boy frowned.

"Do you expect to be commissioned one in the immediate future?"

"No sir, not the *immediate* future."

Jackson and Van Allen laughed, right along with everyone else standing there. Cartwright was shaking his head, one hand over his bespectacled eyes, the other holding onto the boy.

"If you think it more romantic to go into battle on horseback, you should have joined the cavalry." Sherman walked away.

"Sir, *you* are not in the cavalry!" called out the boy, finally breaking Cartwright's grip and running after the commander.

Sherman expelled an irritated breath. The boy was trotting along just in front of him now, moving backward, trying to keep ahead of the fast-walking commander. "Sir, when . . . I become an officer . . . may I have Quicksand as my own?"

"Damn you, boy—*yes*, when you receive your first commission you may take the horse. You have my word. Now go away or you will not live to earn that commission."

"Thank you, sir." The boy saluted smartly as befitted a soldier who had just extracted a promise from the commander of the Fifth Division of the Army of the Tennessee.

Sherman mounted up, and from atop his sorrel, the cigar-coarsened voice said, "*This* is the kind of mount an experienced officer would choose, my boy, fleet as a deer, very easy in her movements, and sweet-natured." He urged his beautiful race mare directly into a canter.

"Gen'al's right, boy," Jackson told Jesse as he swung up onto his own large gray mare. "This here's Sally, steady as a rock and even-tempered as yer maiden aunt." He looked at Cartwright from under his large hat. "See, Doc, all that hollerin' was fer nuthin', the boy's still in one piece, *just!*" He burst into laughter and cantered off after his commander.

"You've had a busy few days, Private Davis, first Reb cavalry, now a crazy horse. What's next, I wonder, a trip to a whorehouse? How are your bowels?" The surgeon poked and prodded at the boy's cuts and bruises. My God, he had not felt this inspired since trapping a fly under one of his mother's empty preservative jars in the dark basement of their house and cutting it open to see how it worked. "Have you had any of the usual childhood diseases, measles, mumps, scarlet fever? Remember, Private, when you take a chill, it can turn overnight into bronchitis or pneumonia in young recruits unaccustomed to sleeping in the wet. How about intestinal and digestive ailments? Badly prepared food can make life very miserable, at best you'll be disabled for life, at worst, given the medicines prescribed by most of my colleagues, you'll be dead. You'll have a scar but I would say it serves you damn right and you're damn lucky not to have broken your damn neck. Open wide." The boy obeyed. "Ever had whooping cough, strep throat, or croup?"

"Aaarrr—"

"Remove your shirt and pants. I want to give you a thorough examination." As Cartwright gave this order, he narrowed his eyes to scrutinize the bruised face for signs of panic. There was none, in fact the boy started quite calmly to ease his slim arms out of the shreds of his shirt. "What *the hell* are you doing? Are you crazy?" Cartwright attacked him with a blanket as he glanced over his shoulder to make sure no one was watching.

"You told me to remove my clothes, sir."

"Well . . . well . . . I know . . . but . . ." Suddenly he straightened up, pushed the errant hair out of his eyes, and said, "Okay, okay, if that's the way you want it, we'll stop playing games. What you did out there today was irresponsible in the extreme. What you did yesterday was downright suicidal. Next time you might find yourself going home in a damn box, or worse. Do you know what could happen to you if the Rebs get ahold of you?"

"You said you wished to God you could give the sick men some fresh fruit," he reminded him and Cartwright stared at him, blinking rapidly behind his small lenses. "I *wanted* you to be able to give the men fresh fruit."

"So it's *my* fault you nearly got your head blown off?"

"No sir, of course not."

"Goddamn it—" He turned around and turned back again, pushing a hand through his hair, exhaling loudly. "Here was I thinking, you and that pompous—well, never mind what I was thinking—you sure had me fooled, about that, anyway." He leaned over and thrust his half-shaved face close to the bloodied one, then he said in an insistent whisper, "Just tell me *one* thing, will you? Just one goddamn thing—what the *hell* are you going to do when Sherman finds out you're a girl?"

6

"Let us pause in life's pleasures . . ."

A man said to the universe:
"Sir, I exist!"
"However," replied the universe,
"The fact has not created in me
A sense of obligation."

—STEPHEN CRANE, *War Is Kind & Other Lines*, XXI, 1899

The carved wooden sign hanging over the entrance to Seth Cartwright's tent read, "Gone fishing, back after the war."

Jesse took the leather pouch from her pocket and slipped it under the canvas. As she turned, the flap flew up and the surgeon stood there, barefoot in his red woolen long johns, his voice demanding angrily, "Where the hell are you sneaking off to?"

"I wasn't sneaking off to anywhere, sir. I assumed you'd gone fishing."

"Do you know anyone who goes fishing at night?" With a contemptuous snort, he disappeared back into the tent and let the flap drop on her head. After a moment, his irritated voice inquired from within, "Well, are you coming in or ain't you?"

Jesse gazed around the claustrophobic interior of the small "A" tent which gave off a vague and not unpleasant aroma of whiskey and tobacco and, despite the mess, a cozy warmth. The surgeon stretched out on his cot; an empty whiskey bottle was just visible amid a tangle of blanket and soiled clothing.

Because none of the other officers would share with him, Seth Cartwright bivouacked alone, which suited him fine. Now Jesse could see why. Not merely was he unsociable and bad-tempered, but he was plainly a man who could not keep house. The tent was a mess of clothing, empty whiskey bottles, and medical journals, and everywhere, like a recent snowstorm, were scraps of paper and envelopes covered by notations in his illegible hand.

"You'll excuse my not being dressed. I wasn't expecting company." There was a letter on the cot.

"News from home?" Jesse asked conversationally, with a gentle smile.

"Nothing I can't handle."

"I'm sorry, I didn't mean to pry into your private business."

"No one has private business here. You might as well have your damn life story printed up and circulated around the camps. My sister wants to get married." He looked at her and held up the tobacco pouch. "What's this, a bribe to keep my mouth shut? You should have saved your money. I won't tell, I'd be cutting off my nose to spite my face." He leaned forward and curled his lip as he gave the two pristine-looking stripes on her sleeve a desultory flick with his finger. "So, they made you a corporal, huh, if that ain't the meat in the gravy. What's the story, you here to fight beside your sweetheart? Or maybe you lost your brother at Bull Run and you signed up looking for vengeance?" He made the motion of a bayonet thrust.

"I have no brother and no sweetheart," Jesse told him quietly.

Cartwright wondered why his mouth felt the urge to jerk at the corners, as if with satisfaction. Indeed the right side of his firm mouth did jerk. "No sweetheart, huh? Not for lack of trying, I'd say, not from the way you eyed up that pompous colonel. What they got you doing up at division?"

"I'm working as a copy clerk, making copies of orders for distribution to brigade commanders. Captain Van Allen says as the youngest member of staff I shall be division headquarters mascot."

"Wise choice. You're marginally better-looking than a goat, and you eat less. Have you made out your last will and testament, by the way? Damn you," he said suddenly very angry, "I could have taught you to be a good nurse, a *great* nurse, instead you're gonna throw it all away to do what? Spend your days scribbling in a ledger." His gaze went to the cut above her left eyebrow and he relented, but only a little. "You're crazy, you know that, don't you? Crazy—you'll never get away with it. Sit down."

"I can't stay long, sir."

"I didn't ask you to stay long. I didn't ask you to stay at all. I didn't ask you to come here. We ain't friends or anything. Friends are something you don't need in a war."

"Surely war makes friendship even more precious?"

"Barely out of your mama's womb and you know everything. Wait until you start seeing those *precious* friends laid out in a burial trench, you'll learn. Read this, I cut it from a newspaper for you."

While she read, he awaited a reaction. It was a story about a young female spy found in the ranks of the Army of the Potomac, a Southern sympathizer masquerading as a Yankee soldier. She was to be confined through the war's duration at hard labor, a ball weighing twenty-four pounds attached to her left leg by a log chain. The letters *F S* for "female spy" were to be marked with indelible ink on her left hip. Jesse folded the paper and placed it on the cot without comment.

"How'd you like that to happen to you?" the surgeon asked.

"I'm not a Rebel spy," Jesse said, "I noticed your tobacco pouch had a hole in it. The sutler recommended the leather variety because of the saddle stitching, they use leather throngs instead of thread, that way it lasts longer. It's good tobacco, too."

"Good or bad. I smoke what I can get." Cartwright drew open the throngs, found the pouch brim-full of leaf and held it up to his nose, drinking in the aroma. Then he set about filling his pipe. He puffed, holding the bowl in the cup of his hand with an intimacy born of solitary use. A more relaxed expression came over his features.

"You must be very happy about your sister's marriage?"

"Yer, I would be if we weren't in the middle of a goddamn war. Jack Coopersmith has been my closest friend since medical school."

"You just said you don't have any friends."

"I said I don't need any. I didn't say I ain't got any. Don't stick that ugly nose into matters you don't understand and that don't concern you."

Self-consciously, with a frown, Jesse touched her nose.

Despite it not being her business, Cartwright told her anyway. "Helen's best friend lost her fiancé to typhoid. It spooked her. Now she wants to get married. Right now Jack's on his way to Richmond with McClellan and I'm stuck here in Tennessee. Neither of us knows when we can get a furlough but Helen wants to get married. I don't wanna talk about it." He held up the tobacco pouch. "Where did you get the money for this? When I asked you for a loan you said you didn't have a cent."

"Poker winnings."

"Poker winnings? You play poker?"

"I didn't until Thursday night. I appear to have picked up the rudimentary points. It seems to be all about fooling the other players into believing you have a bad hand when you have a good one and a good hand when you don't." She shrugged. "It's called bluffing."

Cartwright looked at her. With a face like hers, she could outbluff the devil himself, "ugly nose" notwithstanding. "How much did you win?"

"Ten dollars and some change."

"God Almighty—" he exclaimed excitedly, "that's a goddamn fortune. You can buy me a bottle of whiskey." He showed her the empty one he'd been nursing under his thigh.

"I've spent it all. I bought your leather pouch and tobacco, a pair of socks for Jakob, the rest went on jellies, lemonade, ginger cookies, and fruitcake for the sick men."

"Damn you, and damn the sick men. How about the sick surgeons? Hasn't anyone taught you that charity begins at home and stop calling me *sir*." He tossed a pair of rolled-up socks at her head. They were hard with caked dirt. "I've got a name, use it or get out, and sit down, you're giving me a pain in the neck." The surgeon leapt off the bed, tipped the medical journals off the camp chair, and placed it near his cot. "Sit," he commanded. When she was seated, he said, "*Chess,* now there's a game. Nothing like it. I'd have taken the trouble to teach you chess, but it's a well-established fact, females can't learn such an intricate, subtle game. You need a very logical mind." He tapped his temple. "You have to think ahead, plan your moves in advance, anticipate your opponents' moves. The game requires vast powers of concentration. That's why females can't play. They've always got their minds someplace else."

"You make it sound very like war. You have to think ahead, plan your moves, and anticipate your opponents' moves. General Sherman plays chess. A good commander must be like a good chess player."

"God, no." Cartwright was horrified. "That's sacrilege, comparing the greatest game in the world to the greatest scourge of mankind."

"I'd like to learn to play chess, if you'll teach me?"

"Forget it, I'd be wasting my time." He looked at her out of the corner of his eye.

After a moment's silence, she said, "You like to fish?"

He looked confused, then he said, "The sign is a joke. Jacob carved it for me. You know what a joke is, don't you? Fishin's good. But I prefer to lie on the riverbank under the shade of a tree and doze, with the reflection of the sun on the water just tickling under my eyelids, that's what Helen and me used to do when we were kids. That's what I dream about—that's *all* I dream about, my shady old tree by the riverbank." He placed his hands behind his head and closed his eyes. An otherworldly smile turned up the corners of his mouth, as though even now in this low-ceiling canvas bolt hole miles from home and loved ones, surrounded by hostile forces, worn down by the sight of death, destruction, disease, and on the verge of what everyone agreed would be a great battle, he could imagine this *utterly* perfect scene.

"What is Quincy like?"

He opened his eyes, lifted his head slightly, and looked at her. "Well, for one thing, it sits on a bluff overlooking the Mississippi. If you go north of town on a good day, you can stand on that bluff and get a view of the river and its wide valley that will just take your breath away. It's a great spot to watch the migrating ducks and geese fly south for the winter. Helen and me used to watch them heading out for the Gulf states, you know"—he propped himself on one elbow—"where it's warm. We'd try and count them, guess how many would return, try and think up ways to recognize them when they got back." He laughed. "But they all looked the same and we used to wonder how they could tell each other apart. Do you know *why* I like Quincy?" Since this was a rhetorical question, Jesse was silent. "Because there are a hundred places along the riverbank where a boy can sit, all alone, surrounded by nothing but trees. Hidden by those trees, watch the muddy water flow by and *think*, with no one to disturb him, no one to pull his ear or pinch his cheek, no one to say, '*Why don't you speak up, boy? Are you sick, boy?*' A boy needs somewhere to go to when his home is filled with strangers." He rested on his pillow. "You don't really wanna know about me. You're good at making men feel as though you care. I've seen you in the hospital. You ask all the right questions; give all the right responses. How do I know you're not humoring me? You'd like Quincy. It's considered, by those that know, a very exciting place, especially now with the war on. My mother wrote me they have five general hospitals and a cannon factory supplying guns to this very army. Now *there's* a thought, taking pieces of lead out of a Rebel soldier that might have come from a cannon made in my own hometown. Makes you feel kinda warm all over, kinda proud. Quincy, where there's always something happening, ships steaming in and steaming out again, carrying Illinois's finest to death or destruction, leaving behind future widows, orphans—"

"Tell me more about your childhood," Jesse interrupted, trying to steer him away from the subject that occupied his mind twenty-four hours a day.

"Let me think, it's been so long since I was a child." He was staring up at the canvas apex, his hands behind his head again. "Okay—across from the town, across Quincy Bay, about a hundred yards or so out, we have Bay Island. In the summer folks can take a canoe or rowboat out there and spend the day picnicking. There's always music, and the kids play around near the water's edge, the girls look pretty in their best store-bought summer dresses, their hair all teased up, shining in the sun, flirting too much with the boys, making their parents mad. Do you like to picnic?"

"I've never tried it, sir."

"You don't *try it*, it ain't like whiskey or ice cream. You don't *try* a picnic, you *go on* one." He sat up suddenly and stared at her. "Okay, Tom Thumb, I'll take you on a picnic first chance we get. That's a promise. Maybe I'll take you back to Quincy and we'll have a picnic on Bay Island or along the riverbank. I'll give you the grand tour. We'll skip the general hospitals and the cannon factory. I'll show you my favorite fishing hole, where Helen and me used to dangle our feet while we fished. Sometimes we would tie the string to our big toes and just lie back on the grass—"

"—And doze, with the reflection of the sun on the water just tickling under your eyelids," Jesse interrupted laughingly.

"Hey, now you're gettin' the idea—other times we would get a sturdy rod with a hook and find us some fat juicy worms and really fish. Would you like to see my favorite fishing hole?" When she hesitated a second he said coldly, "Forget it," and lay down again, covering his eyes with his arm.

"I *would* so like to go to Quincy—" Jesse said plaintively into the tense silence.

"Drop me a line when you get there."

"Tell me some more about the town."

"Ask a Quincy boy. There are plenty camped around Shiloh Church. They're all homesick, they all want to talk about their homes. We've all got the same story and they're all boring as hell." He elevated and then lowered his eyebrows with dramatic significance and propped himself once more on his elbow. "There's gonna be a battle, you'd have to be stupid not to know that. What do you propose to do then?"

"The same as I do now, remain close to General Sherman."

He removed his spectacles and started to clean the lenses. As usual, the left lens came away. "Goddamn it—" After this man, whose sensitive, lifesaving hands worked miracles every day, had made three abortive attempts to force the lens back into the frail wire frame, the girl took the lens and carefully eased it home.

"You really ought to get these spectacles repaired, sir."

"You don't have a sweetheart or a brother, you didn't come here to nurse the men, because if you did you wouldn't be up at division scribbling into a ledger and I *know* you're not a camp follower, so why in hell *are* you here? The tragedy is you'll end up as a laundress, and the last thing on a soldier's mind is his soiled clothes if you catch my drift." He snatched the spectacles and eased the wire over his ears. He was like an absentminded professor searching among the tangle of blanket and clothing on his cot muttering to himself. "Sir Ransom thinks you a fine and brave little fellow." He started to laugh. "Don't you think that's funny?"

"Sir Ransom?"

"You called him a knight, so I knighted him. Sir Ransom of Illinois." His too disdainful laughter had a tinge of green and he seemed to realize it. He stretched out on the bed again and stared up at the ceiling. "I reckon Sir Ransom could win this war single-handed. The rest of us can just go home."

"Why do you dislike the colonel so?"

"If you don't know, you're more stupid than you look." He didn't bother to stifle a yawn.

"I'd better go," Jesse said, "I'm obviously overstimulating you with my conversation." She stood up and the surgeon's eyes traveled from her red curls to her feet in the army-issue brogues. Normally he went for more shapely females, and he liked long hair, the way it flowed over a girl's shoulders, held back off a plump face by a ribbon, and he liked them sweet and gentle, not sassy. But there was no denying the appeal of this girl's freckled face and boyish body, not to mention her steadfast character. That she was so appealing to him made him angry. "I'll tell you one thing, when Sherman finds out you're a girl he'll show you a little glimpse of hell you won't forget in a hurry."

"I've seen a little glimpse of hell many times, sir, the prospect of seeing it again doesn't frighten me." She watched him scoop the black graying hair off his brow. "Can I ask you what do you write in all these note-books of yours?"

"They're histories, medical histories." He looked at her earnest face, and the facetious tone vanished from his voice. "I make notes from the bed cards of the patients, name, age, company, date of admission, date of injury, date of operation, if any, and then a closing date according to whether they were discharged cured, sent north to a general hospital, or died. I write down my observations and when I have a moment, I try to figure out why one man dies while his comrade survives when they both have the same wound and get the same treatment." He bit on his pipe stem. He was off now on the single most involving passion of his life, medicine. "I study a patient's reaction to shock, loss of blood, how much blood, inflammations, fevers, types of fever, why some wounds bleed more than others. I can't go much further because after the patients are sent back north I lose track of them. I also have a column for comments like 'no visit today from his messmates,' 'wife ran off with a traveling preacher,' 'homesickness,' 'maybe he's worried that his cows aren't giv-ing enough milk.' You'd be surprised at how often a patient's state of mind can affect his ability to recover from physical injury."

"What will you do with the notes?"

"Who knows, maybe I'll publish my findings, write a textbook that will revolutionize medical science into the next century, get rich and famous." He was mocking himself. "Find a nice wealthy widow for old Jacob, have a hospital named after me in Chicago or New York, marry a beautiful socialite, and spend the rest of my life lecturing to audiences of surgeons who will nod their venerable heads and worship me from afar. On the other hand maybe no one gives a damn and I'll have a bonfire and burn the lot and sink into a drunken stupor from which, with luck, I will never awake."

"Do you ever have to note 'makes too many jokes,' " the girl said, "or 'uses anger to conceal his true feelings, afraid someone will guess he really cares about people'?"

"No, but sometimes I have to write 'should mind her own business because she's still wet behind the ears.' "

Jesse laughed.

"There are women nurses down the river at Savannah," Cartwright mentioned casually. "There's a woman called Bickersley, they say she takes good care of the men. You could stay with her until I can figure something out."

"Mother Bickerdyke," Jesse corrected. This dedicated Ohioan woman and her companion "the Cairo Angel" were in the newspapers every day now since they nursed the soldiers brought in after Fort Donelson. They had followed Grant's army in anticipation of their services being needed for another battle. "Thank you for your concern, but I'll be fine."

"It's no trouble. When Sherman catches on, and you can bet he will, I'll talk up for you, it's the least I can do." He felt obliged to say this, and he meant it, though he knew no power on earth would stop Sherman sending her back where she came from. "I'll tell him about your work in the hospital, that should count for something. If he won't budge I'll go to Grant, maybe I could appeal to him as one drunk to another." To his disappointment the girl didn't throw herself into his arms and swoon with gratitude. Instead, she held back the tent flap, paused to frown at the soiled clothing, and said,

"Don't you think it about time you had a visit from a laundress?"

"What . . . eh . . . yes . . . I'll . . . eh . . ." Cartwright felt his cheeks catch fire. By the time he had managed to control his sudden stammer, the girl was gone.

Jesse had been to collect that morning's mail. Perhaps the most exciting time in camp for soldiers, who lived for two words: *"mail call."* Only arrival of the paymaster came close to arousing such ecstasy. One glance at a man's face told the whole story—whether or not he had a letter from home. An expression of unrestrained joy, a loud hootin' and a hollerin', a jumping into the air, a clutching of a letter and kissing it until it was too wet to read, meant only one thing, a missive from sweetheart or wife. Just a few words, no more was needed, written testament that family and friends had not forgotten them. Those without mail, on the other hand, seemed like the loneliest creatures on earth, unloved and unwanted, except by the duty sergeant.

"Sweet Lord in Heaven, if I ain't got me three in one go!" Captain Jackson announced as he held up the envelopes for all to see. "Two from Gracie, and one from the girls." His great gray mustache was literally bristling with joy.

"Captain Van Allen has *eight* letters, sir," Jesse told him proudly as though this profusion of correspondence in some way reflected upon her personally.

"Let me see those—" Captain Jackson stared over Van Allen's shoulder. The New Englander was placing one behind the other as he studied the handwriting and sniffed the envelopes. "—Darn it, Marcus, I swear to the Lord you got one a those hair-ims like those sull-tans in Arabia." He snatched a letter and breathed in the aroma. "Par-fumed and the paper matches the envelopes. I'll be gall-darned. I can just imagine what Gracie would say 'bout such foolishness." Mrs. Jackson reused envelopes of a tobacco brown color, and urged her husband to do likewise.

"May I, sir?" asked Jesse. Marcus held the envelopes under her nose and she drew her full lips back in a grin. "The paper smells sweet," she announced.

"Sweet as gardenias," agreed Marcus, placing them carefully into his pocket, with a self-satisfied smile. "As do the gentle doves who write them."

The urbane captain with the romantic looks of a Byron, only son of a Boston property tycoon, could have stayed home in comfort and safety. Instead, he had joined the cavalry. At Bull Run, nursing a wounded shoulder, he had found himself drafted as an aide to a beleaguered Sherman, who was so impressed with the uncomplaining officer he taken him to Kentucky as a member of his permanent staff despite his being on convalescent leave. Andrew Jackson had come to his commander via a different route. When war broke out, at forty-two the Hoosier was considered too old for a three-month enlistment. To compound his unsuitability to serve his country in its direst hour, he suffered from chronic back pain that worsened at the slightest sign of rain. He'd been turned away from the recruitment office on *four* separate occasions. Not that he wanted to go to war. He was a farmer, he had crops to plant and a wife and four daughters to take care of, but no self-respecting Northerner could stay home while the country was biting off its own tail and let others do the fighting. So he took himself directly to Washington and there he'd literally bumped into Sherman on the street, drunk and complaining bitterly about stubborn recruitment officers. Something about the Hoosier had impressed the Ohioan, who felt that such loyal, determined men should not go begging. Jackson became the oldest courier at Sherman's headquarters, the average age being eighteen. But it was a way into the war. Now he was Sherman's oldest, most trusted aide.

"My *mail*, Corporal?" General Sherman demanded hoarsely. He stood at the entrance of the headquarters tent, cigar in place, long thin legs apart, hand extended in anticipation, eyebrows raised.

"Ten." Jesse saluted briskly, and gave him his letters. "Two from *Mrs.* Sherman." Sherman's narrow-eyed gaze marched all over her face with big, muddy boots.

"I recognized the handwriting," she explained with a wry, apologetic smile.

"Where's *your* mail, boy?" Andy asked her. "Don't you get no letters?"

"No sir."

"Ain't you got no kin folk?" This seemed inconceivable to a man with an extended family spread over five counties of Brown Township, Indiana.

"No family at all, Jesse?" Van Allen asked.

"Everyone's got someone, ain't that so?" Andy appealed to Marcus and to the division commander, who now had his sharp nose buried in a letter. "Here, take a look at this—" Jackson placed a dog-eared photograph in Jesse's hands, announcing proudly, "Four girls, beautiful, ain't they? Amy, twelve; Sadie, eleven; Sophie, ten; little Grace, named for ma wife, she's nine, and Gracie." They were indeed beautiful young women, with thick braids wrapped around their heads and sturdy bodies, standing beside their mother, a tall, statuesque woman with strong features, wearing a plain dress and a very serious expression. An expression which seemed to disdain the very idea of posing for a photo as nothing short of ridiculous when there were cows to milk and butter to churn.

Jesse returned the photo. "You're very fortunate, sir."

"Darn right I am. Gracie's not only handsome, she's smart too, and not the kind of smart that comes from book learnin' neither. She's got practical sense. She ain't one a those frivolous types. I never known a week go by that she didn't save a little something for a rainy day." Jackson's manly voice was brimful with pride, the small gray eyes nothing but points of light amid the crinkled skin surrounding them. "And any farmer will tell yer, those rainy days have a bad habit a turnin' up when you least expect them."

Jesse looked at Sherman's scowling face as he managed to read his letter, listen to the conversation, smoke his cigar, and fiddle with the buttons on his coat, all at the same time. He cleared his throat and stuffed this missive and the others, unopened, into his pants pocket with a great display of irritation.

"Letters from home are overrated, my boy, they invariably mean one thing, family squabbles that I, hundreds of miles away, must settle, as if I had nothing more important on my mind. I'm sure Captain Jackson will confirm what I say?" Sherman fixed Andy with a meaningful stare.

Marcus was less subtle; he gave the Hoosier a dig in the ribs with his elbow.

"Huh—? Oh yer, Lord knows—letters from home, nuthin' but trouble."

"There," Sherman said, before disappearing back into the tent. He had presented irrefutable proof to back his pronouncement, despite the fact that Jesse had only ten minutes before witnessed grown men behaving like complete fools at the approach of the United States mail wagon.

In his tent that evening, Sherman stood before the near empty pigeonholes of the portable bureau balanced precariously on the empty cracker box, and threw Jesse an interrogative glance as she cleaned away his uneaten supper things.

"How is it that I am getting through so much paper and stamps these days? And where are my pencils? Do you still write letters for the men in the hospital?"

Jesse's answering expression was a touching, if somewhat confusing, mix of innocence and guilt, admission and denial.

"Never mind," Sherman said.

The girl lit his cigar, cupping the flame in her small hands as he sucked.

"I like the way you do everything without a fuss. I'd hardly know you were around, yet you are at my elbow whenever I need you."

Jesse grinned her delight at such a compliment.

He puffed his cigar; he was in philosophical mood. "Don't marry too young, my boy, see the world. A man must accept that the condition of matrimony is a natural, if often constraining, state, but he doesn't have to jump right in. If I hadn't been married I would have remained in California, roamed the country like a vagabond, only my horse for companionship, slept under the stars, with saddle and blanket, but I had responsibilities, as you no doubt will have one day." He looked at her, suddenly narrowing his eyes and suspicious. "Why would you insinuate yourself into my camp and want to serve me, I wonder? I hope you're not expecting any kind of reward?"

Jesse called on every ounce of indignation she could muster. "Captains Van Allen and Jackson take care of you, sir, and Private Holliday, you said yourself he rides at your side, carbine at the ready, to protect you. Would you ask that question of those gentlemen? We serve you merely for the *honor* itself, sir."

The Ohioan's steady gaze held her earnest one. There was no hint of obsequiousness about this soldier's manner or tone, none of the lickspittle toadying often encountered in the flunkies who gravitated toward the high-ranking officers, hoping for a crumb off the table. Some commanders, McClellan came readily to mind, could not have existed without their ever-expanding entourage, which now included half the nation's newspaper scribblers. "My officers and staff *all* do their duty, Corporal," he said finally, and changed the subject. "I have written my brother Senator Sherman about recommending you to the United States Military Academy." He tapped the letter book on his desk with the two fingers that held his cigar. He read aloud from his letter. " 'This boy is bright, handsome, and energetic as a thoroughbred colt. He is transparently honest, reliable, and faithful, exhibiting an unselfish and noble charity toward his fellow soldiers and a courage that is by no means reckless of others. He is correct in his habits, and can carry out an errand promptly and without fuss. He is every inch a real boy, no hint of the crybaby or complainer about him. I'll warrant this boy has in him the elements of the man and I commend him to the Government as one worthy of the fostering care of one of its most treasured National Institutes—the United States Military Academy at West Point. I know he will grow into a fine young man, and make me proud to have been the instrument of his advancement.' Well, what do you say to that?"

Jesse didn't say anything, because Sherman was still talking, which was fortunate since she would not have been able to think of anything to say.

"Well, I expect you're eager to discover this world of knowledge and instruction, but you'll have to suppress your natural excitement, soldier, for your application could take months to process. In the meantime, do your duty. I'm sure you will find plenty to occupy you here with me. That's all."

7

"What is grand strategy?"

★ ★ ★ ★

The art of war is simple enough.

—U. S. GRANT, *Personal Memoirs,* 1885

It was already suppertime on Saturday evening, April 5, when Sherman and Lieutenant Colonel James McPherson returned to the division commander's headquarters in a torrential rainstorm. The two Ohioans had been on a reconnaissance to Second Brigade, camped over a mile and a half away from the rest of the division, as they covered the Hamburg-Savannah Road, the first of the two most important approaches to Pittsburg Landing from the south.

With sweat running down his strained face and still wearing his dripping oilskin, Sherman went to meet an aide from General W. H. L. Wallace, waiting to see him with a report from his chief. Eager to get back to his own camps he refused the offer of a hot drink and there in the pouring rain told Sherman that he had been on the picket line that afternoon and had seen squads of enemy cavalry both in front of Prentiss's division and farther to the right, in Sherman's own front. The Ohioan listened intently, the stub of a well-chewed cigar jammed into the left-hand corner of his mouth, bone weary, gaunt-eyed and grim, as befitted a man who had been in the saddle for nearly six hours. Hearing him out Sherman readily agreed there was more than the usual enemy activity, though after scouting the east bank with his usual thoroughness, incredibly, he personally had seen none of it.

"Yes, yes, it's true, they have been up on the right, three times, and fired on McDowell. But what does General Wallace want me to do, sir," he said suddenly, tearing the cigar stub from his mouth and tossing it away. "My hands are tied. Buell and the rest of the Army of the Ohio should have been here ten days ago. Where is Buell? Thank General Wallace for the information, Captain Rumsey, but tell him, sir, I have positive orders from Grant to do nothing that will have a tendency to bring on a 'general engagement' until Buell arrives."

The aide accepted this information with an anxious frown, saluted, remounted, and rode off.

Turning toward the welcome interior of his tent Sherman suddenly stopped to stare at the small figure standing in the steamy rain-soaked shadows. "What are you doing there?" he demanded.

"Waiting for you, sir."

To McPherson's utter astonishment, the commander grabbed a handful of the corporal's jacket and propelled backward into him. "Damn you, boy, don't you have the sense of a stray dog to come in out of the rain?" He had removed his battered slouch hat and was wiping his wide damp brow on the sleeve of his frock coat as he spoke. "Get out of your wet things, Mac," he told his young subordinate.

Both men removed their dripping oilskins to find Jesse holding out towels to them, while she stood there dripping. Sherman used the towel to wipe his face then told McPherson, "To think, I believed this soldier smart enough for the military academy." He dropped his towel over Jesse's head.

Her big blue eyes gazed out from under the towel as she grinned at both men.

"Impudent wretch," Sherman said and gave her one of his well-aimed cuffs about the head. He glanced through the opening at the sheet of rain that was driving into any face unlucky or stupid enough to show itself. He looked at McPherson. "Well, Mac, what do you think, should we toss him out in the rain or give him something useful to do?" He winked at the young engineer.

Jesse poured two glasses of whiskey and gave one each to the officers.

"Ah, just what the doctor ordered," Sherman said.

"Thank you, Corporal," McPherson said to Jesse.

"You're very welcome, sir."

"The boy is too saucy," Sherman explained. He touched his glass against McPherson's. "Your good health, Mac."

"Yours too, sir, and if I may add, to the end of the rebellion."

"To the end of the rebellion." Both men smiled.

Jesse hovered.

"If you're staying in here, make yourself useful," Sherman told her. "Roll up those maps over there and don't let me hear a word out of you."

It was, McPherson observed, as though the commander was speaking not to a young soldier, but to one of his own children allowed to play in his father's study. He saw the older man wince slightly as he drank his whiskey and pass a hand over his stomach region.

"Is it still the diarrhea, sir?" he asked with genuine concern.

"I can't shake the damn thing off," Sherman confessed.

"Did the surgeon's remedy of blue mass not help you, sir? I hear Mr. Lincoln takes nothing else for his stomach ailments."

"That's *why* he still has them." A voice spoke up from the corner of the tent, a voice that both men ignored.

"The surgeon says, like thousands of others in this army, I have an organic inflammation and must flush out any poisons with this purgative." Sherman took the bottle from the table and held it up. "When I complained that the medicine had no effect he said I had to increase the dose. But the cramps have gotten worse and I'm still not in control." If anything was destined to make William T. Sherman mad as hell, it was not being in control.

"Sir—" Jesse stopped rolling maps, took her haversack off the floor beside her, and brought a small phial from the mysterious depths. "—May I suggest something to help you?" Sherman looked at McPherson and then at the girl as she came toward them. "It's paregoric—powdered opium, anise oil, camphor, glycerine, and alcohol, and taken by mouth it'll relieve your cramps in a matter of hours, sir. Dr. Cartwright swears by it." The girl smiled. "And, more importantly, so do his patients."

"I have medicine," Sherman stated, and that, as they say, was that. He turned to McPherson, drank some whiskey, and said, "Sit down, Mac. Kick off your boots, sir, if you feel inclined."

Jesse returned to the maps. McPherson sat down but kept his boots on and while the commander started to pace, the two men discussed the events of the past week. Among the more general reports from pickets, one said they'd seen Rebel cavalry roaming the area, and there had been a positive sighting of a Rebel brass field gun glinting in the sun southeast of the Widow Howell's house, not one mile from Shiloh Church. Ten Rebel prisoners taken during a skirmish and kept at the church had been taunting their captors with warnings that they were only one advanced unit of a fearful army that would drive them into the Tennessee.

The following day came and no fearful army appeared to drive them into the river. But overwrought messengers rode in and out of Sherman's camp from morning 'til night. Colonel Hildebrand had marched his Seventy-seventh Ohio out to investigate why pickets at the Seay House had been driven back by a large number of gray cavalry. Then a party of Rebel horsemen had calmly sat upon their horses and watched the Seventieth Ohio drilling in a field near their camp. Perhaps the same who had rousted Captain Shotwell's party. Federal riflemen had exchanged brisk fire with a dozen of their opposite number amidst the thistles and cockleburs in Fraley Field and so on.

That very morning, eight pickets on duty at Jack Chamber's house out on the Corinth Road had gone missing. Colonel Buckland had ordered two companies forward to rescue the pickets. When artillery fire was heard all the way to Sherman's camp, the Ohioan went himself with a brigade of infantry to investigate. By the time Sherman arrived at the picket line, Buckland's men were already bringing back their dead and wounded, and finding an angry division commander waiting with a battery and two regiments of infantry drawn up in line of battle. Blue-clad men, muskets glinting in the warm sunshine that had followed hard on the heels of the rain, features set grimly against an enemy that lay beyond the strip of fallen timber, watched over by diligent officers, pistols drawn in anticipation of the order to attack.

Buckland reported he'd met and fought Beauregard's advance guard. Sherman however had not been pleased. "Damn you, Buckland," he had shouted, "what *the hell* did you think you were doing? You might have drawn the whole army into a battle before we're ready."

When an agitated courier arrived on an overheated, ill-used animal, to report sightings of enemy cavalry at the end of Rhea Field, south of the camp of the Fifty-third Ohio, Sherman really lost his temper. He had told the courier, "Tell your colonel to *take your damn regiment back to Ohio!*"

Whole regiments were spooked, but Sherman refused to be agitated, or perhaps more accurately he refused to show his agitation.

"I think that Beauregard would not be such a fool as to leave his base of operations and attack us in ours, they're merely reconnaissance in force," he told McPherson, finally alighting on a chair. "I can't afford to be panicked by these stories. I'm acting on the supposition that we're an *invading* army, that our purpose is to move forward in force and repeat the grand tactics of Fort Donelson, by separating the Rebels in the interior from those at Memphis and on the Mississippi River." Sherman offered his young companion a cigar and then lit it for him.

Unlike Sherman and Grant, McPherson's attachment to the cigar was not an addiction; he smoked for pleasure, in a social setting, the way he drank. This tall officer in his early thirties was not a conventionally handsome man, but his curly beard, small pleasing features, hair thinning and dark, robust form, bright smile and sunny nature made him popular with everyone. Now he watched with growing amusement as the man whose friendship he had gained five years ago continued his march around the interior of the tent, dropping an inch-long sphere of ash on a vest already soiled and gray.

They had met when both had lodged in the same boardinghouse at 100 Prince Street, New York City. During that difficult, eventful time, William T. Sherman had been a depressed and rudderless man. His wife and father-in-law had forced resignation from the army upon him. Sherman had found employment in a profession wholly unsuited to any man with integrity and moral fiber, that of trying to manage a grossly under-funded bank. In that year of 1857 Sherman's employers sent him to New York to open yet another branch, a venture that ended in failure. McPherson had been a second lieutenant in the elite corps of engineers, assigned to fortify New York Harbor. Now he was Grant's chief engi-neer, and Sherman a brigadier general, and though he was far from rud-derless he was still depressed and sick and their beloved nation was now fighting for its life.

"Thank you, sir," McPherson said, taking the seat that Sherman had belatedly offered him. The commander was neither a rude man nor a neglectful host, just so preoccupied by more weighty matters that he for-got social graces.

Yes, much had happened to both men in the past five years. However, the young Ohioan was gratified to see that the wild-eyed, disheveled fig-ure he had seen pace, smoke, and talk incessantly of every subject under God's sun, through long nights in the parlor of that boardinghouse, was the very same man he had grown to love and admire. Only now, he was back where he belonged, in the army of the United States. Sherman sud-denly looked at his young friend.

"Forgive me, Mac, I should have asked. How is your fiancée?"

"In low spirits, I fear, sir. My friend Lieutenant Elliott wrote that Emily hardly smiles at all. He said Emily told him that all her family in Baltimore are opposed to us marrying, despite my promotion. They are insisting that Emily leave San Francisco and go home while the war lasts, but her sister Sophie wrote their mother that she still needs Emily, in order to keep her there. Elliott blames me for Emily's present disposi-tion. He says my dispirited letters have a depressing affect on her." McPherson smiled wanly. "He says that while I pour out my sadness in letters to her, Emily refrains from telling me all that assails her heart. But I am not to mention any word of what he has confided to me."

"Well, now, Mac, sounds as if I should have Grant send *you* home and request Miss Emily join us in your place? This young lady sounds as true and strong as our bravest soldier." Sherman slapped the younger man on the back. Poor McPherson, Miss Hoffman's parents were devout Secessionists. Before states rights had gripped the South they had wholeheart-edly approved their daughter's engagement to a United States officer of so much promise, but now they had cruelly withdrawn it again. "Come along, bear up, be patient, I have no doubt that Miss Emily's parents will soon come to their senses. In the meantime the staunch young lady flies the flag of affection in her heart for her gallant soldier."

"Thank you for your reassurance, sir, I shall try to do as you say, bear up and be patient."

"Splendid," Sherman said. That aside he now returned to the subject uppermost in his mind. "The talk around the camps has been the same since we embarked here. When General Buell gets here . . . when General Halleck arrives . . . the men are as fed up of hearing this as I am. They're ready to leave at General Grant's command and can't understand why we're still here, still waiting. When men are on the edge this way we jump at the slightest shadows." Sherman made a noise of disgust. "I'm not sure if the men have infected the officers or the other way around. I do know I'm sick to death of listening to timid officers whose nerves are being worn down by pickets rushing around my camps repeating wild stories of legions of Rebels out there." He indicated the failing light beyond the canvas wall with his glass. "Every time we search out these ghost legions we find *nothing* or we find small parties of enemy cavalry who flee at our approach. I had enough of these camp rumors at Kentucky, rumors that almost finished my career—finished *me*." After a few seconds of fingering the buttons on his vest, he was up again, his long, thin legs covering the distance of the tent in an erratic circle, compulsively smoking his cigar. "Tell me, Mac, what do you suppose would happen if I suddenly started to endorse these rumors to Grant or to Halleck? What do you think would happen if the newspaper hounds learned that I could be unnerved by the sight of a few enemy field guns in our front?" He swept his arm up in a gesture of dismissal. "I'll tell you what would happen," he said as McPherson opened his mouth to speak. "They'd say old Sherman is scaremongering again like he did in Kentucky—gone in the head again—predicting the demise of the entire Tennessee army—allowing his own fears to get the better of his good sense.

No, Mac, damn it all." He waved the glass in the air. "*Never again*. I permit myself mistakes, but I do not permit myself to make the same mistake twice."

Evening brought a visit from U. S. Grant. He made the trip upriver on the *Tigress*, every day now apparently deaf to those who whispered that a commander of an army should be *with* that army not in a comfortable two-story dwelling owned by Mr. John Cherry of Savannah, Tennessee, especially when a large Rebel army was only twenty miles down the river.

Maybe it was the presence of the much-admired General Smith in an upstairs bedroom that kept him there, lulling him into a false sense of security. Though others had reasoned that if Grant felt confident enough to remain ten miles away *and* on the opposite side of the riverbank, there was no danger, even with the increased skirmishing, pickets carried off hourly by the enemy, and frequent sightings of Rebel cavalry.

Tonight Grant had a well-padded crutch strapped to his saddle and a very swollen ankle attached to his leg. The previous day his horse had stumbled in the mud, trapping his master's ankle. The whisper was that this short, slight, slouching little man in crumpled dusty blue blouse and pants, beneath a crumpled dusty frock coat, topped off with a crumpled dusty hat, had been drunk. Though he looked sober enough now being helped off his horse by John Rawlins.

Rawlins wedged the crutch under his commander's armpit and watched anxiously as he headed off with an awkward limp toward the corral, where Jesse was attending to Sherman's sorrel mare, tethered to a tree in company with a number of his equine companions.

"Good evening, sir," Jesse said boldly, though she had never spoken to the tanner's son before.

"Corporal." Grant's gravelly monotone sounded as though even this single word of greeting was too great a burden on a man so comfortable with silence. He placed his cigar in his trapdoor mouth, and used the one free hand to stroke the horse's neck. "Fine animal." He spoke with a nostalgic look on his face, as though he was remembering something that had happened long ago, but that was more vivid in his mind than something that had happened five minutes hence.

"Yes sir. The general captured him from a Rebel cavalryman."

"Give him a good groomin' there, soldier. Remember to wash his eyes gently—and the mane and the tail should be last to get cleaned and never untangle the tail with a brush, lift the tail away to the side and draw your fingers down in a kind of combing action, like this, always draw the tail downward." The blue-coated horse lover demonstrated with his one free hand, giving Jesse the distinct impression that this was the most pleasant few moments he had known for many a long, bloody day. Grant watched as the sorrel nuzzled his flaring nostrils into Jesse's neck while the other horses moved in close around her, pushing and teasing her as though to share the attention this once Rebel-owned interloper was receiving. "You like horses, Corporal?" The detachment in his voice was thawing slightly, but she suspected it had less to do with her and more to do with the subject.

"I love them," she said simply. "All horses are beautiful."

Grant smiled, it was nothing much, just a slender thread, but it said he understood and concurred. The smile grew a little, blossoming over a mouth that was all but concealed by the beard. "Horses have better instincts than humans, they know who to trust, who to be wary of." This was not mere rhetoric speaking, but the stuff of personal experience.

Jesse watched him comb the horse's mane with his fingers, tipped with broken and grimy nails. He had withdrawn into himself now, and appeared to be reflecting on that old, yet vivid memory again. Slight and not above five foot five, he had a head of thick dark-brown hair, sprinkled with a little gray, and a full beard of the same color that hugged closely to a square jaw. His eyes too were brown, the expression turned inward as though he was listening to some silent voice within him, even when others were speaking, of seeming not to be either physically or mentally present. They were soft and sad, indeed, his tentative demeanor, emphasized by the crutch, belied the tenacity that now underlined his reputation. Congress and Northern newspapers considered Sam Grant the "coming man." The general who could give them the military successes they had so long craved. Overnight he had been taken up as a national hero, a man with a most unlikely pedigree for such a role. Son of a merchant and with a mother some said was slow in the head, or maybe just slow. Like her son, they said; no great talker and no great thinker, a man more comfortable in the company of his wife and children.

At that moment, Jesse heard him mumble something under his breath.

"When I graduated the military academy I'd hoped to join the cavalry. All I ever wanted, even as a lad, was to be 'round horses. I love to train young colts." The childlike longing with which he said this belied the popular image of Grant the commander sitting coolly upon his horse at Donelson, chewing a cigar while his bleeding men perished in the snow.

"Perhaps when the war is over, sir, you'll get your wish."

The commander in chief drew his introverted gaze from the animal to Jesse's handsome, grimy face, his expression vague and uncertain, as though he had not been aware of talking his thoughts aloud and therefore had not expected a response.

"Grant!" The small man was startled as Sherman's loud rasping voice carried easily the distance from his tent to the picket rope, and in a few seconds his rapid walk had carried him just as easily to the army commander's side.

"I stopped to admire the sorrel," Grant explained, defensively, a boy caught messing about instead of doing his chores, even testily, as if reluctant to have this welcome connection with horses disrupted by an embodiment of harsh reality called William Tecumseh Sherman.

"Fine animal," Sherman agreed in his terse way, "grown attached to her." He touched a gentle hand to the horse's face and was rewarded with a loud neighing and a tossing of the head. "Yes. I've grown mighty fond of you, haven't I, mighty fond."

Jesse's head popped up. Her dirty face wore a saucy white-toothed grin. "Thank you, sir."

"I was talking to the horse," the Ohioan said irritably, treating her to one of his looks.

"I was just saying, Sherman, when I get old I'll ask nothing more from life than to hold a colt's leading line and watch him run around the training ground."

"Yes, yes, Grant, admirable ambition, admirable, sir. Any sign of Buell?"

"No, not Buell himself, but Nelson's advanced units have arrived at Savannah. Nelson says Buell will be here shortly. He wanted to pitch his tents on Pittsburg Landing, but I told him to encamp for the present at Savannah, that it would be impossible to march his division through the swamps of the east bank. I'll send boats for him Monday or Tuesday or sometime early next week." As Grant related this, Sherman took his free arm and led him off in the direction of his headquarters tent. A mite too swift, since the younger man, limping badly, was bound to the slower pace of a temporary cripple, dependent upon a crutch and hard-pressed to keep up with the always fast-walking Ohioan, who had two good, strong legs and knew how to use them. "Nelson is worried that Beauregard will attack us. I told him I have more troops here than I did at Fort Donelson and we could hold against anything they have. I took him to see General Smith, who assured him the enemy are all at Corinth, and when our transportation arrives we shall go there and, as General Smith put it, 'Draw them out, as you would draw a badger out of a hole.' "

Jesse brought tin cups and poured the whiskey. Grant was staring at the whiskey bottle, the way he had stared at the sorrel, a tad longingly.

"No whiskey for General Grant or myself, Corporal," said Rawlins, the man who was called "Grant's conscience." The self-educated Galena lawyer, now Grant's adjutant, with the feverish eyes and full black beard, let his voice rise loudly like a preacher in a pulpit, reaching the climax of his sermon. He dropped an arm across the table between the bottle and the commander, a zealot rushing to place his own mortal flesh between the temptation and the tempted. It was said only Rawlins or the presence of Mrs. Grant could stop Grant from going on a bender. "The general adheres to a strict policy of abstinence and has done so for the last six years."

Either the "conscience" had been asleep or was a bold-faced liar.

Not that Sherman was averse to the bottle. At Kentucky he'd drunk too much, it was true, but it was a temporary aberration. He needed no man, nor woman, to keep *him* on a sober path. As for Dr. Cartwright, he could stop drinking any time he wanted to, the trouble was he didn't want to.

As she was pouring Grant and Rawlins coffee, Sherman said, "Jesse, get some se-gars."

First she lit Sherman's "se-gar" and then Grant's. He looked at her with a vague recognition that quickly passed into oblivion beneath the slightly hooded lids as the conversation turned as usual to recent Rebel sightings in the area.

"Before encamping my division here at Shiloh Church, Mac and I rode out the three miles toward Bethel Station to make a personal reconnaissance," said Sherman. "We had found the area between there and Pittsburg Landing clear. We then rode out ten miles toward Corinth to Monterey, you recall the Rebels had a cavalry regiment there, Mac," Sherman placed a hand on the younger man's broad shoulder as he passed on his usual pace around the tent, "which of course decamped on our approach. Apart from the Rebel cavalry patrols and the two infantry regiments and battery six miles out, my division in front is clear."

"The locals told us that trains were bringing large masses of men from every direction into Corinth," McPherson said.

"Well, there's no doubting that A. S. Johnston has a large army at Corinth." As usual Grant's tired voice belied the tenacity of its owner. "None of us have ever doubted that fact. Even if reports are exaggerating, I have to take the threat seriously. My concern is not for Pittsburg Landing, but for our base of supplies at Crumps Landing."

The five men continued their discussion, Sherman's hoarse tones dominating the conversation, while Grant and Rawlins spoke as one man. McPherson inclined his view toward his superiors. He reminded them that though he had been ordered by Grant to lay out a fortified line, he'd found that it would have to be placed in the rear of the line of encampments, which certainly appeared to undermine the point of the exercise, which was to attack. Grant repeatedly quoted General C. F. Smith. The venerable old soldier, forced to give up his division of Grant's army because he had scraped his shin on a rowboat coming ashore at the Landing, was laid up with gangrene and dysentery at the Cherry Mansion, but still offering advice to his old West Point cadet.

Sherman, as always, was restless, unable to remain seated for more than a few minutes. He tapped with his fingernails on the table and spoke somewhat disjointedly of the increased "sauciness" of the Rebel cavalry in their front as he paced back and forth behind his companions' chairs, his vest flying open, his hair standing on end. He looked like a man on a precipice unable to decide whether to stay put and chance being rescued, or jump. When he asked Grant if he'd questioned the Alabama prisoners sent up some days ago by him the tanner's son admitted that he hadn't yet got around to it. If Grant appeared too eager to follow the ailing General Smith, Sherman appeared, for reasons already stated most forcefully to James McPherson, gratefully willing to accept Grant's view that Beauregard would have to be flushed out of Corinth if there was to be any battle. Though the continued absence of Don Carlos Buell's Army of the Ohio evidently made him more nervous than he cared to admit, even to himself. However, at the end, all agreed, theirs was to be the offensive move.

Grant, bolstered up on both sides by a crutch, one wooden, the other flesh, departed with words that might have lulled an entire army, but brought only a sharp inclination of Sherman's large red head before the tent flap dropped.

"Sherman, I have scarcely the faintest idea of an attack being made upon us. Good night."

The Ohioan may have exuded an air of certainty during the discussion, repeating what he had told his officers that morning, but the persuasive manner, the forceful voice, the assertive gestures of those heavily veined hands, masked a genuine fear, that, as he had told McPherson, if he expressed his true feelings they would again call him crazy.

Sherman stood in his tent and removed the stopper from the bottle of medicine his own surgeon had given him. Before he could swallow any of the contents, a voice said, "For a man who professes *never* to make the same mistake twice, you are, sir, about to do just that." Jesse stepped out of the shadows.

The Ohioan stared at her. "How *dare* you talk to me that way? What are you doing in my quarters?"

"Making sure you take Dr. Cartwright's medicine, not that rubbish."

To Sherman's speechless amazement she took the bottle from his hand and poured the liquid between the duckboards.

"What your surgeon has given you is a purgative, a cathartic, to cause evacuation of the bowels. It's for treating constipation, sir, not diarrhea. I've seen what can happen when you dose a diarrhea sufferer with laxatives. The more you complain to your surgeon that his purgatives are not working the more he'll increase the dosage until you will become so sick you'll have to go to the hospital. You need something to calm your stomach lining, *not inflame* it still further, which is precisely what a purgative will do. The bottle should have a skull and crossbones painted on the label." She tossed it out of the tent. "As for blue mass, that contains, among other things, *mercury*, which I'm sure you know is a metal poison. I shudder to think what those pills are doing to Mr. Lincoln's poor stomach." She took Sherman's hand and put the other bottle on the palm. "Dr. Cartwright has treated dozens of suffering soldiers with this, and within three days, sir, they were back on their feet, ready to fight for the Union. Paregoric is just a tincture of opium and therefore not as strong or sedating as pure opium. Dr. Cartwright says that the origin of the term 'paregoric' comes from the Greek word *paregorkos*, which means 'soothing.'" She moved closer to him and stared up into his eyes; her expression so appealing, so steadfast, that Sherman swallowed a dose of her medicine without another word. She replaced the stopper for him. He rubbed his left shoulder with his right hand. He looked exhausted. While the commander of the Army of the Tennessee may have been enjoying the luxurious surroundings of the Cherry Mansion, the man actually taking care of that army was here at Pittsburg Landing.

"If you sit down, sir, I'll massage your arm."

He stared at her a moment longer from out of narrowed eyes and then perched on the edge of his cot. She began by working her fingers over his neck, slowly, soothingly, then moved along to his left shoulder and down his arm, massaging where she knew the pain to be most acute. After a second, his eyes closed and the tension around his mouth and between his constantly frowning brows had all but melted away.

"Damn rain—" he said in a subdued voice.

"The rheumatism has gotten into your shoulder where you dislocated the bone falling from your horse."

The Ohioan's eyes opened. "How in God's name do you know about that?" In January '45 while deer hunting with Lieutenant, now, General John Reynolds of Pennsylvania, on the plantation of their friend John Poyas, up the Cooper River from Fort Moultrie, Lieutenant Sherman had fallen from his horse and injured his shoulder seriously enough to be sent home on furlough. Jesse went on massaging the arm. "I told you before I don't believe in ghosts and spirits and things that go bump in the night." He looked at her sideways, critically. "You should grow a beard. Your face is too smooth. It's hard to believe it now, looking at our army's leaders, but there was a time when general officers disapproved of facial hair. I served under Brigadier General Stephen Kearny in California. One day he sent for me and suggested I borrow his razors." Sherman rubbed his nails over that coarse cinnamon-colored growth, making a scratching sound. "All the Sherman men possess tender skin and a wiry beard that makes shaving painful. But I did as I was told, shaved it off and continued to shave until Kearny was gone. My face became red and raw. Since then I have never shaved my face. It is a mystery to me why soldiers ever shave, for the beard is the best possible protection against cold, heat, and dust. You were right, Corporal, at Louisville I smoked too many segars, wrote too many letters by candlelight, and drank too much whiskey because of a nervous anxiety about matters that seemed then *and* now to be beyond my control. I have a division composed of raw soldiers, most of whom have received their muskets on the way from enlistment station to field. They have as much idea about war as children." He looked at this child out of the corner of his eye and said, "Less than children, and not a clue how to fire their arms or make sense of their instruction manuals. The officers are hardly better. We are constantly in the presence of enemy pickets and cavalry. I know that. I am neither blind nor stupid. If we don't get away soon the leaves will be out and the whole country an ambush."

"Then you *do* believe the Rebels will attack?"

"What *I* believe don't count. I have nothing to do with the plans and can therefore be at ease and do my best. I want only to acquit myself with courage and have my family remember me with respect. Once, not a life-time ago, Corporal, I picked up a newspaper to learn that I was 'insane.' 'Gone in the head' because I tried to warn my superiors that the Union generals in Kentucky did not have sufficient arms or men. People do not easily forgive or forget accusations of insanity in their generals, and should their memories be short the newspapers will quickly refresh them. For myself I do not give a damn, they can accuse me of insanity all they wish, my former associations with the South *had* rendered me almost crazy, as one by one all links of hope were parted, but I have children who must be protected from the vile slanders of the newspapers. When I was relieved in Kentucky my son Tommy came home from school one day in tears—the other children had told him that the news-paper declared his father was *insane*. Do you think their father would willingly put them once more through such torment? *No.* I keep my views to myself. As I said, here at Pittsburg Landing, I am not in com-mand. I play a subordinate role. I prefer to shrink from the responsibili-ties others seem to court. I have stopped looking into the future and no longer wish to guide events. They are too momentous to be a subject of personal ambition." In early January that year, he had written his brother,

> I am so sensible now of my disgrace from having exaggerated the force of our enemy in Kentucky that I do think I should have com-mitted suicide were it not for my children. I do not think that I can again be entrusted with a command.

However, he did have a command; one he had raised himself for duty in the field. Despite what their commander might say, he was as eager as they were to find out if he could be entrusted with their lives.

He looked at her closely. "Do you understand *anything* of what I am saying?"

"I understand *all* of what you are saying, sir," the girl said.

"Yes." His voice was a harsh, hoarse whisper. "I believe you do."

"I'll massage your shoulder again tomorrow. Let me help you with your boots."

"No, no, I'm going out for a stroll around my camps. I can't sleep. Did you read those books I loaned you?"

"Oh yes, I particularly enjoyed Mr. Dickens's *Tale of Two Cities*. I shall read that again if I may keep it a little longer?"

"Fiction is fine, but you should be reading books of geography, history, science—it is most important that young boys and men keep well up in the scientific developments of our own and other lands. That's what I used to tell my students in Louisiana. Also you should study your fellowman, to know men, their nature, strength, powers of endurance, the influences which impel them to action, is even a higher branch of knowledge." He went to his footlocker and as he rummaged around inside, he said, "Here, take these. Mrs. Sherman's mother sent them to me but I already have far too many. The lady wouldn't object since you are a most deserving case." He thrust a brown paper package at her chest. Inside were two pairs of drawers and a calico shirt. "The shirt will be too large for you but you'll grow into it. Like you, I have always loved books. I paid my debts, sent money to my mother, but I always kept money enough to purchase books. Scott, Dickens, and Washington Irving are as necessary to fix the tastes of the young as is the Bible and Shakespeare, and you will remember that no home is complete without them. I abhor what they call dime novels, newspaper comics, and trashy literature. You may help yourself to the books you find in my trunk, provided you treat them with respect and return them in due course and, most important, do not neglect your duties." He blew out the candle. "And grow a beard!"

In the darkness she saw the glow of his cigar, heard the sound of the tent flap, and then there was silence. He had gone for his nightly stroll. Jesse took the lantern and followed.

Someone close by was coaxing the melancholic strains of "Tenting Tonight" from a harmonica. The fires were softly dying. The camps had never seemed so peaceful, perhaps in anticipation of the morrow. The *Lord's Day*—the officers and men would stir at sunrise. There would be roll call as usual, then they would prepare a nice, leisurely breakfast and sit down to contemplate the pleasant, lazy day ahead. For the gratification of those with a religious bent, there would be energetic hymn singing and pious sermonizing, and for others a game of chuck-a-luck or letter writing. Five-day-old Northern newspapers would be passed around, together with the inevitable dime novels. Some men would even crawl back inside their blankets and contemplate a world where drill sergeants, army beans, picket duty, and loneliness did not exist. Some enlisted men might already have been anticipating their diary entries for the next day:

SUNDAY APRIL 6, 1862 —

Did nothing today. No drilling. No reviewing.
No musket practice. Perfect day. Just a day of peace
and quiet beside a log church called Shiloh.

8

"... Our lives, our fortunes, and our sacred honor"

★ ★ ★ ★

Who but a living witness can adequately portray those scenes on Shiloh's field, when our wounded men, mingled with rebels, charred and blackened by the burning tents and underbrush, were crawling about, begging for someone to end their misery? Who can describe the plunging shot shattering the strong oak as with a thunderbolt, and beating down horse and rider to the ground? Who but one who has heard them can describe the peculiar sizzing of the minie ball, or the crash and roar of a volley fire? Who can describe the last look of the stricken soldier as he appeals for help that no man can give or describe the dread scene of the surgeon's work, or the burial trench?

—General William T. Sherman,
address to the Society of the Army of the Tennessee, 1881

Sherman reined in his small, swift mount and brought her to a halt under a tree, speaking softly to her as he patted her neck. He waited for his staff to catch up, as usual, and then demanded to know of Major Sanger, "What do you make of that, Dan?"

"Picket firing," replied the inspector general unhesitatingly, his black mustaches twitching. He pointed in the direction of the camps of the Fifty-third, whose commander had evidently not taken Sherman's order seriously, and *not* taken his regiment back to Ohio. "From the direction of Colonel Appler's camps, sir." His expression turned dubious, for he knew that Sherman was at the very end of his rope with the nervous officer.

"I'll ride over and find out what's going on, sir," volunteered Captain Van Allen.

Before Sherman could reply they heard the sound of a hard-driven horse and into the clearing rode one of Appler's staff officers. While he was still ten yards away he started to shout on top of his lungs, "The Rebels are coming—the Rebels are crossing the field in front of our camp! We're being attacked by the Rebels—the Rebels are upon us!"

"Get a grip on yourself, sir!" Sherman bellowed as the captain reined in his sweating mount, the poor done-in animal panting as hard as his rider, who had torn the hat from his head and was wringing it with despair.

"But, sir—we're finished—the Rebels—are pouring out of the woods—thousands of them—all heading this way—what must we do? *What must we do?*"

"Right now, do nothing but get a goddamn grip on yourself!" Sherman ordered.

"What do you think, sir?" Sanger calmly asked his commander.

This lack of urgency on the part of general and staff was due in no small part to Appler himself. He had cried wolf so often in the past few days, he was now in danger of being completely ignored.

"I *think* that Appler is a chronic worrier, but still he must be badly scared over there." Sherman turned to the courier. "Tell the colonel I will be over to see for myself."

The courier jerked his animal's head to the right and galloped off, whether to carry the commander's message to Colonel Appler or to the safety of the rear no one could have said for certain.

About four hundred yards in front of Appler's camps, Sherman held tight to the reins of his excited mare and raised his glasses onto a part of the field that appeared at first glance to be free from any gray-clad sightings. Behind him a small but courageous number of Appler's men were ready to do their duty, but they were very much in a minority, and without officers were firing erratically at the unseen enemy in their front.

Many more were in a state of outright panic, running between the tents, banging into each other, some in their underclothes, some half-shaved, others with their breakfast still in their hands.

The majority of the regiment were simply staring at their equally stunned officers, their pathetic expressions begging mutely for instructions, pleading to know what to do to prevent being taken prisoner or shot, despite the past weeks of preparing for just such an attack.

They would get no sense from Appler himself, who was shouting orders in every direction, immediately countermanding one order to issue another, as he stood helplessly beside the unattended breakfast fire, trembling with fear.

"Can't see any Rebels," Hammond announced from his place at the back of the headquarters party. Since he was using only his naked eye to survey Rhea Field he was not in the best place to judge.

"There's sumpthin' glintin' offa those bushes," said Captain Jackson to Marcus Van Allen as the latter raised his own fine pair of field glasses to survey the scene. "Over there, Marcus, to the right." The Hoosier pointed and spoke to Sherman at the same time. "Gen'al, over there, just about two hundred yards."

As Sherman adjusted his glasses to follow Andy's directions, the ever-vigilant Private Holliday shouted, "General, look to your right, sir! To your right!"

Sherman turned and stared in amazement. A line of gray uniforms had risen up from the swaying corn, the early-morning sun glinting on their rifle barrels as they aimed and fired once before moving forward.

"My *God*, we're *attacked*!" he cried as they came sweeping across the field, their muskets held at shoulder height, yelling at the tops of their lungs, a yell that would have turned to ice water even the blood of the most courageous veterans.

As Sherman spoke, enemy pickets concealed in the bushes opened fire. Instinctively, the Ohioan threw up a hand as though to protect himself. Beside him, Private Holliday uttered a tiny, surprised cry, before he fell from his horse and lay motionless on the ground, shot through the head. With barely a moment taken to register the loss of his favorite riding companion, Sherman spoke urgently to Captain Jackson.

"Ride to General McClernand, tell him the Rebels have attacked, ask him to send me three regiments to protect Waterhouse's battery and the left flank of my line."

Andy's hand was still raised in salute as he spurred Sally away in the direction of First Division headquarters. In swift succession, Sherman had sent Captain Van Allen to warn General Prentiss and Lieutenant Taylor to alert General Hurlbut. Next, the Ohioan turned his attention to the commander of the Fifty-third Ohio, still muttering orders that no one was obeying, least of all himself.

Sherman had now accepted that the unexpected was happening. This was *not* a sharp skirmish but an all-out Rebel attack.

"Hold your ground," he ordered Appler, who was the color of cold ashes. "You are the left flank of the first line of defense, sir, our first line of battle. You have a good battery on your right, and strong support to your rear. Your regiment is protecting one of our two batteries. I'll send you reinforcements, but you must hold your ground at all hazards!" As he spoke, he drew a handkerchief from his pocket and wrapped it carelessly around his bleeding hand. In the initial onslaught that had felled poor Holliday, buckshot had struck the third finger of his right hand and had burrowed under the skin, but the seriousness of the injury was of no interest to him at that moment. He rode away, followed by his staff, less one officer, whose body was being removed by men of Appler's brigade.

Around the camps of Sherman's division close to Shiloh Church chaos reigned.

Half-dressed, wild-eyed soldiers, who only moments before had been contemplating the joys of a lazy Sunday, were now running up and down the tent streets yelling incoherently at each other and praying for deliverance through clenched teeth. Those who still had their wits had grabbed a musket from the stand as they ran, they knew not where, uttering a different shade of prayer under their labored breath. They asked God for a steady hand, a clear eye, a shot of iron in their soul.

Others, more intent on escaping the battle rather than joining it, simply ran.

In the frantic struggle to shoot fast and reload, to shoot and reload, boys who had never before been under fire wept with fear and excitement, tore cartridges with their teeth and then forgot completely the sequence of loading and firing. Faces changed as they leveled their muskets and fired. The innocent youth became an animal with the taste of blood in his mouth, his fury unrestrained. "*Kill Rebels! Kill Rebels!*" they screamed, and others took up the bloodthirsty cry, while the bodies of their companions piled up around them. Oh, they had not guessed, these boys and men, that Death in person would visit them this quiet Sabbath morning, causing them to perish on a battlefield far from home and loved ones.

As the rattle of musketry increased and the enemy batteries in the woods threw shells into the camps, steadfast officers of lower rank shouted orders, desperately trying to rally these frightened, excited men into a command that would meet the opposing skirmishers in the warm spring air.

There were cheers amidst the rattling fusillade and monstrous cries of "*Forward!*" or "*Stand fast! Don't run away and hide! Meet the enemy onslaught, men of the—!*"

Then the firing slowed down, dropped away, and soon it became merely spasmodic. Gripped with fear and the excitement of sudden battle, the men could not get their minié balls down and they rammed them hard and harder and then— *Oh dear Lord, here they come—the enemy—the Rebels—run for your lives!*

The panicked wailing of fleeing men was drowned out only by the deafening sounds of canister exploding against trees and flesh. They ran unheeding, among bursting shell and whistling bullets through breakfast fires, sending coffeepots flying, scrambling over tin plates, scattering books, letters, magazines, billowing canvas, shot torn colors, splintered flagpoles.

They fell, boys not yet old enough to shave, men with gray beards, blood and flesh exploding in thick clots, a head flies, a hand disintegrates, a leg is severed, a face loses its humanity, destroyed by grapeshot. That way, that way, run, flee for your lives.

Over fences, they leapt, pushing against each other, elbowing and kicking; it was a stampede. Men were trampled as they ran for the open fields, where the golden corn looked so peaceful swaying in the light breeze. *Is this Sunday morning?* What a beautiful place for a battle.

Meanwhile, those who remain load and fire, load and fire, load and fire, mechanically, with a kind of maniacal rage.

One hour into the fighting and it still required a moment of intense realization to absorb the fact that a full-scale battle was underway.

The Rebel army that was supposed to be at Corinth, that everyone said was at Corinth, was clearly not in Corinth, but here. Johnston and Beauregard had not waited for Buell to arrive. They had attacked first.

While many officers and men of the Federal army had panicked, William Tecumseh Sherman was behaving exactly as expected, cool and intense, a picture of concentrated courage and determined leadership that inspired all those around him. In a single hour, he had placed his entire division in line to meet the Rebel advance. He seemed to be everywhere. He seemed to anticipate everything.

As for Jesse Davis, after the first few moments of pandemonium around her, she had become oblivious to the danger, swept up in the excitement of living, moment to moment. She rode unnoticed with Sherman and his officers, as the general, heedless of his own safety, his injured hand tucked inside the breast of his frock coat, dashed about the field, re-forming regiments, instructing artillery crews, and plugging up lines which had broken.

It was at Shiloh Church itself that Jesse witnessed the demise of Sherman's first horse. As Sherman rode between the ranks of frightened infantrymen, trying to rally the spirits of these green recruits who had received their muskets only days before, the poor sorrel mare she had so lovingly groomed was struck by solid shot, and bleeding profusely from the chest, sunk to the ground with a terrified whinny. She would race no more. Jesse watched in envy as Lieutenant Taylor promptly dismounted and handed Sherman his reins. As he swung into the saddle, she heard the commander tell the younger man, "Well, my boy, didn't I promise you all the fighting you could do!"

Appler got his reinforcements, even though he personally was not there to receive them. After venturing out from behind his tree, the brave colonel had broken for the rear, shouting, "*Save yourselves! We are whipped for sure!*" taking with him his own boys and those of Colonel Mungen, along with the colonel himself, leaving Waterhouse's battery exposed and the remainder of the ranks to fight and save the reputation of their regiments. The reinforcements came from McClernand who, responding with surprising speed to Sherman's request, sent three regiments from his own division to protect Captain Waterhouse's battery and the left flank of Sherman's line.

Albert Sidney Johnston, commander of the Rebel army of the Mississippi, had lined up his force and was sending his troops obliquely from Sherman's right to his left in attacking waves, trying to overwhelm Sherman, and pass on toward Prentiss's Sixth and McClernand's First Divisions, whose line of camps was almost parallel with the Tennessee River, two miles back. Sherman saw this at once, and while the enemy's forces were still passing across the field to their left, the intensified sound of artillery and musket fire told all who had ears to listen that Prentiss's brigades were already drawn into battle.

By 9:00 A.M., the Rebel three-line formations had quickly broken down into one extended single line, but still it kept on, relentlessly driving the Yankees back. Sherman, McClernand, and W. H. L. Wallace extended the Union line to Prentiss's left, while Hurlbut's men drew it out on the right. However, it was soon clear to Sherman that despite Prentiss's determined stand he was falling back.

Three Illinois regiments remained to support Waterhouse's battery, but when their colonel was severely wounded they too fell back in disorder and the battery was captured.

The colonel of the Fifty-third was not the only one to desert his men just when they needed him most. News came that Colonel Mason of the Seventy-first Ohio had taken one look at the oncoming Rebels and spurred his horse for the rear. His second in command had taken up the challenge and almost immediately been killed. The Seventy-first were now in total disarray. Sherman's left, although offering a furious resistance, had been turned, and the Rebels were pressing the entire Federal line. He sent couriers to colonels Buckland and McDowell to hold their ground, but no sooner had the couriers returned than Sherman was forced to issue new orders. The Rebels had their artillery to the rear of the Union left flank and maneuvering on the part of the Yankees had become vital.

Grabbing Marcus by the shoulder and shouting to be heard above the noise of artillery shells bursting to their rear, the commander instructed him, "Tell Captain Taylor to bring his battery from Shiloh Church and to fall back as far as the Purdy-Hamburg Road." To Major McCoy he said, "Tell Buckland and McDowell to adopt the Purdy-Hamburg Road as their new line of defense."

He then rode off with the remainder of his staff to meet Captain Behr. Now it was the fate of his second mount, the one donated by Lieutenant Taylor, to fall, struck by canister as the general greeted the young battery commander at the intersection of the Corinth and Purdy Roads. Ordering him immediately into action, Sherman paused only to help capture a riderless and panicked horse, the mount of an officer who now lay dead upon the ground, his chest a mass of blood and exposed ribs.

Dogged Federal infantrymen loaded and fired as they went, fell back to fire from behind trees and fallen logs, to rally around the batteries, but would not allow themselves to be completely driven from the field, although one after another, they were falling. Cut down also was the young and eager Captain Behr, shot from his horse at the very moment that he was giving the orders for his guns to be unlimbered. With the loss of their captain, the drivers and artillerymen fled, taking with them the caissons, but abandoning five of the six guns to the enemy, without having fired a single shot.

Now Sherman was forced to abandon the line of defense beside the log church and with it all his division's original camps, and choose another, but he was a man possessed with an unclouded vision.

This morning during his forty-second year, if the insane, nervous, overwrought W. T. Sherman of Kentucky and Missouri had ever existed he was to die on the battlefield at Pittsburg Landing during the first few hours of combat, and a new inspired and inspiring Sherman would be born. At Jones Field, he sent his aides to conduct McDowell and Buckland and their commands to join on McClernand's right. Not long after this, Sam Grant arrived. It was only 10:00 A.M. It seemed as though a day, a year, an entire lifetime had already passed.

With Rawlins's guiding hand Grant dismounted, snatched the padded crutch off his saddle and hobbled toward a dust-covered Sherman, barely flinching as a shell exploded close to their rear, sending a shower of earth and bark and leaves over their heads, but both making damn sure they saved their segars. This was their first meeting under fire.

"Sherman—" said Grant, incorporating greeting and inquiry in one word, not a man to waste words, even in the heat of battle, especially in the heat of battle.

Jesse, standing behind the Ohioan, heard him reply with steady voice, "The situation is none too bad, Grant. My men have checked the enemy and are holding their ground."

"Good—" Grant said almost distractedly. "Things do not look too well with Prentiss on your left," he added, shifting his weight on the crutch and wincing. "He's been forced slowly backward and has anchored his regiments in a sunken road where he's fighting like a demon." To the left of that sunken road was the peach orchard where Jesse had picked the Widow Howell's fruit. Now they rained their petals, like pink teardrops, onto the broken and lifeless bodies of the rough men who had so recently admired their delicate nature. "I've told him to maintain that position at all costs."

"Any news of Lew Wallace or Nelson?" Sherman shouted above the exploding shells and booming cannon.

"I stopped at Crump's Landing on the way up here 'bout seven-thirty," Grant shouted back. The two men, stalwartly, perhaps stubbornly, standing their ground as members of their staff scattered at the telltale sounds of an approaching barrage. The crashing came, the blinding flash, the streaks of flame, fragments struck the earth. When the smoke cleared, there was Grant, still talking, and Sherman, still listening. "And called across to Lew Wallace to hold himself in readiness, send out patrols and await my orders. When I found what was happening here I sent one of my staff officers back to order him to march by the river road and come up on your right. He should be here by now, or near."

Sherman bent low for Jesse to light his cigar. They heard the rapid-fire of massed muskets and another shower of leaves came down upon their heads. "Good boy," he said to her. "Running does no good when the whole earth is exploding around you. And Nelson?" the Ohioan asked of Grant and puffed.

The continued absence of the Ohio Army's brigade commander perplexed Grant even more than Lew Wallace's whereabouts. "Before I left Savannah I sent him a note ordering him to move his entire command to the river opposite Pittsburg. I told him he could easily obtain a guide in the village. I also sent a note to Buell telling him we are attacked and that I had directed Nelson to move his division up the river."

"Then we will have to await his arrival with patience." Waiting was not a virtue normally associated with the redheaded division commander.

"Sherman, what do you need?"

"Ammunition."

"Arrangements have already been made."

"Then—" Sherman pushed his cigar between his lips and used the free hand to wipe sweat from his face, blackened by gunpowder. There was blood on his brow, smeared with dust. His coat was gray with dust and his trousers encrusted with mud. He *looked* like a man who had been in the heat of battle for four hours.

Grant suddenly noticed the arm half-concealed inside the older man's coat and moved his eyes questioningly to the red-bearded face.

"Scratch," Sherman announced in reply to Grant's mute inquiry.

"Sherman, take care. A wound that forces you from the field today will be disastrous for us, for the Union cause. If you need to find me send someone to the cabin near the rim of the bluff. We'll talk later, sir, meanwhile I am needed more elsewhere."

Sherman looked at the younger man for a moment before his red head snapped in a gesture that said he understood the implication of Grant's words. The entire exchange took no more than ten minutes. Then Rawlins, who hooked the crutch to the saddle, helped Grant onto his horse. Sherman glanced down at Jesse. She was staring up at him. Briefly, roughly even, he removed some of the broken leaves from her shoulder with a sweep of his good hand. She smiled, her teeth the only white in a near-blackened face, and he nodded reassurance, not merely for her, but for his entire division, his entire country.

Thirty minutes later news came that the enemy had made a furious attack on McClernand's whole front. Responding to the pressure on this Illinois politician, Sherman moved McDowell's brigade directly against the Rebels' left flank, forcing them back some distance. While personally instructing the men of McDowell's brigade on where to conceal themselves, behind trees, fallen timber, and a wooded valley to their right, Jesse saw the general lose his third horse of the day. The poor stricken animal went down on its forelegs, blood streaming from its mouth, barely giving Sherman a moment to leap clear, before collapsing, the smashed body jerking and shivering for a few seconds, before life deserted it. The loss of another horse seemed strangely poignant in the midst of all this carnage.

Sherman's new mount was a strong beast, an artillery horse, which Jesse herself proudly helped disentangle from the remains of an overturned caisson.

He now rode up and down the lines re-forming regiments as their numbers dwindled, instructing his raw artillerymen on such shockingly basic skills as how to cut the fuses of their shells. Without a care for his own safety, without apparent cognizance of the Rebel batteries, nor of the volleys of musket balls and buckshot that swept the ground and pattered away at the green leaves overhead, he halted his spurring progress by each battery of guns. Around him, the battle raged but he calmly ordered an artillery battery into position just in time to stop a charging enemy column. When Rebel infantry tried to overrun the guns, he shifted some of his own infantry and beat back the attempt. More than ever now, he seemed to be everywhere, maneuvering companies, complimenting officers, encouraging individuals, his severe features animated with excitement, his red-bearded face easily recognized by his grateful men.

To an impartial onlooker he must have appeared like a man who believes himself arrogantly invincible. This was untrue. He simply cared least of all for his own safety and knew that his men would do their best, risk their lives for a commander who led by example.

Up and down he rode, the men inspired by the sight of their commander, face blackened by gunpowder, streaked with sweat and blood from his wound, whose seriousness they could only speculate upon, since he kept the injured hand concealed inside his frock coat. Some said the hand had been shattered, others whispered that it was completely gone and that the frock coat concealed a bloody stump.

For the next four hours Sherman's divisions held their position, at one time gaining ground, at other times losing it. Sherman himself remained a model of intense concentration. He rallied his forces and they gave ground grudgingly. He did not puff on those interminable cigars with his usual fury, he had no choice, they kept going out as he spurred his horse up and down the lines of infantry and cannon. He ceased to wave his arms when he talked, nor did he talk much, except to issue orders, clear-cut and curt, anticipating everything that happened. When a line broke he was there, tight-lipped, his eyes narrowed to slits, urging his men into the breach, and when the Rebels swept over and by his cannon he had those guns turned around to fire on the enemy as they surged forward. He seemed to be in rapture, finding himself, for the first time, a man suddenly, miraculously face-to-face with his own destiny.

During this time Captain Rowley, one of Grant's aides, arrived to ask, on behalf of his chief, how the battle was progressing and to tell him that both Colonel McPherson *and* Captain Rawlins had now been urgently dispatched by General Grant to find out what had happened to Lew Wallace and his division. Sherman chewed a cigar stub and without removing his eyes from the field of combat said, "Tell Grant, if he has men to spare I can use them, if not, I will do the best I can. We are hold-ing them pretty well just now—pretty well—but it's hot as hell."

At midafternoon, they had another visit from Grant. This time, how-ever, he did not even deem it necessary to dismount as he told the Ohioan, "I sent another note to Buell telling him we've been attacked since early morning and suggesting that the sight of fresh troops on the field now would raise the spirit of our men and greatly dishearten the enemy. I still don't know if Buell is actually at Savannah. I'd hoped to talk with him before coming up here."

Buell had a rank commensurate with Grant's: They were both com-manders of powerful Federal armies. To anyone listening it would have seemed quite clear that Grant was loath, if not unwilling, to *order* the Ohio Army chief to bring the remainder of his considerable force up to Pittsburg Landing to join with Nelson's division and support Grant's army. Whether or not the bombastic Buell would have obeyed a direct order, even if it had come from a Federal major general and meant the difference between victory and defeat for his side, remained an unan-swered question. Perhaps Grant felt that a request might more quickly induce Buell to come to the support of a fellow general under pressure, whereas an order might encourage him to dally. Though surely a man of Buell's experience did not need to be ordered or even advised, surely he would fairly rush to support his suffering comrades under arms?

When General McClernand rode up around 3:30, looking bemused and alarmed and accompanied by an entire entourage of staff and orderlies, all wearing equally despairing faces, to tell of how Hurlbut's line had been driven back to the river, Sherman assured him most vigorously that *they* could hold until Lew Wallace appeared, whenever that might be.

"But we *must* hold the bridge we built over Snake Creek for just such a purpose 'til he does get here." Sherman used Jesse's back to open a map, select and point out to McClernand where the new line of defense was to be placed, with its right covering the bridge. Finished, he thrust the map at her chest and went on talking to McClernand, gave a short speech to his staff officers about the importance of knowing when one is beaten and retreating with dignity. He ceased only when Sherman interrupted to state most categorically that surrender was an option that neither he nor Grant would even consider. Finally the political general rode off, convinced, for the moment at least, that he should be in control of his own men, not hanging onto Sherman's coattails.

Sherman's brief but telling lecture had evidently had the desired effect, for in due course the word came through that McClernand's First Division had made a fine show against the enemy and driven him back with a bayonet charge. The Ohioan looked relieved, if not gratified, as he listened to this news.

"How is your hand, sir?" Jesse asked, after he had formed the new line on the right of Owl Creek Bridge, when they were briefly alone between messengers coming and going.

"My hand?" He brought it from his frock coat and frowned at it wrapped in the blood-soaked handkerchief, as though it and the appendage belonged to someone else. "I'd forgotten. Now I come to think of it—it throbs." He grimaced around his cigar stub, though it might have been a smile.

"I was negligent, sir, afraid and excited, there was so much going on— I lost concentration—just for a moment—"

He was barely listening to her; he was watching a spirited cavalry charge by the enemy, characterizing it as a "*handsome repulse*" when the men of the Twenty-ninth Illinois did their work with a will. He searched in his pockets for a fresh cigar, but he had none. Falling back, they had left everything in their old camps, including his cigars!

"Sir, will you take some whiskey for the shock?" Jesse rummaged inside her haversack.

"Stop fussing, boy." He pushed her aside and shoved the hand back inside his coat as a captain from the Fortieth Illinois rode up at a lick, excitedly calling for ammunition.

"General Grant sent up boxes of ammunition hours ago, Captain," Sherman told him with the confidence of one who completely trusts his commander in chief.

"It's true, sir, but out of the five different cartridges that were sent up none were of the caliber needed in the Fortieth."

This was a different story. Sherman looked around him. Van Allen,

Jackson, Sanger, McCoy, Taylor, all had been sent off with messages to various parts of the field, and poor Holliday, dead at the very start of the battle. Slowly his intense gaze moved down to Jesse. There was no one else to send.

"Tell me, boy, do you think you can take a message to General Grant, last seen at the wharf?" Without awaiting an answer, he was already giving her a leg up into the battered saddle atop her battered horse.

This was her moment to prove her mettle. It was her chance to prove that she was capable of more than merely copying orders. She was trembling, not with apprehension, but with excitement as she looked down at the Ohioan's strained features. Gunpowder had turned his short-cropped beard almost black now, and his face was red where it was not black and rivulets of sweat ran down his neck into his upturned shirt collar. He blazed with a fierce unquenchable energy, intoxicated and intoxicating, exhilarated and exhilarating. He had never looked nor felt more alive as he grabbed her leg.

"Tell General Grant that the Fortieth Illinois is holding its ground under heavy fire, though their cartridge boxes are empty." Sherman looked to the artillery captain, who quickly told Jesse the caliber required, twice, as though he didn't trust this tiny soldier to carry out this life-or-death task. Then Sherman said, "Ride, Corporal, don't let down our brave boys!" He struck the animal's hindquarters and it shot away across the field with an energy and purpose that for a moment shocked even the girl fighting to stay upright in the saddle. Was it possible that this curmudgeonly steed knew that the lives of the men of the Fortieth Illinois rested on his tired old haunches?

"Think he'll make it, sir?" asked the artillery captain, wishing he had written down the caliber instead of trusting to a young, excitable boy's memory.

"Yes," Sherman replied staunchly, grabbing the captain's shoulder and squeezing tightly. "He'll make it—I know that boy, know him well, future West Point cadet."

From out of the corner of her eye, as she and Ironsides, for that was her horse's name, galloped across Jones Field to the relative safety of the tangled undergrowth to her left, in the direction of the Landing, Jesse saw a line of men rise up from the cover of the long grass, their uniforms indistinguishable under blood, gunpowder, and dust. For a second she knew such intense fear that her chest seemed to squeeze the heart that lay inside and a roaring started up in her ears. Then a blaze of color. Stars and Stripes on a staff held aloft, flapping defiantly in a sudden gust of wind. Yankees. In a few seconds the steady blue line moving resolutely, inexorably forward had been raked with a furious fire of canister and grape, which exploded from the densely wooded area in their front, severing limbs from bodies, cutting branches from trees, sending fence rails and pieces of tree bark and strips of blood-soaked cloth flying into the air.

"Lay down!" she screamed. "Take cover!" Or thought she did.

Oh, dear God, they could have lain down. Why did they come on as if they were immortal? They could have hidden in the tall grass, or broke and run, those left standing after the first assault, but they just kept on coming, grabbing up the colors, as one after another fell, crossing that open field.

Suddenly there was a gigantic explosion, like a thunderclap, a man-made tornado that gathered up the groaning, mangled blue line in a smoke-filled, flaming din of splintered trees, whirling metal, pieces of canteen, musket, shoe and hat, flying clods of earth, uprooted brush and bloody body parts flinging all into the smoke-filled air.

When the sheet of flame that had burned and engulfed them had at last died away, a hundred years or perhaps a hundred seconds later, leaving only the swirling black acrid-smelling smoke of gunpowder, Jesse saw not men, but a horrifying twisted tangle of wreckage that had once been men.

Across a field thickly carpeted with dead and wounded they staggered, those still miraculously able to walk or drag themselves forward, coming on, coming toward her, closer and closer. Arms outstretched, arms without hands, shoulders without arms, men without legs, men on bloodied stumps, hair and beards clotted with blood, men with faces shot away, gray matter exposed, jaws gone, temples torn away, men with their insides hanging out. Those who could not walk or drag their shattered remains crawled, until it seemed to her horrified gaze as if the very field itself was alive with crawling flesh.

Then one of these shocking visions spoke to her, or it seemed that he had spoken; the sighing sound of a ghost carried to her ears, though nothing but whimpering noises issued from what remained of his shattered face, as he lifted the stump of his arm. Eyes protruding with a glassy stare, he was asking for something. *Water? Mercy? Death? Something.* Was this war? Was this the glory and the honor?

Jesse sat motionless in the still air, listening to the buzzing of maddened flies and the rumbling of the cannon, like a distant thunderstorm. The flag was limp now. Lifeless. Time had stood still. Reality had ceased to exist. This place was not a cornfield in the middle of a warm spring afternoon, and these hideous, grisly images searing themselves onto her eyeballs were not men. The world she had inhabited that morning, last evening, last week, last century, had fallen away. *She* had fallen away, into hell. She had told Dr. Cartwright, I have seen hell many times before, but every time it had been a recognizable, unmistakable, demoniacal pit, wherein was raging a death struggle, a wrestle between good and evil. This was different. This was a new kind of hell. In this place, even the devil quailed.

As the sighing of these ghostly shapes accosted her ears, she seemed to become aware of the weight of her haversack slung across her narrow chest. The haversack that was as much a part of her now as her arms and legs. The haversack filled with lint, bandages, morphine, whiskey, and chloroform, for momentary oblivion. God forgive her, she could not stop to help these men that were already dead. If she did, men who were still alive would die. She had already wasted too much time. She was breathless as she turned Ironsides's head and kicked him into a trot. He seemed to hesitate, his haunches quivering between her thighs. She kicked again, hard as she had ever kicked and the animal went forward, though reluctantly.

Her chest was tightening again, her eyes had started to burn and smart and fill up with water. She would not have been able to say if it was the smoke or tears and if it were tears, she could not have said if it were tears of sorrow or tears of anger and if it were anger, she could not have said if she was angry with herself or with humankind.

In less than twenty minutes, the artillery captain reported in person to General Sherman that boxes of cartridges of the correct caliber had started to arrive from the rear.

"Splendid, Captain, splendid—you sound surprised, sir, did I not tell you the boy would complete his mission?"

"Yes sir, you told me."

By four o'clock McClernand and Sherman, still awaiting Lew Wallace's seven thousand men and Buell's Army of the Ohio, decided to pull back yet again.

Indeed, the Rebels had pushed the Yankees to within a quarter of a mile of the Landing.

Could it possibly be true, was the Rebel army well on its way to winning a decisive victory along the banks of the Tennessee River?

9

"What a piece of work is man?"

In peace there's nothing so becomes a man
As modest stillness and humility,
But when the blast of war blows in our ears,
Then imitate the action of the tiger:
Stiffen the sinews, summon up the blood,
Disguise fair nature with hard-favored rage,
Then lend the eye a terrible aspect.

—WILLIAM SHAKESPEARE, *Henry V*, act 3, scene 1

It was along the banks of the Tennessee River, at the Landing, that Jesse had earlier found Sam Grant. The short crumpled man had given his full, undivided attention to her request, had her wait while he gave the order, and then moved off to greet a tall, heavyset, balding man with a trimmed gray beard, whose prominent light-colored eyes betrayed an anxious expression as he approached. Grant's greeting had conveyed more emotion than usual. The emotion he had conveyed at that moment was relief.

"General Buell."

So the commander of the Army of the Ohio was here at last, if not the army itself. The two men had spoken briefly. Grant asked Buell to bring his forces to the Landing as soon as possible and Buell asked Grant what preparations he was making for retreat. Grant had repeated the word as though its meaning was totally foreign to him, then he had replied, "None. We are going to win." As always, he spoke with a quiet simplicity that could have been mistaken for lack of imagination in a plain man, or tenacity of character in a wise one. History had yet to decide in which category the tanner's son belonged.

Could Don Carlos Buell be blamed for lacking Grant's focused optimism? Whether grounded in reality or not, for at the staging area in sight of the wooden Federal gunboats *Tyler* and *Lexington*, anchored in the Tennessee River, boys and men, soldiers in name if not deed, were hiding under the bluffs, cowering in fear—hundreds, if not thousands and more. The dead were piling up like cordwood.

No one could possibly have said how many soldiers had run away from the fighting. Grant himself tried to persuade these panicked soldiers to return to the battle and support their comrades. When his heartfelt entreaties fell on deaf ears he did what any self-respecting army commander would do, he unleashed a squad of cavalry into their midst, driving many of the skulkers to the water's edge, where some jumped and drowned and others were crushed by the transports.

Jesse clutched Ironsides's lead rein tightly in her hand, watching more in sorrow than in shame as men, out of control, near hysterical with fear, stampeded through the ranks of Buell's fresh troops, at last arriving at the Landing. They threw their muskets upon the ground, crying, "We're whipped, whipped all to hell—retreat—turn back while you still can— run for your lives! It's Bull Run—I tell you—Bull Run—our regiments are all cut to pieces. We're the only survivors."

"Stand and fight or die by the hand of your own countrymen," a captain of artillery bellowed as he waved his pistol in the air, searching in vain for men to fill the places of those who had perished beside their guns.

"It's no use," cried a soldier trying to rid himself of his equipment, strewing the ground with canteen, kepi, knapsack, rubber blanket, and finally his musket. "We'll be pushed into the Tennessee, go back, go back while you still can."

"Why you lousy stinking coward!" shouted a second officer and struck the man full in the mouth with the barrel of his pistol, sending him reeling to the ground, blood spurting from his mouth. No sooner had he fallen than he was up again, fear of the enemy greater than his fear of the officer. A few seconds later Jesse saw him jump into the river.

She was knocked sideways by a member of Grant's staff as he caught hold of a youth who was trying to make good his escape to a transport. He shook the boy roughly, and screamed into his ashen face, "You cowardly son of a bitch!" but the boy was quivering from head to toe, muttering to himself like someone gone stark raving mad. Just one of thousands, running in every direction. The officer, suddenly seeing the hopelessness of his cause, released him, and he ran on.

Lying on their bellies under the bluffs were farm boys no older than Jesse, trembling and incoherent with fear, unable to fight, unable even to move or respond to the entreaties and threats of the officers who ran around waving their sabers in the air and shouting. Side by side with the cowards, and those genuinely paralyzed with fear, were the wounded, the dead, and the dying. Those who had been carried off the field and abandoned along the riverbanks, to lie there like dirty bundles of clothing until they could be transferred to the steamers or moved to the dressing stations and operating areas that had been set up all over the yellow clay bluff.

Wide-eyed, sweating, her heart thumping in her narrow chest, Jesse stared at this vision. They were everywhere; they covered the ground like a human carpet, making it impossible in some places to walk without stepping on a broken arm, a mangled leg, a cracked skull. In some instances, they had been deposited so close together they lay two deep, as if rehearsing for the burial trench and yet more were arriving by the second. On litters, blankets, fence rails, doors torn from their hinges, left without shade, without water, without hope. She wanted to shout, to scream into their faces. There was no more room, no solitary spot for a man to make peace with his God. A girl alone with a single canteen and a small haversack filled with bandages could do very little. She must do *something*. If they would not stand shoulder to shoulder with these brave men, would they not comfort them in their final moments?

Desperately she rallied some of the walking wounded, those who had been patched up and were able to move; they must help those who could not help themselves. She shouted at the skulkers to carry the seriously wounded to shelter, to the shade of a tree. A few emerged from their hiding places and passed among the groaning blood-soaked men with their canteens, as Jesse bode them. Once her back was turned they disappeared again.

To those who remained Jesse demonstrated how to use a blanket to carry a wounded man. Four men could tie a corner of a blanket to a musket and steady the muskets on their shoulders, forming a carrying cot. She showed them how to wind a bandage around a bleeding stump and press a hand to the wound so that the pressure stopped the bleeding. How to cool a fevered brow or steady a trembling hand.

As she knelt beside a soldier with her canteen, Grant passed, alongside him rode James McPherson.

"Di'we win, Gen'al," asked the soldier, heaving himself up with a gargantuan effort. One of his legs was gone, gone from the knee down; in its place was a mess of dirty, bloodied rags. Around his empty left eye socket, Jesse had wrapped a strip she had torn from the bottom of her corporal's blouse. She was all out of bandages.

"Tomorrow, for certain." The words barely made it out of the trapdoor mouth before it closed and the commander passed on, averting his gaze. McPherson, recognizing her, pursed his mouth in a sorrowful little smile and handed down his full canteen, his compassionate gaze on her face. He looked just a little the worse for wear, but still very much the booted and gauntleted soldier, though his gauntlets were now grubby and his boots caked in mud. Earlier he had halted his mount to watch her giving a dozen young farm boys instruction on how to load and fire a musket. Going through each stage slowly and patiently as Sherman had done for her that first night in his bivouac near Shiloh Church, in what now seemed an age ago. Halfway through this impromptu class most of the students had crawled back into their hiding places, leaving their firearms on the ground, as if divesting themselves of these symbols of the war, ridding themselves of all responsibility to fight. The three who remained had wiped their runny noses on the backs of their hands, steadied their trembling lower lips, and marched off to the sound of the guns, one of them still sobbing, but from fear or shame, no one could say.

"You are an example to us all, Corporal," he said from atop his large chestnut mare and saluted, his eyes filling with tears before he spurred away.

Half-covered by a blanket Jesse found a child in the elaborate uniform of a musician, with soft brown hair and pale skin. The front of his shirt was rags and what must have been a fragment of shell casing had ripped a huge jagged gash right across his small chest. His breastbone was split in two and unidentifiable bony fragments protruded from the mangled flesh. She could see one of the lungs feebly attempting to expand with each labored respiration. A young cavalry officer, a bloodied bandage around his head and an arrogant expression on his face, passed at a slow walk on his tired-looking mount. Failing to look away fast enough to avoid seeing the blood-soaked child with the insides of his chest exposed he sat forward suddenly and vomited from his saddle. Jesse poured the last few drops of water from McPherson's canteen onto a piece of rag and passed it up wordlessly to the officer.

He snatched it from her hand and held it to his mouth. When his retching had ceased he tossed the rag into her face, saying angrily, "Damn *you*—it was something I ate—something I ate—" He jerked his horse's head around, trotting off, almost running into a riderless mount that had careened into the side of a wagon before being subdued by the teamsters.

A dismounted officer slowly approached this excited, sweating animal, stared at him hard for a moment and spoke to Grant, who was standing nearby. "Sir," his voice shaking as he spoke, rivulets of grimy sweat running down his brow, "I'd know this fine animal anywhere, it's Prince, my brother's horse. Will Wallace, commander of the Second Division."

She remounted Ironsides, lately munching grass under a tree with all the nonchalance of a horse unhitched from a barouche at a church social, and started back to join her general by way of Jones Field.

The closer she got the more deafening became the clamor of battle. The artillery and billows of dirty-white smoke that rose chokingly above the green-leafed trees had set the woodland afire. Here in the once peaceful fields were the real soldiers; here the fighting was in deadly earnest. She had left the panicked mob in the rear where they belonged, where their stories of defeat could not infect those striving to do their duty. It was impossible to judge if the Federals were retreating and the Rebels advancing, or if it was the other way around. Masses of men seemed to roll back and forth, yelling and screaming and dropping to their knees to load and fire, many crumbling, never to fire again, while the crash of field artillery rumbled on in the background.

At the south end of Jones Field she halted Ironsides, touched a soothing hand to his panting flanks. Never give a sweating horse cold water, Private Holliday had told her.

As she stopped to slake her own thirst, she saw a ragged, terrified rush of men in blue come howling from the underbrush, arms raised, muskets held aloft, as they gave themselves up to headlong flight, some crying at the top of their lungs,

"The Rebels are coming! The Rebels are upon us! Retreat! Retreat! Save yourselves!"

Jesse stared beyond the blue-clad fugitives, to the officer pursuing them at full gallop, leaping fallen timber, splashing through creeks and streams, hatless, a saber raised above his dark blond hair, and blood from a head wound running down his distorted features. Jesse blinked and blinked again, a look of rampant excitement and chilled horror filling her eyes. It was *Lieutenant Colonel Ransom*. Yet it wasn't him. The Vermonter's compassionate, handsome face was converted into something supernatural, so completely different from the man who had spoken to her almost as an equal.

"Retreat, will you? Run in the face of the enemy?" he screamed. "I'll give you retreat! I'll teach you to desert your comrades—you spineless cowards! I'll give you reason to run! Stand and fight, you cowards! You filthy cowardly traitors! Come back and fight like men! Stand to it, I say!"

But they would not come back or stand to it, or fight. They were completely out of control. Running headlong across the field, tossing away equipment and muskets, trampling over fallen comrades, disappearing into the woods, throwing themselves behind large oaks, clambering through the cornfields, stumbling over tangled timber, clearing fallen logs, knocking each other aside in their panic to fall back from the enemy and this officer, in their rear.

Moments later Jesse's blood had turned to ice.

An infantryman, his uniform disheveled, coat trailing, hat gone, shirt flung open as if he had tried to tear it from his body, went splashing through the shallow creek in a desperate attempt to escape the horse and rider that was bearing down on him. He scrambled up the steep incline and with crazed red eyes starting from his head, spun suddenly around. In a frenzy of violence, screaming so loudly his eyes bulged from their sockets, he brought up his musket and plunged his bayonet into Old Bob's exposed flank. A roar like thunder broke from the Vermonter's throat. He rose up in his saddle, blood streaming from the wound in his scalp, and slashed out at the soldier with his saber, slicing the side of his head clean away. The man staggered forward, clawed at thin air and fell face down into the creek. Ransom wheeled his injured horse around, slender threads of blood and sweat flying in every direction from a face made inhumanly ugly by rage, and seemed to notice Jesse for the first time. He stared at her without the slightest sign of recognition, and for a heart-stopping moment it seemed she would suffer the same fate as the infantryman.

Instead, he gathered up his reins and charged in the direction of the thick oak forest. He didn't make it. Abruptly Jesse heard a single shot. She saw Old Bob reel and then twist to the side as though slamming up against an invisible wall. The wounded animal went down on his front knees, swayed, and then keeled over, half-pinning his master's left leg.

Jesse rode up as the colonel was crawling out from under the heaving animal. She shouted his name, then her own name, tore off her hat so that the startling color of her hair might help him know her, but he did not respond, did not even look at her now. She seemed to be in one world while he existed in another. He wrenched his sidearm from the saddle holster with clumsy fingers and staggered into the trees, using his free hand to wipe blood from his eyes.

Jesse dismounted and followed. She watched him weave like a

drunken man over the uneven ground, stumbling, struck in the face again and again by the low brambles, almost tripping on the tangled undergrowth, willpower alone keeping him on his feet. Even in his injured, half-maddened state, he was in command, of himself and of his men. With no horse, he was pursuing the skulkers on foot. There they were, dozens of them, snatches of blue uniform, red eyes, pale sweating faces, cowering in the thickets, hiding behind oaks, beside logs, lying on their bellies in the tall grass, awaiting their fate, either at the hands of this apparently insane officer or the Rebels, they neither knew nor cared anymore. The colonel waved his army Colt in the air, threatening to shoot every last man, unless they obeyed. With a gargantuan effort, he got those who still carried a musket to their feet, and into the line of battle.

"Stand to it—" he kept saying, "stand to it—stand and fight—yes, that's it—stand and fight. You'll not dare run to the rear while I stand with you—" On his slurred command, they raised their weapons, aimed at where they supposed the enemy to be, and fired, enveloped briefly in a cloud of acrid blue smoke.

They fired once, but did not reload. Rather they stared at him as one man.

"What . . . what are . . . you waiting for?" he screamed, his cultured New England accent now reduced to a hysterical croak. "Load and fire—load and fire—and keep firing—don't stop until we drive them into the river!"

One volley was all he would see. Jesse watched him sink exhausted to his knees and wave the gun weakly at chest level before he fell headlong into the grass and lay still. This was their cue. This was what the cowards had been waiting for; loss of blood had weakened the officer to unconsciousness.

Up they sprung, throwing their weapons aside and fleeing in every direction, urging each other to an effort they had never shown while facing the enemy.

Jesse, tearing a length of cloth from her shirt as she went, rushed to the colonel's side. While she was trying to stanch the flow of blood from the dreadful gash on his scalp, two men appeared from nowhere, private soldiers, perhaps men of his own regiment. Without waiting for her to finish binding his wound, they bundled him onto a litter just before a Rebel battery started to pour charges of canister into the field. Explosions were ripping up trees by their very roots.

"Where are you taking him?" she shouted, grabbing one of their arms, as the earth seemed to shatter into pieces around them.

"To the Landing—to the Landing—" The man barely had time to reply before he trotted off, crouching low, beneath the whizzing lead, the canister and grape, the injured colonel raving and ranting, calling loudly for Old Bob and his sword, the already blood-soaked length of makeshift bandage trailing in the mud.

Jesse crouched behind a tree. She remained thus for a full minute, her hands pressed over her ears, her eyes tightly shut, then a moment longer. Her lips were atremble; her eyes had filled up with hot, burning tears. Her entire body was shaking, just as badly as those men she had nursed in the full throes of ague. She was suffering a different kind of fever. This was excitement, fear, exhilaration, a heating of her blood as it rushed to her temples, beating there with such force that she thought she would faint. She tried to breathe deeply, to calm herself, and stop her chest from heaving.

She listened. Silence.

Apart from the constant buzzing of the insects, was she alone in the world? Where were the enemy? Their six-pounders only moments before had been splitting the earth asunder. Where were the skulkers? Where was Thomas Ransom? What had happened to the guns, the two privates, the litter, and the raving colonel? All had disappeared.

She fell back against the tree and rubbed the palms of her hands over the hard, rough bark. That was real enough. She could hardly breathe and sweat was dripping from her face. Then she lowered her gaze and saw it. There in the long grass where it had slipped from his fingers lay evidence that the last ten minutes had been no nightmare.

Ransom's sidearm.

She reached out with a shaking hand.

She turned and walked back into the clearing, retracing the officer's erratic steps. In a while, she found his sword, and, if further proof were needed, there was Old Bob, blood seeping from the bayonet wound in his side and pouring from a hole in his hindquarters. The animal's big, moist eyes were still open, pleading with her to end his agony. She knew what must be done and she would not flinch from doing it. She checked the colonel's pistol as Captain Van Allen had taught her. It was loaded. With tears streaming from her eyes she placed the muzzle to the side of the animal's head, cocked the hammer, and pulled the trigger. The loud report and kick of the gun drove her off her feet. She sat there with closed, burning eyes, muttering to herself. Was it wrong to mourn the loss of so faithful a creature when thousands were falling in these golden cornfields?

She struggled up. Ironsides was trotting toward her, watching her, gratitude in those old eyes. Now he knew if, like Old Bob, he took a wound, he would not be abandoned to his suffering. As Jesse fastened the colonel's sword and pistol securely to her saddle the animal nudged her gently with his head. "I know—" she said softly, weeping, "—*I know*—"

She arrived back at Sherman's side to hear the shocking news of Prentiss's surrender in the sunken road.

Prentiss had held out all day and had only now given in to save the lives of his remaining two thousand men. Hurlbut, it was said, in defending the peach orchard, had placed his men on their stomachs in a double row to shoot Johnston's men like rabbits. Grant, using the men who had broken from ranks, had patched up a solid front line again, Sherman and McClernand had fallen back into a more solid array, and the Federals were waiting for the next assault.

It never came. There was a rumor that the Rebel general Johnston was dead. Perhaps Beauregard succeeding to command realized his men had also had enough. The Rebels had not driven the Federals into either Owl or Snake creek as they had predicted, or into the Tennessee River. The Union force had established a strong line of defense around Pittsburg Landing and now that was how the day would end.

The battle dwindled as twilight spread. But members of Sherman's staff were to witness the mystery of yet another narrow escape by their commander. Swinging into his saddle, the Ohioan's horse pranced sufficiently to tangle the reins around the animal's neck, as they were being held by Major Hammond. As the general leaned down to retrieve them a minié ball cut the straps two inches below the major's hand, and tore the crown and back rim of Sherman's hat.

There were no tents, even for the wounded, so orderlies had thrown a sheet of canvas across low-hanging branches to make a fly tent, under which the division commander was now sitting on an empty hardtack box, surrounded by staff and messengers, all of whom appeared to be talking at once. While Jesse lay out bandages, lint, and the contents of her small surgical kit, Captain Jackson arrived to confirm the fate of the Rebel commander. During the vicious fighting at the peach orchard Albert Sidney Johnston was mortally wounded. He had bled to death for want of any officer who knew how to apply a tourniquet.

Far more important and tragic for the Federals was the loss of General William Wallace, shot in the head and left for dead at a place the Rebels called the "Hornet's Nest" when a sudden advance by the enemy had forced a retreat.

"Sherman!" It was a very evidently relieved Grant, pushing his way through the throng of officers. "They told me you'd been mortally wounded and was dying in your tent. Then they said your hand was shot off!"

"Well, Grant, I have no tent in which to expire, I hear that Beauregard now occupies it, and as for my hand, sir, that as you can see, is still attached to my arm." He wiggled it for Grant's benefit, despite the blood and stiffness before Jesse laid it carefully on the upturned barrel beside the surgical instruments, and requested respectfully, if insistently, that he keep it still. But it was like asking the world to stop spinning on its axis for a second.

Grant's uniform was spattered with the brains of an aide who had been decapitated earlier by a six-pounder, but apart from being blackened in the face by gunpowder he looked no different from the usual crumpled little man with the chewed cigar.

Sherman shifted his weight so that Captain Jackson could light his stub of a cigar. He took the tin cup that Marcus gave him and swallowed a mouthful. He knew better than to offer Grant, who licked his lips. Although Rawlins was not around to scold and lecture, now was not the time to partake of intoxicating liquor. The Tennessee Army chief watched as Jesse examined the entrance wound in Sherman's hand, palpating the buckshot between the skin and bone, pressing the nail bed for a second or two, as Dr. Cartwright had shown her.

"Will it have to come off?" Sherman asked matter-of-factly, not stipulating if he meant the finger, the hand, or indeed the entire arm. He might have been asking if it was raining or if the mail had arrived. He drained the liquid in the cup. As he moved, Jesse could smell the sweat on his body. Rather than offensive, it was exhilarating. The male smell of him.

"No sir," she said, watching the nail bed pink up as blood returned to the small, vital arteries in the finger. "The blood supply is fine."

"If Beauregard's in command we'll be finished for now. He'll want to regroup, think it out, I know him well, he's not a rash man, given to excitable outbursts, but not rash," Sherman said as the girl began to scrub the wound with a small sponge moistened with clean water from her canteen.

Grant's gaze was fixed on what Jesse was now confidently doing with the forceps. She was probing for the buckshot pellet that had struck the third finger of the general's right hand, penetrating it to the bone. Dirt, small pieces of dead skin, and a slither of muscle dropped to the earth at her feet.

"Nelson's division of Buell's army has arrived." Grant's voice was more monotone than usual, he was fixated on Jesse's ministering, almost hypnotized. "And Lew Wallace arrived ten minutes ago."

"Better late than never," Sherman replied, but he wasn't meaning to be funny. The failure of Buell and Lew Wallace to arrive in time to fight on what would surely only be the first day of the battle was no matter for amusement. Wallace had started early on Sunday morning to cover the five miles to Shiloh Meeting House, but had wandered around the country all day within sound of the battle without being able to find it. Not even the combined entreaties of Rawlins and McPherson, sent to find him, could persuade the Indianan that he was marching in the wrong direction, and the farther he marched away the fainter grew the sound of battle. It had cost them dearly. Tonight they could have been celebrating a great victory instead of trying to see the best in what was almost an outright and disastrous defeat.

The notoriously squeamish Grant was now half-watching the operation, half-turning away. As confidently as any experienced surgeon, Jesse had now located the buckshot. She grasped it with the small bullet extractor and removed it, with little fuss and even less blood. If there was pain, Sherman was keeping it to himself. He winced very slightly and bit down on his cigar stub.

"Does the boy know what he's doing, Sherman?" It was a reasonable question, since the last time Grant had seen Jesse it was not as a surgeon, wound dresser, or even medical orderly, but as a courier flying back across the field on a bowlegged nag after delivering a message to hurry forward more ammunition. This boy seemed to be everywhere and everything. Surely there was more than one of him? Had Mrs. Davis given birth to triplets, all of whom were serving at Sherman's headquarters?

Sherman laughed and chewed hard on his cigar and squirmed about on the box, eager to be up and pacing, as always. "The boy's bright as a silver dollar," he said.

Jesse placed the pellet on the top of the barrel beside his hand. "There."

At that moment, Colonel McPherson rode up, dismounted, and saluted both generals.

"What'd you have to tell me, Mac?" asked Grant.

"At least a third of the army is out of commission, sir, and the balance greatly disheartened. Those who fought bravely and were pushed back saw the skulkers and cowards along the bluff and it was all their officers could do to stop them shooting their own kind. I believe neither side can claim to have organized armies at this moment, sir, officers have lost their regiments, regiments are intermingled, and companies all scrambled together, Ohio with Iowa, and Indiana with Illinois and so on.

Should we make preparations for a retreat, sir?" McPherson concluded, his mouth slightly open, and watched as Jesse confidently controlled the minor bleeding in Sherman's hand with a styptic before closing the small neat wound with adhesive plaster strips.

"Retreat? No!" Grant was saying. "They can't break our lines tonight, it's too late, they've spent their force. Tomorrow we'll attack them with fresh troops from Wallace and Buell, and drive them off. At Fort Donelson, when both sides seemed defeated, I saw that the one who took the offensive the next day won. I propose to attack at daylight and whip 'em!" He looked at Sherman, who, though obviously not as convinced as the commander, nodded his large head in agreement.

"Enough!" he suddenly bellowed, staring at Jesse with piercing bloodshot eyes as she started to apply the cotton dressing. "Stop bandaging me up like a goddamn Egyptian mummy. By the time you're finished, Beauregard will be across the Ohio and we'll all be whistling Dixie." The narrowed eyes twinkled with amusement, though the tension at the corners of his firm mouth showed he was in pain. He extended the finished article for Grant and McPherson to see, cleaned, probed, and dressed. However, Jesse wasn't finished yet. She was trying to unbutton his blouse. "What in hell—?" She explained that he had taken a second wound, in his shoulder. He looked to the right shoulder and then to the left. To his amazement, the strap was severed and the bloodied flesh exposed. "Another scratch," he said, covering it up with the piece of cloth that now hung loose.

"The wound needs to be cleaned and dressed, sir, otherwise it'll become inflamed."

"I told you, it's a scratch," his hoarse voice declared as his eyes glared at her.

"Sorry. The *scratch* on your shoulder needs to be cleaned and dressed, otherwise it'll become inflamed," Jesse said again, holding his gaze with arched red brows.

"Damn *you*, Corporal, I can't decide if you're insolent, obsequious, or dim-witted, but when I have decided you may be sure you'll receive the appropriate punishment. Get on with it." He jammed the cigar into his mouth.

He was now sitting on the edge of the hardtack box, his hat far down over narrowed eyes, a cigar in his mouth, stripped to the waist, looking like a bad-tempered comical old bird stripped of his feathers and perched on a branch. His skin was very white, with nothing to relieve the pallor but a patch of red hair on his narrow chest. His shoulders and arms were spare, the sinews stood out in his neck like cords. He was truly a bony man, with an almost feminine slenderness, but by no means lacking in physical strength.

As Jesse poured a little fresh water onto a piece of lint and used it to clean the wound on his shoulder she gazed up to see James McPherson watching her with a queer, inquisitive, even puzzled expression in those kindly brown eyes. What he could see was a look of utterly rapt devotion. She smiled at him and he looked away, almost uncomfortably. She placed a fresh wad of lint on the wound and used two strips of adhesive tape to keep it in place.

"Very professional," Sherman said, putting on his frock coat and wincing. "Now get away before *you* need the attentions of a surgeon."

Unfazed, Jesse made a sling from some rag she had in the bottom of her haversack and before he knew what was happening she'd drawn his arm through. Words of loud and angry protest formed on his lips, but it was Grant who forestalled them.

"You should keep the arm rested overnight, Sherman."

Sherman's response would have made a seasoned sailor blush.

For a while, the two men discussed what had transpired on other parts of the battlefield. Then Grant said, "We can afford to be optimistic, time is on our side. The enemy has done all he can today. Tomorrow morning, with Lew Wallace's division and fresh troops of the Ohio Army, we'll soon finish him up." He laid a hand on the Ohioan's arm. "Be ready to assume the offensive in the morning."

"Corporal Davis, you did a splendid job on my hand, splendid." Sherman half-flexed his fingers and winced, winking at McPherson. "Don't hurt a bit, not a bit."

She had wiped and replaced her instruments in their little plush-lined case and packed her haversack. Now she asked, "Sir, may I have some time to deal with a personal matter?"

"Of course, my boy," he said, leaning over to squeeze her shoulder, "you earned it." As she prepared to leave, Sherman called her name, then in a loud voice so that all standing by could hear he said, "You acquitted yourself with much personal courage today, you stood your ground when many others, older than you, and far more experienced, broke and ran. Here," He tossed her a "segar," which she caught easily with one hand. "Despite the fact you appear unable to grow a beard, you're no longer a boy, but a man."

For the second time that day Jesse found herself staring at the endless rows of dead and wounded, laid out along the Landing.

"*The City of Memphis* is the only hospital boat," the orderly replied in response to her inquiry, as he paused to squeeze the blood from a piece of rag he was using to dampen the bandages on the stump of an amputated leg. "She's been up to Savannah a'ready. Got seven hundred wounded onboard this trip. Them three," he pointed at the transports still hugging the shore at the lower end of the Landing while several more sat motionless in midriver, "they got plenty a wounded on there, end to end wounded you might say. Not a inch of space between them. I was on there earlier. Your wounded officer might a been taken there, or the others. No tellin' which. I heard tell they got every buildin' upriver filled with wounded, every schoolhouse, hotel, church, and residence. There ain't no room for no more. See them boats there, they might look like wooden tubs floatin' in the water all peaceful like but when it gets real dark they're gonna wake up those Rebels who are sleepin' mighty peaceful in our old camps. Have yer taken a look at them laid out here fer yer colonel?"

A young cavalry lieutenant walked by and ripped off one of the blankets, revealing a body without a head.

"Goddamn it," said the medical orderly, "ain't yer got no respect?"

"To hell with you, I lost my horse, lost my outfit, near lost my life. *He* don't need it no more and *I'm* getting wet." With that, he wrapped the blanket around his shoulders Indian-style, clasped his carbine to his chest, and strode away.

Jesse gazed up to heaven. It had started to rain. Many of the wounded left under the blazing sun since early morning had become dehydrated, and were groaning for water; their dressings, or rather the makeshift bandages that had been applied, were already filthy and blood-soaked. There were few medical attendants and still fewer surgeons. "I'm sorry to keep asking you—" she began, crouching beside the orderly.

"Ain't your fault if'in yer lookin' fer a friend. Hey, Jamie?" he called down the row of prostrate men. "Eleventh Illinoise? Seen any?"

"Boy over there," Jamie shouted back immediately, "the one nursin' his hand, I think he's Eleventh."

Jesse looked across the crowded wood landing to the boy with straw-colored hair sitting up against a barrel cupping a blood-soaked hand against his chest like a child protecting a bird with a broken wing.

"Water—" said the boy on the next litter. "—Please—"

"I'm comin', old friend," said the orderly. "—Hold yer horses, I'm comin'."

But Jesse had already gone to him with her canteen.

"Much 'bliged," said the orderly, "we ain't got much a anythin' here 'cept wounded. No beddin', no tents, no hay for beddin', no salves nor stimulants. A lot a the regiments lost their medical supplies in the attack. Left 'em behind in the old camps. Rebs got 'em now, I reckon."

He watched with interest as Jesse opened her haversack and proceeded to clean the exposed wound on the boy's left shoulder. "You dun this afore, I can tell." She gave the boy another drink, then pushed the stopper back into the neck.

"I'd leave you the canteen and my haversack," she told the orderly, "but if I find the colonel he may need my help."

"That's okay, we got plenty a water. Water we got, it's willin' hands we need. I hope yer find yer officer."

"Mama—" cried the boy whose shoulder Jesse had dressed, "mama— I want ma mama—"

"Well, I ain't yer mama, boy, that's for damn sure, but I guess I'll have to do."

Jesse went to the soldier with the mangled hand. When he lifted his blood-besmirched face, she was amazed to recognize one of the two

enlisted men who had carried Thomas Ransom from the field that afternoon. "Private?" she said gently, "I'm sorry to bother you. Colonel Ransom, where did you take him?"

He stared at her, eyes half-closed with pain and fatigue. "Company
K," he said. "Private Martin Baker, Company K. Captain Carter's gone.
Shot through the head—I saw his brains spurting out, just as the battle
commenced, saw them spurting out all over the ground."

"I'm sorry," Jesse said, "I'm sorry about Captain Carter, but do you
remember where you took Colonel Ransom?"

"Oh my Lord—they say Colonel Wallace is gone. I heard the officers
talking. Is that true, do you reckon? Colonel Wallace used ter command
the Eleventh afore they made him a gen'al. He used to be our commanding officer afore Colonel Ransom." The boy stared into her eyes blankly.
"Now they're all gone—all gone, Captain Carter—General Wallace—"

"Please, try and remember, this afternoon you carried Colonel Ransom from Jones Field." She gave Private Baker a little shake as his eyes
drooped closed. *"Where did you take him?"*

"Colonel Ransom?" His eyes opened again and showed recognition.
"We took him to the commissary ship. There was no room on the *Memphis.*"

"Let me look at your hand," she said removing the blood-soaked
piece of torn shirt he had wrapped around the wound. A minié ball had
gone clean through the center of the palm. She applied a clean bandage,
putting as much pressure as she dared to stem the flow of blood, for she
couldn't trust this boy to remain conscious enough to loosen a tourniquet and there was no one else to do it. The orderlies already had
enough on their plate. She slipped the hand into his shirt, made him as
comfortable as she could, gave him a little morphine, and held the bottle
as he swallowed a mouthful of the whiskey she brought from her haversack. When the shock wore off he would be in great pain, but for now,
she could delay the inevitable. Seeing the young soldier's dazed smile
surface above the dirt- and blood-besmirched features she silently
blessed Dr. Cartwright and Jacob for taking the trouble to teach her
these basic skills. It was impossible to offer comfort and solace to all, but

to be unable to help just one of these suffering men would have been intolerable.

The scene that greeted Jesse on the commissary ship *Continental* was shocking. She moved up the side of the gangway so as not to take up too much space as the wounded were littered from the Landing to the hurricane deck, already crammed to capacity. Straw and hay had been scattered around to absorb the blood. Wounded men, forced to remain on their feet because there was nowhere to sit, let alone lie down, were swaying with exhaustion, loss of blood, and pain. As she passed, searching every haggard face for those admired features, hands stretched out begging weakly for water. Others merely stood and stared into nothingness. Here and there, she stopped when a moan, a sigh, became too much for her to bear. She gave water, words of comfort, but with a pang of desperation and guilt she realized she would never find the colonel if she stopped every few seconds to help.

Her clumsy brogues slipped on the blood-soaked stairway as she went below. Here the chaos was compounded by the smell. In the close confines, the stench was almost overpowering. Every inch of space had been taken with the wounded, cabin, stairs, gangways, some with the most ghastly wounds, faces mangled, stomachs torn open, arms or legs gone, joints splintered and shattered, vile testimony to the devastating power of Captain Claude Minié's conical ball. Horrified she watched as the few medical orderlies trampled helplessly over the wounded in their efforts to reach those furthest away.

"Sir—" She stopped a man in midflight, spotting the caduceus on his sleeve. "—Please—I'm looking for—"

"See the orderlies!" he barked and ran on, a distracted look on his face, a severed foot just visible in the scrap of blanket he held in his arms.

"No time!" an elderly man in a civilian suit stained with blood shouted into her face, when she spoke to him, and then "If you're not here to help, for pity's sake get out of the way. Get out of the way, you little fool!" He ran off responding to the cry of "Surgeon! Surgeon needed here!"

As she stepped carefully over the wounded, cold, bloodless hands clutched at her. Looking down she noticed for the first time that the bottoms of her trousers were soaked in blood and hanging heavy about her ankles.

She entered a large area that had been stripped of furniture. Here the wounded were laid side by side with barely a breath between them. There were no cots, just coarse feed sacks loosely stuffed with hay, no thicker than a blanket, called bed-sacks.

Standing in the midst of this suffering humanity she suddenly, miraculously, saw him, third bed-sack from the end, covered with an army blanket that was moth-eaten and dirty. The pillow beneath his head, if a filthy linen envelope no wider than a handkerchief stuffed with a few hay stalks could be termed as such, was stained with blood.

The colonel came to himself, his eyelids fluttering open as she knelt beside him. He stared at her with those big, deep-set eyes, soft now in pain, without any hint of the murderous steeliness she had seen that afternoon in Jones Field. "Water—" he murmured.

She lifted his head and put the canteen to his thin sculptured lips. He drank thirstily, his bewildered gaze on her face.

"It's Jesse, sir," she told him, tears starting to her eyes, "Jesse—Corporal Davis. Do you know me?"

His bewilderment turned to incredulity. "Corporal Davis? What . . . what are . . . you doing . . . here?"

"I came to find out how badly you'd been injured—" Before she finished speaking, he had faded again with a feeble moan.

She laid his head carefully on the pillow and dripped a little water on the piece of shirt she had wrapped around his head; dried blood had stuck it fast to his scalp. Then she used a clean piece of cloth to bind the wound. It would do the trick until he reached the hospital; at least the wound had stopped bleeding. She wished she could find a clean blanket and a proper pillow. She stared at the colonel's face. Lying there helpless, drawn and pale from loss of blood, he looked younger than his twenty-eight years, not the same man who had sliced away the top of a man's head with his saber, albeit one that had just plunged his bayonet into Old Bob's side.

While she cleaned the tiny cuts on his cheeks and forehead, he came once more to consciousness. This time he knew her immediately.

"Oh, give me a drink, Corporal—I'm dying of thirst, for God's sake a drink—I beg of you." She raised his head and put the canteen to his parched lips. He drank so greedily that the water overflowed his mouth, he coughed, nearly choking, and then abruptly he pushed her hand away, grabbing instead to her blouse. "Cowards—I showed them—stand to it—stand and fight like men—dirty filthy cowards. Load and fire—what are you waiting for? *Fall in Eleventh! Face to the rear and charge cavalry!* Corporal Davis?" he said sharply. "What are you doing here . . . soldier . . . why aren't you fighting?"

"The fighting is over for the day, sir." She wiped his chin and smiled at him.

"Tell Colonel Wallace—the Eleventh are ready and will follow him onto hell." He grabbed her blouse again. "*You must* bring me news—of my regiment—do you understand?" His pain-filled eyes clouded over suddenly. "And bring me news of Colonel Wallace—and my Eleventh—"

"Yes sir." She had decided to say nothing of Captain Carter or General Wallace. "Sir, I have your sword and pistol. I'll keep them safe for you."

"How did it go—the battle—did we drive back the Rebels?"

Jesse recalled General Grant's words to the boy lying on the litter. "Tomorrow for certain, sir."

His eyes had closed and his head sank to the side of the pillow.

By the time she had emerged from that hellhole, it was dark and the stars were out. Corporal Tucker was right, as she came down the gangway gasping fresh air into her lungs, the "wooden tubs" *Tyler* and *Lexington* were lobbing shells into the Rebel army encampment, where Union soldiers had slept the previous night.

Tonight, only the dead would get any rest, and even that was doubtful.

Back at General Sherman's makeshift headquarters Don Carlos Buell was just leaving. Jesse caught the conclusion of their exchange.

"With these reinforcements, we will have a numerical advantage over the Rebels and tomorrow we can sweep the field," Sherman was saying. "General Grant has already talked to me about taking the offensive. He said he recalled that at Donelson there came a moment when either side was ready to give way if the other showed a bold front. He has decided to be the bold one. He believes that the enemy has shot its bolt and with your force available by morning, victory is sure."

"That wasn't the impression Grant gave me when I met him on the wharf."

"Then not only is your conclusion erroneous but also your impressions." Sherman removed the cigar from his lips, blew out smoke, and stood very straight.

"Sherman"—Buell's smile was not only sudden, it was greasy—"come now, surely that is a poor way to welcome the savior of the day?"

"General Buell, I'm glad you've come, sir, but think victory certain even without you."

Don Carlos Buell crossed over the rest of his troops. These fresh regiments from the Army of the Ohio marched off the transports past men bathed in blood, and led by brass bands playing patriotic tunes, much to the disgust of the rain-sodden and battle-weary soldiers trying to sleep along the sheltered strip of beach between the riverbank and the water.

The occasional rattle of muskets could be heard in the distance, a sputter and an answering sputter, breaking out and stopping, as though a few stubborn men on both sides were unwilling to give up the fight, now and then accompanied by a solitary shell from a faraway battery. Lethargic and only token, the last word in an argument the reason for which no one could recall.

Meanwhile the skulkers, white-faced harbingers of doom, lankhaired and hollow-eyed, had crawled out of their holes to predict a bloody fate for the new arrivals. But they were drowned out by rousing music, and silenced by Buell's officers who, afraid that these cowards would infect their own men, treated them none too kindly, and by the men themselves who called them every kind of base creature, even hitting out in rage.

At 11:00 P.M. Sherman decided to seek out Grant.

"Grant, at last!" the division commander bellowed, plowing his way through the mud toward the huddled figure backed up against a tree trunk, hat pulled down over sorrowful eyes and coat collar pulled up around his ears, a lantern wedged into an overhead branch, the inevitable cigar glowing between his teeth. "I thought you had retired for the night, then one of your staff told me you'd made your headquarters under this tree."

"I have nowhere to retire to, Sherman, and I couldn't sleep even if I did, they're using the *Tigress* for the wounded. They kindly offered me a spot in a cabin, but I confess the shouts of the injured were too much for me, that and the ankle." He passed his saddened gaze over Sherman's arm, resting in the sling. "How's the hand?"

"Fine. Fine," Sherman replied honestly, "I can flex my fingers. The boy did a good job."

"You look all done in, Sherman."

The Ohioan, not normally known for his sartorial elegance, this evening in the torrential rain, after ten hours of intense pressure in battle, against a formidable, courageous, and determined foe, was encrusted in mud from boots to hat. The brim already hanging off was drooping with the weight of rainwater, his cigar stub was played out, and his black tie, never where it ought to be, was all the way around under his right ear. However, it should be noted for posterity, his eyes were as alert as ever, two penetrating orbs in a face whose wrinkles were edged in grime.

"Well, *you* don't look as if you could lead the prettiest girl around the floor in a polka!"

The younger man's thin lips confirmed this fact with a rueful smile. Not that he would have led the prettiest girl around the floor in a polka, even if he could, unless the prettiest girl happened to be his wife. He used his cigar to point into the near distance, and said incredulously, "Isn't that your orderly coming there, Sherman?"

Jesse was trudging carefully through the muddy potholes, splashing along, up to her ankles in water, past those once beautiful white oaks and red buds, splintered and scarred, toward them, guided, it seemed, by the light from Grant's lantern, for how else could she have found these two great generals in that crowded, noisy, rain-soaked, despairing darkness? Then, reaching them, from under her dripping oilskin, like a magician producing a rabbit from a hat, she produced two tin cups of steaming coffee. Sherman was beyond astonishment. He merely drank a mouthful of coffee and said with satisfaction, "Hot toddy."

"Mighty fine." Grant sipped the liquid, wincing as he shifted his weight from one side of his body to the other. "Touches the spot, huh, Sherman? Thank you, Corporal, very welcome."

"Get under a blanket somewhere dry and snatch some sleep," Sherman advised her.

But she had much to do before she saw her blanket. She lingered a moment, sheltering under the tree, turning up the collar of her oilskin. On the other side, the shorter man brought two fresh cigars from his pocket, one of which he gave his companion, saying quietly, "Whichever side takes the initiative in the morning will make the other retire. Beauregard will be mighty smart if he attacks before I do."

For a moment, Jesse waited as the two men smoked in silence, doubtlessly thinking of what had transpired through that long and bloody day, and what would be the fate of their army on the morrow. Then the red-bearded soldier said with emotion, "Well, Grant, we've had the devil's own day, haven't we?"

"Yes," said Grant, with a short sharp puff of the cigar, "lick 'em tomorrow, though."

10

A blanket for a shroud

★ ★ ★ ★

If I were to speak of war, it would not be to show you the glories
of conquering armies but the mischief and misery they strew in
their track; and how, while they march on with tread of iron and
plumes proudly tossing in the breeze, some one must follow
closely in their steps, crouching to the earth, toiling in the rain
and darkness, shelter-less like themselves, with no thought of
pride or glory, fame or praise, or reward; hearts breaking with
pity, faces bathed in tears and hands in blood. This is the side
which history never shows.

—CLARA BARTON, excerpt from a speech given between 1866 and 1868

Around the rough-hewn log cabin on the bluff, during that first chaotic
day, had mushroomed a canvas city.

"What do you think of it?" Jacob asked her proudly. "The ambulances come up from the battlefield, the surgeons work their miracles,
and then the wounded are littered away to the recovery area." He indicated orderlies hastily carrying litters from the operating area inside and
around the cabin to the large wall tents. "We are making history. They

are calling it the first 'field hospital.' " Suddenly his smile vanished as he followed the direction of Jesse's bleak gaze.

The wounded and the dying disgorged by the wagons had been laid out on straw pallets, on blankets, on coats and on the wet ground, as far as the eye could see. For them there was no shelter. There were pitifully few orderlies to organize; like the surgeons, they were swamped.

"God knows," the Dutchman raised his sorrowful gaze to heaven, "it is not perfect, but you had to see it this morning to understand."

Jesse looked into the cabin where three surgeons were at work in the cramped interior, Dr. Fitzjohn, the elderly Dr. Lowenfels, and Dr. Cartwright. Cartwright, his apron smeared with blood and every manner of human waste, up to his elbows in blood, his face and spectacles speckled with blood, the bottoms of his trousers soaked in blood, bent over a patient, a bone saw in one hand and a wad of bloody lint in the other. Finishing his gruesome task, and quickly sewing, he looked around and took a deep breath, as two orderlies removed the victim from his table.

"How many more?" His voice was a croak.

"Ain't no countin' 'em, Doc," said the orderly. "How many fleas on a dawg?"

The surgeon went to the door, stared with burning eyes at the row upon row of wounded, trying to gauge how long it might take to fight through this flood of human misery. A week? A year? A lifetime?

"Sir, I'm sorry to bother you—" Jesse began.

"Where the hell have you been?" he said with quiet intensity. "I needed you, goddamn it, look around. Where have you been? I ought to put you on a charge."

She stared at him. It had never even occurred to her that he would expect her to be with him during the battle, attending the wounded, and as for putting her on a charge . . .

"Get to work," he ordered. "Find an apron. Then get to work—" He pushed himself off the splintered door frame with an effort and limped slowly across the yard. She didn't have to ask why he was limping. His feet and ankles were swollen.

She followed. "May I have a brief word with you, sir?"

"No. There's work to be done." He gestured toward the line of sway-ing, jolting vehicles coming along the dirt road to the bluff, a line that never seemed to get any shorter, never seemed to tail off, despite the speed and efficiency which the surgeons brought to their work. He needed a drink. Not whiskey, God help him, water. *Water.* He'd breathed so much chloroform, the lining of his throat was on fire. Jesse watched him snatch up the overflowing ladle and gulp it so fast half the contents went down his chin and onto his blood-soaked apron. He looked like a man possessed. Only one thing kept him going. A searing, perpetuating anger against whatever or whoever it was that had put him and these men in this place. He should have dropped hours ago, his back breaking, but he would not rest, could not rest, until every suffering soldier, Rebel or Yankee, brought to his table, was tended.

Jesse let him walk to the tin washbasin set up on the rain barrel, then she joined him. As he tore off his filthy apron, she told him about Colonel Ransom, lying injured on the *Continental,* and what she had in mind. He stopped trying, with trembling hands, to pick the dried blood spots from his eyeglasses and faced her, eyes wild with anger.

"Let me get this straight, in the midst of all this, you've got the god-damn nerve to come here to ask me to authorize the removal of one offi-cer from the transport to the hospital here so you can nurse him personally? Is that right? Is that what you're asking?"

"The transport stinks; it's a disease-ridden, floating hell hole. There are no beds; the surgeons are stretched to the limit—"

"And we're not!" Cartwright laughed maniacally, arms thrown wide to take in the hellish scene.

"The wounded can't even get a drink of water. They have no blankets, no pillows, no medicines, very few orderlies. The colonel is suffering—"

"Like thousands of others. He's strong. He survived other wounds without *you.* He knew what he was doing when he enlisted. Save your sympathy for the ignorant deluded farm boys." Cartwright splashed water over his face and flinging the tiny slither of soap back in with a snort of disgust, shouted, "Orderly! Fresh soap."

"Ain't nun."

"Find some!"

"Told yer, ain't nun!" Cartwright took a menacing step toward him. "Ah'll find some."

"Sir, do I have your permission to—"

Cartwright rounded on the girl. "You have my permission to do one damn thing, and one damn thing only, that's get to work on the wounded. Stop mooning over one lousy officer when we have a whole damn army to care for."

"Mooning? I don't understand."

"Mooning. You never heard that word? It's what impressionable young girls do when they see a brass-plated officer. Ransom's better off in a general hospital in Cincinnati or Saint Louis, and his own people should take care of him anyway." He started back to the cabin.

Doggedly, Jesse followed. "The Eleventh have been cut to pieces," she said. "So many were lost they say not much more than a company remains. Doctor," she gripped his arm, "have I asked you for one single favor since I've been here?" Her expression hardened. "You were the one who struck a fellow surgeon because he refused to care for a soldier from another regiment."

Cartwright stopped abruptly. "Who the hell told you that? Jacob. I never struck him, I pushed him. He fell. And stop wasting my goddamn time. If you think I'm going to let you take an ambulance wagon, an orderly, and a teamster for one man you're crazy—"

"I never asked for an ambulance wagon, I'll use that—" She pointed. Cartwright looked at the broken-down go-to-market one-mule cart that soldiers had taken from a local farm to bring their own dying colonel to the hospital that morning. Only now, there were no soldiers. "If you loan me a mule I'll drive it myself and find someone at the Landing to help me carry the colonel."

"And if I don't loan you a mule?"

"I'll harness the cart to my back with a rope and drag it down to the Landing and up again." Tears of determination had sprung into her eyes.

"And if I take the cart away?" The surgeon gave a vindictive twist of his mouth.

Her lower lip trembled and the clefted chin raised a notch. "Colonel

Ransom was kind to me. He's my friend. I would carry a friend on my back if I had to. I would carry you. I would carry Jakob."

There was no question in Cartwright's mind that she would too. "Your friend?" His expression was one of amused disdain. "Colonels don't make friends with corporals." After a second's silence he said, "It means that much to you?"

"Yes sir—" she said intensely, holding his gaze. "It means that much to me."

He stared at her a moment longer before bellowing "Jacob!" as the Dutchman crossed the yard. "Find someone who can handle a cart without driving it into the Tennessee," he told the steward. Then to Jesse he said, "Satisfied, damn you?"

"Yes sir, thank you, sir."

He grabbed hold of her by the collar, pulled her up onto her toes, and thrust his haggard face close to hers. *"Don't—call—me—sir. Don't ever call me sir. Is that clear?"*

She stared at him with her large eyes brimming tears and smiled.

She eased the unconscious colonel's head carefully to the center of the stained canvas and covered him to the chin with a clean blanket. She laid his coat over the top of the blanket to keep him warm, then she and the silent young bandsman Jacob had sent with her lifted the litter and made their slow, painstaking way back to the stairs, trying not to step on the wounded, and down the gangplank.

Outside the earlier cold sleet had turned to hail. What had happened to the warm Southern spring?

She sat in the back of the tottering cart as it bounced and jolted over the uneven track, the canvas tarpaulin cover supported by a sturdy tree branch, as she steadied Thomas Ransom's injured head in her lap. His elegant features looked bony and drawn. She put a little water on a cloth and held it to his cracked lips. He stirred, moaned a little. "You're safe now," she whispered, stroking the hair off his pale, moist brow. "We'll take good care of you." She rubbed his cold hands, put them inside her jacket, and smiled to herself, a tiny self-satisfied smile.

The good and faithful Jacob came to meet them. He stood in the rain like an oak and stared at the bedraggled girl under the dripping canvas in the rickety old cart and she stared back at him, blinking rainwater, but still smiling, her injured colonel cradled in her lap.

"I have him," she said, excitedly, as though in possession of a rare species that must be protected. "I have him safe, Jakob."

"Yes, my child, I see that you have him safe and I rejoice. It's all right—all right—leave him—" He told a second orderly who had joined the bandsman to remove the litter from the cart. Instead, the Dutchman wrapped the young Vermonter in the blanket and carried him into the cabin in his own strong arms. Yes, *such* an inestimable prize must be nurtured.

Nevertheless, not all agreed.

"What's this?" Cartwright demanded as Jacob laid the colonel gently on the table and began to clean the wound for the surgeon to examine. "What the hell are you doing? You know the rules, for God's sake—"

Oh yes, the rules. The rules were ruthlessly followed. There was never *any* exception. The Dutchman had explained them to Jesse. The mortally wounded were carried off to the far end of the yard to die. They usually wanted only water and a comforting word. Those with minor injuries were placed near the trees, in a barn, a stable, a tent if any were available, to shelter them from the rain, the sun, where they nursed their own hurts as best they could until it was their turn to see a surgeon or wound dresser. The third category, the seriously wounded, but with a chance of survival, also waited for treatment, but they were first to see a surgeon.

"Get him off the table and put him with the others." Cartwright gestured to the orderlies. Jacob the oak barred their way. He spoke to Cartwright. "The rules are important, it is true, without them there is chaos, but once in a while we are permitted to bend them a little for those we care for."

The surgeon looked from the Dutchman to the girl and frowned his puzzlement. The girl took his hand and placed it against the colonel's bloody face. "*Please—*" she said.

"Minor wound," Cartwright stated finally, with his usual display of sympathy, after what had to be admitted was a thorough examination of the colonel's scalp, the application of a styptic to stop the bleeding, and a lint dressing. "Minié ball, probably, ripped through the scalp. That bright red blood was from small blood vessels in the scalp, no major bleeders and no skull fracture. He's lucky, inch lower—*fatal*." He wiped his bloody hands on his bloodstained apron. "You made it sound as if half his damn head was blown away." Was that regret in his voice?

"He lost a lot of blood," Jesse explained. "He was dizzy, I saw him fall over on the battlefield."

"Maybe he was drunk. I often get dizzy and fall over when I'm drunk." Jesse's expression said this wasn't funny. "Loss of blood, that's all, if he'd done the sensible thing and got the wound dressed he wouldn't be lying here right now. Most wounds like this just go through the scalp. The skull is protected by a dense layer of tissue, called the *galea aponeu-rotica*." Even now, he was giving her a medical lesson. "Scalp always bleeds a lot. Easy to control with a pressure dressing. You should know that by now, unless this calf love has wiped out everything you've learned in the past few weeks? Put him in one of the recovery tents. If the wound starts bleeding again you might need to suture it and use a bulky dressing to keep more pressure on the wound." He laughed. "He'll have one hell of a headache when he wakes up. Give him some morphine. Keep the wound moist." He stared at the girl's face as she stared at the unconscious colonel, and a lump of anger, like a sudden ball of dyspepsia, rose so high in his throat he thought he would choke. "Look, for chrissake, you know all this, or you should, he didn't need a surgeon. You wasted my time." His anger was all out of proportion. Jesse stood on tiptoe and to his utter astonishment pressed a kiss to his bristled cheek. He looked around the cabin, but everyone had more important matters on their mind. Which reminded him, "And for chrissake, show a little tact, he's a man and you're a *boy*. Get my drift?"

Ten minutes later, after making the Vermonter comfortable in one of the recovery tents, Jesse found an apron and got to work, but where in God's name to begin? Those outside and conscious, awaiting the surgeon, heard the screams of those about to go under the knife, not yet fully anesthetized, and in most cases it scared them more than their own wounds.

She watched Jacob working along the opposite row, his large fleshy features animated with anguish and dedication, as he moved from one soldier to another. He was dressing wounds, giving water to fight the dehydration, whiskey to combat shock, administering morphine, and often, almost as important, a few words of comfort. General McPherson had been right, so intermingled had the companies, regiments, and brigades become in battle that these injured soldiers represented every division in the Tennessee Army. Would any surgeon today dare to refuse help to a soldier not from his own regiment or brigade?

She went down the line with her haversack.

Private Lawrie of the Eleventh Iowa had next of kin written on a piece of bloody paper pinned to his blouse. He'd lost his right leg, blown off at the knee. Although unconscious, his eyes were half-open, the eyelids flickering disconcertingly. His breathing was loud and labored. Jesse felt for his pulse, it was racing. She opened his collar and settled him into a more comfortable position that did not restrict his airways. She poured water over the dried, soiled rags that had been placed around the stump by a litter bearer to make them easier to remove, then carefully put on a fresh dressing. In a few seconds, it was soaked with bright red arterial blood. Secondary hemorrhaging had begun. She applied the tourniquet, and called an orderly from across the way, telling him with authority, "This soldier must go immediately into surgery." He and another of the bandsmen carried him off to the cabin.

Corporal Cooper of the Forty-eighth Illinois had his right hand blown clean off. She gave him some morphine for the pain, which had turned him the color of candle wax and appeared to have robbed him of his power of speech. He sat quietly, staring blankly ahead of him. Private Owen Davidson, Fourteenth Missouri, had taken two balls in the shoulder blade and one in the right leg. He wanted only water and to be left alone with his misery.

Private Kuhn, Twenty-fifth Indiana, hit twice, thanked her profusely for her attentions as she examined the wound in his cheek where a minié ball had passed clean through, exiting behind his left ear. He said he wasn't in pain, but more likely, Jesse reflected, he was in deep shock. She got him to swallow a morphine pill for the moment when the shock wore off.

Private Alonzo Miller of the Seventy-seventh Ohio, who continually yelled to keep up the charge, until his lower jaw was shattered by a minié ball and left hanging by a strip of skin. Somehow, he had been placed in line to see the surgeon, instead of at the far corner with the dead and dying, the hopeless cases. She put a padded dressing of dampened muslin to the gaping hole in his lower face and moved on to the next man.

Private Rogers was also Seventy-seventh Ohio. He'd taken shrapnel in both eyes and was miraculously conscious. She made him more comfortable on the hay-filled pillow slip. There was very little else she could do for him or the brave Private Miller.

"I ketched ma foot in a gall darn ditch," Corporal Sylvester Braddock told her when she removed his brogan. "T'aint much but gall darn bad luck." His sock was soaked with caked blood. The end of the tibia was sticking out of the skin. "We got separated from the rest a the brigade and had to pick our way through the woods north a the Purdy-Hamburg Road. We come across a large reggiement headin' toward us. Old Col'nal Cockerill he reckoned they weren't our boys, even though they's wearin' blue jest like us, he says he dudn't quite know jest how they could be our boys, but he daren't open fire. Jest then the wind shifted and out that flag a their's was a flyin', jest like God was givin' us a sign. They were Louisiani boys a flyin' their state flag. Old Col'nal Cockerill he gets us to unleash a volley and we scattered that whole damn reggiement. I reckon they're still runnin' and we was runnin' after 'em, that's how I snagged ma ankle thataways. I had me such awful damn luck. I wanted real bad to ketch me a Louisiani boy."

Corporal Frank Haynes had a minié ball in his thigh. There had been an early loss of blood judging by the makeshift dressing of the corporal's army-issue woolen sock, which, once gray, was now a mauve-red, as though it had been dyed in a vat of claret. But it had stopped now. He talked fast and did not stop from the moment Jesse knelt beside him to the second she passed him the canteen, mainly to shut him up. Shock affected men in many different ways. Some became silent and lethargic, others, like Corporals Haynes and Braddock, could not still their tongues long enough even to slake their thirst, but must tell their stories, all different, all unique—and yet all the same. This soldier wanted to know too about a young man across the way coughing up blood and sputum as Jacob tried to comfort him. The rules had already broken down long before the Dutchman had placed the young colonel on the table. Bandsmen and overworked orderlies deposited their burdens wherever they could find space, before rushing back to fetch another from the wagons.

"The barrels of the weapons got hot from constant firing—little pellets of melted lead fell out of the muzzles after each shot." Private Jack Taggart told her, "You ever seen that, Corporal, little pellets of melted lead just falling at your feet?"

Before she could answer, a young infantry officer, perhaps no more than seventeen, with a tumble of yellow hair and soft blond mustaches, got unsteadily to his feet, blinked away the blood that was gushing from a head wound, and staggered forward, stiff-legged, waving an imaginary saber in the air. "Forward Company C, give 'em hell, boys, give 'em hell!" he yelled and in a few moments his lower lip had begun to tremble, he swung around, stared sightlessly at the wounded laid out on the blood-soaked pallets, then became very rigid, and finally collapsed. The boy with the shrapnel in his eyes sat up and began to yell deliriously for "Lizzie," thrashing about blindly, trying to tear off the bloody rags that covered the top half of his face. Jacob went to him, as he screamed repeatedly, "Come get me, Lizzie—come get me, Lizzie—oh, come get me, Lizzie—oh, I wish you'd come get me, Lizzie—" His plea like a lament.

Another soldier, his shirt pulled up and left, perhaps by his own restless hands, had exposed a nasty abdominal wound from which a loop of small bowel was poking out. Jesse saw one of the little drummer boys approach him tentatively with a canteen. As he got close, the soldier went into a coughing fit, the small gut protruding farther and farther from the wound. The drummer boy, his face gaunt and streaked with tear-stained sweat and mud, seemed to steel himself bravely as he bent down and held the canteen to the man's mouth. No sooner had the man drunk the water than it ran out through a second large wound on the side of his chest. The expression of naked horror on the wounded man's face was matched and exceeded only by the look of disbelief on the grimy face of the drummer boy. For another orderly, clutching precariously to one end of a blanket stretcher, this was too much. He let go and the unfortunate on the blanket rolled off onto the wet ground and lay there groaning pitifully, the stumps of both arms held up for all to see, while the stretcher boy vomited. Jesse ran to the soldier with the wounds in his chest and tried to poke the small gut back into the abdominal cavity with her fingers, while the drummer boy looked on open-mouthed. It was useless, for every time the man coughed, out would pop the intestine.

Hastily she and Jacob, working in perfect unison, as though they were two pairs of hands on the same body, applied bandages over this mortal wound and secured them with strips of adhesive plaster. The man was quickly littered to what the orderlies called the "dead area," the isolated section across the yard, where the wounded gasped out their last mortal seconds.

The stretcher bearer wiped the vomit from around his mouth, and with eyes streaming tears, he confronted Jacob bitterly. "I seen you read that Barble Dutchman, so you must know all the answers. I used ter believe in God Almighty, but he ain't lookin' out fer us this day, no sir, he ain't givin' us a gall darn thought, else he wouldna let this happen, no sir, never would a let this happen, not in a million years—not in a million years—" He walked away muttering to himself. The wounds were not all physical.

"Oh Lord—I been shot," said the sergeant far down the line, who was big and strong as an artillery horse, and had hair and heavy beard the color of a carrot. "I been shot and I'm bleedin' like a stuck pig!" Jesse rushed to his litter. "It won't stop bleedin'," he told her, weeping hysterically.

She moved the filthy rag he was holding to the knee and would have needed a magnifying glass to locate the scratch.

"I been shot," he said, using the rag to mop at his wet eyes. "Lord, I gonna die."

"It's nothing, sir." She gave him a piece of lint soaked in alcohol to place over the "wound," just to keep him quiet, but it didn't work.

"Damn you, boy, what good's this, I been shot, I tell you. I been shot. I really been shot. I been shot. This ain't gonna help me, boy—not when I been shot—I need help—God—help me—"

Beside him sat a boy with a man's fortitude, patiently, silently holding a filthy blood-soaked handkerchief to a facial wound, as he waited his turn on the operating table. Blood was running through his fingers and down his youthful stoic features. Jesse knelt beside him, gently lifted the bloody rags. His left eye was gone. In its place was a bloody, mush-filled mess. He looked at her with his right eye and said softly, "It's God's will. He wants me to come home. He says to me, Peter, it's your time."

"I been shot!" shouted the sergeant, grabbing ahold of Jesse's shoulder and yanking her backward off her feet as she crouched there. "Oh God—I'm gonna die—I'm really gonna die." He shook her until her head looked as if it would work loose and then started tearing at his chest, tearing at his shirt, and screaming hysterically. "I gonna die—!" Then he passed out.

Not a moment too soon, for Jacob was lumbering toward them, his fists already clenched. He helped Jesse to her feet, inspected her most solicitously for harm and glared at the sergeant laid out in a dead faint. Jesse smiled up at him. It was the first time she had ever seen the Dutchman display the slightest anger.

Dead company officers were laid out on the end of the line, side by side. As Jesse stood there, two bandsmen arrived and rolled a body off a litter onto the ground. They left him face down in the mud. No time. No time. She turned him gently over onto his back. In a so-called civilized society, they cover the faces of the dead. Why? As a mark of respect? More likely the living are afraid to look upon the faces of the dead. In a war there's no place for such delicacies. These dead were exposed. There were not enough blankets to cover them—*so to hell with the dead*—*or to heaven*. But there was little to be afraid of here. There was little blood.

These dead looked as though they were asleep, but for the small round holes in the lieutenant's brow, chest, and left shoulder, the two neat matching holes in the chests and throats of the two captains, and the single hole in the major's chest right about where his heart had once beat, and the two strangely close together in his left shoulder. You might think they were asleep.

Ambulance wagons rolled from side to side across the uneven road, jolting along, before depositing their suffering load on the grass, now soaked with all that man is made of, and then starting once more for the battlefields. Blood dripped steadily from the bottom of these wagons. It seeped through the wooden slates as the dejected-looking horses trudged through the blood-soaked grass. The teamsters looked like death.

Leaning against a tree were a matching pair of what were laughingly called "medical orderlies," chewing leisurely on some tobacco, and watching with dispassionate interest as Jesse tended a man horribly burned when he was caught between the company tents, set on fire by a bursting shell. At that moment, Cartwright came out of the cabin, a lantern held aloft.

"Ah, you men taking a rest?" he inquired with a deceptively friendly smile. The men grinned. Just then, an orderly was leaving the cabin with a pail of bloodied water. Cartwright grabbed the pail and threw the contents over both men. It happened so quickly that Jesse could only stare as a snatch of hysterical laughter sprang from her throat. The two boys stood there soaked to the skin, smelling like slaughtered animals, and raising a howl.

"Now get to work, you lousy sons of bitches, before I put you both on a charge." It was evidently Dr. Cartwright's day for putting everyone on a charge. "You! *In here*. I need you." He meant her.

No time to speak, except to give instructions through gritted teeth, and the smell. The smell and the grating of the saw. You get accustomed to it, like the smell, said Jacob, and the feeling of plunging away into hell. *Into hell's hell.*

Around the room, swinging lanterns streamed their fitful light upon the half-naked figures of the wounded writhing on the makeshift operating tables, before going under. It illuminated the bare arms of the steadfast surgeons, soaked in blood, and gave a yellowish hue to their bloodshot eyes, from which all vestige of human emotion seemed to have drained. Even exhaustion. Was this why they accused army surgeons of being inhuman? Oh, so unjust—so unjust.

A soldier, bloodied and battered, caked in mud, but apparently uninjured, had followed his littered comrade into the crowded cabin. He wanted to know, *must know*, would his friend live? Tell me, Doc, he demanded of Fitzjohn, is he gonna make it? Let me die, screams his friend, because both legs are shattered above the knee and one arm is gone. He knows he cannot live, so why not let him die now and spare him the suffering? *Let me die!* Oh no, Charlie, wails his friend, at least ten years his junior, no, don't say it, Charlie, don't even think it. Why can't those bastards have got me instead? Orderly! Orderly! Get this man out of here! The friend is removed, shouting that Charlie must live.

Others have the same object in mind; wander in, faces ashen, arm in a sling, to support a fallen comrade. They often come in pairs for moral support. Their brother, not so lucky, is under the knife. Oh God, oh God—he sure looks dead—what will I tell our ma—they ask each other and Fitzjohn. He has them removed. There is little room for the wounded and for the surgeons, never mind visitors, he declares, and who can blame him?

Is this why the surgeons are branded destitute of feeling?

Oh so unjust. *So dreadfully unjust.*

A wounded man was heaved onto the table, handled so roughly he shrieked with pain. Shrieks that penetrate the eardrum. Cartwright, linen apron smeared with blood and human liquid. How many types of sticky liquid does a human body hold? But the smell—you get accustomed to it? Is that possible? The smell of death? Takes a moment to examine and decide. Amputation? Hands always busy, always occupied, beloved hands. Yes. She can say that without fear of being misunderstood. Pools of blood on the floor. Bring more straw! Wake up, you useless bastards! Orderlies scatter the straw. Slipping and sliding, their shirts soaked with blood from carrying the injured. A dead soldier is removed.

His broken body has barely cleared the table when another is thudding down in its place. Between littering and straw scattering, and washing the bloodstained tables with blood-soaked sponges, the orderlies take away piles of amputated limbs. Armfuls of arms. Hands and feet in buckets. Legs wrapped in blankets. Is there one whole and healthy soldier left out there?

God knows, can't leave them around to pile up here, so they pile up outside. Shoulder high.

As Cartwright violently sponged off his table, awash with blood, the blood spattered Jesse's face and apron.

"See him?" Cartwright inquired, pointing at the young assistant surgeon who had replaced the exhausted Lowefels, a loyal Union man who could not bear to remain comfortably home with his grandchildren when his countrymen are dying, standing frozen to the spot, staring at the patient stretched out on his table. "Go poke a scalpel up his backside!"

Jesse touched the young surgeon's arm. An expression of repugnance, even horror, was contorting his pleasant features. He was sobbing silently. The moment of truth had knocked on his door, and he wasn't home.

"I can't—" was all he said before dropping the forceps he'd been holding and bolting from the cabin, sobs of pity for self and mankind accompanying his flight toward the bluff.

Jesse saw what he had seen and could not look at. She glanced around for a surgeon, there was just Dr. Fitzjohn and Dr. Cartwright now, and both were occupied. She picked up the wad of lint and started to blot the liquid that was oozing from what remained of the boy's cheeks, nose, eyes, beneath a head of thick, black, curly hair, grasping his twitching hand as she worked, speaking to him in a reassuring whisper. His fingers tried to tighten around hers, as though grateful to feel the touch of another human being. An otherworldly moan, like an animal that sees the reflection of its own terrible wounds, emerged from the gaping hole that had once been his mouth.

Jesse dropped the lint on the floor and instead lifted the boy by the shoulders. She held him to her, embracing him as tightly as she could,

resting his poor destroyed face upon her chest, feeling convulsions rip-
ple through his body. The final death throes, the agony that would soon
become the ecstasy of nonexistence, when all pain and memory would be
wiped clean.

She held him until that moment, that moment of release, of letting
go, and then she kissed his head.

"Orderly!" she heard Cartwright shout and the boy was taken
roughly from her embrace. They needed the table. They needed her.

What time was it? Who could say? Was this still the night of the same
day that started out as Sunday morning? It was still raining. Torrents that
fell on the injured and those who sought to comfort them.

In the cabin, the boards at which the surgeons worked were covered
with layers of dry blood under the fresh, bright red variety, and the floor
had become so slippery and wet that the straw squelched underfoot.
Around the room flies hovered and congregated in black clouds of anticipation over every brutal, festering, rancid pan filled with bloody water,
every bloodied rag, every stained bandage and soiled dressing. It was,
Jesse found, a hopeless task to swat them away.

Occasionally Cartwright or Fitzjohn would holler for an orderly to
change the water in their pan so the amputating knives and saws could be
rinsed of blood, but this took a second, and a second was too long to wait
between the man hauled away and the man hauled in, and in the last few
hours a new torment.

The Federal wooden gunboats *Tyler* and *Lexington*, the same "wooden
buckets" that had escorted Buell's army in its advance up the Tennessee,
had been throwing shells into the Rebel lines, pounding the camps that
had once been occupied by the Yankees, and in which this night neither
Rebels nor their tormentors would get a moment's peace.

The pounding of the shells shook the tables, deafening everyone and
drowning out the rasping sound as knives and saws cut through bone.
This and the screams of the men before they went under the anesthetic,
was all too much for some orderlies; scared, disgusted, shocked, several
ran away, but not Jesse. She held fast to the board at which Cartwright

was working, feeling it shudder and buck every time artillery burst on its target, more than two miles away.

"Damn them all to hell, I can hardly hear myself think," Cartwright said bitterly, cutting through a man's flesh. As shells found their target, a dull, heavy, monotonous boom-boom could be heard.

"They're ours," said the orderly with patriotic pride as he cheerfully sponged fresh blood off the table into his wooden bucket.

"I don't give a goddamn if they're the Queen of Sheba's, they're driving me mad."

Bang! Bang! Boom! Boom! went the guns.

"I don't reckon the Queen a Sheb got anythin' like *that*," said the orderly with a serious but uncertain frown.

The surgeon paused to stare at Jesse, who was wiping the sweat from the victim's youthful features. "Tell me," he said, "am I really the only sane person left on earth or are *you* all sane and *I'm the mad one*?" Then, "Damn your eyes!" he bellowed at an orderly who all but dropped a soldier onto the board. "Why the hell don't you throw him on the floor and be done with it?"

"You make them clumsy when you shout at them," Jesse told him as he waited with his bone saw for her to administer the chloroform. "They're doing their best, but you make them nervous."

"Their best stinks. They're clumsy, dirty, and lazy."

"Not all. Be kinder. Results might surprise you." She was learning to speak, like everyone else working here, in monosyllables, wasting no breath. She placed the precious can on the side table. The supplies of morphine, chloroform, and especially bandages were rapidly disappearing. The boy was under.

"You be kinder, got no time—" Cartwright was sawing through what remained of the boy's upper arm. "I'm a surgeon, not a chaplain—"

Next.

As this boy began to stir, he was littered away and another took his place. Again, the routine was repeated, and again Cartwright bellowed at the orderly.

"I'm sorry, Doc—ma hands slipped—" The boy showed his palms, slippery with blood. "I would'na done it otherwise. I know these boys is in pain. I know it." He was about to cry.

Cartwright glanced at Jesse, who was positioning the injured man's head more comfortably on the board, prior to administering the chloroform, and pointedly ignoring this exchange.

"Well—" Cartwright muttered inconclusively, wiping the blade of his bone saw on his apron.

The boy hesitated. "Twertn't ma fault, Doc, honest, ma hands sure are slippery."

"You already said that. Wipe your goddamn nose and go rinse off your hands." The doctor looked at the boy's earnest little face and at the blood which had soaked into his private's blouse from the patient's chest. His eyes were mournful and tired and he was really crying now. "How long you been on duty?"

"Same as you, Doc, though can't rightly recall how long that might be. I never learned to tell time."

"Don't cry, damn it—you're doing a good job." This came out grudgingly as he worked on the patient's chest.

The boy looked startled, his features worked, wet eyes blinked, lips twitched. "Why thank yer, Doc, I sure do 'ppreciate those kind words." He walked off with a new spring in his step, wiping away his tears. The next wounded man this boy helped to carry was deposited on the table with extra care, and he showed Cartwright his dry hands.

"Don't *say a damn word*," Cartwright warned Jesse through clenched teeth, "if you say a damn word *you'll* be stretched out on this table."

More pairs of hands were needed. Two boys from the regimental band found themselves assigned as litter bearers. One was so small, perhaps eleven years old, he could barely have lifted an empty bucket, never mind a full-grown man on a stretcher. The other looked older, but not much so, perhaps fourteen.

"They're useless to us," Fitzjohn announced sorrowfully. "What are they thinking about up at brigade to send such youngsters to help out?" It was a rhetorical question, since no one, least of all Cartwright, could furnish an answer. "They only get in the way."

"They stay," said Cartwright, "or I go." His last patient had died on the table. A twelve-year-old with abdominal wounds. Useless, his skills, with abdominal wounds. Experience and precocious talent counted for shit with abdominal wounds.

"The doctor wants them detailed to hospital duties," whispered Jacob in Jesse's ear, "otherwise they will march with the infantrymen into battle. At least here they are safe."

"Very well," agreed Fitzjohn, who was not a hard man, despite his reputation and demeanor, "then you sir, must be responsible for their conduct."

"Come back here—" Cartwright called out after the departing chief surgeon. "I don't want them." He stared at the two boys, the smaller, who was dragging a snare drum, had very obviously been crying. His child's eyes were puffy and red where he had rubbed at them, and was rubbing at them now with balled fist. The other boy appeared more philosophical about his fate and clutched tightly to his fife, apparently ready and willing to face anything the war and this glowering doctor could throw at him. Cartwright swallowed. "You heard the officer, don't get under our feet else I'll shoot you myself, and make no mistake I'm the man for it. This corporal will show you what to do. Okay? Good. You're safe here." He spoke gruffly and negligently patted the younger boy on the head.

The boy looked as if he would rather take his chances with the Rebs and indeed said, "I don't wanna be safe." He then burst into tears and stamped his feet. "I *wanna kill Rebs.*"

Cartwright stared at him a moment, blinked, then ran both trembling hands through his untidy thatch of hair. "Get him out of my sight," he said softly.

Between patients Jesse tried to clean and lay out Cartwright's amputation set, Liston's small amputation knife, sharp along one side, the Catling, which cut in either direction, Wood's circular amputation knife, the scalpels and curved knives. All of which had started the morning in a neat row but were now in a heap on the windowsill, their edges dulled by use. It was an impossible task, no sooner had she started than they were needed. This time an officer was carried in shrieking and cursing God, the army, and the government that brought him to this place. Jesse took the chloroform off the windowsill, instructing the still-cursing captain to take slow, deep breaths as she gradually brought the cone closer to his mouth and nose.

When it was only a half inch from his face his one good arm shot up and smashed against her mouth as he shouted, "They're going to cut off my arm, Mother! Help, help me!"

Almost instantly a trickle of blood appeared at the corner of Jesse's lower lip. She licked it away.

"Get him under!" Cartwright said through gritted teeth.

Jesse poured a little more fluid into the cone and in a few seconds the struggling man on the table was only able to whimper.

"Do just as I say," the surgeon commanded, as he had commanded all night.

She did as he said, as she had done all night, applying the tourniquet as high up the arm as possible and tightening it. She held the upper arm with one hand and the forearm with the other and no sooner did she get into position, as commanded, then Cartwright had plunged the Catling knife through the center of the arm midway between the elbow and the shoulder. He cut a flap of tissue from inside out on the front of the upper arm. The wounded captain's fingers quivered as the sharp knife stimulated and divided the nerves in the arm. Just as quickly, Cartwright cut the back flap and told the girl to grab the bloody flaps with her fingers and pull them up the arm. The humerus was then widely exposed. Jesse watched as the surgeon expertly scraped the remaining soft tissue from the bone. With a half-turn behind him, a half-turn he had made dozens and dozens of times that night, and through the previous day, he grabbed the capital bone saw. He gave her one rapid look, just a second's eye contact as though he were checking to see if she was watching, and then with rapid strokes he cut the humerus. As soon as the bone was severed from the body, the limb came free. "Out the window," Cartwright instructed without glancing up. How many times did he need to say it?

Out the window. Next. Out the window. Next. Out the window. Next.

Jesse took the amputated limb to the window and dropped it out, hardly glancing at the pile that now reached to the frame itself.

"Think you can do an amputation now?" the surgeon asked her as she put adhesive straps on the skin between the sutures, again as she had been taught. She looked at him. "Just joking," he said and while she was still applying the dressing, he called loudly, "Next!"

In the dim candlelight now supplanting the lantern, orderlies were placing an elderly soldier on the table, as quiet and calm as the captain was loud and hysterical. Another amputation, this time of the right leg.

"It comin' off, Doc?" he asked philosophically. He wore the uniform of an artilleryman and he was already short three fingers on his right hand.

"Yes." Cartwright didn't even look at the soldier's face. "I'll cut below the knee. Less pain for a false limb."

"That's a hell of a damn consolation, Doc, if yer don't mind ma sayin' so."

"I *do* mind you saying so, as it happens. If you're not happy with the service around here, you're free to go someplace else."

"Didn't mean no harm, Doc," said the man, looking at Jesse sorrowfully and back at the doctor. "Hell, Doc, I didn't mean no harm."

"Damn light—" Cartwright took off his spectacles and wiped them on his apron. "Can't see a damn thing in this damn light. Have you noticed how there's always enough light for the battle and never enough to operate." Then he had grabbed up his Catling and was cutting.

And next.

And next. And next. And next. And next. And . . .

Cartwright wiped his stiff hands on his apron and went toward the open door. Jesse saw him draw in a deep breath. It was all he wanted, just a deep breath, a glimpse of sky, confirmation that death hadn't completely overwhelmed the universe. Yes, there was a tree, a blade of grass, a star still twinkling, rain falling. Not all was darkness, not yet. He held his face up to the rain then took the canteen of water she gave him. When he returned to the table, she wiped his brow for him with a piece of toweling and he laughed.

"Where's your precious colonel?" he wanted to know.

"Resting," she said, stifling a yawn.

"It's the chloroform fumes," he said. It wasn't exhaustion. "Get some fresh air, and while you're out there, empty the buckets." He kicked at the bucket for emphasis.

It was while Jesse was on one of these bucket-emptying runs that General Grant hobbled to the doorway of the log house, which had been his headquarters earlier in the day. She saw him move awkwardly aside to allow wounded men to be carried through in a never-ending stream, some lying ominously still as they were jostled on makeshift stretchers.

As Jesse went by, he stopped her, looked at her face spotted with dried blood and streaked with grimy sweat. Large patches of sweat showed under her arms and the cuffs of her too-long pants hung heavy with blood. He dropped his gaze to stare into the bucket she was carrying. It contained three severed hands and one foot. Then he gazed into the interior, dimly lit by flickering candles, and one single lantern that swung hypnotically from a roof beam on a length of string in the center of the room. He listened a moment to the screams of men whose courage had held steadfast in the wheat fields and Peach Orchard, but which now deserted them at the sight of the surgeon's knife.

"Sir, are you quite well?" Jesse asked, as the army commander seemed to ruminate on some mystery, and then perhaps decide against overtaxing his limited intelligence, which would be in demand for matters of a more military and less philosophical nature in the morning. On the other hand, maybe he wasn't ruminating at all and the inhuman clamor and foul smell had merely caught him unawares.

His croaky monotone barely audible, he said, "Do you need anything, Corporal?"

"Yes sir, lamp oil," she said. If daylight didn't come soon they would be working blind. "And tents, we need more tents."

"I'll have some of both sent up."

If Grant remembered to send the lamp oil, it never arrived, but the tents came.

"If there was a damn *God* he'd give us daylight—strong . . . steady daylight," Cartwright muttered as he paused in his task to pull the lamp that the orderly was holding aloft closer to the patient's groin, ripped open by shell fragments still lodged in the torn flesh.

"I'll pray for daylight," said the boy fifer. He went down on his knees by the door and put his hands together, a child before his bed. As Jesse passed, she placed a hand briefly on the top of his head. No more than a minute passed before the orderly with the lamp gazed up and out at the soft blue, almost iridescent light that was spreading through the night sky.

"Well, I'll be—and it ain't even dawn yet," he said in surprise.

A couple of the walking wounded trying to shelter from the rain came to the doorway and gazed up into the sky to the east.

"It's lightnin'," said one. "Some poor bastards are in for a soakin'."

In a few moments, the cabin itself seemed to be flooded with light.

"Don't worry about what it is," called out Cartwright, ever the realist, "just use it!"

At 7:00 A.M. of Monday, April 7, the bombardment by Federal gunboats ceased. Grant's orders were simple, to advance, to counterattack, and to recapture their original camps. They must be determined to redeem today the losses of yesterday.

There was to be nothing complicated and grand about the assault. The combined armies of Buell and Grant would simply drive forward and overpower the Rebels by sheer weight of numbers. The addition of Lew Wallace's and Buell's forces gave the Union army another twenty-seven thousand men, surely more than enough to gain the second day. Now it was the Rebels turn to fall back. *Today* the tide would turn.

At the appointed time, what remained of Sherman's Fifth Division, along with the Thirteenth Missouri, moved forward and reoccupied the right of McClernand's camp. Here, while the Rebel artillery bombarded them with a vengeance, for even if the Yankees knew the Rebs were on their last legs, the Rebs themselves did not know it, or did not care to know it, General Sherman waited patiently for four hours before the sounds of Buell's advance could be heard on the Corinth Road. Either Buell needed to change his timepiece or, like the guest of honor, he liked to arrive late, even for a war.

It was only fitting that Sherman personally direct the howitzers that silenced the enemy's guns at the Shiloh Meeting House. By 3:00 P.M., the enemy was giving way at every point, and an hour later, the Ohioan had regained the ground of his original front and immediately directed his brigades to resume their old camps.

By twilight the Rebel army of Beauregard, Bragg, Hardee, and Polk had retreated in disarray and the Battle of Shiloh was over.

11

Dreadful days

★ ★ ★ ★

Give back the foolish flags whose bearers fell,
   Too valiant to forsake them.
Is it presumptuous, this counsel? Well,
   I helped to take them.

— AMBROSE BIERCE, "The Confederate Flags, 1905"

Sherman sat restlessly on a campstool staring through the open flaps at the Federal soldiers detailed to remove the corpses, their own and the enemy, from what remained of the tents and camps while Jesse put a fresh dressing on his hand. The wound was inflamed, but it was no worse than expected considering the Ohioan had been in the saddle since daybreak. His own tent was so full of holes it was no more than canvas strips fluttering in the breeze. Sherman had fared no better. His rough-hewn Yankee features were smeared with grime and sweat, his red beard darkened with gunpowder, his shoulder strap still ripped asunder, and his hat brim torn from the crown, hanging down the back of his neck. The Rebels had stolen his cot, ransacked his trunk, bayoneted some of his books, made off with much of his new underwear and his spare uniform, none of which appeared to bother him unduly as he demanded of Captain Jackson, "Did you hear them, Andy? My Muldraugh's Hill men—remember how they used to call me 'Old Pills'?" Andy remembered, "Old Pills" because he was hard to swallow—"Now they cheer me as I ride down the line—you heard them—they would have marched on Richmond." His staccato voice, normally hoarse, but now almost a croak from shouting orders at his men as he rode the line, shot out the words like bullets, without breath or punctuation. "Yes, one word from their old commander and they would have marched on Richmond!"

Horatio had disappeared. Last seen he had been running toward the undergrowth behind the church on Sunday morning. Now the general declared himself suddenly hungry, a condition shared by most of his staff. Orderlies were dispatched to search for edibles among the debris.

Jesse made straight for the surgeon's tent. To be sure, he had nothing of value to steal, unless the Rebels coveted his dirty laundry and empty whiskey bottles. His home-sweet-home-from-home looked as it always did. Undoubtedly, any thieving Rebel stumbling on this mess would have thought it already plundered.

His loose papers were scattered and some pages of his notebooks ripped in half, but if all the pages were present, there was no reason why they could not be patiently pieced together again; after all, he pieced together the bodies of broken men. Jesse put them carefully in her haversack with his spare eyeglasses, which she'd found wrapped inside a rancid-smelling sock under his upturned cot. She gathered some of his soiled laundry into a small canvas sack and went off to continue her foraging.

Before heading back to headquarters, she visited the old hospital area of the Seventieth Ohio. Orderlies were already in the process of trying to salvage something of the ripped tents, overturned cots, sabered sheets, and torn blankets. Even the medicine chests had been vandalized, their precious contents poured away and the vials and bottles smashed. The utter stupidity of such a waste by an army that was reportedly low on medicines was unimaginable. Inside what remained of the hospital were the dead, patients unable to protect themselves from the Rebel advance, cut down from behind by a saber slash or a minié ball, trying to escape from their sickbeds. Jesse helped herself to some bandages, lint, sticking plaster, and rags, stuffing all into her haversack, with the doctor's papers.

Back at division she laid out her contribution to the booty, a potato with more eyes than a sutler has in the back of his head, two pieces of hard-tack, a tin of beans, a chunk of moldy cheese, three handfuls of rice, and two cans of condensed milk. She kept back one can of condensed milk, an apple, two pieces of hard candy, and a quart bottle containing about three mouthfuls of whiskey. Since the surgeon would not touch the alcohol in medical supplies this was a particularly choice find, taken from the frozen hand of a dead Federal captain, who was certainly dead drunk before he was dead.

The scene of carnage and slaughter near Shiloh Church was unbelievable. Bringing order to this chaos would take weeks.

First, they would have to bury the dead.

As the ambulance moved heavily in the fading light, rolling from side to side over muddy roads and rutted, uneven tracks, Jesse stared out into the night. By the light of the lantern swinging drunkenly above her head, she could just make out the overturned artillery caissons and upended limber boxes. Here lay a stricken axle, there a twisted wheel, there splinters and wreckage where solid shot had met solid iron and wood, along with the grotesque contortions of dead or dying horses, still in harness, their guts spilling out, smeared across the ground.

For most of that day, the Army of the Tennessee had advanced over ground soaked by the night-long rain, littered with the dead and wounded from the previous day, and now frozen into shocking, macabre poses. Twenty-four-pounder howitzers had rolled over this earth, breaking the bones of the dead and wounded beneath the wheels, crushing arms and legs, grinding pieces of bloody flesh to pulp. Muskets, their barrels bent and twisted, the stocks splintered, knapsacks bulging open, their contents disgorged and trodden heedlessly into the mud, lay everywhere. Letters and photographs, precious personal items left on the field by soldiers who would never now return to claim them, had been scattered to the four winds. Black smoke filled the air, a choking black smoke that obliterated the setting sun, made eyes burn, and caused tears to roll down grimy cheeks, and everywhere the smell of burning flesh, man and the beasts that had served him so faithfully.

Some of these dead horses remained in the most bizarre attitudes of death, down on fetlocks, on their backs, their legs stiffly in the air, indecipherable shapes against the darkening sky. Shockingly, even now, others were still dashing around, riderless, horribly injured and unable in their pain and madness to simply lie down and die. By morning these pain-crazed creatures would have been caught and burned, for highlighted against the skyline were funeral pyres upon which the carcasses of dead animals were being heaped.

The Peach Orchard, Rhea Field, Jones Field, the Sunken Road, the Hornet's Nest, all had been battered by shells, trees blasted by canister and grape, branches rent asunder, hanging from the heart of the oak, like mere straws, as though struck by lightning. The foe had withdrawn. The battlefield was now alive with another kind of horror, men half-alive, their upturned faces and open eyes imploring mutely for help. The night was alive with their screams. They lay about in ditches, and creeks, strewn across brush, and wooded areas and buried by fallen timber. Lantern lights danced in the darkness, held aloft by soldiers moving across the fields, like Jesse and Jacob, searching for the wounded.

"There's an awful bad smell, ain't there, Jess?" said Olly, the boy fifer, starting to cough.

Jesse untied the neckerchief from around her throat and showed the boy how to fasten it around his mouth and nose, to block out the smell and the bad air. Others stuffed leaves up their nostrils.

"How 'bout you?" he asked, his voice muffled and only his big eyes visible between the peak of his low-slung forage cap and the spotted bandanna.

"I'm accustomed to it now," she said. Jacob's prediction had come to pass.

In a few moments, the Dutchman had joined them, together with a teamster and his partner, who, after settling his mules, stood in stunned silence staring at the sight that met their gaze.

In the lush green grass beneath the tall stately white oaks, as insects buzzed about them in the warm damp air, were three rows of Rebel dead, twenty to a row, dirty gray bundles that had once been men, and one row of Yankees, dirty blue bundles, laid out, all awaiting interment. Even the weary animals hung their sad heads over their harnesses and wept for man's folly.

"A'mighty God—" said the teamster, dragging off his slouch hat and spitting tobacco juice away from the sight. "—Lord knows, I ain't never seen nuthin' ter compare, not so neat an tidy like. Now who'd yer suppose laid them out thataways, so neat and everythin'?" He looked at Jacob, who he assumed, as the medical steward, would be the one to take charge, the one to have all the answers. But there were no answers.

"Let us get started," the Dutchman said.

The stench of rotting, bloated, blackened bodies under the midday sun was overpowering; some boys gagged, others simply ran away. But most stuck it out, their eyes streaming, their noses running, their jaws set grimly, determined to "plant the Rebs" with no less dignity than they planted their own. They used bayonets bent into hooks or blankets to drag these dirty blue and gray bundles to the chosen burial site where men, strong not only in body but also in stomach, had dug long, shallow trenches. "Wagons hauling in dead men and dumping them on the ground as cordwood, for burial in long trenches, like sardines in a box." Sherman's words came back to Jesse. The bodies were then placed in these mass graves, two or more deep, and covered with a layer of earth, sometimes gentle, other times thrown down with less than reverential haste because there were more that needed burying and the smell was like nothing anyone had ever experienced. A piece of splintered wood or the side of a cracker box was used as a marker, then someone with a pocketknife or a stub of pencil would scratch, "30 Rebel Dead" or "28 Union Dead" and the date: "April 1862."

On one part of the field, Jesse helped bury forty-seven Rebel soldiers, among them a major and three captains, one of them with fine gray mustaches like the Hoosier aide. That happened a lot lately; Jesse saw the faces of those she loved in the faces of those who had perished. This fine, big, manly-looking individual with dirt in his mouth and blood in his nostrils and a bullet hole in the center of his brow reminded her of Captain Jackson. The expression of the eyes only imagined, since death had closed the lids forever.

"Don't make too much fuss a the Rebs" was the casually given advice of a well-groomed lieutenant who appeared out of nowhere and spent his time leaning on his dress sword and smoking a cigar. "It ain't even like yer buryin' yer favorite hound dog, now is it?"

"They look so darn peaceful—some 'er 'em," said one boy.

"They look damn angry, most of 'em," said his partner, "and they smell awful bad."

"Reckon them Rebs is short a footwear, some a 'em ain't got no shoes."

"Some ain't got no feet."

Some had no faces. The first boy backed away from the pile of rotting copses before he heaved up his breakfast and then, looking at his companions with undisguised horror, started to run for the trees. The lieutenant, who up until then had expended little energy above lighting a fresh cigar, brought his pistol from his holster and sighted.

Before he could get off a shot, a sergeant who had buried soldiers before at Donelson, among them two brothers and a son, had clamped a hand over the weapon and said, "Now there ain't no call fer that, Lieutenant. Ain't we had 'nough killing, *sir*?"

Five minutes later, after watching how the men disentangled that faceless corpse from the rest of the decomposing pile with a meat hook, the lieutenant was sick into the silk handkerchief he was holding to his mouth. However, no one laughed, no one thought it funny.

"Yer dig a hole in the ground, lay 'em side by side without any coffin, and then cover their bodies with earth, *Tennessee* earth," said the sergeant who had buried three men of his family at Donelson. Unfortunately, there never was enough time for the traditional military salute. Nor even a short prayer. The sight of a chaplain at the burial trench was also rare. It fell to the soldiers who had fought with and fought against these men to offer up a word of spiritual comfort.

Some, more familiar with the lyrics of a melancholy song than the scriptures, would speak or sing, bringing a genuine sorrow to the occasion. Appreciated by the mourners as well as the mourned, this was infinitely more relevant than the pious sanctity of a chaplain, eager to be back in his tent with his communion wine. Across the way, Jesse watched one such dedication, led by an infantry major, a handsome, heavily bearded man near as big as Jacob, whose baritone voice rose reverentially, stirringly, to the treetops.

> *"Just before the battle, Mother*
> *I am thinking most of you*
> *While upon the field, we're watching*
> *With the enemy in view*
> *Comrades brave are round me lying*
> *Filled with thoughts of Home and God*
> *For well they know that, on the morrow*
> *Some will sleep beneath the sod*
> *Farewell, Mother, you may never*
> *You may never, Mother*
> *Press me to your breast again*
> *But O, you'll not forget me*
> *Mother, you will not forget me*
> *If I'm numbered with the slain."*

The Dutchman brought the wagon to a halt and sat motionless on the hard wooden seat, the reins held loosely in his enormous hands. This was their fourth trip. Jacob fought with all his considerable strength to steady the mules and the ambulance while Jesse tried in vain to ease the suffering of the men who lay on the rude wooden boards. She bathed clammy brows, stanched blood, dressed mangled limbs, quietened frenzied souls, whispered prayers.

Beside him other wagons had stopped, their drivers, like Jacob, taken aback by the sight that met their weary eyes. Jesse poked her red head through the opening, a hand on the steward's shoulder to steady herself. She recognized the small body of water, not far from where she had seen Colonel Ransom fall in Jones Field. To this place, swollen with rainwater, wounded men in blue and gray had dragged their broken bodies, bathed their wounds, and quenched their thirst. Some exhausted and in shock collapsed as they drank. In a while so many men had died there, their life's blood running into the water, turning it red, that the place became known as "Bloody Pond." They lay there now, their bodies swollen and turning black.

They had already lost one man. A Rebel lieutenant, his body bearing four wounds, had breathed his last even as Jacob was easing him into the wagon. With a sigh that could have rocked the universe off its axis, the Dutchman had laid him gently back on the ground. They must save space in the wagon for the living.

The roads and fields were impassable in some places, littered with foliage and branches and abandoned equipment, and by the walking wounded, hobbling some, on makeshift crutches, a musket, or tree branch, as they made their slow, exhausted way to the field hospitals, and everywhere mud. Mud, sucking at and clinging to brawny arms and sinewy necks, manly chests and iron-clad muscles that had once held the reins of a steaming horse, sighted a trusty musket, wielded the saber or rammed home the cannon's deadly load, all still now.

No more rank and file, no more coward nor hero, no more Rebel or Yankee, officer and enlisted man, no more meaningless distinctions. In death, all are simply men, without pretensions to fame or glory.

As she knelt beside a wounded soldier in her old stamping ground near the Widow Howell's cabin, Jesse watched a macabre scene being played out in the moonlit darkness among the once beautiful, wooded oaks. A Rebel color bearer was crawling away on a bloody stump, dragging with him the blood-spattered pelican flag of Louisiana. Suddenly, like carrion, two Yankee soldiers swept down out of the branches of a tree and faced him off.

"Git the flag!" cried one, jabbing a hand in that direction. Whereupon the second Yankee tried to drag the flag from the Rebel, who was more dead than alive, yet his grip upon the flag was stronger than ever. "Git the goddamn flag, why don't yer!" shouted the first soldier, himself now trying to pry the Rebel's fingers from the flag, while the other soldier was to make off with it.

"Ah'm tryin', goddamn it. Kain't yer see ah'm tryin'? He ain't 'bout to let go."

It was to be a life and death struggle. This was, apparently, not how they had rehearsed it from their perch in the tree, but the second soldier was correct, the Rebel was not about to let go. He was lying down now, close to exhaustion, the torn and bloody flag wrapped around his torso, what was left of his leg bleeding onto the precious colors. The young blue-clad soldiers stood there, uncertain, where before they had been cocky and filled with confidence, and stared down at the Reb color sergeant in his agonizing death throes.

"Git it, ah say," said the first soldier finally, with another jerk of his hand.

"Goddamn it, okay . . . okay . . ." said the second the soldier, ". . . why don't you git it?"

Neither moved. Then all of a sudden, the Rebel stopped twitching, and lay very still, his eyes wide open to heaven, his fingers wound so tightly around the flag that they would have had to use their bayonets or their pocketknives to cut it loose. The two Yankee soldiers stood there and stared at the older Rebel, who was just as determined in death as in life to hold onto his regimental colors.

"Help me move his body," said the first soldier. "Help me git his body off the flag, why don't yer?" He was crying. Jesse could clearly hear him sobbing as he spoke.

"Let him keep the goddamn thing, why don't yer—" said the second soldier. "He's dead anyhow. Let him keep the goddamn thing. It's tattered anyways. Let him keep the goddamn thing—he wonts it so bad—let him have the goddamn thing—ah say—"

"Damn you *and him*," said the first soldier, sobbing loudly, but he didn't touch the flag or the dead Rebel. "It wess yer goddamn i-dear all along. Ah didn't wont the goddamn flag—"

The second soldier bent down and drew what was left of the flag over the Rebel soldier's face, then he walked away.

"Damn you *and him*," called out the first soldier hysterically, throwing his kepi on to the ground and stomping on it. "Ah dint wont the goddamn flag anyways, it was yer i-dear."

Bluish-white smoke of burned powder still hung over the trees in the Peach Orchard. It was acrid in her nostrils. Jesse raised her lantern to shoulder height. There were no more blossoms on the Widow Howell's trees; they had been cut down by musketry and artillery fire, like the dead who lay beneath, covered by the pink and white blossoms. Nature's own wreath laid over the corpse-strewn ground.

By the yellow light of one single lantern tied to a pole and driven into the earth, two aged and bent gray-bearded civilians in coats that hung from their thin bodies like shrouds were doggedly digging a trench; beside them on the ground was what looked like bundles of rags. Jesse blinked. It was a scene from the vale of tears.

Jacob met her as she came shakily out of the clearing; put an arm about her shoulders. "Stay close by me, child," he counseled. "These are sights that a soul should not witness alone."

"Eerie, ain't it?" asked a soldier staying real close beside the Dutchman. The moonlight was bright enough to reveal ghostlike human forms on the ground, illuminated by the sudden flashes of lightning. It was raining again. "Hey, what's that sound?" A strange sound, snuffling, or was it crying? "What kinda creature cries thata way?" Horrible shrieks—a strange sound, yes, neither human nor animal.

"Jakob," Jesse said softly. "What *is* that sound?"

"Hogs. Hogs are after the bodies. They don't care if they dead or half-dead."

Another sudden lightning flash illuminated the hellish scene.

Coming on a group of wounded Rebels by a creek Jesse knelt down with her haversack.

"I just want to look at your leg," she said gently, trying to get the nervous soldier to lie back on the litter. These men had already had their wounds dressed but blood was seeping through the bandage on this soldier's thigh.

"Thank yer, kindly—" said the boy.

Stretched out beside him, his arms under his bandaged head, was another gray-clad soldier, whose begrimed, bloodied condition had only increased his sense of grievance against the "enemy."

"Why you thankin' that nigger lover?" he wanted to know of his comrade. "Bet that lille shit is a nigger lover. All Yankees is shit-assed nigger lovers. There ain't a one a 'em who wouldn't let hiss sister go with a nigger for a plug nickel, ain't that right, Lincoln mud-sill-nigger-lover?"

Suddenly Jacob loomed over him, one enormous, mud-encrusted boot planted on either side of his prostrate body, a giant oak looming over an insignificant little acorn, threatening to block out the sunlight, *forever.*

The angry Rebel soldier swallowed hard. "Kant yer take no joshin'?" he asked Jesse reasonably. "Hell, I dudn't mean nuthin', I *like* niggers, it's damn Yankees I can't stomach." He burst into laughter.

As Jacob lifted him up by the lapels, the soldier's legs dangling uselessly, his laughter turned to screams of sheer terror. Now it was Jesse's turn to laugh as the giant dropped him in the creek.

"We leave you where we found you," he said. "Until you learn your manners."

"Damn Yankee nigger-loving—" Jacob turned back and the Rebel stopped. "Never did take no joshin', that's a trouble with you damn Yankees," he concluded as Jacob finally walked away.

This was by far the lightest moment of a bleak and ghastly day.

At the field hospital, Jesse sat by his cot and cooled Thomas Ransom with the fan Jacob had fashioned out of interlaced leaves in a wooden frame, fastened with hospital sutures. The young colonel was restless in his sleep, murmuring, about "Will," his father, and in between issuing feverish orders to his regiment. She bathed his face, caressed his side-burns, quietening him in the flickering light of the candle beside his cot.

Beyond the tent flaps cook fires had been started, despite advice from those who should know not to start fires, lest the Rebels find the range with their artillery. Nevertheless, some had been lit anyway, so that a little hot food could be given the wounded. Coffee was brewing and soup steamed in a large rusty container. "Stick it all in, boys," the cook had instructed, "all you can find, rice, vegetables, meat, apple peel, hardtack and salt horse, we need it good and thick, boys, good and thick." Trembling hands came with tin plates, bowls, and cups, anything that would hold the hot broth, even their kepis. The food was ladled and color returned to blanched cheeks. The cook grinned around his "jawin'" tobacco. It was the bag of pepper that got dropped in the pot, he declared, that and Sam Grant's socks, but he was proud to be of help to his suffering comrades instead of boiling new-laid eggs for some pampered officer.

Under her caressing hands the colonel's brow was warm. She turned the sheet down to his slender waist, opened his nightshirt, squeezed the surplus water from the cloth, and laid it across his chest and shoulders, to soothe him, to reduce the fever, as Jacob had taught her.

His skin was very white, on his chest a few stray blond hairs, his body slender and youthful. The flesh on his shoulders where he'd taken Rebel balls at Missouri and Donelson was puckered and scarred, the left shoulder wound hadn't totally healed. She touched it tenderly with her fingertips, massaged some of the doctor's salve into the skin. She moistened the dressing on his scalp, bathed his closed eyes at the corners, along the pale lashes, and touched a little water to his sculptured lips with her fingers. Spoke to him softly. His eyes opened, their wavering attention drawn to where the lights from a hundred lanterns were ranged along the bluff to guide the ambulance wagons to the field hospital. They swayed and dazzled on their poles driven into the soft clay, the yellow light drawing an ephemeral arc in the darkness as men passed wearily by, carrying litters, many themselves bearing the bloody, bandaged result of that day's madness.

His drowsy gaze moved back to the dim interior, to an orderly moving silently between the cots, his apron dyed red. Another orderly across the aisle drew a blanket over a face on a pillow. The distressing sounds of men in mortal pain, groaning in their semiconsciousness, a sighing last breath, a sudden shriek, a poignant cry, carrying a woman's name. Someone calling urgently for a surgeon, and the man in the white apron turns from the cot, now being emptied in seemingly undue haste by two orderlies. A youthful voice cries out for a beloved mother, a family pet, a priest. The murmuring continues, and the unmistakable fetid stale and nauseating smells that permeate the warm-damp night air drifts in, over fever-racked bodies, tossing and turning beneath soiled blankets inside the euphemistically called "recovery" tent.

At the entrance a few soldiers are gathered, whispering, one very young, red-eyed and openly weeping, the rest are older, uneasy, perhaps ashamed that they still have legs to walk on and hands to fill a pipe, eyes to gaze upon a loved one. They are searching for a wounded comrade, brought in here, they think, earlier in the day, after going under the surgeon's knife. Yes, brought in here and swallowed up. The living go in and the dead come out and not even the most stalwart of them dares to ask what goes on in between. They look and look away, a prayer uttered perhaps in desperation to a God whose existence they seriously doubt after today, yet can they do less than thank him for delivering *them* from such terrors. Still there is always tomorrow. How can civilized man come to this?

The young Vermonter's intense stare was on his nurse's face, her curling red hair, her striking blue-glass eyes, her full mouth, smiling reassuringly, then finally to her hand holding tightly to his on the sheet and his expression was wondering, confused, and not merely because he could not recognize his surroundings. The girl blotted the perspiration from his glistening face.

"Hello," she said with a smile. "How fine to see you awake. Can you take a little nourishment?" she asked encouragingly and was already lifting his head to put the tin cup to his lips. She wiped his chin where the pale white liquid ran down. "Condensed milk." She had saved the can for him.

He gave her a tiny smile of gratitude. "It's wonderful—may I have a little more?" Then after he had swallowed a second mouthful, "Where . . . where is this place?"

"You're still at Pittsburg Landing, sir. You were on a steamer but now you're in Dr. Cartwright's field hospital," she answered, her fingers straying to his hair, to his moist brow, and caressing tenderly.

"Dr. Cartwright? Is *he* my savior?" That broad touchingly boyish smile, ragged around the edges, made a faltering appearance. "Why would he do that, I wonder? I thought he disapproved of me."

"The doctor's skills are available to all who need them."

Ransom's sad, compassionate gaze traveled over her face for a moment. Then he said humbly, "Forgive me, my young friend, I meant no offense, it was a lame attempt at humor." He stared up at her as she blotted the threads of sweat running down his neck and rebuttoned his nightshirt, telling him, "You'll take a chill." She gave him a little more of the condensed milk and stroked the damp hair off his brow.

Her dedication to his well-being brought tears to his eyes. There were hundreds and hundreds of wounded, all with as much claim on this little boy as he, more so, since his wound seemed minor compared to the horrors he had seen. He squinted at her, blinked tired eyes.

"What day is this, Corporal?"

"Tuesday, sir. Yesterday the battle was renewed and we drove the Rebels from the field. It's said they're retreating back to Corinth."

"Thank *God*." He closed his eyes. "Not, I would wager, through any great skill of some of our generals," he added bitterly, turning his head away. Since Jesse couldn't possibly guess to which generals he might be referring she let that statement pass without comment. "Have you any news of my regiment?"

"Lieutenant Dickey and several other officers came to see you. You were sleeping so they sat with you for a while and said they'd return later. The lieutenant told me to say he had no further news of General Wallace's condition."

"Thank you. Cyrus, Lieutenant Dickey, is General Wallace's brother-in-law and my good friend. He was with the general when he was hit by a Rebel musket ball. Cyrus dismounted and went to the general. It was a terrible wound that had shattered the side of his head and exited through one eye. Cyrus was convinced that the general was dead." He paused, moistened his lips. "May I have something to drink, Corporal?"

Jesse lifted his head and gave him some water. "You really should sleep, sir."

"General Wallace is like a father to me," he explained, because there were tears in his eyes. "Cyrus was determined to save the general's body from the indignities of a battlefield." He continued, equally determined to tell the story of the unfortunate general's fate. "So he enlisted the help of two orderlies and together they carried General Wallace for a quarter of a mile or more before the firing became so hot that the orderlies ran away. Alone poor Cyrus had no alternative, he dragged the body off the road and laid it gently against some ammunition boxes. He escaped just in time. But General Wallace wasn't dead. Union men found him on Monday morning, encrusted with blood and soaked to the very marrow by the rain, but miraculously still alive. He was taken to Savannah, to the Cherry Mansion. His beloved wife had only that morning arrived with the single desire, to pay her husband a surprise visit. Mrs. Wallace has been by Will's side ever since." Tears were now running from the corners of his eyes into his hair. "Poor . . . Will . . ." his trembling lips murmured.

His lids drooped closed. She fanned him as he slept.

Outside the stream of wounded was ceaseless, up the hundred-foot yellow clay bluff they came, in wagons, on carts, in blankets, on makeshift litters of doors and fences, over shoulders, moaning, weeping, crying, bleeding men. Many of whom had been lying out in the torrential rain since early Sunday morning, soaked to the skin at night, and during the day parched by the heat of the sun.

The army had run out of coffins. The coffins were for the higher-ranking officers. As quickly as the carpenters knocked them together, they were used up. Now the crude wooden boxes stood side by side with those officers whose final remains had been wrapped in blankets.

"Tomorrow we bury the dead," Jacob said, surveying the awful scene. "First we attend to the living, *then* we bury the dead."

"How's your friend, the colonel?" Cartwright asked Jesse as they stood together at the water basin, washing their hands.

"Resting. Thank you for taking care of him."

"It's my job. You're enjoying all this, ain't you? You're *actually* enthralled by all this carnage and chaos."

"It might seem like chaos to the private soldier, but General Sherman and General Grant know exactly what they're doing." The surgeon was wiping his hands and looking at her out of the corner of his eye. "There were moments when I felt excited," Jesse admitted belatedly, "and inspired. But I didn't enjoy it—" She fell silent.

"What excited you most, the torn flesh, the rivers of gore, the piles of amputated limbs, the cabin floors awash with blood and sawdust, the smell of fresh blood and stale urine, the agony of men whose insides were torn out, whose limbs were shattered, by hunks of metal—? Why in hell are you so besotted with men like Sherman and Ransom, who romanticize war, who talk about carnage and mutilation as though it were something to be sought after. To have the honor of 'falling in battle,' to see your guts spilled out, to be buried in an unmarked grave and have your comrades say so politely what a jolly brave fellow you were, how you went forward and charged the enemy without fear."

"The finest officers do feel that way. If they must fall, they want to die with honor."

"You're right, Jesse, they *do* feel that way, and that's what makes it all the more obscene. They genuinely do feel that it's glorious to die for one's country. But, okay, if they're stupid enough to charge some impregnable enemy breastworks and be blown to pieces that's *their* decision, *their* life to waste, what bothers me, what keeps me awake nights, is the thought of how many innocent boys they take with them."

"The enlisted men want to fight for their country too. They volunteered to stop the Rebels' destroying their country."

"Horseshit. The truth is they don't know what they volunteered for, they heard the military bands in their little backwater towns, they saw the officers with their shiny brass buttons and fancy mustaches, and they followed like children, believing they were going on some exciting adventure. Then someone put a musket in their hand and told them to stand in line, fight and not run away even when their friends and brothers were being blown to pieces and they saw that the adventure wasn't exciting at all, but a nightmare from which most of them will never wake." He threw his towel into the basin and walked away. Jesse followed.

"That's unfair," she accused. "You're presuming that all enlisted men are too ignorant to understand why they are fighting their own country-men. They *do* know what this war is about; they might not all have the same reason, for some it's slavery, for most it's the survival of the Union, but they're not all fools who marched blindly to war because of a military band and a brass button! They know their country is being torn apart and they must fight to save it."

Cartwright halted. "Just listen to yourself," he said, shook his head disgustedly, and walked on.

There was nothing to compare with what men had witnessed these past two days and nights across the fields and woods near Shiloh Meeting House and on the bluffs of Pittsburg Landing by the Tennessee River.

Dr. Fitzjohn and Dr. Cartwright, both of whom had been operating since early the previous morning, without rest or nourishment, had swollen ankles and stiff swollen fingers. Poor Dr. Lowefels had collapsed, pushing his elderly body too far. Even Jacob, whose strength and energy had appeared infinite, looked all done in.

Little wonder that he and Jesse found Seth Cartwright baying at the waning moon like a crazy, wounded animal and demanding of the heavens in a strange confused voice, "Why bring the wounded here? I'm not a surgeon, I'm a butcher and this"—he swung around to gesture at the cabin with red, swollen hands—"*this is a charnel house.*"

12

The hearts of men

We are but shadows—we are not endowed with real life, and all
that seems most real about us is but the thinnest substance of a
dream—till the heart is touched. That touch creates us,—then
we begin to be—thereby we are beings of reality, and inheritors
of eternity.

—NATHANIEL HAWTHORNE, *Passages from the American Notebooks,*
volume I

"Doctor," Thomas Ransom called softly, opening his eyes to see
Cartwright at the next cot, "are you able to spare me a moment?"

The surgeon made no reply, but when he'd finished attending his
patient he walked to the foot of Ransom's cot and muttered, "What do
you want? You feeling lonely now all your admirers have gone?" The
young colonel had been receiving visitors throughout the day. The
tallest of the group, a broad-shouldered, strikingly handsome young
man, was Lieutenant Cyrus Dickey. The other men were Captain Wad-
dell, a hollow-cheeked individual with black mustaches and a stern manner, commanding the Eleventh while Ransom was indisposed, and
Lieutenant Doug Hapeman, who looked like a strong, intelligent farm

boy. They had sat around Ransom's cot analyzing the battle and criticizing the generals who had led them. Including Sherman.

"I wanted to thank you for having me brought off the steamer to your hospital. I don't know why you acted as you did, I can only—" The Vermonter stopped and looked pained because Cartwright had burst into laughter.

"*I* didn't take you off the steamer. *I* didn't bring you here. To me you're just another puffed-up, swaggering, brass-plated officer. It was Jesse."

As he turned to leave, Ransom called, "Doctor . . . wait . . . wait a moment . . . please—"

With an exaggerated show of irritation, and a loud sigh, the surgeon waited.

"Do you know *why* the corporal brought me off the steamer?" Ransom said.

"Ask—" He nearly said "her," he *nearly* said it, just for the sheer bloody-mindedness of it, but deep down a tiny spark of decency stopped him. "Ask the boy." He was laughing again as he walked off.

When the Vermonter opened his eyes again, the girl was by his cot, her cool hand against his brow.

"How do you feel?" she whispered.

"Light-headed," he said.

"You have a slight fever." She held his head and put the cup to his lips. All the while, his eyes were on her face, asking a question. They said, *This is strange.* This is a mystery—the easy informality, a corporal and a lieutenant colonel, a boy and a man, what is this strong bond between us?

"Why do they call you Green?" she asked and he found himself telling her.

"For Greenfield, my mother's maiden name."

"I prefer Thomas," she said softly, with a smile, stroking his brow.

He stared at her. His eyes flickered, and in a hushed whisper, he said, "Now I remember . . . it was you . . . in Jones Field . . . you were there . . . and in the wagon . . . the jolting . . . you were cradling me in your arms . . . the rain was falling. I heard the good sergeant's voice . . . he was lifting me—" He closed his eyes. His lips trembled; he could not finish the sentence. His excited voice had woken the youthful officer in the next cot, who started to weep. "What is it?" Ransom asked anxiously, sadly. "What's wrong with him?"

"It's his sixteenth birthday," Jesse said. "Dr. Cartwright amputated his left leg this morning."

"Here, please, give him this package." He reached under his pillow. "Fruit jellies." One of his officers had brought them. "Say it's a birthday gift from you. Please, it's the least I can do."

Jesse opened the package for the boy. He sucked a jelly and grinned. When she returned to Ransom, he said, "Will Wallace is dying."

"Yes, I know." At dawn a handsome, middle-aged cavalry colonel name of T. Lyle Dickey, father of Cyrus, had come to Sherman's tent with tears in his eyes. He had begged leave of the Ohioan to visit his son-in-law, Will Wallace, lying near death in Savannah, and attended by his daughter, the general's wife. It had indeed been a moving story, but if Sherman was moved, he didn't show it. Duty came first, he had told the colonel, and since *this* colonel commanded the Fourth Illinois cavalry, Sherman's only cavalry, he was required to command them. Only after they had seen the Rebels on their way had Sherman given Colonel Dickey permission to go upriver to Savannah to see his dying son-in-law. She lifted Ransom's hand from the blanket and gently stroked the bruised knuckles. "I'm so sorry. But love does not end with death."

He stared intently into her face. Out of the corner of his eye, he saw a young soldier hovering close by, trying to catch her attention.

"I'm mighty sorry—I don't wanna bother you," the soldier said, squeezing his kepi between his small hands, tears running down his freckled cheeks. "My brother says—for you to come. He says it's time."

Jesse got to her feet. She drew the cover to Ransom's shoulders, but he struggled to sit up, watching her follow the boy to a cot opposite.

"I brung him, Orrin, I brung him just like you said. *Orrin?*" The boy's voice turned panicky as he shook his brother.

"I'm still here," said Orrin, opening his eyes.

On the first day of battle in the Peach Orchard Corporal Orrin Flagg had received a dreadful wound in the abdomen. To Jesse both brothers were special. They were from the surgeon's hometown. Orrin beckoned Jesse to come closer and then whispered in her ear, "I'm fixin' to die, Jess, stay with me now like you promised. Lyle ain't never seen none a his kin die before, he's just a boy. He's real scared. If'in he sees I ain't scared he'll feel better 'bout ma goin'. Stay with me and read somethin' from ma Bible, but I don't want nuthin' sad. I marked the place. Hey, Lyle, you stop that blubberin' now, yer hear?"

Lyle wiped at his child's tears and stared at Jesse like she alone knew the reasons for being born and for dying and for all the good and evil that went on in between.

"Sit on the edge of the cot and hold your brother's hand," she told him.

The boy did as he was told. He could not stop crying. He was making loud sobbing noises, the kind a child makes when crying so much he cannot breathe and the crying has gone beyond the point where he can recall the reason for his agony. Jesse took Orrin's well-thumbed Bible from his night table and opened to the page he had marked for her, to the last words he wished to hear. She began to read in her wondrous voice, a voice that was neither feminine nor masculine but something strong in between, which could lift the lowest of spirits and transport the most downhearted, to a place of optimism and light.

" 'Let not your heart be troubled: ye believe in God, believe also in me. In my Father's house are many mansions: if it were not so, I would have told you. I go to prepare a place for you.' "

Orrin's mouth, so twisted with pain, twitched now with a smile. "That's it, Jess," he said weakly, "that's just what I wanna hear. Read it good and loud—let the whole darn world know—where I'm goin'—ain't I the luckiest son of a gun?"

" 'And if I go and prepare a place for you, I will come again, and receive you unto myself; that where I am, there you may be also.' "

A small group had gathered around the dying man's cot. Young Olly, the fifer, was standing by her side, his hand resting lightly on her shoulder, his head bowed respectfully. Three orderlies, ministering to the sick and dying every moment of the day and night, themselves in need of some comforting words, now pushed in close to listen. A few of the more mobile patients, on makeshift crutches, another with his head swathed in bandages, had left their own sickbeds to give support to a comrade in his last moments on earth. At the rear of this small impromptu congregation was the young colonel.

"—'I will not leave you comfortless' "; Orrin took over in a suddenly strong voice, quoting from memory. " 'I will come to you. Yet a little while, and the world seeth me no more; but ye shall see me: because I live, ye shall live also.' " With that he sighed deeply and was silent.

"*Orrin?*" said the boy in an anguished voice. He could not stop sobbing, his breath was coming in short, sharp gasps, as though he had hiccups and could not properly catch his breath. "Orrin? Please, Orrin. Oh, Orrin. For the Lord's sake, Orrin. Orrin. Oh Lord—Orrin."

Orrin's eyes had closed, his hand in Lyle's had grown limp. On his face that had lately been distorted with pain and suffering was a contented, almost wise smile.

Jesse put the dead soldier's Bible in his hand. She took Lyle into her arms, stroked his soft brown hair, and spoke gently to him, like a brother. All who stood there touched the boy's head, his shoulder, sought somehow to share a portion of his grief.

Jacob De Groot scolded Thomas Ransom for leaving his bed. He held the younger man's elbow to steady him as he faltered and in a moment had lifted him like a baby and returned him safely to his cot.

"I've never seen anything like that, Sergeant," Ransom said as the Dutchman covered him with the blanket. "I've never seen a man give up life with such noble resignation, have you? Did you see him, he smiled as though he's seen the secrets that await us beyond the grave and was no longer afraid."

Jacob perched his bulky rear on the edge of the cot. He squeezed the moisture from the cloth and laid it across the colonel's brow, holding it there with his enormous hand.

"Do you know what I hope, Sergeant, I hope that when I meet death I can embrace it with as much dignity as that man. How often since my father's death have I wondered what lies in the hereafter for us. But I cannot picture myself knowing such a peaceful death, or dying anywhere but on a battlefield." He moved his head on the pillow that the Dutchman puffed gently beneath his dark blond head so that he could watch Jesse pass between the cots. "That boy—Jesse."

"You must try to rest. Sleep is the best restorative."

"Who is he—? Where does he come from? If you know, Sergeant, please tell me—"

"If you cannot sleep, then you must take some nourishment. I shall bring you some condensed milk. Jesse told me you like condensed milk."

"No, wait, please, listen to me—I've watched him quieting the suffering with a gesture, listened to him easing pain with a word—shall I tell you what I think?" He gripped Jacob's hand, which sought to ease him back on the pillow. "I think he is one of those through whom God works his miracles on earth. You're silent, Sergeant, but your eyes are filled with sadness; you of all people must believe in such creatures?" Jacob stroked the hand that held his as though it were the hand of a small child.

"God must have his mysteries, my gentle colonel," he said, his full lips pulling back in an encouraging smile. "How about some rice pudding with a little jam to tempt you?"

"Jesse," Ransom called her as she passed, "would you mind, I forgot to ask Lieutenant Dickey to mail my letters." He held out two envelopes, neatly addressed and stamped.

"Yes sir."

As she went to walk away he said, "There's a letter to my mother— and to my friend, Dodge, he's just made brigadier general. I thought I'd be the first to congratulate him. His wife calls me Ned. Ned, for Edwin. One of my middle names. We've been friends since university days. Thomas Edwin Greenfield—Ransom." He was staring at her. Suddenly he brought a trembling hand to his brow. "I'm sorry," he murmured, aware he was talking for the sake of it. "If you would just mail my letters, I'd be very grateful."

"Yes sir." She saluted and left.

Jacob had prepared a veritable feast for his companions. Rice, a morsel of rabbit, shot by an orderly, and some mashed potato, followed by two Dutch cookies, somewhat crushed but still edible. He gave one to the doctor and one to the girl. Cartwright broke the cookie in two and offered it to the generous donor.

The Dutchman grinned and nodded. He looked at his two friends with a munificent grin.

"We shall recall this meal in years to come as a feast, not because of the food we shared, but because of the companionship."

"Yer—" Cartwright said with a twist of his mouth, and his usual vigorous contempt for sentimentality. "By the way, I forgot to ask, do we know who won the battle?"

"*We did,*" said Jesse and Jacob at the same time.

"*We?* We, meaning the Federal army? *I* certainly didn't win any battles." Cartwright looked from one to the other.

Jesse bit lustily into the apple Sherman had given her from his mess table and then passed it to Jacob, who did the same, and offered it to Cartwright, who shook his head. "Too much excitement for one day." He puffed on his pipe for a few seconds and then said casually, "Is it true your *friend* the brave colonel killed some of his own men?"

Jesse's expression said it all. She looked at Jacob and spoke directly to him, as though fearing his judgment upon a man he had helped to bring back to health would count far more against him than the surgeon's, who detested anything military anyway and would condemn whatever words she put forth in the colonel's defense. "There was just one. I saw it happen. The soldier had plunged his bayonet into Old Bob."

"Old Bob?" Cartwright said.

"The colonel's horse."

The surgeon laughed shortly, brutally. "Well, I guess that makes it all right, then, doesn't it? That makes it even, a man's life for a goddamn horse."

"Those men were running away from the battle," Jesse pointed out.

"I don't blame them. I also wanted to run away."

"*But you didn't,*" Jesse reminded him forcefully, "you stayed and you did what had to be done. You stood on your poor swollen ankles for over forty-eight hours and saved countless lives. Colonel Ransom attacked those men because they were deserting their comrades in the heat of battle."

"By slicing them through with a saber? Damn him and damn you if you can sit there and find excuses for an officer who kills his own men. I should have let him rot on that steamer."

"Perhaps injured as he was, the shock made him behave in a way he would not normally have done," Jacob said after a little reflection. "I am trying to understand what he did," the Dutchman added because Cartwright was looking at him, "as I try to understand you." Jacob raised both bushy eyebrows.

"Don't try and understand me. I don't need understanding."

"As you don't need friends," Jesse said.

"You got that damn right."

"I've talked with him," Jacob continued. "He's a good man. A Christian of deep moral sensibility. He talks of making his family financially independent, of making their lives pleasant. His character is built squarely upon determination, iron will, and devotion to responsibility. He is the sole support of a widowed mother, a young sister, and before the boy joined the army, his brother, Eugene. Also since the death of his uncle he has willingly taken on the responsibility of that man's family, a wife and four children, none above school age. He is paying for their education. He comes from a family of soldiers, men who have always stepped forward to serve their country in time of war and revolution. In his dedication to his family and his duty, is the colonel not very like you, Doctor?"

When Cartwright snorted, Jacob struggled to his feet. "I am going to turn in. I have a sore rear from that wagon seat. If I lie down it redistributes the weight." He laughed, Jesse laughed, and he kissed her on the top of the head.

"How about me?" the surgeon asked with a grin. "Don't I get a kiss?"

"Jesse—"

She stopped by the colonel's cot. Beyond the tent flaps, night was lying across the glittering waters of the Tennessee, and the river looked aflame with the lights of myriad campfires. As always, music, voices, and a harmonica drifted through the still spring air.

"Did you mail my letters?"

"Yes sir."

He lowered his gaze. "Of course you did. Forgive me; I just wanted an excuse to . . . to talk with you—"

"You don't need an excuse. I would enjoy talking with you."

"You're busy. The wounded need you."

She smoothed out his blanket, stroked his hand. He moved it self-consciously out of her reach. Their gazes clashed and he lowered his again, his hollow cheeks coloring. "Sergeant De Groot . . . said—" He halted, feeling foolish. What had the Dutchman said? That God must have his mysteries. Yes, impenetrable to man. Nevertheless, it did not stop men from trying to penetrate them. "I've been wondering—why do you show me such dedication?" His clear, innocent, suffering gaze rested upon the girl's face.

"Friends look out for each other. Would you like some tea, Thomas?"

He shook his head and turned his face away. The boy seemed to enjoy saying his name. It tripped so naturally from those full lips, and he, he felt no desire to tell the boy not to use it.

"Thomas?" She touched his shoulder. "What would you like to talk about?"

"Nothing. Nothing. I'm . . . I'm more tired than I thought." He was trembling as she said, "I understand. Good night, sir. God bless you."

"Yes—" he murmured, shamefaced. "And you also—"

In the commander's tent at midnight, Sherman told the girl about his close shave with death that morning in the guise of a Rebel colonel called Nathan Bedford Forrest.

"I am sure," he said, as Jesse, with the minimum of fuss, went about changing the dressing on his hand, "had his pistols not jammed it would have been the end of my career, the end of old Sherman." He looked at her. "Yes, you missed a spectacular show this morning, my boy; Sherman was at the mercy of a Rebel colonel. God alone knows how he did not shoot old Sherman out of his saddle."

"God alone—" agreed the girl, with a self-satisfied smile, fastening the buckle on her haversack.

He showed her the contents of an old segar box, holding it under her pug nose so she could see the musket balls, bits of shot and shell, a single spur. "For my sons," he announced proudly. "Willy will examine them, wide-eyed and wondrous and show all his friends. The spur came from the boot of a dead Rebel captain. Their mother will paste them on a little paper and write of how they were picked up near my tent on the battlefield of Shiloh, souvenirs of their father's honorable redemption. Mrs. Sherman will cut paragraphs from the paper with my name for Willy's future study." He closed the box with a snap, narrowly missing her nose, obviously thinking it highly amusing, since he laughed that hoarse hiccuping laughter, and even more vigorously when she looked indignant. "At last Sherman stands redeemed from the accusations of insanity in Kentucky." His wild eyes glistened in the shadowy interior. "Did you know that poor Holliday was the first man killed in the battle? The shot that killed him was meant for me. What do you think of that? I'm told I avoided death so many times on that first day they lost account. Four horses shot from under me and more holes in my uniform than your grandmother's sieve." He started to laugh again.

Jesse looked at him. He was in a highly agitated state, and had been since the close of battle on Monday afternoon. It was not the agitation of sickness, but of a man whose explosive nerves lie close to the surface and whose senses are attuned to an almost unbearable pitch. It was not the agitation of insanity, but joy. He was pleased with himself and his performance in battle, to a degree where he could conceivably be accused of vanity. He was in what he liked to term "high feather."

"Have you heard what they're saying about Albert Sidney Johnston? That he purposely put himself in situations of the greatest danger." She was turning back his blanket, placing a cup of whiskey on the tiny stool by his cot, along with two cigars and some matches, should he wake in the night and want a drink or a smoke, to calm those restless nerves. "Perhaps he felt that dying in battle was preferable to living under a cloud of uncertainty? Better to die a fallen hero than live under those alleged inadequacies as a commander."

Sherman was staring at her, his glittering eyes darting all over her freckled face. He was still staring at her as she eased the right sleeve carefully over the bruised shoulder and bandaged hand.

"I thought I told you to grow a beard?" he said finally. "It will make you look older and less like a milksop."

"Do I look like a milksop?"

"No, you look like a street rough. Are you wearing the drawers I gave you?"

She turned down the top of her overlarge pants and showed him the edge of the graying cotton cloth. "They don't make my skin itch like the red woolen army drawers," she told him and he nodded his approval.

He sat down on his rickety old cot, all that could be found for him on the morning of the seventh. Though all things considered, it was far superior to the wet blanket he'd slept on during Sunday night. "Where were you this afternoon?" He grabbed her collar and his cigar breath seared her face. "I'll tell you where you were. In the hospital helping the wounded."

"If you know where I was, why do you ask?"

Sherman stared at her, his mouth working, but no sound came. She started to massage his shoulders. "God in heaven, you should have seen the desolation and misery in that Rebel hospital camp this morning, Jesse. That poor man, Surgeon Lyle, the medical director, not knowing which way to turn. Wagons hauling in dead men and dumping them on the ground as cordwood, for burial in long trenches, like sardines in a box. Wounded men with mangled legs and arms, and heads half shot away horrible to behold, and still more of them appealing for water and for any help they could get." He ran his bony hand over his spiky red hair, picked and plucked at his short-cropped beard. Without available wagons to transport the wounded back to the Federal hospitals Sherman had ordered Colonel Dickey to accept a surrender and a pledge by Surgeon Lyle and his staff to report themselves to General Grant in due time, as prisoners of war, and give up the Federal wounded as soon as wagons could be sent out for them. Sherman in return pledged medical supplies and help for the enemy wounded.

"You've done a fine job on my hand, there's hardly any soreness even though I was in the saddle most of the day. What do you think of war now, Corporal? Have you had enough?"

"Enough of the fighting, yes, sir," she confessed.

"Fighting? That's the exception in a soldier's life. The easiest thing. Marching, countermarching, dust, thirst, short rations, sickness, wagon mules, and all the complications—fighting is a small part of a soldier's life. Do you know if I had not been a soldier I'd have been a farmer. If I had resigned my commission earlier than I did to make my fortune in civilian life"—he puffed up his chest comically, perhaps parodying himself at an earlier age—"it would have been to raise enough money to buy a good farm in Iowa." Jesse lit his fresh cigar. "I'll miss you when you go north to the Academy, to be sure, my boy, I'll miss you."

She closed her eyes and let the vigor and vitality of this strange, contradictory, ambivalent man enter her soul as his hiccuping laughter filled the tent. He smelled of tobacco, gunpowder, and sweat mixed with a little whiskey and warm horseflesh, to give it extra pungency. He smelled of *life*. The aroma could not have been more welcome in her nostrils after three days of chloroform, stale urine, fear, fresh blood, and death.

13

The fire-eyed maid of smoky war

Is there more? More than Love and Death?
Then tell me its name!

—EMILY DICKINSON, *The Complete Poems*

At the hospital the next morning Jacob handed Jesse a small package. It was from Thomas Ransom. Cartwright burst into disdainful laughter as she unwrapped an eight-inch Bowie knife with carved bone handle in a brown leather sheaf. He read Ransom's accompanying note over her shoulder.

Corporal Davis, I am sorry to have missed the opportunity to thank you in person for all that you have done to facilitate my swift recovery. But I know you will understand when I say I have just heard from Lieutenant Dickey that General Wallace, after show-ing signs of recovery, has become delirious and that if I hurry I may, as a convalescent, claim passage on the *Mound City* which is about to depart for Savannah and see my nearest friend. I leave you this token of my gratitude, taken from a Rebel at Charleston, Missouri, not the same who deposited the ball in my shoulder, but another whose aim was not so accurate, and assure you of my friendship at all times.

Kind regards,
Lieutenant Colonel T.E.G. Ransom,
commanding 11th Illinois.

"Personally I would have given you a red velvet dress to match your red velvet hair, but then, despite what *I* know, maybe *he* knows you better. Jacob told him to rest up a couple more days, but he wouldn't listen. He had rebellions to put down, cowards to saber, duty, honor, patriotism." The surgeon wielded an imaginary sword above his disheveled head.

So magnificent a gift surely deserved a sturdy leather belt, but she had none, so she threaded the length of string that held up her baggy pants through the slit in the leather sheaf and tied it around her narrow waist. She gave the note to Jacob to read and his gaze turned introspective as he stroked down his beard.

"The *Mound City* does not leave the Landing until midday," he said. "The colonel had plenty of time to thank you in person. I am disappointed. But he is afraid, afraid and confused, so he runs away, and who can blame him."

Jesse was about to ask why the young colonel should be afraid and run away when he had faced the enemy so courageously, but Jacob had already gone back to his work.

Surgeon Fitzjohn gathered together the motley crew that made up the lower echelons of his "medical department" and informed them in his clanging funereal tones that, "The division commander himself has asked every regimental hospital to provide volunteers to help at the Confederate hospital camps of Surgeon Lyle on the Corinth Road, to nurse the wounded until they can be shipped out to a prison in the North, and to bury the dead. So you might look upon this as a mission of mercy."

The volunteers stepped forward, among them Jesse, Jacob, and Olly, the boy fifer. Fitzjohn looked at them and nodded somberly. "You will have your commander's gratitude."

Jesse jumped from the back of the slowly moving wagon as it rolled into a clearing dotted about with small stunted trees whose branches had been broken during the shelling. Beyond the hospital tents, she recognized the vast area of fallen timber where the previous day a slave-owning traitor had failed in his bid to kill a United States general.

Outside the camps of Confederate surgeon Lyle a Rebel private, shot in the leg during Sherman's pursuit of Rebels on the Corinth Road, had come slowly to himself. He had sat up, thrown off his dead, gray-clad comrades under whom he lay half-buried, and stared glassy-eyed at the small redheaded figure in blue, kneeling over his sergeant, a man worshipped by his entire company.

"Ho!" the Rebel boy called, watching the corporal open the buttons on the sergeant's coat and slip a hand inside. "Ho, what yer doin' there, Lincoln boy? You git 'way from Sergeant Toomey now, yer hear me?" This Rebel boy was weak from loss of blood and had never felt thirstier in his life, never known such an all-consuming, maddening thirst, but no one, least of all a Lincoln boy, was going to manhandle Sergeant Toomey or rob him blind, not while there was breath in his body.

"He's still alive," Jesse said without looking up. "I'm trying to find the wound."

"Did yer hear me, Yankee boy . . . leave him be . . . leave him be, I tell yer—take your filthy Yankee hands offa him." The Rebel soldier was crying now, wiping tears and dried blood off his freckled face with one sweep of his hand. "Leave him be, I tell yer, dear Lord, don't yer speak English—you son-of-a-bitch thieving Lincoln boy!"

"I'm trying to help him," Jesse said, her sensitive fingers making contact at last with a hole in the man's back. "It's a miracle he's still alive."

"I said leave him be . . . now do it . . . do it . . . yer hear me . . . yer son-of-a-bitch Yankee? I ain't messin', Lincoln boy—I swear I ain't messin'." The boy's voice rose hysterically as he produced a pistol from beneath his thigh, which he cocked and aimed with shaking hands. "I mean it . . . Yankee boy . . . I mean it, so help me . . . I ain't kiddin' . . . I swear to the Lord I ain't kiddin' . . . I can't have no Yankee boy messin' with Sergeant Toomey . . . I jest can't allow it . . . no sir . . . I can't—" Tears were streaming down his bloodied cheeks, his hands were trembling, and the gun shook. Suddenly there was a crack.

To Jesse, searching in her haversack, it seemed as though something snapped inside her head, a kind of smacking sound against her ear, a twig snapping or breaking close to her ear, a momentary pain, followed by a strange liquid warmth, and then a falling sensation.

It happened so quickly, so unexpectedly, that even though Jacob, searching for wounded among the dead, heard the unmistakable report of the pistol, saw the Rebel boy with the smoking gun in his trembling hands, and saw Jesse lying across the prostrate sergeant, still required a second to understand, to grasp the reality of what had happened.

Then he bellowed his rage to heaven. *"Noooo!"* He dropped his haversack, grabbed up a musket lying nearby and came at the dazed private with the inexorable momentum of an enraged bull, making the very ground shake beneath his feet. He plunged the bayonet into the boy's skinny chest with all the power behind his three-hundred-pound body, driving it clear through to the other side, pinning him, as though on the end of a stake.

The Rebel boy, his freckles fading into the waxiness of his face, sat there, profound shock making his light blue eyes start from their sockets. He remained sitting, his surprised expression deepening to utter confusion, as he stared at the giant standing over him. Then he dropped his gaze and stared down at the blade buried in his chest up to the hilt, and his mouth dropped open. He seemed about to speak, to ask a most profound question, but Jacob had withdrawn the instrument of death and the boy fell immediately backward with a light thudding sound. His sightless eyes now stared at eternity, while blood spurted up through the slit in his chest, running freely, to stain his gray tunic.

Fitzjohn was standing in front of a blanket that had been thrown over a roped-off area to the rear of a recovery tent, blocking it off from public view.

"You wanted to see me?" Cartwright said. "Let me guess, there's a bedpan missing and I'm chief suspect?"

Without a word, the older surgeon drew Cartwright behind the curtain.

In the cot lay a slender form, the blanket slowly rising and falling, so there was no need to ask the obvious question, which was just as well since Cartwright's mouth had gone dry and the bottom had fallen out of his stomach. It was Jesse. On the side of her head, just above her ear, was a dressing, from which still seeped a trickle of blood. Fitzjohn turned back the blanket. Her blouse was soaked with blood. A noise of shock came from Cartwright's throat and one single word, as close to a prayer as he had got since his father's death. "*No*—" Fitzjohn's undertaker voice said without emotion, "I made the same mistake, but the blood on the blouse belongs to a Rebel soldier. I didn't know that when your steward came in here. During my examination, I made a startling discovery. But, then, you already know what I found?"

Cartwright was no longer listening. As his fingers gently began to examine the head wound, a low moan escaped the girl's full lips. Her eyes opened, dazed and confused.

"Hey." He stroked her brow. "It's me, ole Cartwright—rest easy. I'll take good care of you."

"I think you've answered my question," Fitzjohn said, turning to leave.

Cartwright grabbed his arm. "What are you going to do?" he asked desperately.

"What do you think? I've given instructions that only you are to attend this patient." He walked out.

As Cartwright followed, he stopped one of the orderlies to demand, "Where's Sergeant De Groot?"

"Ain't seen him, Doc, not since he brung in the boy."

Fitzjohn's horse was gone from the corral. Cartwright tried to calm himself. His satanic majesty was going home tomorrow; surely, he had better things to do with his time than report the girl? Maybe he could intercept him on the way to Sherman's headquarters and persuade him to stay silent. And if he couldn't, did he offer him a bribe? If he refused, should he kill him?

He couldn't find Fitzjohn but Jacob was lying on his cot in his tent, his Bible clutched to his chest.

"Jacob," the surgeon said harshly from the entrance, "get up. I need you. Jesse's alive. That's the important thing. The ball broke the skin, there was blood, that's all. You've seen enough superficial head wounds to know if you keep them clean, change the dressing regularly, they're not dangerous. Are you going to lie there for the rest of this goddamn war? We've gotta think of some way to stop Sherman sending her away. That's the important thing now. Damn it, if you did *anything* wrong it was letting Fitzjohn get his hands on her. That was just plain stupid." He lunged forward and gripped the man's enormous shoulder and shook him. "Did you hear me, Jacob, stop blaming yourself—we haven't got time for self-pity. I need you."

Jacob turned his suffering gaze on the surgeon's angry face. It was obvious he had been crying for some time, his eyelids were swollen, his eyes bloodshot. "I killed a man." He pronounced the words slowly, wonderingly, his beard and cheeks still wet with tears.

"What? What man? What are you talking about?"

"The young soldier—who shot Jesse—I killed him. I took another man's life. I have prayed to God over and over, to take me. I no longer deserve to live."

Sherman was in the midst of dictating a report of the battle.

"Shortly after seven in the morning with my entire staff, I rode along a portion of our front, and in the open field before Appler's regiment, the enemy's pickets opened a brisk fire upon my party killing my orderly, Thomas D. Holliday, of Company H, Second Illinois Cavalry."

"Sir," the assistant adjutant general interrupted the commander's bullet-fast delivery as he marched up and down before the hardtack box the captain was using as a desk.

The Ohioan halted, turned, rammed the cigar butt into the corner of his mouth, and demanded irritably, "What is it, Hammond? Am I going too fast for you, sir?"

"Frankly, sir, yes." Sherman only had two speeds—fast and *very* fast.

"My damn hand, I dislike having to dictate these reports. Where is the boy, have you found him yet?" he demanded of Captain Van Allen.

"He's probably at the hospital with Surgeon Cartwright, sir. You gave him permission to go over there to help with the wounded when he wasn't needed at division."

"Well, he *is* needed, his *commander* needs him. I want my dressing changed. This one is too bulky. If I had a smaller dressing I could hold a damn pen."

"Shall I ask Surgeon Hartshorn to pay you a call, sir?" asked Hammond hopefully. After two hours of rapid-fire dictation and choking on cigar smoke, he needed to escape.

"Certainly not. Do you think those overworked surgeons have nothing better to do than make house calls?"

"Tent calls," Hammond muttered under his breath.

If Sherman's eyesight was excellent, his hearing was batlike. "Hammond, I think your stomach is affecting your brain, sir."

"Gen'al?" Captain Jackson came into the tent.

"Have you found the boy yet?" was all Sherman wanted to know at that moment, flexing his fingers uncomfortably.

"No, Gen'al, can't say I've been lookin', but Surgeon Fitzjohn's outside askin' a word with you. He says it's urgent."

"He probably wants to say good-bye. Everything is urgent with these people. Show him in. Hammond?"

"Sir?"

"Let's continue: Fire came from the bushes which lined a small stream that rises in the field in front of Appler's camp, and flows to the north along my whole front."

It never failed to amaze anyone listening how Sherman could simply pick up the thread of a conversation or an idea that had been dangling there for some time past while he pursued another thought or another conversation. He could manage it while a regimental band played a noisy selection of patriotic quicksteps outside his tent, as now, or while excitable couriers were garbling out their messages in unison, and during a thunderstorm, or in the middle of a raging battle, or when all these were happening at once. His powers of concentration and his energy were awe-inspiring, whereas poor old Hammond, sick with diarrhea and fever, was losing the struggle to keep up.

Fitzjohn entered in Captain Jackson's wake, the chief pallbearer at the funeral.

"Dr. Fitzjohn, you leave us tomorrow. You've done good work here, sir," Sherman said.

"Thank you, sir. I have something rather delicate to report to you, though it affords me no pleasure."

"Sir, may I excuse myself for just a moment?" Hammond rose to his feet clutching his stomach.

"Yes, go on, go on, we'll finish the report later." Sherman had little time for his own ailments, and none at all for other people's. He sat down, leaned back, and crossed his legs on top of the hardtack box, hooking his thumbs over his vest pockets, the cigar firmly entrenched in the left-hand corner of his mouth, adopting his favorite pose. He was still very much in high spirits, despite the discomfort of the wound.

Hammond left and Van Allen came into the tent as Fitzjohn said, "It's the boy, sir. Private Davis."

"Jesse?" Sherman displayed the first spark of interest. "Have you seen him, Fitzjohn? I want my dressing changed. I can hardly lift a damn pen or hold the reins with this thing wound around my hand. Send him to me immediately before I have him horse-whipped."

"You yourself asked for volunteers to help the Rebel wounded in the hospital camps of Surgeon Lyles. Corporal Davis was one of those who volunteered. He was shot this morning by a wounded Rebel soldier whom he was trying to help."

"Oh God no—" Marcus whispered.

"Damn—" Andy exploded. "—*God damn those Rebs!*"

Sherman removed the smoldering cigar from between his clenched teeth. He even took his legs down from the box and sat forward to ask, "How bad is it?"

"He was shot in the head, not seriously—"

"Not seriously injured, you say, Fitzjohn," Sherman interrupted, glancing at his two aides, all three men sharing a moment of relief. "Then we must be grateful. Let me know if he needs anything. If he's conscious tell him his commander will visit with him this evening and fetch along something to cheer a young invalid."

As far as Sherman was concerned that was the end of the matter. Fitzjohn didn't budge.

"Whilst examining the boy I made a quite extraordinary discovery." He raised both dark eyebrows. "*The boy* is not a boy—"

Now he had Sherman's attention again. "What are you talking about?" he demanded very quietly, staring.

Marcus laughed and Andy smiled somewhat stupidly. There was silence inside the tent.

"There must be some mistake." Marcus was the first one to find his voice.

"I have been a surgeon for over twenty years, Captain. I believe I can tell the difference between the anatomy of a male and a female. The patient called Jesse Davis, whom I examined not more than an hour ago, is not a boy, sir"—he coughed to denote that something delicate was coming—"in the most anatomically important respect."

Fitzjohn looked from Marcus to Andy, whose face was distorted by an inappropriate smile, half-shocked, half-quizzical, then to Sherman's rapidly reddening face. His left hand, the good one, balled into a fist, the knuckles turning bone-white.

As Marcus released the tent flap behind him, all three men heard the thunderous shout of rage that broke from within, as something hard and heavy was thrown at the canvas wall. Marcus looked at Dr. Fitzjohn. "Is the boy going to be all right?"

"The girl—is comfortable and will receive the best of care from Dr. Cartwright. I will of course keep the matter confidential. Now if you will excuse me, I have to finish my packing."

Around midnight Sherman rode alone to the hospital area. An orderly pointed him to the rear of the tent.

There she lay, a child wounded in battle, trying to tend a fallen enemy, a bloodied bandage around her head, a soiled army blanket pulled up to her clefted chin, her small naked feet poking out, touchingly exposed. Sherman put the tips of his fingers to the soles. They were cold. He cursed. He covered her feet with the blanket as best he could. He stared grim-faced at her, feelings of anger and compassion, resentment and betrayal, passing in succession over his sharp features. He straightened suddenly and narrowed his eyes. To hell with any feelings of sympathy. She had no business being there—*in battle*. War was war and no Sunday-school picnic. If she *was* a Rebel spy, she had gotten what she deserved. The Yankees would bury her here in an unmarked grave, and her family would never learn of her ignoble end. Thus was the fate of all spies and Rebels. But of course he knew she was no Rebel spy. Then what in God's name was she?

Spy or not he had taken what he thought to be a courageous, intelligent, and highly personable boy-soldier to his heart and been betrayed. *It was unthinkable—unspeakable.*

The girl stirred, moaned, pushed the blanket away fitfully, and lifted her hand to the stained bandage. Sherman arrested her arm, tucked it beneath the cover again and patted her shoulder, with uncharacteristic timidity. Her vivid blue eyes opened for a brief second, stared at him without recognition and closed again.

"Yes," he said gruffly as she settled back into unconsciousness. "You are quite safe, rest easy."

His hand was still on the blanket when a voice behind him said angrily, "I thought I gave instructions that no one was—"

Drawing back his hand as though he had touched hot coals, Sherman said, "How quickly can she be moved?"

So startled was Cartwright to see the division commander that he could only think four words—*Damn Fitzjohn to hell*—and say one, "*She?*"

"Look at me, Dr. Cartwright, do I strike you as a stupid man?"

Cartwright stared at the firm mouth, the thin lips, the scimitar nose, the pitted skin across the hollow cheeks, the broad brow beneath the receding red hair and matching grizzled beard. He even let his gaze move up and down the long spare frame and slightly stooping shoulders.

Most of all he looked at the eyes, those fierce, glowering eyes, the eyes of a predator. He unpeeled the thin wire that held his spectacles to his ears, pinched the corners of his tired eyes, and sniffed. "With head wounds it's always difficult to say. It can be dangerous to jolt a patient in a wagon. Jesse lost a lot of blood, as you can see." Carefully he moved the girl's head, exposing a bloodstain on the pillow, directly beneath the wound. If this action was calculated to solicit sympathy from the Ohioan, it failed, miserably.

"There will be no jolting. Transports travel very smoothly along the water."

"What transport? Damn it, you can't seriously be considering sending her back North on one of those steamers?"

"I am not seriously considering it, Doctor, I have *decided.* Make her ready to leave in the morning."

"I can't allow that—" Cartwright blurted, laying a hand on the girl's shoulder as though protecting her from the ogre's clutches. "—I . . . I strongly protest. I won't allow her to be placed on one of those ships, exposed to typhoid, pneumonia—she'll be dead long before she ever reaches land. Do you want her death on your conscience? At least let me take care of her until she's fit to go home."

"And when, Doctor, do you suppose that will be?"

"Hard to say." Cartwright's tone and eyes grew shifty.

"I strongly advise you make an effort, sir."

"A week. Maybe ten days." Involuntarily Cartwright found his gaze moving to the girl's face, his expression softening behind the spectacle lenses. She had never looked as vulnerable as she did now, with the bloodied bandage and her full lips slightly open as she slept. For a moment, he had let his guard down and Sherman had seen it.

The division commander would make no such mistake. Suddenly realization flooded those perceptive eyes. "You *knew,* didn't you? You've known all along."

Cartwright stroked the red-gold curls off the pale brow. "No, not all along." He raised his eyes to Sherman's face and allowed his twisted smile to twitch at the corner of his mouth. "Whereas you had no idea."

Sherman ignored this observation. Instead, he asked, "Don't you have any clean blankets?" Sherman indicated the bloodstains and other soiled areas on the covering.

"They're all dirty. You take it off the dead and you give it to the living." As Sherman left the tent Cartwright's voice pursued him into the night, "She got to you as well—you can't deny it. She got under your damn skin!"

Half an hour later an orderly delivered two clean blankets, a pillow-case, a pair of thick woolen socks, and a calico shirt, directly into the surgeon's hands. "For the boy" was written on a piece of paper in Sherman's own hand.

The weak rosy glow of dawn was just visible above the horizon. Sherman sat in his small tent and struggled to write a letter with his injured hand by the flickering light of the single candle. He put down his pen and squeezed the corners of his smarting eyes. His shoulder ached. His hand ached. The Ohioan looked like a man who could commit a murder. He glanced up just as Cartwright's head came around the tent flap and demanded, "What do you want, as if I couldn't guess?" He released his breath in a long-suffering sigh.

"Captain Van Allen said it was okay to speak with you."

"Did he indeed—"

Cartwright came inside and hovered. He looked at the bottle of whiskey and tin cup remaining there from the previous night and moistened his lips ostentatiously.

"At least have the decency to wait until the sun is over the yardarm, Doctor."

"I've been up all night. I can't even see the sun, let alone the yardarm."

Sherman pushed the cup and the bottle across the table. Then he walked to the entrance, where he stood squinting up at the predawn sky, lost in contemplation. "I sometimes believe I have seen more coming of more dawns than any of God's creatures. There were nights in California during the winter of '55 and '56 when my asthma was so bad—I truly believed if I once went to sleep, I would never again wake up. I even went as far as to swear out a will and power of attorney, convinced I would soon die." He was speaking quietly, reflectively, almost as though he were alone with his thoughts. He had grown accustomed to speaking to the boy that way. Speaking his thoughts aloud.

Cartwright had already filled the cup and swallowed two large mouthfuls. Normally he wouldn't have the slightest interest in the melancholy memories of this grim-faced old bastard, but if offering him a shoulder to cry on would help his cause, then go right ahead, he was all ears, or all shoulder, and as long as the whiskey held out, so could he.

"I suppose you tried burning niter papers to help you breathe?" the surgeon said.

"I tried everything, everything my doctor gave me. Morphine, quinine—"

"For asthma?" Trying to use restraint, Cartwright topped up his cup, no point in killing the goose that was at this moment laying a golden egg. "You sure it wasn't malaria?"

"Save your breath, Doctor. Pretending to show interest in my health will not change my mind. As far as I am concerned, the boy I befriended that first night is dead, buried, like hundreds of other soldiers who fought at Shiloh. That is what I have written Senator Sherman. She leaves in the morning."

Well, thought Cartwright, looking regretfully at the remaining whiskey in the bottle, that glimpse into the far reaches of the grim Sherman soul was short-lived.

"All I require from you, sir, is an address to which I can send her."

Cartwright shrugged his shoulders. "She never told me where she comes from."

"You expect me to believe that, Doctor? She was close to the Dutchman; she must have talked to him?"

"She did, but not about her home. Believe it or not, I'm telling you the truth. The only people I've come across more tight-lipped than her were dead. Maybe she doesn't want her folks finding out where she is—she's not easy to know."

"People with something to hide rarely are."

"I wouldn't know about that, all I know is since she arrived, it's like

I've grown a second pair of hands." Cartwright gave a brutal twist of his mouth and laughed. "And you must have thought she was pretty special too, or you wouldn't have recommended her for West Point."

That tore it. Sherman's eyes flashed wildly. He rose to his feet, his face a dark shade of purple as he bellowed, "If you come here to my headquarters again to plead this girl's case I'll have you *both* sent back North where you will wash dirty linen and empty bedpans! Is that clear?"

It was clear as crystal then and it was still clear two days later as Cartwright planted his backside on the dispensary table and stared at Jesse's face as she patiently relabeled the bottles. Most had become smudged or obliterated by blood and other bodily fluids during the madness of April 6 and 7, and its aftermath. He had given his permission for her to perform light duties in the hospital.

"Why do you think we ain't heard anything from Sherman about you going home?" he asked, getting out his pipe and cleaning the bowl with one of the inky pens she was using. "I guess he's too busy patting himself on the back. Good to see Jacob up and around." Since the Dutchman's display of uncharacteristic violence he had been lying in his tent, consumed with guilt and shame. "Too bad he's been at the lamp oil."

Jesse's big plaintive eyes displayed shock, so he laughed to show it was a joke.

"Well, he's been at something. He told me you drove him down to the Landing this morning and he saw that Rebel boy, the one he stuck with his bayonet, right as rain, going off on a steamer to a prison camp. He said the boy took off his hat and waved it at him, friendly as you please." Cartwright scratched his bristled chin reflectively with the pipe stem and sighed. "Maybe it's the old fool's way of dealing with his guilt. Not that he ought to feel any guilt, mind you."

"People see what they want to see, hear what they want to hear," Jesse observed in a quiet voice.

"That's true enough. 'Specially when a person's head is filled with all those stupid Bible stories." He turned the collar of Jesse's sack jacket down, smoothed it, looked into her face intimately and said, "For a while there, I thought I might have to find myself a new orderly *and* a new steward. Why *do* you think we ain't heard anything from Sherman about you going home?"

"Because General Sherman doesn't *want* me to go home," Jesse said, smiling at him.

Cartwright threw his head back and laughed. "Looks like old Jacob ain't the only one who's been imbibing lamp oil."

14

Wag the world how you will

All that we see or seem
Is but a dream within a dream.

—Edgar Allan Poe, "A Dream Within a Dream"

There had never been, in the whole history of Pitts Tucker's Landing, such feverish activity.

The injured were being loaded onto steamers for hospitals on the Ohio River, at Evansville, New Albany, Louisville, Saint Louis, and Cincinnati.

For some this would be their last journey, but it would be more bearable now because of the presence of physicians, nurses, medical orderlies, Sisters of Charity, and agents of the Sanitary Commission, all steaming up the Tennessee, their ships filled with medical supplies, their hearts overflowing with tenderness and mercy.

While the men organized, the women, mostly matrons, displayed no-nonsense manners tempered with kindness as they tended the wounded and read from the Bible. The civilian surgeons applied a dressing and then disappeared. Unfortunately, the women with the Bibles *didn't* disappear, much to Cartwright's ire. As he was often heard to say now, he had nothing against women as nurses, it was the demanding, dictating, counterordering; the purity and self-righteous piety, he couldn't take. These sharp-eyed creatures had seen him swigging from the bottle he kept in his apron. Now they watched his every move. On and off duty.

"Not so very charitable" was Jacob's opinion of these charity workers.

That morning charity was the last thing on William Sherman's mind.

"Pestiferous newspaper fellows, they don't fight, they merely hang about the enlisted men searching for malicious stories and rumors they can print in their scurrilous rags!" He was talking to members of his staff as he stood outside his headquarters tent, watching a small group of these "pestiferous fellows" scribbling into their notebooks, surrounded by soldiers only too willing to tell a story, be it truth or fiction, for a cheap cigar. "Look at them, spies, every one of them, catering to the crassest appetite of our people. *By God*, I feel a loathing toward these people." A loathing that had taken root in San Francisco in '54, when exaggerated newspaper reports had helped start a run on the financial institutions of that fledgling city, eventually ending Sherman's unsuitable, troublesome career in banking. That same disgust had flared up again in Kentucky, when those accusations of "insanity" had appeared on the front pages. The Ohioan started forward, striking his riding crop against his thigh with his left hand.

"Here we go—" murmured Captain Jackson. "—Now the darn fur'll fly. It'll be fricasseed reporter for supper."

"Get away from here." Sherman marched directly into the group, waving his stick into the reporters' astonished faces, scattering the soldiers, as well as the reporters. "Go on, I say, get away from here, before I have you all shot!" He tried to drive them off like dogs, but even dogs can protest their treatment, and these particular dogs could do more than just bark.

"You have no right to talk to us that way, General Sherman, we're just doing our jobs," came the whinging protest.

"The people are anxious to know what's happening on the battlefield," called out another, as he retreated swiftly from the inexorably advancing division commander with the wild eyes and the energy of a whirling dervish.

"Yes sir, is it not our business to tell the truth of what we see and hear?" demanded another, waving his chewed pencil.

"We do not want the truth told about things," Sherman stated emphatically, circling this last reporter like a predator trying to decide if he will devour his prey on the spot, or drag it off to a lair for a midnight snack. "We do not want the enemy any better informed about what's going on here than he is!" He tapped the man's notebook with his stick. "You write your stories telling how many troops we have deployed here, when and where we shall be moving, and you print them in your scurrilous rags for *our enemies to read*. You give aid and comfort to the enemy, is that not clear to you!"

"You already have enemy spies in your camp, General!" said this reporter, so keen to give the public *and* the enemy this elusive thing called "truth."

"Yes *sir, you sir!*" Sherman thrust his crop up under the man's nose. "You newspaper reporters are the biggest enemies of this army, libeling our best officers, telling filthy lies about the men who fought the hardest, and praising those who ran away. This hue and cry against General Grant is scandalous, all wrong!" He swung around to address them all. "The real truth, if you have the nerve to print it, is that the private soldiers in battle left the ranks, ran away, and raised these false issues and *you*, hiding on the boats, believed them! The political leaders dare not lay the blame where it belongs lest they lose the votes of their constituents. It is far easier to blame the generals than the sons and fathers and brothers who vote!"

"They're writin' it all down—" Andy whispered to Marcus as they stood and watched. "—His words'll be all over the damn papers in a few days."

"The politicians are afraid of the men," Sherman was lecturing, "but I'll speak the truth and I believe there are still honest men enough to believe me!"

"Sir, can we quote you?"

"You quote me, sir. It would offer me real pleasure to personally shoot one or two of you Cincinnati boys and save the government the money."

It was easy to spot the Buckeye scribblers, for they all, as one man, took a step to the rear, while the general requested that Captain Van Allen pass him his sidearm.

"We're trying to get an idea of how it feels to be a soldier," explained the reporter who was "just doing his job," a smart-looking man in civilian clothes, well-fed and well-watered, judging by the full cheeks glowing under a shining brandy hue.

Sherman confronted him square on, for he knew no other way. "If you *want* to get a better understanding of how it feels to be a soldier why don't you pick up a musket and *fight* instead of asking your endless questions?" He marched to a nearby stand, snatched up a musket, and tossed it at the reporter, who tried to catch it before it clattered to the ground, the stock striking his foot. There was laughter, which Sherman curtailed with a wave of his arm. "You're cowards, the whole damn lot of you," he spat with utter contempt, "cowards and fawning sycophants. If this war were left to you and the politicians, Varina Davis would be taking inventory in the Executive Mansion right now. Make no mistake"—he raised the Colt to eye level, his clear, resonant voice booming out—"if you're still clinging to the edges of my camp by nightfall like some pestilent vermin, I'll shoot you myself and save the country the trouble of hanging you as spies!" There was silence as he turned on his heel. "Same game as Bull Run," he asserted, going back into his tent. "Men run away, won't obey their officers, won't listen to threats, remonstrance, and prayers of their superiors, but after the danger is passed they raise false issues to cover their infamy. Same damn game as Bull Run."

For once Sherman was not the target of their malicious campaign to discredit a Union general. He was described as "dashing along the line, encouraging his troops everywhere by his presence, and exposing his own life with the same freedom with which he demanded their offer of theirs." But no flattering reports of his own role on April 6 could calm him. In fact, this sycophantic rubbish made him angrier.

"Today I'm the hero of the people. Tomorrow they'll be attacking me again. Next month Grant will be their hero and I'll be accused of insanity. Vox populi, vox *humbug*! Newspapers now rule, and for one to prosper one must ignore the old government and acknowledge the new Power of the Press."

Most reporters had printed stories of the battle so full of errors they might have been reporting a completely different battle. Grant's name was being maligned in the capital and the newspapers had gone to town on him, like hyenas tearing apart a half-dead sheep. He was drunk, absent for most of the battle, and when he did arrive he stood about confused and afraid. Buell and McClernand had wasted no time in giving good accounts of themselves. "It is our opinion," wrote one reporter, after interviewing Buell, "that while Grant had allowed his men to be bayoneted in their beds, only General Buell emerges from this slaughter as a hero." And McClernand, in his battlefield report to his friend Abe Lincoln, had written, "My division as usual has borne the brunt. We pushed back the continuous Rebel onslaught by repeatedly changing front."

Sherman sat down at his desk and stared hard for a moment at his injured hand. When he looked at the hand, he thought of the girl, and when he thought of the girl, his face got very red, his eyes glittered, and he got mad all over again. The fingers had stiffened almost to the point where he could no longer flex them without severe pain. He looked up at Jackson and said quietly, "Find *her*." He was holding hard to the desk as though he could barely contain his rage, and he might be tempted to fling it and the papers across the tent. "It's time. Bring her to me *at once*. Frog-march her here if you have to, under armed guard. Take a company of Missouri cavalry, the meanest set of men you can find and place her under arrest. Lash her to the back of a horse. If Dr. Cartwright tries to prevent you, place *him* under arrest and the Dutchman, place them both under arrest. But find her and bring her here to me *now*, do you understand, Captain Jackson?"

"Yes, sir, Gen'al—" Andy said smartly, his hand snapping up to salute. "I just about got the drift," he muttered, leaving the tent. "Though I reckon that's overdoin' it, even for that sneekin' lyin' little female."

"The gen'al sent me for the girl," the aide told the surgeon, who was outside in the bright April sunshine checking the latest batch of wounded before they were transferred to the wagons for the short journey to the Landing.

"What girl?" Cartwright gently patted the soldier's foot. "How's the leg feel, Sergeant?"

"Still there, Doc, thanks to you." With feverish eyes, now swelling with tears, and abruptly dropping the forced cheer, the soldier reached up and clutched tightly onto Cartwright's hand. "I don't know how I'll ever repay you, you were the only one who—"

Without waiting for the soldier to finish Cartwright snatched back his hand and moved to the next litter. "When did the orderly last change this dressing?" he asked the patient sitting against the tree with a bloodied, bandaged stump on the end of the arm held across the young officer's knee that Jackson could smell long before he reached the surgeon's side. The patient didn't know. Cartwright crouched to inspect the dressing more closely. "Orderly!" The boy who was supposed to be assisting him that morning came slouching over. "When did you last change this dressing?"

"Kain't ra'tly re-call," admitted the orderly, blinking at the stump.

"You *kain't ra'tly re-call*?" Cartwright repeated, shading his eyes from the sun.

"Nope," the orderly confirmed crisply.

"Jacob!" Cartwright bellowed before turning back to the boy and saying bitterly, "Get away from me. Go way, go wash bedpans, that's all you're fit for, you dried-up piece of cow dung." He drove a trembling hand through his untidy hair and let rip with a string of curses.

"The girl, Doc," Jackson said, keeping his voice low, trying not to breathe too deeply, in fact trying not to breathe at all, or look at the green and brown ooze on the soldier's filthy dressing. "The gen'al sent me for the girl."

"So you said—what girl might that be? I'm not aware of any females around here." He nodded toward the female representatives of the Sanitary and Christian Commissions moving between the litters with fresh

fruit and comforting passages from the scriptures. "Unless you're referring to those Bible-thumping old biddies."

"Come on now, Doc, don't insult my intelligence."

"I wish to hell you'd have Sherman come out here and see what we
have to work with—"

"Doc," Jackson said in a tone that warned his patience was wearing thin.

"I don't know where she is, but when I see her I'll tell her you were
asking after her."

Andy grabbed his shoulder as he turned away. "You go in there now,
Doc," he said quietly, "and you tell her I'm waitin' right here, cos if I go
back without her the gen'al will send the provost marshal."

"For one itty bitty little girl?" Cartwright grinned incredulously.

"For one itty bitty little girl, and keep your darn voice down."

Cartwright's grin waned and then vanished completely, to be replaced
by a hopeful smile. "Well, I guess he's had time to calm down by now,
right?"

"Don't go stakin' yer egg money on that, Doc. He's been fightin' with
those gall-darn reporters most a the mornin' and right now he's fixin' to
spit nails."

"And you? You think she oughta stay, right?"

"If it were up to me I'd have her and you sent to the Dry Tortugas."

"Thanks for your support. She's down at the Landing. I sent her there
with two patients."

"I'll wait." The aide settled down under a tree with his pipe.

Half an hour later, when Jesse drove the ambulance wagon into the hospital camp Cartwright made sure he was there to meet her. She stood
beside Jackson's outstretched booted legs and said, "I'm ready, sir," like
she was going most nobly to her own execution.

The Hoosier removed the hat from his leather face, blinked small
gray eyes against the sunlight, got lazily to his feet, and rammed his
enormous hat over his thick gray hair. Not a word was exchanged as they
rode to Sherman's headquarters. Jesse tried, but finally gave in to the
aide's stony, disapproving silence.

Sherman glanced up furtively and saw the girl standing just beyond the tent flaps, Captain Jackson close beside her, looking stern. She seemed smaller somehow or perhaps it was because the aide was so large by comparison. "That will be all for the time being, Captain Hammond," he told his adjutant. He wanted to have this unpleasant interview out of the way as quickly as possible. "Enclose the sketch done by Captain Kossack of the engineers. As soon as the detailed reports from the brigadiers and colonels are in your possession, give them to me for endorsement and such remarks, as I deem proper. Until all the brigadiers and colonels make their reports I cannot venture to name individuals, but all can be certain that in due season I will name all those who preferred to keep back near the steamboat landing as well as those who kept in our front line. Also find out what's happened to Colonel Stuart's report of his operations during the time his brigade was detached."

"Yes sir." Hammond got to his feet. He saluted Sherman and looked briefly at Jesse as she passed.

"Sir—" she murmured, for hadn't he always treated her kindly during their brief contact?

Hammond smiled sympathetically. He had no idea why this boy was suddenly out of favor with Sherman, but the Ohioan was notoriously unpredictable. He could change from friend to foe overnight, leaving the victim confused as to how and why he had fallen from grace. Andy gave her a little push into the commander's presence.

"Captain Jackson and Captain Van Allen, please remain. I may need witnesses."

Jackson gave a brisk "Gen'al." He was prepared to be witness, judge, and executioner.

Marcus said, "Sir, with your permission I would rather be excused."

"Permission denied." Sherman's face was already red, his hair already bristling on the crown of his large head. His gaze moved slowly and with contempt over Jesse's attire as she stood quite still and straight before his desk, the bandage just visible beneath her hat, her enormous eyes on his face, not afraid, but wary, as though knowing she would have to keep her wits about her, and always, *always* soft with worship.

Unwisely, she spoke first. "How is your hand, sir?" She leaned across the desk to touch it.

"Never mind my damn hand." He winced as he rested it on his lap, out of her sight as well as out of her reach.

"If you had allowed me to continue to treat the wound it would have been completely healed by now."

"Shut up!" he shouted, raising his good hand. "I didn't have you brought here to discuss my hand—and remove that hat! It's government property."

Jackson removed it for her, snatching it from her head. Now it was her turn to wince with pain. The bandage beneath had revealed itself to be bloodied at the spot where the ball had struck flesh, and was now sitting at an unintentionally comic angle.

Sherman's eyes flickered but his voice remained wrathful. "Why are you *still* wearing the uniform and rank of a corporal in the United States Army?"

"I have no other clothes, sir."

"You may keep the coat and pants until clothing more suitable to your gender can be found. Captain Jackson"—he tossed a small pocketknife across the table. "Remove the badge of rank, sir."

Jesse's hand went instantly up, her small fingers enclosing the now grubby, hard-earned stripes, protecting them from the aide's onslaught. Without a word, he removed her fingers and began to cut away at the meticulous little stitches she had used to sew the precious chevrons to the sleeve of her oversized jacket. Jesse's gaze remained unflinchingly on the commander, who was reading, or was pretending to read, a report open on his desk, while she stood rigidly to attention.

Marcus lowered his gaze; more than uncomfortable now, he was mortified.

Finished, the Hoosier placed the knife and the stripes on the table. Jesse's hand returned to examine the empty space on the sleeve, as if unwilling to believe that this awful deed had been done. Then the hand dropped once more to her side.

Throughout the proceedings, Sherman had kept his eyes on the report open before him. Now he raised his eyes and his hoarse intense voice was like thunder. "How *dare* you inveigle your way into the good graces of me and my officers with this outrageous deception?" He removed the cigar stub from his mouth. "You passed yourself off, for reasons best known to yourself, reasons I cannot begin to understand, nor would I wish to, as something that you are not!"

"I am whatever you wish me to be."

"I *wish* you to be gone from my camps!" He closed one set of papers and opened another, in reality neither had any bearing on this interview, but as always, he was nervy and restless. He got to his feet. The hands were now playing with the tarnished buttons on his frock coat. "I have reports here of your behavior during the battle. I am reliably informed that you were seen giving soldiers at the Landing instruction on the loading and firing of their weapons?" He spoke laughingly, with disdain, but his eyes were like silver darts that pierced her neck, shoulders, back, as he circled her like a hunter circles its prey.

One of Sherman's reliable informants had been James McPherson, and another, none other than Sam Grant himself, and along with the information had gone a recommendation, that the boy be promoted. Outrageous!

"In the terrible noise they couldn't hear their rifles firing or feel the kick of the butt against their shoulder," Jesse said. "They just kept on loading and loading without realizing that their muskets had failed to discharge. Some of them were so afraid that they had forgotten to bite the end off the paper cartridge before ramming it home—they were cramming the breeches with unfired rounds."

"And you, a *female*, took up your musket and demonstrated how to shoot Rebels?"

"No sir, I didn't use a musket. I was busy showing others how to use theirs."

"Because, of course, *you* are an expert."

"Not an expert, but I did have the best of teachers." She turned her head to look up at him. "Do you recall you instructed me on the use and loading of a rifle on my first night at Pittsburg Landing? You advised me to learn the necessities of camp life from my elders so that I would stand a better chance of survival. Those boys did not have the benefit of your advice. Had they, so many more would now be alive."

Sherman took himself off to the opening, held up the tent flap a moment, shook his head briefly that he wanted nothing from the officer in charge of the headquarters guard, and let the flap fall again. He stood there a second longer staring at the canvas, fumbling with those buttons, then he turned, taking a fresh cigar from his pocket. Andy stepped forward to light it for him. The Hoosier frowned. There was something wet on the old man's lashes.

Then he had once more composed himself. He sat down and started to drum his fingers on the table. "Where is your home?"

"This encampment is the only home I know."

Sherman placed his cigar on the edge of the table, clasped his hands together, rested his elbows on the table and his bewhiskered chin against his hands as he studied her in silence a long-drawn-out moment. His eyes glittered. After an inconclusive growling noise, he replaced the cigar in his mouth and went back to tapping. "Are you a runaway or an orphan? Why are you here?"

"I came to serve you."

Sherman bit down hard on the cigar, so hard, in fact, that it broke off and fell to the desk.

Marcus closed his eyes as Sherman said, "Do you know what an insane asylum is? Do you want to spend the rest of your life locked away, because that will be your fate if this . . . this game . . . continues." Making an effort to become more restrained he said, "I am beginning to suspect you are in some way mentally"—he flicked his fingers against his temple—"deranged, mentally enfeebled—"

Sherman stared at Andy, who misunderstood the look and said obligingly, "Crazy as a coot, dotty as a daisy, mad as a—"

Sherman stopped him with a glare.

"Have I not served you loyally in the past six weeks, sir?" Jesse said quietly.

"Your loyalty is not in question. Only your gender." He paused, significantly. "And it would seem *your sanity.*"

Jesse's sudden smile was indulgent, and her tone chiding. "You know I'm not insane, sir."

"You are *strictly* confined to the hospital until I can arrange for your departure. If I see your ugly nose back here for any reason, any damn reason at all, I will personally chop it off! You will also return your mount to the teamsters. The horse belongs to the United States army; it is for use by soldiers, not civilians, especially not female civilians. You will tell no one, *no one*, about any of this. Is that perfectly clear? Now get out of my sight—*and stay out!*"

At the tent flaps, she paused and turned around: "Would you also like me to return your drawers, sir?" She showed him the bleached cotton just visible above her pants.

That afternoon Sherman discussed the matter with a Miss Pinchot of the Sanitary Commission and it seemed his description of the girl was hardly designed to enthuse the woman. In fact, when he was finished, Andy removed his hat, scratched his head, and was forced to remark to his fellow aide, "If that's how the old man sells a bill a goods, it's darn lucky he ain't a snake-oil salesman, his family'd starve to death before he sold a single bottle."

There were a few new faces in the recovery tent that morning, one of those faces belonged to a Southern soldier Dr. Nash had treated for a leg wound. The wound was improving; his cough, however, appeared to be getting worse. As Jesse plumped up the young officer's pillows, she found a double tintype in a velvet-lined silver-plated case, of the kind carried by wealthy officers. One photo showed a likeness of typical proud Southern parents, the other photo was of a boy in an elaborate cadet uniform. Jesse just had time to rub blood off the glass with her sleeve and read the first half of the inscription before the young man snatched it away.

"Please, that's mine—" he said fearfully, holding the case tightly to his narrow chest.

"Louisiana Seminary of Learning and Military Academy," Jesse said, "General Sherman's Academy at Rapides Parish?"

"You know it?" The boy stared at her in amazement.

"If you tell me your name, sir, I'll ride over to division and let General Sherman know that you're here."

"That would be wonderful, Corporal." The boy's sudden excitement faded as quickly as it had come. He lowered his gaze. "Oh, but he wouldn't remember me." He opened the case and gazed at it dreamily.

"This photograph was taken in November '60." He was convulsed then with a coughing fit.

When Jesse called Nash's attention to thick mucus tinged with red, which the boy had coughed up into a handkerchief, he said, "Let the doctor at the prison camp worry about him."

The surgeons tried not to interfere with each other's patients, unless asked, but there was nothing else for it. Jesse told Cartwright.

"What do yer want?" Captain Jackson inquired in his deep growling voice as he stood before the entrance to the headquarters tent, effectively barring the way to the girl. "Didn't the gen'al tell yer not to stick yer ugly nose outside the hospital?"

"When General Sherman returns would you please give him this message, sir? He'll want to know."

Jackson took the note and nodded his head in his slow, deliberate way. He stared at her suspiciously for a full minute, his eyes getting smaller and his wrinkles getting deeper, before he hoisted his large hat aloft and scratched his head. She was too clever for a female, too clever by half.

"How'd you know the gen'al ain't here? And where'd yer get the horse? You were told that horses ain't for female civilians."

"I loaned him from Surgeon Cartwright, sir. All the wagons are being used to transport the wounded to the Landing. I had no other way of getting here."

"You ever heard a walkin'?" asked the man who had once insisted on carrying her *and* her sack of peaches on his horse. "Get along with yer— go on—" he said brutally, shooing her away with his hat as though she were a scavenging dog. "Get along now, go on, get."

Jesse got.

If she'd "got" with a little less alacrity, she'd have met up with a young colonel of her acquaintance.

Five minutes after her departure, Thomas Ransom dismounted, thanked the orderly who led his horse to the corral, and walked the short distance to the Fifth Division Headquarters tent, where he was met by

Marcus Van Allen. Marcus felt deep admiration for the fellow New Englander. Stories of his heroism during the battle had come to headquarters from various sources. How he had rallied the hodgepodge of
regiments, and led them forward, together with the shattered remnants
of his own Eleventh, under a heavy fire, pushed them gallantly on, blood
gushing from the head wound he'd got earlier in the day, until they were
but two hundred yards from Cobb's Rebel artillery. He had then ridden
up and down the line, waving his saber and directing small arms fire into
the Rebel battery, encouraging and rallying his men around Jones Field
until the reluctant Ohio boys had fled. At this moment, he looked tired,
no doubt still suffering the effects of his latest wound.

"Captain, where I can find Corporal Davis?"

"Jesse?" Marcus's expressive eyes flickered with surprise, but were
almost immediately masked. Now he remembered, something about
Jesse bringing the colonel off the hospital ship and nursing him. Perhaps
Ransom merely wished to thank "the boy." Surely the old man couldn't
object to that? He thought quickly. "He's no longer at division. The
medical department was short of orderlies. General Sherman had him
transferred to Dr. Cartwright's hospital. If you would care to write down
any message I'll have it delivered to the—to Jesse."

"No, Captain, that won't be necessary. Thank you for your time."

"Wait—" Van Allen blurted out after the departing figure, "—sir—
are you intending to ride over there yourself? I only ask because—well,
you should inquire simply for Jesse Davis, not *Corporal* Davis."

Ransom stared at him a moment, then walked slowly back. "I don't
think I understand."

"General Sherman would be the one to explain, sir." Marcus winced
then, at his own cowardice, and saw himself transferred to a small out-
post on the Gulf Coast for the duration.

"In that case, would you ask General Sherman if he has a moment to
spare me?"

"The general took an expedition to break up the Charleston and
Memphis Railroad, sir."

"I'll await his return."

Sherman, caked in mud, thoroughly exhausted, but most gratified by his successful expedition, had just dismounted when Andy gave him Jesse's note. Sherman read it.

"Cadet Wylie Leander Jarreau of the Louisiana Military Academy, now lieutenant, Company F, Fourth Louisiana Infantry, is in Dr. Cartwright's care. Lieutenant Jarreau is comfortable and not in any danger."

"The girl said you'd wanna know, Gen'al," Jackson said.

"Yes. One of my old cadets is in the hospital. I'll take five minutes for a hot drink and then I'll ride over there."

The Hoosier then broke the news about his other visitor, adding, "Marcus said he seemed mighty determined to get some answers from you."

"Did he indeed." Sherman frowned. All right, determination deserved the truth. Damn it, the girl had fooled both of them. He rubbed his uninjured hand over his horse's face. "Well done, boy, you did your full share of work today, didn't you? You deserve a rest. Have a fresh mount saddled," he told the orderly who came to lead the animal away. "And give this animal a good rubdown and some oats." He looked at Andy. "I'll see Colonel Ransom and then visit my cadet."

"Come in, Colonel, come in, sir. Sit down," Sherman said in his usual sharp manner, gesturing with his unlit cigar toward the camp chair before his desk. "Do you smoke?" he asked the Vermonter as his orderly lit the cigar for him. "Bring coffee, will you." He had heard much about Thomas E. G. Ransom, all of it highly complimentary, even from John McClernand, who usually reserved his greatest praise for himself.

"Thank you, sir," Ransom said formally, resting his sword against his thigh as he seated himself, crossing his long slender legs. "I don't smoke."

"You find me in high feather, Colonel Ransom, high feather, sir. General Halleck wanted me to destroy the bridge and trestles over the Memphis and Charleston Railroad. I left early this morning with one hundred troops of the Fourth Illinois cavalry and a brigade of infantry to go up the Tennessee thirty-two miles to Chickasaw Landing onboard the *White Cloud*, took along two gunboats. We reached the railroad bridge across Bear Creek, just at the corner of Alabama, drove off its defenders, and burned the span along with five hundred feet of trestles, a good day's work."

The orderly brought coffee. When he had gone, Sherman tasted the pale liquid and made a face. "Can't make coffee worth a damn—not like—" He stopped, looked pained a moment, and returned to a more comfortable subject. "—Yes, my men succeeded perfectly. General Halleck is delighted—delighted. This has been a chief object with him. Whiskey?" He reached behind him and snatched up the half-empty bottle with his right hand. "Pass your cup, Colonel."

"Not for me, thank you, sir."

"Then I'll have your shot as well as my own." Nothing was going to destroy the general's great good humor—not this strikingly handsome officer with his rather pompous manner, or the disturbing news that one of his old cadets was in the hospital. Not when he had a copy of a letter given him by Henry Halleck that "Old Brains" had written to Secretary of War Stanton commending his performance in the battle as "contributing largely to the glorious victory of the 7th," and recommending him for promotion to major general of U.S. Volunteers, to be dated April 6. "How's the head?" he asked, using his cigar to point.

Ransom no longer wore a bandage but the raw furrow plowed by the Rebel ball was still very visible on his scalp. "Better, thank you."

"Your head—my hand—we make a fine pair, sir, a fine pair." Sherman could have added, and we both had the same fine nurse, but he didn't. "I heard the enemy tried to get you twice before. Was it their bad aim, do you suppose, or your good luck?" Sherman laughed his strange hiccuping laughter. "I survived so many near misses on the sixth that my staff lost count. You and I will survive this war, Ransom, what do you say, sir?"

"I'd like to believe so, sir."

Sherman drank his whiskey. He tried to decide if this officer was hostile or merely frosty.

"Major Jackson tells me you want to know why I sent Jesse Davis to the hospital to work?"

Ransom sat forward, his sculptured jaw, bordered on both sides by the bushy side whiskers, thrust out determinedly. A slight color had risen in those pale cheeks.

"Yes sir, that's true. I cannot begin to imagine what misdemeanor Corporal Davis has committed to earn your displeasure, and since I know him to be of the highest character, an honest, compassionate, and courageous little fellow, incapable of any crime that would warrant such treatment, I would like to protest most strongly."

Sherman held the Vermonter's steady gaze.

"In that case, Colonel, what I am about to tell you will come as something of a shock."

15

Our immortal ranks

> If even worms are inclined to be in love with one another, how
> can we expect people not to do so?
>
> —Pawnee Indian song

Despite his persistent coughing, Cadet Wylie Leander Jarreau, now feeling he was among friends, liked to talk, and the subject he chose while
Cartwright examined him was not one destined to improve the surgeon's
mood.

"Superintendent Sherman was a good friend to us all, like a father. All
the cadets loved him, even those he was forced to discipline. He encouraged us to visit him in his private quarters at the weekends. We would fill
his room to overflowing while we listened enthralled to his wonderful
stories of army life and his adventures in California. He did not wish to
leave us at all, you know, when Louisiana seceded, he believed he had no
choice, but must leave and go back North. I recall it as if it were yesterday, he came into the classroom that mornin' and began to explain to us
how he felt about *us*, about the impendin' war and how we would be
fightin' on different sides. How he could not bear to think of us as his
enemies—he became so choked that he could not continue his little

speech and he merely put his hand on his heart and said, *You are all here—*"

At midnight, the man himself came to the hospital. Jesse was waiting for him. With a "Good evening, sir," she raised her hand in salute. Remaining there in silence as if she did not exist, the grim-featured Ohioan squinted into the dimly lit interior.

"Cadet Farreau is in the third cot on the left-hand side, sir," Jesse told him. Sherman started in that direction, Jesse followed. The general leaned over the cot and lifted the slender white hand. "Cadet Farreau?" he said softly.

The boy opened dulled blue eyes.

"Wylie, do you not remember your old superintendent?" Sherman's pretense of mortified indignation did the trick. Recognition flooded the pain-filled depths.

"Oh yes . . . yes . . . sir—" The boy's hand tightened around the general's hand. "I was afraid—that you, sir, would not recall your humble pupil."

"Come now, sir, how could I forget one of my favorite students?"

"You were . . . the only one who ever could get my name . . . quite right."

Sherman growled with laughter. "Yes, yes, I remember, you were called Willie by some, William by others, and I believe Mr. Vallas even called you *Wilhelm* on more than one occasion."

This made the poor lieutenant laugh so much that he began to cough and then to choke. Jesse raised his head and put the canteen to his lips, wiping the excess liquid from the corners of his mouth. She passed the wooden fan slowly back and forth over the boy's face. When she turned from the cot she saw Sherman staring at her, but he looked quickly away and spoke to young Wylie.

"How are you feeling, Cadet Farreau? Well, now, we'll send you home as soon as we can arrange your parole. You look as if you've been living on army rations too long, my boy. Tell Jeff Davis I said he has to feed my old cadets better food than we served at the seminary or else he too may expect a riot on his hands."

Wylie was laughing so much his entire frail body gave into a fit of coughing. Jesse put a cloth to the boy's mouth as he brought up a small lump of rusty-colored sputum. Sherman frowned his concern. The boy held the cloth in his hand. He was having trouble catching his breath. "Excuse . . . excuse me, sir—"

"Excuse you for what, my boy?" Sherman pushed the damp hair off the cadet's pale brow. "Tell me, how many of my old boys were here during the battle?"

Farreau began to name those who had fought on Sunday and Monday and Sherman slowly nodded that large tufted head of his, his eyes clouding with sadness as the faces of those mentioned paraded once more through his memory, as they had paraded that day in early February, before he left Louisiana to go back North.

"Sir, do you remember our half-holiday Saturday evenings, when we were privileged to be allowed to drop in on you in Professor Boyd's quarters and listen to your instructive conversation? The evening, sir, one of our number asked you the question, sir, if we have a war, what are *you* going to do? You were silent for a long . . . while, sir . . . and then you said, my boy, you don't know what war is. I do and sincerely hope we will have no war, for it is a terrible thing. But if we do I will say that I was reared and educated by the United States—I will not live *out* of the United States. My duty I owe to the United States and I am going there—"

Jesse saw the boy's lips begin to tremble and saw tears fall from the corners of his eyes to disappear into his curly brown hair. She saw Sherman, the old superintendent, touch his fingertips to those tears while his own eyes grew moist.

"War did come . . . sir . . . and it *is* a terrible thing, yes it is terrible—"

"You shouldn't talk anymore, Wylie," Sherman told him in a thickened voice. "You must save your strength. We'll talk again in a day or so, I promise."

"Sir—will you please write my mother. She will think me negligent if I do . . . not let her know my situation."

"I'll write your mother this very night, and let her know that *I personally* will try to arrange for your exchange or parole. You will be home with her very soon, my boy, and sincerely hope you shall remain there."

As Sherman turned from the cot, he looked beyond Jesse, again, as though she were invisible and addressed instead the orderly beside the next cot.

"Ask Dr. Cartwright if he has a moment to talk with me." He blinked his eyes and moisture stood out on his sandy-colored lashes. He wiped it away with the back of his hand.

Ten minutes later the surgeon explained, "It's not the leg wound that bothers me, that's healing well. It's that cough. Mucus gets that color due to bleeding in the lung tissue. It might be pneumonia. But he admits that his losing weight and that the cough has been troubling him for a long time—it could be the early stages of consumption."

"Thank you, Doctor, for all you're doing for the boy. You can of course have no idea the depth of feeling I have for my old students at the seminary."

"Oh, I think I can guess." Cartwright compressed his lips and struck Sherman lightly on the chest, just over the heart region. "They're all there."

It took the brilliant mind but a moment to grasp the significance of these words, then he said, "Can you do anything to alleviate his condition?"

"I can certainly suggest some forms of treatment. If it is the beginnings of consumption he'll need lots of rest in a clean place with dry air, close attention to diet, plenty of eggs, milk, cod liver oil. I'll start him on a general tonic containing iron and quinine, perhaps some fortifying herbs—and lots of fluids." The surgeon scooped the heavy fringe out of tired eyes. "He won't get any of that in a prison camp. He needs to go home. But if he doesn't take care of himself the disease will come back and in a couple of years he'll be dead."

"Don't worry, Doctor, I will see that he's exchanged as soon as possible. If you would be so kind as to write out your recommendations for treatment and recovery, I'll enclose the letter to his mother with my own. I'm sure she would be most grateful to you."

"Waste of time. We both know when his leg heals he'll be back trying to kill Yankees."

"I'm sure he'll have the good sense to stay home. I believe he's had enough of war in his young life."

"You wouldn't like to make a bet on that, would you?" Since the commander chose to remain silent, the surgeon said, "One more thing, if you want to thank anyone, thank Jesse. If it wasn't for her diligence the boy would have coughed his lungs out. Maybe that'll get you to reconsider your decision and let her stay with me." His eyes blinked behind the small round lenses. "I mean with the medical department."

"Had she saved the lives of every cadet in my seminary, Dr. Cartwright, I would not, sir, reconsider my decision. I'll send some clothing and a change of underwear for Cadet Farreau. Good night, sir, and again, thank you."

Sherman found Jesse waiting beside his horse.

"What do you want?" He snatched the reins from the orderly's hand, his pitted cheeks reddening.

"To see you, sir."

"Well, you've seen me." He mounted up and sat there a moment staring into the horizon, lit up by a hundred camps fires. When finally he spoke, he might have been thinking aloud. "Imagine, only one year ago I had charge of General Beauregard's own sons—Henri and Rene—in my academy. Their father had set his heart on West Point for Rene after his time with us, he was an intelligent student, in fact I made him my adjutant. Then came the war. I believe he is now at the military academy of South Carolina. I presume that state was grateful to their father for presenting them with the ruins of Fort Sumter." He took out a cigar and turned it over in his fingers as he said, "That fellow Farreau, a fine young man, he was only at the academy from November '59 'til spring '61, so had very little time to achieve anything of note, but he liked to read, and was a keen observer of human nature." He drew his gaze back to the girl's face, his expression hardening as if he had just remembered her treachery. "Be at my headquarters tomorrow at dawn."

If the commander's ability at selling a bill of goods left much to be desired his "advice" to the girl on how to conduct herself in her conversation with Miss Pinchot was another revelation that left Jackson and Van Allen in a state of confusion.

"Change into those." Sherman used his cigar to indicate the dress, Quaker bonnet, and shawl on the campstool. "Tuck all that hair under the bonnet, we don't want anyone identifying you. If you wish to become a nurse for the Sanitary Commission you must make a good impression on this woman. If you scratch and seem at all dim-witted she will refuse to take you and that's an end of it. Speak only when you are asked a question and do not reply with chapter and verse. Do not ramble."

Just like *you're* doin' now, thought Captain Jackson, looking at Marcus out of the corner of his eye.

The woman from the Sanitary Commission looked at Jesse and Jesse looked at the woman from the Sanitary Commission. The woman smelled of carbolic soap. Jesse on the other hand smelled of horseshit. That she smelled of horseshit was no accident. She had made certain of that by walking back and forth across the corral dragging her oversized brogans through fresh deposits of the steaming waste until they formed an extra-thick layer on the scuffed black leather. After all, no institution with the word "sanitary" in its title would want a nurse who smelled of horseshit. Her face, thanks to deposits of gunpowder from the barrel of a cannon, was streaked with dirt, and her features, though barely visible, it was true, were made uncharacteristically ugly by a scowl she'd been practicing all morning in Cartwright's cracked shaving mirror, coached, it had to be said, by the surgeon. Her diminutive frame was overwhelmed by a calico dress of a horrid dark green around which she had thrown a brown woolen shawl that would have caused even the most pious of New England grannies to shudder. Though the crowning glory was the Quaker bonnet, concealing as it did Jesse's crowning glory, those magnificent short red curls. What's more, she spent the entire interview scratching. It was a brief interview, two minutes and forty-two seconds, to be exact.

Miss Pinchot's interview with Sherman was of equal brevity. "General Sherman, it's entirely out of the question. I cannot possibly take her. She scratches constantly. She is moronic." The woman snorted and waved a hand under her nose as the general purposely blew cigar smoke in her direction. "I had heard from my colleagues that you were *not a gentleman*, and I see with my own eyes that they are quite correct."

"Madam, if that is the worst crime of which I am accused by the time this war is over I shall consider myself a candidate for sainthood. *Good day to you!*"

"I should have pressed the point," said Sherman a tad defensively, Marcus thought, when the Sanitary representative had left. "I should have asked if she could suggest an orphanage, but that damn woman was obviously not open to rational discussion."

"Not open at all, sir," the New Englander agreed.

In a fluster of righteous indignation Miss Pinchot found herself colliding with a redheaded soldier not far from the general's tent. "Get out of the way, you clumsy little pup!" said the woman, giving this soldier a bad-tempered push.

Jesse Davis grinned as the woman flew off into the distance, a clever trick indeed without a broomstick.

"Get in here!" Sherman bellowed as Jesse hovered. "Damn you, and damn the Sanitary Commission. I'm stuck with you until I can think of some place else to send you. What in hell did you say to that woman to make her so agitated—and what's that confounded smell?" The sharp scimitar-shaped nose lifted. A few seconds were sufficient for all in the tent to find their eyes watering; Sherman had ordered a large cake of lye soap to be brought, which he banged on the edge of his table, flakes flying in every direction. "Take yourself off to a private spot along Owl Creek, where you will thoroughly wash yourself from head to toe, including your hair, and do not imagine that you can remain here one second longer than it will take me to write to Mrs. Sherman's cousin, Sister Angela, who runs the Union hospital at Memphis. If that pious lady doesn't want you, I will contact the bishop of New York, who is a family friend, but be advised, girl, I will not rest until I have you off my hands."

The Sunken Road was really no more than an old eroded wagon trail running through the center of heavily wooded areas on both sides, now known to the soldiers engaged in that Union position on the Sunday as the "Hornet's Nest." Some grayback, it was said, had told his comrades, "It's a hornet's nest in there—" and thus the name had stuck.

Here on the afternoon of the sixth, men of General Prentiss's division had hunkered down in the shallow trench to make a last stand. Here the Illinois politician who had fought with Grant over rank and swore he would never serve under a drunkard had redeemed his reputation, even as his call to cease fire had sounded, and he had surrendered himself and what remained of his command: half the men he had started out with that fateful day.

It was said the place was now haunted. Of course there were ghosts. They existed as tenuously as ghosts can be said to exist. Ghosts were merely memories. There were ghosts in every place that armies clashed. But Shiloh was special. Soldiers felt these ghosts, these memories, were close by on a warm spring day as they drilled, or as night was falling in camp. In the plaintive notes of a harmonica or in the poignant words of a favorite song. When they marched, a glance over the shoulder would reveal their ghostly comrades in the ranks, as if reluctant to be left behind. Yes, ghosts would always cling to Shiloh, to the Sunken Road and the Hornet's Nest, to Bloody Pond and to all those other places where men had breathed their last, as long as their comrades, their families, remembered.

This night Jesse had ridden out into the darkness of the Hornet's Nest looking not for ethereal beings, but for a young man with iron in his soul and a steely heart. As she walked Sable down the wagon road from the west she saw the tall, slender figure dismounted up ahead, his horse tied to the half-destroyed fence rail running alongside Duncan Field. She saw the glint of the scabbard that hung from the belt around his narrow waist, as it caught the silver moonlight, saw him remove his hat and bow his head in an attitude of prayer. She waited until he lifted his head once more, then she put her mount into a trot. As the officer turned to watch her approach, he wiped negligently at his eyes with the back of his hand and came to meet her, his hat still in his hands.

"Jesse . . ." he said with a frown and a nervous laugh.

"Lieutenant Hapeman said I would find you here, sir," she explained. "I'm *so sorry* about General Wallace." For the newly promoted commander of the Second Division it had been a short war. He'd died on Thursday night.

He nodded. "Thank you." His smile was sad and gentle. "He was like a father to me. Ever since I enlisted at Bird's Point. He was the first colonel of the Eleventh." The Vermonter's eyes filled with tears. "When the last breath went out of Will's body, the words you spoke to me at the hospital were all I could think of—*love does not end with death*."

"You have the consolation of knowing that General Wallace's adoring wife was with him at the end. They were together at the moment of his passing—her beloved face was the last thing he saw."

"What more can a man ask? God must surely have brought Anne to the landing that day."

"Captain Van Allen told me you went to the general to protest his treatment of me."

Ransom lowered his gaze.

"Thank you, sir." Jesse's smile was rueful. "I'm sorry if I embarrassed you."

"No, you didn't, not at all. When he told me I was—" He punctuated the statement with a foreshortened laugh and his frown deepened. "Well, I was relieved." He raised his intense gaze to her face. "Except he made you sound like the daughter of Satan." They both laughed then. "I went to the hospital this afternoon looking for you." He stroked her horse's neck as he spoke. "Dr. Cartwright said you had gone to the landing with some wounded. I rode down there, but I must have missed you again."

"Yes sir." The surgeon had said nothing about the colonel's visit. "Are you well, sir? How is your wound?" she asked anxiously because his face in the threads of moonlight touching the scant branches was deathly pale and he had a drawn look about the eyes and mouth that gave the impression of a man combatting pain. "I sent you a note thanking you for the knife—look, I'm wearing it."

"A Bowie knife." He straightened his shoulders, raised his firm chin.

He *was* embarrassed, despite his denial to the contrary. "It now seems a most unlikely gift."

"Oh no, sir, it's wonderful. I'll treasure it."

He nodded uncertainly. He'd always been strong and self-determined, a man with great ambition and ability, all his young life, and now since the war he had proved himself a courageous and natural commander, who'd gathered his men together in battle to protect and lead them at the expense of his own safety; he had the wounds to prove it. But this young woman dressed as a soldier—well, this was disconcerting. He held her arm as she dismounted. Her smile flickered. He nodded, answered her smile with one of his own, he knew what she was thinking. An officer did not help an orderly off his horse. Some drastic readjustment of his thinking was called for. His deep-set emotional eyes passed over her red-gold curls as she removed her kepi and pushed it into her saddlebag. Her hair was a beautiful color in the moonlight, like amber. He cleared his throat.

"Is Jesse your real name?" He laughed again, and shook his handsome head. "That's the least important of a hundred questions I've kept inside my head to ask you." He walked to the fence and stared out at the field beyond, now so silent but for the always present buzzing of insects. He shivered with a sudden chill, though the night was warm. Jesse joined him. "I come out here to look at the place where Will fell," he said quietly. "I stand here and think of my dear noble friend."

"You will meet him again, sir."

He nodded, gazing off again into the distance. Watching that grief-stricken, boyish face now, it was almost impossible to conjure up the distorted blood-soaked features of the man Jesse had seen slashing away at the cowards in Jones Field.

"Why do you call me *sir* now, when you called me Thomas at the hospital?" he asked.

"You're a colonel and I'm a corporal. In the hospital it was different. I could be more informal, sir."

"A colonel and a corporal?" He looked at her. "Ah yes—" He began to walk and Jesse followed.

"It was around here," he said. "Will rode out into the very center of the firestorm. They say the opposing lines were only one hundred fifty yards apart, the Rebel infantry closing to within seventy paces. The place the men now call 'Hell's Hollow.' Cyrus was with him. He pointed out the approaching Rebels, Will rose in his saddle for a better view, and the ball struck him. He always called me '*his particular friend.*' "

A few yards ahead two leg bones protruded from the earth, already bleached by the sun, and a skull nestled in the grass. Inside those sightless eye sockets worms writhed and slithered.

"I've heard soldiers say they are prepared to die if only they know they will receive a decent Christian burial. What would we say to *these* men?" the Vermonter said bitterly.

"That no matter what horrors befall the flesh, the soul is immortal," Jesse replied. "The soul flies to heaven. The spirit never dies." After a moment's silence she said, "Oh sir, I'm sorry your beloved Eleventh lost so many men. Lieutenant Hapeman said there's even talk of disbanding the regiment and absorbing the men into other commands. What will you do if that happens?"

"I don't know yet. I'll have to wait and see." He wiped his eyes. "Both McClernand and Grant have recommended me for a brigadier generalship, which means I'd get a brigade. Perhaps I'll be able to take my old Eleventh along with me, what remains of it. When I think of the men of the Eleventh who have died—I wonder if any of us will ever be the same again, if our country will ever be the same again. Shall we sit down?" He pointed to a fallen log. When they were seated he said, "Sherman said tell no one about you, we don't want those newspaper hounds sniffing out *this* story. I would be a laughingstock and it would do *your* career no good at all." He turned to face her. "Those questions I want to ask you, Jesse, I don't know where to begin. What are you doing here? Where do you come from? Why are you here? Does your family know what you're doing?"

"I have no other family but the general, Dr. Cartwright, Jakob, you—"

"You're completely alone in the world?" Anguish drew the Vermonter's slender brows into a frown.

"No, I'm not alone. I just told you." She smiled meaningfully into his face.

He responded with a hesitant smile of his own. "How recklessly you behaved, and with what courage! I'm torn between disapproval and admiration. I personally have never heard of such a thing, and I doubt if anyone else has. An overabundance of patriotism and love of the Union cannot explain *any female* risking life and limb to go into battle. Your nursing skills would have earned you a place at any general hospital back at the North. If you wish to nurse our wounded men, why didn't you join one of the agencies and come here in a dress and bonnet like the other ladies of the Sanitary or Christian Commissions? Why go through this complicated and dangerous charade? Now you'll be sent away. What will you do? Will you go home? You must have a home; you must have come from *somewhere*. Will you return there? Now that Sherman has discovered your secret, you cannot remain; you know that as well as I do."

"You said you had a hundred questions, but you didn't say you would ask them all at once!"

"Jesse, I am not meaning to be humorous. Whatever possessed you to pass yourself off as a soldier? Admit now that we have met the situation has changed. Admit of my anxiety for you. You must return home immediately."

Jesse stared at him. "I don't understand, sir. How has my meeting you changed my situation?"

Something flickered in Ransom's eyes. "If . . . if those who . . . were concerned for you . . ." He was choosing his words carefully now, like picking his way through melting ice. ". . . for your safety—believed you should discontinue this charade, then you would go home, wouldn't you?"

Jesse got to her feet as she said, "I have every intention of remaining. Besides, those who care for me, sir, are here. Why would I wish to leave all my friends?"

"Sherman clearly has other ideas." Ransom called after her as she walked off down the shadowy road. "He'll not permit you to remain here a moment longer than he has to." He caught up with her. "Will you give me your address? I shall write you whenever I can and you must give me your word you will write to me. When I have a furlough I'll visit you."

"You already have my address." She looked at him with a mixture of sorrow and irritation. "Corporal Jesse Davis, care of General Sherman's headquarters, Fifth Division, wherever can be found the Army of the Tennessee."

"Jesse, this is no joke."

"*I'm* not meaning to be humorous."

"You are sweet and innocent, you don't know Sherman, he is the most uncharitable of men. He refused to allow Colonel Dickey to go to his dying son-in-law. He is hardly liable to take pity on a poor orphan girl who has shown him up for a fool, even one who has proved her worth and loyalty to the Union. Oh, you'll be going home soon, you may count on it."

"Would you care to make a small wager, sir?"

Ransom looked at her. "Don't be ridiculous. A gentleman does not wager with a female. Besides, you would lose."

"Then you have nothing to fear."

"I'm not afraid," he said indignantly.

"Prove it. Five dollars, sir?"

"I would deem it a great favor if you stopped calling me *sir* and, I told you, a gentleman does not make a wager with a female."

"Okay, we'll make it a gentleman's wager," Jesse suggested with a broad grin. "If I win, you have to give me fencing lessons. Lieutenant Bennett told me you were the best fencer in the whole of Norwich Academy. Agree, sir, or risk being branded a coward!" she challenged, leaping back to wield an imaginary foil and laughing at his shocked expression. "Or let us shake on it." She thrust her hand toward him.

Ransom hesitated a moment before throwing his handsome head back and giving himself up to unrestrained laughter. "You are unbelievable—you are incorrigible—just a moment." His laughter ceased. "What reward do I get if you lose, which you most certainly will."

"I won't lose." Jesse climbed onto the fence and looked at him.

He leaned on the fence beside her and emboldened by her tender smile he said, "A kiss. If you lose, my reward will be a kiss."

Jesse laughed. Then stopped. She frowned her confusion. "A kiss?" Her slender red brows dipped and then rose.

"Oh Jesse, I am fooling," Ransom said, with a casual jerk of his head. "Forgive me." He walked off toward the horses so she wouldn't see his face.

"I think I'll be a fast learner," Jesse said, jumping off the rail and lunging forward in the motions of a cut and thrust. "Don't you? I'm very fast on my feet and not at all clumsy. *En garde!*" she cried, her left arm in an arc above her head and her right once more holding the imaginary foil. The Vermonter turned around and positioned her arm more correctly. "When shall the lessons begin, do you think?" she demanded to know. "As soon as possible?"

Jacob could barely wait until the young man had dismounted before grasping both his hands and shaking them vigorously. "Thank God, you found each other, you found each other," he said, and the ambiguity of this statement was not lost on the younger man.

"Yes, thank God. We found each other," he echoed and laughed when the Dutchman embraced him.

"You will stay for tea and cookies?"

"Thank you, Jacob, but I must get back to my regiment."

"Then I shall make up a little package for you to take with you."

"He is a mother hen," Ransom said as the Dutchman hurried off. "I need time to think about all this—"

"To think about what, sir?"

"When Sherman sends you away, how will I know where to find you?" She stared at him.

"I mean—how will I know where to write to you—if I wish?"

"He won't send me away, sir. I promise."

Ransom didn't look at all convinced, but the Dutchman had returned with a small package, so he let the subject drop.

"Thank you, good, kind Jacob, I shall enjoy these with my coffee in the morning."

Jacob clasped his hand and wrung it. "God bless you and keep you safe under His wing."

"And you." Ransom climbed onto his horse, Jacob's sister's cookies in his saddlebag. "Jesse . . ." he said softly, and could think of nothing more to say.

She saluted smartly. "Please don't forget our wager, sir."

The Vermonter looked at Jacob, looked at Jesse, shook his head in abject confusion and rode off.

16

Too many generals

★ ★ ★ ★

The church so lone, the log-built one,
That echoed to many a parting groan
        And natural prayer
    Of dying foemen mingled there—
Foemen at morn, but friends at eve—
    Fame or country least their care:
(What like a bullet can undeceive!)
    But now they lie low,
While over them the swallows skim,
    And all is hushed at Shiloh.

—HERMAN MELVILLE, "Shiloh, a Requiem (April, 1862)"

In honor of the Shiloh victory, the president had declared a national day
of worship and ordered a hundred-gun salute at the National Armoury
in New York. He'd also approved the joint resolution of Congress calling for gradual emancipation of the slaves.

At the beginning of April, General McClellan had been in the process
of moving his vast Army of the Potomac to the Peninsula, nearer Richmond. By the fourth, he was slowly approaching Yorktown, but despite

vastly superior numbers, he had failed to make a decisive effort to drive the Rebels from Yorktown. Mr. Lincoln had reportedly told McClellan: "—*You must act.*"

Federal mortar boats had bombarded forts along the Mississippi, below New Orleans, and even gone on to capture New Orleans itself. Grant's men had gained the day at Shiloh, but still Little Mac had not acted.

General Henry Halleck, however, had arrived at Pittsburg Landing from Washington and immediately acted. Although he had never led more than a company in the field, "Old Brains" personally took overall command of the three armies now gathered there. Never a Grant supporter, he declared he could not ignore the stories of Grant's "intemperance," or his failure to entrench and protect his army and replaced him with the newly arrived General George H. Thomas, a Virginian who had remained loyal to the Union that had educated and trained him. Sherman was content to serve under his old West Point friend.

Grant on the other hand could not have been more *dis*content, given the meaningless title of "second in command," he was said to be sitting in his tent playing cards, and drinking heavily.

While Mr. Lincoln waited impatiently for news of McClellan's siege at Yorktown, Seth Cartwright waited nervously for the arrival of the provost marshal, who would, any day now, march in and march out again with Jesse Davis held firmly in his clutches. But the days passed. McClellan made no move to attack Joe Johnston, commander of the Rebel Army of Northern Virginia, and Sherman's provost marshal made no attempt to arrest Jesse.

The cots of the "first field hospital in U.S. military history" were all empty and the tents struck. The wounded had all gone North; the dead buried. The hospital wagons had been packed with the surgical instruments, pharmaceutical chests, cots, blankets, bedpans, crutches, and bandages. Litters so stained with blood they'd never be clean were rolled and fastened to the sides of the ambulances. The last hospital transports had steamed away from the Landing with its cargo of human suffering and its decks piled high with pine boxes.

Miss Pinchot and her implacable, bureaucratic companions had departed for fresh fields where their particular brand of stern charity would be applied and appreciated.

On April 25, at two in the morning, in the downstairs front bedroom of the Cherry Mansion, C. F. Smith finally succumbed to the gangrene that had invaded his injured leg and to the dysentery that had hung upon this unfortunate man since Fort Donelson. How strange, said many, that those two exemplary men, Generals Smith and Wallace, who had led the same division, had died in the same house in the same month.

Three days later the Army of the Tennessee began the movement on Corinth, thirty miles away.

When General Sherman's Fifth Division, his four pre-Shiloh brigades now consolidated into three, joined the columns snaking out of the area, Cartwright caught up to the ambulance where Jesse was seated beside the Dutchman. He glanced up into the clear blue sky and commented, "Nice morning." He pushed his kepi rakishly low over his brow as if to emphasize the fact and his rare sociable mood. "How yer doin'?" he asked Jesse.

"I'm still here," she said, smiling at him.

"Yer, I noticed that—" The surgeon allowed himself a grin of satisfaction as he rode alongside the wagon. "I noticed that right off."

If not for the burial trenches, it would have been difficult to believe that such slaughter had ever raged in this place, along fast-moving creeks and in dense woodlands, in peaceful orchards, from behind fallen tangled timbers, in muddy potholes, scarred and sunken roads, Bloody Ponds and Hornet's Nests. As for those who marched and rode in these vast columns, they could rejoice in one fact, they had "seen the elephant," and survived the first big battle in the West. *That* was no mean achievement.

For the entire month of May, marching an average of one mile per day, at a pace that would have shamed a snail, the ponderous legions of the West, artillery, commissary, medical, and headquarters, moved, or rather slithered, toward Corinth.

To a neutral witness it might have appeared that this force was not a force at all, but a sleepy giant lurching harmlessly through the warm spring countryside, stopping to smell the flowers, with no particular place to go, and all the time in the world to get there. Some said it was so slow because George Thomas and Henry Halleck were *extra* slow and *extra* cautious and they encouraged each other in their slowness.

Sherman spent most of his time teaching the still raw, though bloodied, members of his division how to survive, not only in battle, but also in the day-to-day routine of camp life. He issued lengthy papers; written "lectures" on the art of marching and drilling, showed them personally where and how to dig their sinks, downwind of the "bad air," lectured them persistently and severely against the evils of pillaging from the local civilians. "The rules are clear," ran one particular edict. "You may take fodder, hay, and firewood, but you may not take fence rails to make your fires, unless no other wood is available." However, it seemed that no other wood was ever available, since where the army marched and camped the fence rails disappeared as though by magic, went up in a puff of smoke, you might say.

One day Jesse was present as Sherman angrily lectured his men, after a group of civilians had been to see him about their behavior. The shame he felt oozed from every sweating pore, as he stood there under the burning sun with nothing more to shield his red balding head than a small kepi.

"—I will personally beat and kick any man out of a yard for merely going inside. To take a hen is as much stealing as though it had been stolen in our own country."

Very few, if any, knew what in tarnation he was ranting about. They wanted only to get out of the merciless sun into the shade of a tree where they could stretch their aching bodies and imagine themselves somewhere else, *anywhere* else except here in this hostile land with marshes and swamps and about as ornery a bunch of insects as could be found on earth. Goddamn it, these reluctant soldiers did not want to be in this scorching heat, bellowed at by a bony, sweating man with wild eyes and red hair that stood up all over his head like a hedgehog. A crazy man who told them it was wrong to steal one single scrawny chicken from the enemy. *One single scrawny chicken! From the enemy!*

Jesse worried, for his men had started to whisper once more about old Billy Sherman's sanity, or lack of it.

At the end of the long days now as Halleck's ponderous force moved sluggishly toward the Mississippi railroad junction, Jesse often rode Cartwright's horse to Sherman's headquarters and sat at his bivouac fire. At first, Captain Jackson had chased her out of camp like some unwelcome varmint, but when he saw that his commander inexplicably tolerated her presence, he left her alone. Van Allen always had a smile for her, and a kind word. Her visits gradually got longer and more frequent until she could now come and go pretty much as she pleased. Cartwright guessed where she went, but said nothing; as long as Sherman allowed her to remain, he was prepared to share her with the entire Army of the Tennessee, if that's what it took to keep her here.

Some evenings Cartwright and Jesse would eat supper together and then he would lay out the exquisitely hand-carved pieces on the small folding wooden board and proceed to instruct her on how to play chess. Immediately it was obvious that the girl was not only an excellent student of medicine but, if not checked, she would very shortly excel the teacher at the game he had loved since childhood. Between moves, he never wasted an opportunity to try and pry open the clam. That warm May evening was no exception.

"You don't talk about yourself much, do you?" The surgeon studied the board and tried to ignore the insects that buzzed around the lantern. "You yammer, all right, but not about yourself." Only four moves into tonight's challenge and Jesse had already taken the upper hand. She had just captured his white bishop with her black knight, and in retaliation Cartwright had snatched her bishop with his king's bishop's pawn. Jesse had then moved her queen's knight to bishop three. Cartwright narrowed his eyes, removed his spectacles, and blinked at her myopically. "Are you sure you haven't played this game before?"

"You ask me that question every time we play."

"Do *I really*—" he said with an indignant sniff. He put his spectacles on and rubbed his bristly chin. "Well, it just so happens that where I come from it ain't a hanging offense." The surgeon lowered his hand to his bishop and moved it to king two. Jesse moved her knight to king's knight five. The surgeon immediately pushed his pawn to king's rook three and inquired in a more conversational tone, "Which part of this vast land did you say you came from? Was it Ohio?"

"General Sherman says it doesn't matter which part of America you come from, every state is beautiful." The girl studied the surgeon's last move a moment before suggesting, "Perhaps if you took a little longer to ponder your moves, sir, you'd make fewer mistakes."

"*Ponder my moves? Ponder my moves?* You've got your nerve. I don't need *you* or anyone else to tell me how to play chess. I've been playing this game since I was six. So worry about pondering your own damn moves. Now play or resign."

Jesse lifted her knight and used it to capture the surgeon's pawn on king six. She saw his cheeks color and his firm mouth harden, but it had nothing to with her chess game.

"Good evening, Jesse," said Thomas Ransom, stepping into the firelight, "Doctor. Please forgive my intrusion."

In a second, Jesse was on her feet. She saluted and said, "Good evening, sir."

Cartwright shook his head contemptuously. The girl was still playing soldiers and very evidently it made the Vermonter uncomfortable. Tonight Ransom looked as if he'd just been scrubbed. Uniform spotlessly clean, freshly brushed and immaculately pressed, slicked down hair shining, boots shining, smooth skin freshly shaved and shining, sideburns neat, those well-bred New England features softened by a shy smile, hat in hand, the perfect gentleman, come a-calling. Self-consciously the surgeon rubbed a hand over his own stubbled chin. He'd take a shave if Jesse asked him.

"How are the chess lessons coming along?" Ransom asked the girl.

"She's got a lot to learn," the surgeon replied.

Ransom gazed down at the board, saw Jesse's knight threatening the surgeon's queen and suggested in a friendly way, "You must move your queen to bishop one, Doctor."

"When I want your advice, I'll ask for it." Cartwright moved his queen to bishop one and out of immediate danger.

Jesse countered by using her knight to capture the pawn on knight seven, saying briskly, cheerfully, "Check!"

"Thanks for nothing," Cartwright spat at Ransom.

"You're two pawns down," Jesse reminded him.

"I can *count*." He scooped the pieces into the box, a child taking back his toys because his playmates won't play according to his rules. "That's enough for tonight, we don't want to overdo a good thing, do we?"

"Last night you said you can never get enough of a good thing, but then you were winning, at least when we started." Jesse's expression was one of mock innocence.

Cartwright looked briefly at Ransom, whose smile indulged the surgeon's need to retain a vestige of dignity in the face of certain defeat at the hands of a "novice."

"It's an intriguing game," the Vermonter said, to rescue him. "Jesse told me your father taught you to play. My father loved chess also. Jesse says your father was serving as a military surgeon when he was wounded."

"Jesse says a lot about me, doesn't she?" The surgeon folded the board with a thwack.

"It's true, Doctor, Jesse does talk about you a great deal," Ransom said with a wry smile, lowering his gaze and then raising it again to meet the surgeon's resentful gaze directly. Cartwright, if only he knew, had little to resent. On those rare evenings during the slow march to Corinth when Ransom had given himself an hour off duty to visit with Jesse, the main subjects of their conversation seemed to be the doctor and Sherman. In fact, most evenings they were the *only* subjects of conversation. He came very firmly up against the same brick wall as his rival. Try as he might, as many times as he brought the conversation around to Jesse, she managed to redirect it again. He knew as much about her now as he had known the evening they had walked near Jones Field. However, he certainly knew a lot about Cartwright and Sherman.

"Dr. Cartwright's father retired from the army and went into general practice back in Quincy," Jesse said now. "I think you both lost your father around the same age."

Cartwright rounded on her. "You know your trouble, don't you, you read too many damn newspapers, you're beginning to sound like one and my father didn't retire, I told you, he was *kicked out*."

"He took early retirement," Jesse persisted. "He was wounded by a renegade Indian he was trying to treat."

"He was my damn father, not yours, so who knows best, me or you?"

Ransom looked from the girl to the surgeon and back again. They argued the way they did everything, with commitment and energy. "Well, either way," he said, "I'm sorry to have interrupted your game. I came to let Jesse know I'll be leaving in the morning."

"In the morning?" Jesse exclaimed in surprise. Then she noticed the silver eagles on his shoulder straps. The lieutenant colonel was now a full colonel. "Congratulations, sir," she said, saluting again.

"Thank you. I decided to accept General McClernand's offer." Since the Battle of Shiloh the Illinoisan political general had been after Ransom to become his chief of staff. "I'll still be the official commander of the Eleventh Illinois. McClernand's division departs in the morning." He turned to the doctor. "Perhaps you and I could play chess when next we meet?"

"Yes." Jesse looked eagerly from the Vermonter to the surgeon. "That's a wonderful idea."

Cartwright made an indecipherable noise.

"Can you stay for a cup of coffee, sir?" Jesse asked the colonel. "It's fresh."

The surgeon scowled at the girl, got to his feet, grabbed his battered kepi off the floor, swept back his thatch of untidy hair and slapped the cap over it, yanking it low over his brow. Damned if he would have a shave for her, or any other female.

"Please, Doctor, don't go on my account," Ransom said, holding his arm.

"It ain't on your account." He jerked his arm free and walked away.

Jesse looked at Ransom. "Well, sir, I'm surprised you agreed to join General McClernand," she said.

"He has the president's ear, Jesse, and he's given me his word that I'll be a brigadier general before June is out."

"You could join General Sherman's staff?" she suggested half-jokingly.

"I don't believe that would work, for several reasons. Perhaps when next we meet I'll have my first star. Would that please you, Jesse?"

"I'd be very happy for you," she said with a noncommittal tone that made the young officer say, as if he'd been churning it over in his head for some time, "At Pittsburg Landing, although I thought you a boy, when you nursed me you behaved toward me as if you were"—he turned his hat over on his hand—"well, as if you were a female—who liked me."

"I do like you, sir." Jesse laughed; again, it was disengaged, with that matter-of-fact quality, and she even shrugged, as if her liking of him was natural and not in any way special.

After a moment's silence Ransom said, "Has Sherman said anything more about sending you home?"

"Perhaps you could write to me whenever you have a moment?" She was taking her hat off the log where she and Cartwright had been seated. "I don't have anyone to write to me, all my other friends are here with me. The men get so excited when they receive a letter. I always wondered how it would feel. To get a letter."

"I'll write to you every day," the Vermonter said enthusiastically, touching her arm.

"Oh, there's no need for that, sir. You'll be far too busy with your extra duties, and I'll be too busy serving the general. Just write to me when you remember."

"You still believe he'll have you back at his headquarters?" he said, watching the way the freckles danced across her pug nose when she smiled. "Will you send me a likeness of you in a letter?"

"A likeness?"

"A photograph."

"Why?"

Ransom placed his hat on his head and grasped his gauntlets. He blinked at her and then seemed to give himself a mental shake. "I have to go," he said.

"I thought you were staying for coffee?"

"Another time."

"Another time, sir," she agreed with that easy smile, saluting. "I'll miss you."

"Will you?" he asked hopefully. "Will you really miss me, Jesse?"

"Of course I will, sir. We're friends, aren't we?"

"Yes, yes, of course, we're friends."

On the night of the twenty-ninth, blue-clad soldiers were so close to Corinth they could hear the unmistakable whistle of the locomotives, strangely eerie and disconnected in the darkness, as though a procession of ghost trains were passing in and out of the town. Bringing, it was reported by their scouts, not ghosts, but thousands of Rebel soldiers to boost Beauregard's army.

At dawn the following day, Federal soldiers were woken by a series of explosions and a pall of dense smoke rising high over the town. Sherman dispatched six of his regiments to find out what the enemy was up to.

When they moved in to investigate, they found the Rebel parapets abandoned. On May 3 Beauregard had been urging soldiers of the Confederacy to defend Corinth from the "invading despoilers of our homes," now he'd evacuated the town without so much as a skirmish. The loud explosion was discovered to be the magazine going up as the last troops had withdrawn at daybreak. It had all been an elaborate hoax to fool the Federals into believing that the army in Corinth was being reinforced, and it had worked.

Instead of moving on Mobile or directly to Vicksburg, a plan Sherman personally favored, Halleck now announced his intention to break up the magnificent forces under his command and scatter it to the four winds.

By the beginning of June, General John Pope was summoned east to command a new Federal Army of Virginia. General George Thomas was returned to the Army of the Ohio, that army being turned east along the Memphis and Charleston Road, to march for Chattanooga under General Buell.

"This army is the best we have on the continent, and it could go anywhere it pleases," Sherman bewailed when he heard. "I hold General Halleck in high esteem but by one move, he could have solved the whole Mississippi problem."

Alas, Washington had other ideas.

17

The first fluttering of its silken wings

★ ★ ★ ★

Weep not that the world changes—did it keep
A stable changeless state, 'twere cause indeed to weep.

—WILLIAM CULLEN BRYANT, "Mutation"

The quiet period enjoyed by the medical departments after the last of
the wounded and sick had been sent home was over. Jesse, along with
most of the medical staff, now spent her days bathing fevered brows, quieting fevered dreams, and carefully administering the rapidly depleting
supply of quinine.

Commanding generals were not immune to the curse of the Southern
swamplands.

By the time Sherman had moved his division together with General
Hurlburt's Fourth northward fourteen miles to Chewalla, he too was displaying symptoms of the malarial fevers that had affected so many of his
men. Halleck had ordered him to rescue anything of value from the
trains burned and partially destroyed by the Rebels during their evacuation from Corinth. The rolling stock and flat cars, six of them in all, with
about sixty carriages, had been inside Corinth during the night of the
evacuation, loaded up with commissary stores. At daylight, the Rebels

had started the trains west to find the Tuscumbia Bridge already destroyed, by their own picket guards, either in panic or mistakenly. Unable to go back to Corinth or forward to their own lines, engineers and guards had dumped the precious contents of their cars into the surrounding swamps, then hastily disabled the cars and locomotives, set them alight, and pushed them off the track before making good their escape. The result presented a strange scene.

Fermenting sugar, molasses, and flour had sunk to the bottom, and these together with a half-dozen other sundry perishables floating on the putrefying surface caused the swamp to stink to high heaven under the hot, merciless sun. Add to this the stench coming from the fetid, insect-infested marshland, and comparison was possible only with the indescribable smells of the operating tent after battle.

The sun, however, was not the only thing being called merciless. Sherman pushed the work forward relentlessly, some days in a ninety-degree heat, a heat that felled even the most robust men born and bred in the "cold-blooded" Northern climes. They took to their blankets with sunstroke, chills, and fevers and of course malaria, now turning into a full-blown epidemic.

For days, Sherman had been riding up and down the railroad lines supervising the repair of the track, no job too insignificant for him to oversee personally, no soldier too lowly in rank for him to advise and encourage, and no officer too exalted to escape his criticism. Way past dusk and sometimes into the night his unmistakable voice could be heard, giving orders.

"You there, you boys will tear your backs out before you ever move that damn thing! Get rope, men, tie rope to both ends and lash it around that tree to give you leverage!" The general was mounted on a horse before the vast area of swamplands from which sweating men were dragging a burned platform car covered with all manner of swamp life. He waved his riding crop. "Use your brains as well as your brawn. Captain Peters, why are you using men to drag those rails over the embankment when you could use ropes, sir, use ropes and swing them over! Are you an engineering officer, sir, or a wet nurse? Bring more rope!" he would shout above the din of crunching metal and creaking muscles. "You men, come around the other side, that's right, heave with all your might, put your backs into it, don't leave it for the others. Wake up there, Captain!" He would dismount, tear off his frock coat and roll up the sleeves of his blouse. "Here, here, I'll show you how! Heave! One, two, three, heave!" Sweat streamed down his red face, the palms of his hands turned raw, and his hat fell off. But he stuck it out until the locomotive was halfway up the bank, then he would remount and ride off, leaving his coat behind, to dismount again near the charred and twisted wreckage of the Tuscumbia Bridge, to push forward another hapless officer.

He would make up details of men, led by locomotive engineers, to supervise the repairs before riding off to reconnoiter the country westward for about fifty miles in order to estimate the amount of damage to the railroad as far as Grand Junction. Repeatedly Captain Jackson pleaded with him to rest, to seek shelter and a drink. The Ohioan knew only one way to lead, by example. When the men took a break and a drink *he* would take a break and a drink and not before.

While his Fifty-second Indiana, what he called his "railroad regiment," were engaged in repairing these locomotives *he* would remain in the saddle, working alongside them.

"What are you doing sneaking around outside my tent in the middle of the night like an Indian? Did you hope to take advantage of my good humor?"

"Sir, you need help," Jesse Davis told him.

"What are you talking about? I'm fine—I've never felt better in my life. I have—a note here from General Grant. You were right." One morning Jesse had waylaid him as he was on his way to visit Halleck at his headquarters tents outside Corinth and told him that Grant had asked for a thirty-day leave of absence, but actually had no intention of returning. "God knows how—but you were right," he said and knocked over the lighted candle in an effort to extract the said note from the pile of papers on his table.

Jesse ran forward, grabbed up the candle, and replaced it securely in the holder. By its flickering light she could see the sweat that trickled down his wrinkled neck and glistened in the creases around his throat.

His broad forehead and upper lip were all wet with perspiration, running into his beard. There was a look of wildness and fatigue in his eyes and they were red and unfocused, as if he were drunk, and he blinked as the sweat ran into them.

He rubbed the moisture away with a trembling hand. "Why are you staring at me?" he demanded.

Jesse was staring not at him exactly as much as at the small red bumps ranged on his neck.

"Do you wish to know what General Grant said or don't you! When I went to see General Halleck he told me, quite casually in fact, that Grant had asked for a furlough. I rode over to his camp off the Monterey Road and there he was, *packing.* I asked him where he was going. Saint Louis was his reply. He admitted that he had no reason to return. He had requested a transfer and the request was denied. Even his staff tried to get him sent to the Atlantic coast without"—he was glancing around the tent distractedly—"I must have some water—I'm thirsty," he said, licking his lips, running a shaky hand over his thatch of red hair. "Thirsty and cold—the temperature has dropped."

Jesse took the canteen from the table and watched as he greedily gulped the contents. He got unsteadily to his feet, gripped the table, and then righted himself.

"I, of course, begged him to stay. I illustrated his case by my own." He picked up the canteen and had so much trouble unfastening the stopper again that Jesse did it for him, receiving a push in the shoulder for her trouble. He took two large drinks and wiped his mouth on the back of his hand. "Mrs. Sherman thinks I'm sick, Major Sanger wrote to her that I'm sick. The lady wishes to come here and nurse me—she'll take me away again, pat me on the head like some naughty schoolboy and take me home in disgrace just as she did in Kentucky and Missouri. God help me—will I ever recover from the shame I feel from those days." He rubbed and massaged the bony knuckles of his hands and then the wrists and then rubbed the back of his neck. "My head aches—what was I saying?"

"General Grant, sir," she reminded him, "you were saying that he'd decided to stay."

"Yes, that's right. I told him that before Shiloh I'd been cast down by a mere assertion of 'crazy,' but that single battle had given me new life." His hand slipped on the table and he almost fell forward, just grabbing onto the back of his chair for support. "That single battle had given me new life—and I am in high feather . . . high feather—I argued with him that if he went away events would go right along and he would be left out, whereas if he remained, some happy accident might restore him to favor and his true place. He said he would wait awhile, promised not to leave without seeing me—now I have a note . . . from him—he's decided to remain."

"That's wonderful news, sir."

"Wonderful," he agreed, again distracted. "I wrote to him—it's wonderful news—for the country as well as for all who serve under him—" He reached out for the canteen, drained it to the last drop, the residue falling down his beard into the collar of his shirt. Jesse raised the back of her hand to his brow, and felt the burning heat before he pushed her away from him.

"You will kindly observe the proprieties between an unmarried female and a married male and remove yourself from my tent."

As he sat on the edge of his cot gripped by a paroxysm of shaking, she knelt before him, put a blanket around his shoulders, and drew it close. He stared at her from out of fever-racked eyes as she tried to quieten the involuntary movements of his body.

The tent flap was thrown back and Captain Jackson entered. "Who's there? Jesse?" His alert gaze pierced the patchy darkness. "That you, gal?"

"Yes sir."

He glanced around the tent. "There's a darn bird or sumpthin' trapped in here. Did yer hear it and there was a strange shape against the canvas, like a flappin' wing."

"It was probably my coat, sir." She showed him how the open sides hung forward, and silhouetted against the canvas wall might well be mistaken for a wing. "Would you stay with the general while I fetch Dr. Cartwright and get some more blankets?"

For the first time the aide saw Sherman lying, motionless, in the cot.

"Lord above," he exclaimed. "What in hell's going on?" He glanced at the general's uniform folded with uncharacteristic neatness on the camp stool. "Damn it, what are you doing in here?"

"The general is sick, sir."

"Hell, I know that, he's *been* sick for days. Damn it."

Seth Cartwright, trusty bag in hand, came muttering through the night, his breath bearing witness to a last-minute swallow of bust-skull, if not his rolling gait. He wasn't drunk, however, just happy. Sherman was sick. There *was* justice in the world.

"Yup, it's malaria, all right," he announced with undisguised relish, after examining the unconscious commander. "He's burning up." He laid the back of his hand across the wrinkled brow. "Throbbing headache, nausea and vomiting, cold, then sweating. Restless, the rigors, tongue like mule droppings, cramps, weakness, and lassitude. Look there." He pointed to the red bumps on the commander's neck. "He can't say I didn't warn him. He's worked those men through the hottest part of the day, then gets struck down himself. You have to admit there is a nice little irony to it. The next forty-eight hours will tell." He placed several premeasured doses of quinine powder on the small table beside the cot and closed his bag.

Jesse had nursed enough cases of malarial fever to know the routine. She could hear Jacob's instructions: "Once the timing of the patient's paroxysm is known quinine has to be given every two hours before the paroxysm, normally in five-grain doses, but in severe cases the dose may be increased to ten grains."

The surgeon spoke to Marcus Van Allen. "He's in good hands, better than he deserves. If you need a surgeon wake up his own surgeon or one of the brigade men. Me, I'm just an assistant. I shouldn't even be *touching* a major general." He grinned mischievously. "Yes indeed, you have to admit there is a nice irony to it. I might even take a drink or two to celebrate."

Jackson followed Cartwright out of the tent. "Will this quinine cure what ails him?"

"No, but it will control the symptoms. Half the army's down with it. Have you ever had malarial fever, Captain?"

"To tell the truth, Doc, I ain't had nary a chill since I joined up. I got this bad back, hurts like hell when it rains, but otherwise I'm strong as a ox. My old ma used to say all the Jackson men were strong as a ox."

"Well, Captain Jackson, it's early days yet." Cartwright wasn't going to let anything spoil his good mood.

Andy joined Marcus at the foot of Sherman's cot. Jesse was sitting on a camp stool, a bowl of water in her lap as she bathed the commander's sweating face. Both men watched for a moment as the girl turned down the blanket and began to wash his naked shoulders and chest.

"Oh Lord," Jackson said, narrowing his eyes and scratching the back of his neck. "This ain't good, Marcus, this ain't good a'tall. Come on, girl, you can't stay here, you know that."

"Why can't she stay?" Marcus wanted to know. "The general needs a nurse, and you heard what Dr. Cartwright said, he couldn't be in better hands."

"Sure he needs a nurse, so let's get one of those boys from the hospital, or one of our own orderlies, not a darn female."

Jesse stroked the wet matted hair off the general's brow, all the while speaking to him in a soft, soothing voice. She washed his arms, his hands, his wrinkled throat where the sweat ran in rivulets, and then covered him with a cool sheet and several blankets. She soaked the flannel in the cold water, squeezed out the excess, and placed it across his brow. Then she brought her Jacob-made fan from her haversack and sat there moving it back and forth a couple of inches from his face and shoulders. The two captains stood silent witnesses to these acts of devotion.

"I rest my case," Marcus whispered.

No daughter could have nursed a father more devotedly. Every hour spraying his body with cool water, sponging him down when he grew hot, drying him with a towel, blotting the sweat from his face and shoulders, covering him with a clean sheet and blankets. She administered the quinine powders when required, some opium for his restlessness and headaches, got lots of fluids down his throat, and washed him when he became uncomfortable. Jacob came to help change the undersheet and to "spell" her, but she would take no rest, trust no other to nurse him. With Captain Van Allen's "protection" she kept a constant vigil at the commander's bedside.

Cartwright, Van Allen, and Jackson stood near the entrance and listened in fascination as the girl grasped the sick man's hand to her freckled cheek.

"*Minnie?*" asked Cartwright of Marcus, with a dramatic raising and lowering of his eyebrows.

"His eldest daughter," the aide said in a quiet voice, "he appears to believe Jesse is Minnie."

"Minnie?" The general said staring up with feverish eyes as the girl lifted his head and put the tin cup to his lips. "Minnie—is that you? Have you come to nurse your sick papa?"

"Yes, Papa, I'm here, it's Minnie, come all the way from school just to take care of you. I shan't leave you until you're completely well again, I swear it."

"You are . . . a good girl—"

"Thank you, Papa. You have to take another dose of quinine, and drink lots of water. Will you do that for me, Papa?" Jesse raised his red head and held the tin cup to his dry, cracked lips.

Cartwright looked at Marcus again and then at Andy, his brows now dipped in astonishment.

"If you have no respect for the honor . . . and reputation of the generals who . . . lead the armies of your country, you should have some regard for the honor and welfare of the country itself," he said, trying to raise himself from the mattress as he stared feverishly, suspiciously, at his nurse. "Who *are you?*"

"Why, it's Minnie, sir," said the indignant, childish, wholly feminine voice, a voice that Cartwright didn't recognize as Jesse's own clipped boyish tone. "Your *daughter.*"

Two days later General Halleck issued orders not to attempt any further repairs, he said it was pointless, as soon as Sherman's men finished repairing the line the Rebels ripped them up again. Instead he was to concentrate on the rail links between Grand Junction and Memphis.

When the Fifth Division began the march to Grand Junction on June 7, the commander was forced to travel in an ambulance, and much to Captain Jackson's disapproval Marcus gave Jesse permission to stay with him. Most of the time, however, when he wasn't having snatches of conversation with his "daughter," Sherman slept, the expression of tension around his brow and mouth now fading. He looked more rested, more at peace.

By the tenth, to the dismay of all concerned, especially his "railroad regiment," the commander declared himself sufficiently recovered to be carried to the side of the road on a litter, from where he could shout orders, advice, and criticism. Jesse now kept her distance; he was no longer delirious.

So rapidly had his health improved by the end of June, that as July took its place, Sherman was able to march his own and Hurlbut's divisions from Grand Junction to Lagrange, then from Moscow and Lafayette to Holly Springs, center of all roads to and from northern Mississippi, several times, building railroad trestles and bridges, sending a detachment of two brigades to Holly Springs to protect the railroad, and to fight off Rebel cavalry detachments who dashed down out of the south. He was even fit enough to wage what he termed "everlasting quarrels" with planters over their Negroes, liberated by his officers, who used them as servants, and their fences, liberated by the enlisted men who continued to use them to build bivouac fires.

Near Wolf River, Tennessee, in late June, Jesse helped treat men wounded by Southern civilians, "*guerrillas*," who had attacked the Yankee soldiers from ambush. When the commander came to visit them in the hospital she heard him declare angrily that they were now at war with the "entire Southern populace," not merely soldier fighting soldier, army against army, but an occupying force having to fight civilians who took up arms, cowards who shot at his men and then ran home to hide behind their front doors.

"This," he declared wrathfully, standing by the cot of a handsome Federal lieutenant, shot in the eye by a musket ball fired by a citizen of the area, from his house, "is a new kind of war and I will be ready to answer it."

While at the hospital, he made a point of thanking Cartwright for the treatment he had received. "I attribute my attack to a small military cap I wore in the hot sun. I'm sorry if I took you away from others who needed you more. If it's any consolation my death would have left five children without a father."

Cartwright pushed the untidy wedge of graying black hair off his brow with one hand and blinked from behind his small round lenses. He had to admit it; the old bastard had a nice line in self-deprecating humor. He also had a natty line in headgear. If asked, it would not have been easy for Cartwright to describe what the rail-thin, grizzled, and sun-burned Ohioan looked like in his new, wide-brimmed, yellow straw hat sent down from Memphis to keep the sun off his head, but one thing was for certain, he *didn't* look like any major general.

"It was malarial fever," Cartwright said, "and it had nothing to do with your cap. It's the mosquitoes from the swamps." He wasted no opportunity to voice his theory, one that his fellow surgeons did not share. "The little red bumps you had on your neck and arms? I think they were insect bites. My guess is that's how the blood gets inflamed."

"Well, whatever it was that struck me down, Doctor, I am grateful to you and to your steward."

"Well, actually, it wasn't me who—" the surgeon's voice tailed off as Jesse, standing beside him, stamped on his foot. "I'll send you my bill," he concluded.

"Why?" he demanded of her that evening as they snatched a quick supper together; it was a balmy night and the crickets were singing fit to bust their lungs, as the moon coasted slowly across the clear Tennessee sky. On nights like this if it wasn't for the putrid smells coming off the swamps, the groaning of the sick, and the fact that he was on duty twenty-three out of every twenty-four hours, Cartwright could have given himself over to the nostalgia in his own heart. He would have pretended he was home in Quincy on the back porch, an arm around his redheaded sweetheart as they sat on the swing.

"*Proprieties,*" Jesse said, trying to free the sweet corn from the husk with her fork and impale it on the prongs. "He doesn't believe in a female nursing a man who isn't her husband or father. Mrs. Sherman was threatening to travel out here with a trunk full of holy relics that she would have waved in his face like some African witch doctor. Then she would have begged him to embrace Catholicism so that he could be given the last rites and make her happy by dying in the '*one true faith.*' "

"My *God,* that's a pretty cynical statement for someone who believes in God."

"It only *appears* cynical to you because you have no faith, no belief in anything beyond what you can see with your own eyes. Belief and faith have very little to do with holy relics. You're a surgeon, you see miracles every day, if only you'd choose to acknowledge them." She took his hands and held them palms upward. "These hands *perform* miracles every day." He lifted his hand to her smooth freckled cheek but she moved her head out of reach. "Please don't—" she said.

He leaned forward, picked up the husk and bit into the succulent yellow kernels. "See how it's done? Get the idea? For such a clever girl, you can be mighty stupid." He stared at those cushioned mobile lips a second before clearing his throat. No by God, it didn't do for a red-blooded male to let his imagination run away with him, even on such a balmy moonlit night. "Sherman ought to know how you nursed him. It might soften him up. Make my life easier."

"Knowing I nursed him would cause him great embarrassment."

No more embarrassment, Cartwright mused, than if he could see himself as others saw him, in that nifty little straw number he now wore to bully his "railroad regiment."

When newspaper vendors finally caught up with Sherman's division between Lafayette and Holly Springs at the beginning of July, the men learned that Federal gunboats had pushed rapidly down the Mississippi and taken the major seaport of Memphis, an extremely useful base for its campaigning in the heart of the South.

On the twenty-third, Sherman was at Lafayette Station when Grant and his escort arrived from Corinth. Jesse saw the small, dusty man dismount and grasp the tall Ohioan by both hands in a rare display of affection. If not for Sherman's persuasive words and support after Shiloh, the tanner's son would now be on his way to oblivion, not Memphis, where he was to have his headquarters as commander of the District of West Tennessee, and the Union would be down one general it could ill afford to lose.

On July 4, Jesse gave an impromptu concert for the sick and wounded. Her version of "Home Sweet Home" was rendered with such emotion that men of both sides wept in their cots.

Then, twelve days later, as dawn broke at Moscow, Tennessee, she found herself facing General Sherman across a desk littered with papers.

"I suppose you've already heard. I am to take over command of the District of West Tennessee from General Grant and have my headquarters in Memphis."

Yes, she'd heard that and more. McClellan was out, he would "only" command the Army of the Potomac. Halleck had been summoned to Washington. He was now general in chief of the entire U.S. forces. Halleck's command had gone back to Grant.

"From Memphis I shall be able to send you on to Nashville by the cars and thence back to wherever you came from. In the meantime"—he tossed a piece of cloth across the table at her—"wear these."

She stared at the stripes on the table.

"Take them!" Sherman bellowed.

"Thank you, sir."

"Don't thank *me*. These stripes don't make you a soldier. You won't survive a month in this army."

"Really?" She swiveled her eyes to look at him. "I've survived five months. I survived the Battle of Shiloh." Her voice rose with unrestrained pride. "If you find I cannot discharge the duties of a soldier as well anyone in your command then you can send me home."

Marcus thought Sherman, still weakened from the malaria, was about to keel over as he gripped the table, towering above the girl and bellowing into her handsome freckled face, "You may be damned certain I'll send you home before that day!"

Outside the headquarters tent, Jesse looked reflectively at the stripes lying in the palm of her hand. First, she had been a private, and then she had been a corporal, and then nothing, not even a soldier. Now she was a corporal. Well, she would sew the stripes onto her sleeves with big, loose stitches to make it easier for Captain Jackson to cut them off once more when the time came, as surely it would.

18

"All the people are now guerrillas"

★ ★ ★ ★

I told father that war is changing you, you look more lined and wrinkled than most men of 60.

—MRS. ELLEN SHERMAN to W. T. Sherman (August 1862)

To describe the Memphis Union soldiers marched into on July 21, 1862, as a ghost town was inaccurate, for to quote General Sherman, "the place was dead—*even the ghosts had fled.*"

Shops were shuttered, businesses, churches, and schools closed, many houses stood empty and neglected, the occupants departing at the first sight of the blue-clad troops after Farragut's victory. Those residents that remained defiantly flew the Stars and Bars from their rooftops.

This old Mississippi River town had been in Union hands but six weeks and seen three military commanders. The last of them, U. S. Grant, had found it easier to close down the city than to run it. Never a beacon of virtue, what little propriety remained had been undermined to the dislocation of civil war, leaving drunkards, prostitutes, and robbers to rule the nighttime streets, while the decent folk stayed in their parlors and prayed for the "cause."

However, just one week later, Sherman had his new regime firmly in place.

For a man who had served as a quartermaster, worked as a bank manager, a streetcar president, the superintendent of a military academy, and sometime (in his own estimation) unsuccessful lawyer, administration was second nature. If anyone could shake this sluggish flea-bit old hound into life, he could! And, by God, he did!

While his three brigades encamped in and near Fort Pickering, and Hurlbut's division spread out along the riverbank, the new military governor made his own bivouac in tents in a vacant lot near the house of a Mr. Moon. From there he gave his undivided attention to the pressing matters of civil affairs, and the drill and general discipline of the two divisions now under his command. Also the continuing construction of Fort Pickering, to which end he daily took Negroes from their masters to supplement his work force, for which they were paid a small wage and their meals, while other Negroes were employed as teamsters or cooks and hospital orderlies.

Amidst an avalanche of paperwork, pointing out the rules of his jurisdiction, Sherman set the mayor and his municipal bodies back to running the civil government. He reorganized the city police and gave the streets back to civilians unable to walk them unmolested since the Rebel army fled in early June.

The provost marshals' duty was limited to guarding public property held or claimed by the United States and arresting soldiers who were absent without leave or disorderly, and they were kept mighty busy, since every other commercial enterprise on Beale Street was a "grog shop," and that which did not sell booze sold sex.

Surgeons now treated the diseases of passion, not the wounds of war. Cartwright gave it to them straight, but he didn't preach. The men didn't listen anyway. They took their pleasure, paid the penalty, and expected the doctors to deliver relief, not sermons. Most Yankee soldiers agreed they'd rather die from a dose of the clap than lying in the dirt with a Reb bullet in their back. Whoring and boozing had been as much a part of the soldier's life as marching and fighting since Roman times. Sherman was broad-minded. If he disapproved of drunkenness in his own extended family, he did not impose those restraints on his men.

Steamboats had been idle too long; once more they carried trade northward, their decks crammed with bales of "White Gold," their holds groaning with tobacco and whiskey, their shrill emotive whistles rending the air as they passed down the mighty Mississippi. The morally righteous expressed outrage, of course, at the same time as they counted their profits. But most agreed that the city had never been so prosperous, so well policed, since the days of their illustrious founders. Stores, shops, and eating establishments, theaters and churches and schools were open for business.

General Sherman had brought a dead community back to life, even the ghosts were grateful.

As for Jesse, while she waited for Sherman to take her back into his army family, she worked at the hospital and indulged her favorite new pastime of poker. For some reason she could not understand, Thomas Ransom had sent her ten dollars to have her likeness done, so she dragged Jacob and Cartwright to the photographer's studio and all three posed on a long couch with a potted plant. It cost only two dollars, which left her with a nice little stake she had quickly trebled in three consecutive nights of gambling. She had returned the ten dollars to Ransom with interest, in the same envelope as the photograph.

Then at the beginning of August, the summons that Cartwright had been dreading finally came. An eager-beaver lieutenant instructed Jesse: "General Sherman says to pack all your personal belongings and bring them with you."

There weren't many personal belongings to pack. The change of underclothes Sherman had given her, the small wooden cross Jacob had carved for her, letters from Thomas Ransom that she used as bookmarks.

Jesse emerged from the tent still lacing her brogues. "It's all right, sir," she told Cartwright. "My fate will be not be decided here on earth."

"It's not your fate I'm worried about, goddamn it, it's *mine*." He helped to put the strap of her knapsack over her head and across her shoulder lest wounded or sick be found on the short journey to headquarters. He wedged her hat down over her thick red curls, and it might very well have been the morning mists but he looked as if his eyes were watering. "Who's gonna supply my whiskey and tobacco?" His hands were shaking.

He stood with Jacob as officer and prisoner rode away and observed hopefully, "She doesn't *look* like a victim going to the firing squad."

"No, Doctor," Jacob agreed, "but *you* do."

Cartwright stood outside Sherman's office at the Gayoso Hotel kicking his heels. It was a bad morning to be summoned. He'd been up most of the night drinking cheap whiskey in the company of several lively females and he didn't like being jostled by the usual pack of men in blue and excitable civilians, crowded into the narrow corridor. He lifted bleary eyes to Jesse's face as she greeted him. It was three weeks since she'd been taken away. That's how Cartwright thought of it. Taken away. Now he said, "Still washing Sherman's socks?"

"At least he changes his socks every day."

There the exchange ended, for Miss Sarah-Anne Taylor was coming down the corridor toward them. Utterly committed and hardworking, this young woman had arrived South from her home in Springfield, Illinois, to teach school to the Negroes living in the community they had built on the riverbank and named "Happy Valley." Whenever the modest Miss Taylor encountered the bespectacled surgeon, what could only be described as a kind of softening of her features took place, as though her face was melting like a block of ice in the hot midday sun. It was melting right now.

"Dr. Cartwright."

"Miss Taylor." Cartwright was always polite, if his usual amused, rueful self.

"So busy here, isn't it, sir? General Sherman has so *many* visitors."

"He's an important man." Cartwright's rueful smile spread until it became downright twisted.

"Well, yes, he is, but not as important as you, Doctor." Miss Taylor laid a gloved hand briefly on the surgeon's arm. "We must have generals to win our battles for us, but when the smoke has cleared, who is responsible for the wounded? You medical men are the *real* heroes."

"Why thank you, Miss Taylor."

Miss Taylor's lovely face flushed and stayed flushed even after Cartwright had been ushered into Sherman's office. She looked at Jesse, fanned herself rather too energetically with some papers she was carrying, and rushed away.

No one could have accused the Ohioan of reclining in kingly splendor while his men suffered in canvas shelters. Grant had ruled the city from the recently renovated Hunt-Phelan home on Beale Street, convenient for a man who liked a drink and a game of cards. His predecessors, both Federal *and* Rebel, had directed operations from this same hotel, an ugly brick building pretending to be imitation marble, with those large white columns so beloved of the Southern architect, and situated near the lower part of the city, fronting the river. In fact, the view of the Mississippi from the window was just about the only thing that could distract the Ohioan from his duties.

Right now, his tousled red head could be glimpsed behind piles of papers, letter books, order books, and just about every other kind of book. His shirt was already damp with sweat, an ash-stained vest hung open over his narrow chest, and his dusty frock coat was draped across the back of his chair and trailing on the floor. As usual, the length of satin ribbon that passed as a necktie was halfway to the back of his head. It was barely 9:00 A.M. and the room was blue with cigar smoke. Three orderlies stood beside his desk in a pose of absolute alertness. They dare not be otherwise. No one slept around William T. Sherman. Colonel Hammond was swiftly gathering his papers from the floor while a civilian with an unmistakably disgruntled air was being shown the door by Captain Jackson. Hammond said good morning to Cartwright and left, with the distracted air of a man who had a six-day job and three days in which to do it. Sherman, by some trick of eye or ear that Cartwright could not figure out, managed to speak to all three orderlies, write all three sealed orders, followed by detailed verbal instructions, toss some final sardonic barb at the departing civilian, locate a letter he needed to consult, greet the surgeon, gesture him to a chair, and smoke his cigar, all at the same time.

"That was Dr. Cook, Sanitary Commission. *Civilian.*" He made the word sound like the basest of insults. "Come from the North to carry off all our sick. Protested when I said no. I told him, protest away, my answer will still be the same." He halted this monologue only to answer a query from Colonel Hammond, whose head appeared and disappeared so quickly Cartwright got dizzy. "I told Cook, you hold me up to the people of Ohio as a monster because I won't let you carry off our sick." How did he do that, how did he pick up the thread at precisely the place he had let it drop? "What *do you* say, Dr. Cartwright?"

He would have said much, after all this was his subject, he covered sheets of paper with his thoughts, theories, and experiences, but a lieutenant and two more orderlies interrupted and by the time they'd gone he had lost his train of thought, derailed somewhere between a lost commissary report and a short-lived burst of anger against an article in a Memphis newspaper of which Sherman did not approve.

"Sit down, sir, sit down. You know Dr. Derby, the civilian chief at Overton Hospital."

"Well . . . yes . . . I know of him . . . yes . . . I know . . . of him—" Goddamn it, he was starting to repeat himself. He needed a drink.

"Cook's requested that I forcibly vacate the Female Academy on Vance Street and allow him the property for another civilian hospital. The Sisters of Mercy have only just advertised for more scholars to join their academy and I could not easily have found it in my heart to insist upon the forcible removal of these pious ladies and their young charges."

Cartwright narrowed his myopic gaze and stared at the red-bearded man in the ash-stained vest and the crooked tie-bow, as if he were trying to understand something. And he was. Did Sherman actually *care* that those nuns and their prissy little pupils might lose their property? Was it so difficult to accept that this fast-talking, hard-faced old bastard, who always looked slightly mad, might have a small glimmer of humanity buried somewhere inside that pockmarked exterior? His soldiers certainly liked and respected him; his staff was devoted to him. Jesse was devoted to him. Her devotion had been made *very* tangible during Sherman's bout with malaria.

"Is that why you had me ride over here? To discuss nuns and sanitary inspectors?"

"No, that is not why I had you ride over here." Sherman's hoarse voice had lost the conversational tone and was becoming edgy. "Before leaving Pittsburg Landing, Dr. Fitzjohn wrote to the medical director strongly recommending that you take his place as regimental surgeon."

Cartwright, already halfway to the door, swung around and said, "What?"

"You heard me, sir."

"You're joking, right?"

Sherman pushed a form across the desk. "The appointment has been confirmed by the Surgeon-General's Office at Washington, approved by myself and General Grant. I wanted to tell you personally. Congratulations, Dr. Cartwright, you are now a full surgeon and a major."

In August, General John Pope led his newly designated Army of Virginia to a defeat in the battle of Second Bull Run. His army had been disbanded and he was banished to Minnesota to put down the Sioux revolt. McClellan now had full command of the eastern armies. The news upset Sherman, bringing back memories of the first Union rout. The faith that he had lately been feeling in his government, the army, and the men that led it was once more melting away.

Mrs. Sherman's faith, however, was stronger than ever. Her last letter had castigated her husband for attending the city's leading Episcopal church, which she took as a personal slight to her Papist faith, and for suffering her the ignominy of reading about it in the newspapers. "General Burnside has become a Catholic," she wrote peevishly, "why can't you?" All Memphis was still talking about how Sherman had jumped up during a service, and ordered the priest *not* to omit the prayer for the legally elected president, as he'd done on previous occasions. "In future you will speak a blessing for President Abe Lincoln or I will close the church. Is that perfectly clear, sir?" he had warned.

Jeff Davis had authorized a second conscription act, upping the age group. There was also the contentious matter of the substitute. Any wealthy Southern gentleman could pay another to fight in place of himself and his sons so that they might espouse "the cause" from the safety and comfort of their plantation, while looking with pride upon their human property. Jesse had already heard captured Southern soldiers calling it a "a rich man's war, a poor man's fight."

The slavery issue was far more complex, at least for a man fighting not for abolition, but for his nation.

In August '61 and July '62, two Confiscation Acts had been passed freeing slaves used in employment against the United States or owned by anyone who supported the rebellion. The first act had come into being after Ben Butler had seized Negroes coming across his lines in Virginia and coined a new phrase, "contraband of war." Butler had argued that they were captured enemy property, since they had been forced to help keep the Rebels' military machine working smoothly. Now Congress had gone further, declaring any slaves captured or escaping from any person "in armed rebellion or abetting it" could be seized by military commanders, retained by the army, and were "forever free of their servitude and could not again be held as Slaves."

"Are we to free *all* Negroes?" Sherman demanded to know, speaking as if to himself, though Jesse sat across the desk listening. "Men, women, and children? Whether there be work for them or not? We have no District Court in Memphis and none of the machinery to put in motion the Confiscation Act. No army could take care of the wants of niggers, women, and children that would hang about if freed without the condition attached of earning their food and clothing. Instead of helping us, it would be an encumbrance. I have appropriated the labor of Negroes as far as will benefit the army." He drummed his fingers on the table and looked at the girl watching him with profound fascination. "Some system of labor must be devised in connection with these slaves, else the whole system fails. Congress may command 'Slaves shall be free,' but to make them free, and see that they are not converted into thieves, idlers, or worse is a difficult problem and will require much machinery to carry out." He stood up, went through the untidy pile of maps on a side table as if searching for something, then apparently gave up and went to the window to stare out at the night sky, puffing loudly on his cigar. After a moment he said, "When my time comes I'll be buried alongside the Mississippi. At Saint Louis, where I can watch the muddy old waters flow by."

In the sudden melancholy silence Jesse allowed her gaze to wander over the loose pages scattered across the desk, pages covered with Sherman's scrawling hand. The more he wrote the more illegible became his handwriting. This particular letter was addressed to his "Dear Little Minnie" and was a passionate outpouring from a tortured soul pleading that she know him, remember him as a man who did not want to make war on his own countrymen.

"Come look at this view and tell me your youthful heart isn't stirred by its power and majesty."

Jesse went to the window and stared out at the river lit up by the transports moored there in the darkness. Her eyes had grown tears, not for the river, but for the man. She had several times accompanied him on a ride down the river three miles but been unable to share his excitement, or his enthusiasm. To her the Mississippi always seemed dark, even in daylight, impenetrable and fathomless, and strangely uninspiring considering the mix of emotions this muddy expanse stirred up in Sherman. The loneliness of this "Father of Rivers" overwhelmed her, made her feel not exhilarated, but inexplicably sad. But because he loved it so, she said, "It's beautiful."

Here from the window of the Gayoso with the lights and the buildings and the river craft moored up along the banks it was perhaps easier to lie.

"They think I'm heartless, the do-gooders," Sherman was saying. "That I treat the niggers worse than the planters ever did. But I know better than they do."

Jesse looked up at him. He had regained none of the weight lost during his battle with malaria, he still looked thin and gaunt, but his incredible, inspiring energy had retained its full potency, as could be witnessed by the transformation his regime had brought about in Memphis. Now as he declaimed on the subject of the Negro, the compulsive movements of the bony hands and large head, the constant pacing, the apparent searching for papers that could not be found, would convince any Sherman watcher that three months in one place was enough for this restless man. He had risen to and more than met the challenge. It was time to move on.

"Dr. Cartwright employs some of the Negroes in his hospital, sir, he gives them clothing and shoes from dead soldiers and feeds them from the hospital commissary," she told him. "He says they'll never perform anything more than menial tasks, but some are very kind and gentle with the sick men."

"You and Cartwright enjoy a mutual admiration." Sherman went back to the desk and sat down. "It's all right," he added, misinterpreting her uncertainty, as she returned to sit and face him. "I understand the need for young people to form such bonds, even in war. Was the photograph for him? He's very fortunate to have found someone of your intelligence and compassion. Though to be sure you're no great beauty." He lowered his gaze as he said this, as if uncomfortable with what he knew to be clearly untrue. Certainly with her youthful body and strong features she was boyish now, and uncommonly handsome, but one day she would blossom into a beautiful woman. "If Cartwright had any sense," Sherman said, moving papers on the desk, "which he ain't, he'd marry you right now and send you home to his mother. But I fear you're too headstrong for him, like a young colt champing against the bit. What are you staring at? You forget I was young once and could be stirred by flowing ringlets. You too think me the heartless monster I'm painted in the Northern newspapers because I won't embrace the nigger as a brother and won't let the malingering soldiers go home."

"No sir," she said softly, "—I think you a man and a soldier struggling to do what is right for his country, his honor, and his conscience."

Cartwright drained his glass and kicked Jesse's leg under the table. They were together in their favorite dining place, and, as always, Jesse had paid for the supper and the pitcher of cool beer.

"Your *greatest* admirer," Cartwright mimicked.

"It's just a polite soldier phrase," Jesse said. She'd just read him Thomas Ransom's latest missive. "He always signs off that way. It means nothing."

"A polite soldier phrase?" Cartwright laughed. "Either you're as stupid as you look or I'm way out of touch with how lovesick men write to the object of their desires these days."

"What do you mean?" She stared at him as he pushed his chair back.

"Let's take a walk. It's getting too crowded in here."

They meandered silently along, each alone with their own thoughts, staring at the splintered sidewalk. The surgeon had been stunned by the casualty figures from Antietam. Before receiving a brief letter from Jack Coopersmith, assuring him of his well-being, he'd been a man beset by demons, but twenty-six thousand other Americans were not so lucky. The newspapers were calling this last clash between McClellan and Lee in Maryland in early September the bloodiest single day in U.S. history.

"Why didn't you tell me Sir Ransom was a general now? I had to hear it from Jacob."

Jesse looked surprised. "I didn't think you'd be interested."

In a previous letter, the Vermonter had written her:

Do not forget to search for my name among the commanders who have "proved their mettle," for I have left the best news 'til last—I am to be made a Brigadier General!! At last, I shall have my first star. I have received a despatch from Lieutenant Howlett, Second Illinois Cavalry, now at Washington, stating that he saw in the lists that I was appointed on the tenth. I am not officially told but there is nothing to prevent you from sending a note of congratulations to your greatest admirer.

Cartwright leaned on the upright at the edge of the sidewalk. He was looking at her from under the broken visor of his squashed kepi.

"Besides it hasn't yet been confirmed. Senator Washburn spoke on his behalf, urging his appointment as a brigadier general at a private interview in the House but the number of brigadiers for the state of Illinois was already too many."

Cartwright feigned indignation. "That's the last time *I* vote Republican."

"I don't understand why you're so angry. You refused your promotion. Colonel Ransom has been commanding a brigade for two months, so has the responsibility without the rank or the salary. Do you think that's fair, Doctor?"

"Where is he these days, Richmond?"

"Fort Donelson. He's been all over—Paducah, Kentucky; Cairo, Illinois."

Cartwright was staring at her with that funny stare, the aggrieved stare, the one that managed to combine reproach with scorn and defiance, and a pinch of melancholy longing.

"Good evening, Dr. Cartwright," said a quiet voice.

It was the diminutive Miss Taylor.

" 'Evening." Cartwright forced himself to be polite. It wasn't the sweet-natured Miss Taylor's fault that he felt the way he did about that other maddening female.

"Oh, Doctor, is it not wonderful, news of the Emancipation Proclamation?"

On September 22 Mr. Lincoln had issued the first or "preliminary" Proclamation of Emancipation. The papers said he had been waiting for a victory to tell the country and had taken the Antietam "success" as the right time to issue it. "Have you read those stirring words? 'That on the 1st day of January, A.D. 1863, all persons held as slaves within any State or designated part of a State the people whereof shall then be in rebellion against the United States shall be then, thenceforward and forever free—' " An attractive pink flush had risen high in Miss Taylor's smooth cheeks, owing as much to Seth Cartwright's nearness as Mr. Lincoln's proclamation.

"Why, Miss Taylor, you've already memorized the words," the surgeon said, with gentle but mocking admiration.

"I could recount the entire proclamation, sir, for it is truly a noble and blessed document. 'I do order and declare that all persons held as slaves are, and henceforward shall be free—free—free—' " Sarah Taylor intoned in ecstasy. "Now the entire world will see that our blessed Union is fighting a civil war not for states' rights but to end the oppression of Negroes."

Jesse felt compelled to speak up. "President Lincoln and General Sherman have both said this war is being fought to preserve the Union, not to free the slaves. Though the slaves must be freed, General Sherman says this proclamation is a purely military expediency."

The paragon ignored the corporal and took from her purse a card-bound volume entitled *Uncle Tom's Cabin*, which she gave to the surgeon. "I was hoping to see you, sir, I have here the book I promised to loan you. If you read the introduction, by Mrs. Stowe herself, you will see that she believes she has an apostolic mission to put an end to slavery once and for all time." Miss Taylor's eyes were shining as though with an interior light.

"Thank you, Miss Taylor, I'll be sure and take good care of the book."

"Oh, I know you will, sir, and perhaps when you have finished reading, when your sacred duties do not have first claim on your time, we can discuss the contents over tea and cherry cake. I am no slouch at baking, sir, if I say so myself." Her cheeks went from pink to a rosy shade and her smile, though shy, was meaningful.

"Nice girl," the surgeon said on her departure, "but sadly deluded. That proclamation isn't worth the paper it's printed on. Does Lincoln really believe the states in rebellion are going to take any damn notice of his 'proclamation.' It proclaims freedom for slaves in precisely those areas where the United States *can't* make its authority effective and conveniently omits to free them precisely where he has the most authority. Your President Lincoln is either very clever or very stupid."

"You ought to accept Miss Taylor's invitation for tea and cherry cake."

Cartwright gave her that stare. "If I decide to accept Miss Taylor's invitation I won't need your approval."

"All I meant was that Miss Taylor would make a nice companion for you."

"A nice companion for me? You just don't get it, do you? You haven't got a goddamn clue. Those letters from . . . *your greatest admirer* . . . they're not letters from a friend, and that photograph you sent him, he wanted one of you, Jesse, something to gaze at and dream about on a cold, lonely night, not one of me and Jacob. He's in love with you, it's written all over his face when he looks at you. What's the matter?" he demanded because her expression was one of horror, as she grabbed hold of the upright for support.

"You're . . . wrong . . . ," she stammered.

"No, I'm not, I'm not wrong—and you wanna know how I can be so damn certain? Because when I gaze at you I have that same helpless longing in my eyes, that same confused, bemused hangdog look." He grabbed her by the shoulders and shook her until tears started down her cheeks. "And do you know what makes it so much worse—so much more difficult to bear?" He swung her around until she was forced to see her distorted reflection in the store window. "Look at yourself, Jesse, look at your face, you don't look like a young woman who has just found out that two good men would give their lives to make you happy, you look god-damn terrified."

The hot, sultry days and steamy nights of summer were gone. In their place were cold days and even colder nights. Now ice lay on the ground when company cooks lit the breakfast fires at reveille and enlisted men stirred, shivering and reluctant, from their warm blankets. Some said it looked like snow, but though Jesse stared hopefully into the lowering sky, the snow that it looked like never came.

In the east, November had started as badly as possible for the Army of the Potomac. By order of the president, McClellan had again lost his army, this time to General Burnside, who said he didn't want it.

Meanwhile the equally inept General Nathaniel Banks, so confused by Stonewall in the Valley, had replaced General Butler, following charges of cruelty, speculation, and dishonesty, during his reign over New Orleans.

As for Sherman, he could look at his record and be content in knowing that his tenure as military governor at Memphis had been a success. He had itchy feet. He'd fought courageously against the Northern profiteers who'd taken advantage of the war by flocking into Memphis to buy up cheap cotton from Southerners for gold, which they used to buy arms in the British colonies to fight the *very* people who were protecting these speculators and preserving their nation.

Then, one rain-filled, blustery cold morning in mid-November, Jesse watched as the general mounted his new mare, Dolly, a deceptively benign name for a horse with a prickly temperament, and rode down to the river landing accompanied by Major Sanger, Colonel Hammond, and Captain Jackson, to meet up with Grant at Columbus, Kentucky, to discuss their next campaign.

Five long days later, just before midnight, Sherman returned in a torrential downpour. Without pausing to remove his wet clothes or wipe the mud from his face, the general spoke to his assembled staff. Impatiently tossing back his soaking-wet half-cape, he jabbed at the map with the two bony fingers that held his cigar.

"Gentlemen—it's time. We are going for Vicksburg, to open navigation of the Mississippi." He paused to stare at the eager, intense faces ranged before him

There was a loud and generalized murmur of approval, this was the exciting news that Sherman's officers and men had been waiting to hear for months.

"General Grant feels that the way forward is for us to use the plan that has worked so far," Sherman continued, shadows from the lamp playing in the crevices of his gaunt cheeks as the rain beat its loud tattoo upon the canvas above their heads. "The plan that began with the capture of forts Donelson and Henry and won us the Battle of Shiloh, and then gave us Corinth—an advance in land, parallel to the river, flanking all river defenses but well removed from them. I'm sure none of us need reminding that although there was a naval battle for this city, Memphis finally fell because a large Federal force was in its rear. General Grant will move south from Grand Junction, along the line of the Mississippi Central Railroad." Sherman used his finger to trace Grant's proposed route on his map, spread out on the table before them, La Grange, Holly Springs, Wyatt, Abbeville, Grenada, Canton, and finally Jackson, where his finger remained, obliterating the name as he said, "Our ultimate goal, if we want to capture Vicksburg and break the enemy's blockade of the river, must be the Mississippi capital, Jackson, forty-five miles due east of Vicksburg, the railroad hub for the area. If we can take Jackson we will have control of the Mississippi Southern Railroad." His finger left Jackson and followed the railroad line. "Leading directly into Vicksburg, and Vicksburg's only contact with the rest of the Confederacy. We'll be able to get supplies to our own men and stop supplies to the enemy. We move when I hear from General Grant."

"Do we know when that will be, sir?" asked Major Van Allen.

"Right now General Grant is massing his troops at Grand Junction, halfway between here and Corinth and along the Mississippi Central Railroad. He has General McPherson with two divisions and General Hamilton with three."

When everyone had filed out into the stormy night Sherman turned to see Jesse standing in the shadows, watching him with a burning, almost feverish devotion. He unfastened the buttons on his field coat and allowed her to take the coat and the oilskin off his shoulders. Though lines of fatigue had etched themselves deeply into his cheeks and around his firm mouth, his eyes were no less alert than if he had just enjoyed a long night's sleep, and he acted with a decisiveness that belied the long, arduous journey he had just completed. He said not a word. Jesse hung his coat over the chair back before going out into the rain.

When she returned, she was sopping wet. Her jacket bore dark patches, the brim of her battered slouch hat sagged, and her handsome face glistened with water. Sherman tore his gaze away from the map to look at the coffee miraculously appeared on his table by the lantern, and then at the girl.

"Don't you have an oilskin?" He peered more closely at her. "Were you *sick* while I was away?" his hoarse voice demanded to know. "Your eyes are overbright. See Dr. Cartwright." He returned to his map, rubbed a hand up and down his coarse beard, across his thatch of hair, then ran a finger down the river that he loved so well. Perhaps in death his spirit would protect the mighty Mississippi that he sought so determinedly to guard in life.

"I'm not sick, sir, I missed you so terribly while you were gone, and now you are returned, that causes my eyes to shine."

A growl somewhere deep in his throat greeted this ardent declaration. "You have mud on your face," she said.

He rubbed the back of his hand across his gaunt cheek. "I have mud on my trousers and mud on my boots. Mississippi mud. Look out there at that river, nothing like it exists anywhere on this continent, anywhere in the world. There." He struck the map with his balled fist. "The enemy still holds the river from Vicksburg to Baton Rouge, navigating it with his boats, and the possession of it enables him to connect communications and routes of supply, east and west. To deprive him of this would be a severe blow, and if done effectively, will be of great advantage to us, and will probably prove the most decisive act of the war. The Rebels won't allow us to take Vicksburg without a battle, without terrible cost to ourselves and to them." Then, staring at her face, his expression seemed to say, we can no longer ignore reality. "You know what this means? Hard fighting and hard marching, in conditions not fit for man nor beast."

He indicated the entrance beyond which the slanting torrent was turning the ground to a sticky, slippery mire as the wind howled around the canvas.

"Without rest, perhaps for months. Come closer." He was calculating swiftly in his head. "You look at least . . . eight months older than when you first insinuated yourself on me at Pittsburg Landing. For *eight* months, you have been allowed free rein like a colt before he is broken to the bridle. Well, now it's over. I cannot take you with me on such an expedition. I'll give General Hurlbut instructions to ship you back North. If you won't say where you come from, you'll be sent to a workhouse or orphanage. My decision is final, so tell young Cartwright to save his breath. He can gaze fondly upon the photo you gave him and let that be comfort enough on cold nights. Pack your belongings and take leave of your friends in this army and your gambling cronies." Sherman's red head remained stubbornly bowed over the rivers, roads, fields, bridges, and railroads across which he would soon be leading his divisions.

"I have no intention of going home," Jesse said in a balanced but decisive voice. "I will remain beside you until the end, until your work is done."

Sherman looked up. All was silence, except for the sound of the rain, the loud spattering on canvas, and the howling wind. The tent was almost in darkness, the lamp throwing its yellow light over the map, and his grimly furrowed face seemed only to add to the otherworldly atmosphere. His cigar glowed between fingers that were shaking with exhaustion.

Suddenly his brief contemplation was interrupted by a loud crash of thunder, which rolled across the heavens, ending in a whip-strike of lightning that turned night to day beyond the tent flaps, illuminating the girl's solemn young features. For an instant, no more than the blink of an eye, the open sides of her sack jacket, catching a sudden gust of wind, stood out and fluttered, like wings. A shiver passed down Sherman's spine. The last time this vision had appeared, it was at Chewalla, when, so debilitated with malarial fever, he could barely separate fact from illusion. He had regarded it then as the product of his delirium and he dismissed it now as fantastical, superstitious claptrap. Tired eyes played tricks on a man so nearly spent.

Nevertheless, it occurred to him, and he laughed that halting laughter to show he refused to take it seriously, that nature—the heavens, the gods, the Almighty—was displeased with his decision and making it known.

19

Like a pack of hungry wolves

★ ★ ★ ★

See what a lot of land these fellows hold, of which Vicksburg is the key. . . . Let us get Vicksburg and all that country is ours. The war can never be brought to a close until that key is in our pocket.

—PRESIDENT ABRAHAM LINCOLN, 1862

Vicksburg! Vicksburg! Vicksburg!—was all Jesse heard for the next couple of weeks. What it was, why it could not be taken so easily, and why it *had* to be taken.

Admiral Farragut had tried that very year to take it, after capturing New Orleans. He had secured the river for the Federals as far north as Baton Rouge, and then proceeded up the Mississippi, unopposed to Vicksburg. After bombarding the citadel through June and July with gunboats and mortars, he abandoned the attempt and returned to New Orleans and the Gulf declaring, "Vicksburg will never be taken from the river. Ships cannot crawl up hills three hundred feet high."

"The Gibraltar of Dixie" was how many people referred to it, not that Jesse knew what or where Gibraltar was, until Sherman showed her on his Colton's *Atlas*. Gibraltar was situated off the south coast of Spain, built on and around a big rock, in fact, Gibraltar *was* a big rock, and Vicksburg was the same, a city stronghold dominating the vital waterway of the Mississippi.

It sat on top of a high bluff, overlooking the mighty river at a hairpin bend, where the Yazoo River drained into it, and was protected by artillery batteries along the riverfront, its wharves and docks down by the water's edge, its streets climbing to the plateau above, giving an unrivaled field of defensive fire, making it impossible to assail from the river. That wasn't all, to the rear, the city was protected by a maze of bayous north and south, and by a ring of heavily manned forts whose guns guarded all land approaches.

Right now Vicksburg shut off the Mississippi to Northern navigation. Any Yankee ship attempting to get past these riverfront batteries could easily be picked off, especially when heading north against a four-knot current. Vicksburg and the river it commanded also linked the two halves of the Confederacy, on the east Mississippi and Tennessee, the Carolinas, Georgia, Virginia, and Alabama, and on the west Arkansas, Louisiana, and Texas. If Vicksburg could be overcome, and their guns, to the landward side and those facing across the river, silenced, this would cut off the Confederate States west of the Mississippi; they could never again reinforce their comrades in the east. If then the Federals could add Port Hudson, another Rebel strongpoint guarding the river about twenty-five miles north of Baton Rouge, to their successes, they would then have the entire Mississippi, could travel up and down the river, just as they pleased, unhindered, moving troops and supplies and equipment, with control of all the main crossing points.

In late November, Sherman heard from Grant that the first phase of the campaign had been completed. He had captured Holly Springs and set up his supply and ammunition depot. He now wanted Sherman to meet him at his temporary headquarters in the university town of Oxford, Mississippi, to discuss the next leg.

Corporal Jesse Davis was in Sherman's party as they left Memphis on a rainy morning in early December with three small divisions totaling eighteen thousand men. They reached the little town of Wyatt, where the Mississippi Central Railroad crossed the Tallahatchie River, to find the enemy had burned the bridge since Grant had used it. But Sherman had brought along boats.

When the anticipated Rebel resistance did not materialize, he sent his cavalry on to Grant and spent the next couple of days at Wyatt, using the houses of the locals to build a new bridge.

The morning of their departure Jesse watched as the residents of Wyatt whose barns and smokehouses had gone into the construction of the bridge gathered to protest.

Sherman sat atop his impatient mount, a cigar wedged into the left-hand corner of his mouth, turning his animal in an erratic circle so he could face each one, as he told the protesters in his loud, surging voice, "You allowed the Rebel soldiers to burn the bridge that was once here, so I have given you a fine new one. Take damn good care of it, and do not force me to build you another. If you seek compensation for the old bridge, see Jeff Davis!" With that he galloped across this fine new bridge, the clatter of his horse's hooves echoing in the villagers' ears long after he had disappeared into the woods beyond.

Jesse, remembering the young Rebel at Pittsburg Landing, waved her hat in the air and shouted "Yahoo!" at the top of her lungs, as she urged her horse across in the commander's wake. Behind her, so little remained of the town it was from that day on known as Wyatt Bridge.

In the big house Grant was using as a headquarters Jesse, feeling somewhat less boisterous now, curled up on one of the armchairs in front of a roaring fire, and listened to Sherman, Grant himself, and their young protégé, the newly promoted major general James B. McPherson, discussing the next stage of Grant's plan, now slightly amended to accommodate a new enemy, and this one wasn't in gray. John McClernand, Jesse learned, yawning with delicious indulgence, as the warmth penetrated her always cold feet, was planning a naval and army expedition moving from Memphis down the Mississippi to take Vicksburg. She remembered well the Illinois congressman–turned–general, friend of the president, clinging to Sherman's coattails on the second day of Shiloh. Grant had no details of this expedition. He knew only that McClernand was in Springfield, Illinois, recruiting as far as Ohio. Henry Halleck, their overall commander in Washington, was proving, uncharacteristically, to be a Grant ally. He was sending fresh troops to Sherman in Memphis, and had told Grant he had permission to fight the enemy any way he pleased. In other words, Grant had a free hand. As for the Rebel troops in Mississippi, as far as Grant knew, they were down around Grenada, under John Pemberton, a Pennsylvanian, married to a Southern girl, and as loyal to Jeff Davis and the rebellion as any died-in-the-wool, fire-eating Secesh.

"Sherman, I want you to hurry back to Memphis, leaving me two of the divisions you have with you, and assemble the troops Halleck is sending us, along with a further force awaiting you at Helena, Arkansas. Then with that wing of my army I want you to steam up the Yazoo River where it enters the Mississippi, just above Vicksburg, with a gunboat escort provided by Rear Admiral Porter, find a suitable place to disembark your troops, and attack Vicksburg from the north. I believe I can get as far as Grenada. Then if I can keep Pemberton occupied, you can overcome the Rebel garrison at Vicksburg. If all goes well, Sherman, we can trap the Rebels at Vicksburg between two armies. No Rebel force could hope to defend the city from both attacks at the same time. But, Sherman, we must hurry, I want you off from Memphis before McClernand arrives." The tanner's son became suddenly animated. "Sherman, I know you understand that if there is to be a move downriver from Memphis, I want *you* to lead it, not McClernand."

At dawn the following day, Sherman had an unexpected visitor. Major Van Allen showed the tall, lean, handsome officer into the front room of the house, where the Ohioan was still studying the map.

"Colonel Ransom, come in, sir, come in. I heard you had asked to be transferred from McClernand back to a field command in General McPherson's corps?"

"Yes sir. In the past few months I have served as inspector general and chief of staff, commanded the post at Cairo, Illinois, and then at Paducah, Kentucky. Unfortunately, my association with General McClernand did not work out as I had hoped. I now command a regiment in General McArthur's Sixth Division, which is encamped just outside town."

"I see you *still* haven't yet got your star? Too bad. Grant told me he'd given you to McArthur with the understanding that you'd get a brigade."

"General McArthur says he wishes to give me a brigade, sir, but that all the colonels commanding brigades rank me. He is, however, expecting some new brigades and he then intends to give me one of those."

"I hope so. You deserve a brigade."

"Thank you, sir. The president and secretary of war appear to know of my case. I understood that the secretary seemed to think I was already nominated, but when he checked at the adjutant general's office he found out this wasn't so. I'm told that nothing much can be done now before Congress convenes."

"Well, sir, you appear to have all your flanks covered. Grant referred to your Garrettsburg skirmish earlier this month as 'a great success.' He called you an excellent officer. At Riggins Hill I heard you netted sixteen dead Rebels, forty wounded, and sixty captured, occupied Clarksville for twenty-four hours, and seized a whole parcel of government property. It was the second time you'd struck Woodward's guerrilla command in Kentucky, wasn't it?"

"Yes sir."

"Well, what can I do for you?"

"Sir, I come to you on a personal matter. Do you recall her—the young lady who was—with you at Pittsburg Landing—and after, at Memphis, Miss Davis? I was wondering if the young lady had left a forwarding address on her departure."

Sherman's naturally fierce expression softened a little, and his eyes even showed some amusement. Now he came to think of it, the rustling of paper that had been as a backdrop to his thoughts as he drank his morning coffee had ceased in the last few minutes. He seemed very much to enjoy removing the stub of his cigar, jabbing it toward the large chesterfield, and saying, "Jesse Davis hasn't departed, sir, you'll find her behind that sofa, rolling up the maps." He then got to his feet. "Excuse me. I'm starting back to Memphis this morning." And left the room, slamming the door behind him.

Ransom walked to the chesterfield, peered over the top, and stared down at the young girl on the carpet surrounded by map cases, who was staring right back up at him.

"General Ransom," she said and saluted from the kneeling position.

"Jesse, are you hiding from me?"

"No sir."

"Surely you heard me come into the room and speak."

"I didn't want to embarrass you, sir."

"Lying is unworthy of you, Jesse. Why didn't you answer my last letters? I thought you had gone back North and I'd never see you again. It's been nearly seven months. A long time. I've missed you."

"I have to go, sir." She stood up. "You heard the general, we're returning to Memphis."

As she walked by, he gripped her arm. "Why do my feelings for you cause you such distress?" he asked, with a deep frown, his intense blue eyes holding hers. "Why did you return that ten dollars I sent for you to spend on yourself?"

When she said nothing, he released her.

Outside, Jesse and the rest of the party were already mounted. The Vermonter went straight toward her. He reached inside his tunic and brought out a bunch of violets tied around a slender volume. He stood beside her horse, glanced around him to make certain no one was watching, and pressed them into the girl's unwilling hands.

"I intend to get your address from Sherman and post this to you."

Before Jesse could say anything, Sherman's horse was beside her. His bony hand swooped down with all the alacrity of a hawk, snatching the package and putting the flowers to his beak of a nose, his hard, grizzled features softening a fleeting moment before he asked, "Do you know how to press them in a sheet of paper between the pages of a book so they last as long as you do?" He glared at Ransom. "And you, sir, need not look so astonished. You're another one who thinks I was *born* old and crusty?" he stated with a pained, defensive sadness. "Well, think again, sir. I once had as many romantic notions as the next man—and probably far more than you have!" He grinned maliciously and rode off, leaving only his hiccuping laughter to mock the Vermonter's indignant expression.

Jesse pushed the volume of poetry and the flowers at Ransom's chest and galloped after the general.

Four days later Sherman, designated commander Right Wing, Thirteenth Army Corps, was back in Memphis. While the troops characterized by Grant as one wing of his army were loaded onto the transports, the Ohioan met with David Dixon Porter. Since Sherman did not stand on ceremony, he served his visitor, a thickset individual with crinkly, laughing eyes in a face half concealed by a full beard, refreshment in a tin cup, apologizing for the lack of civilized amenities as he did so.

"Not a bit of it, Sherman," said the bluff seaman. "I can drink whiskey out of my hat if I have to."

This set the tone of the friendship, army and navy hit it off immediately, conversing as if they'd known each other for years.

The men who lined the docks in readiness for embarkation on that clear bright winter morning had never seen anything like this grand sight. Sherman had worked miracles to bring about this hurried departure. Bullying quartermasters into stealing mules and horses from civilians, and seizing every vessel they could get their hands on, including coal barges and their cargo. Columns of lively infantry, rumbling artillery and caissons, mounted cavalrymen, marched, rolled, and trotted up the swaying gangplanks onto every conceivable kind of water transport, from ironclads to gunboats, along with commissary wagons loaded with provisions. Filled with confidence Sherman's boys were calling this movement "the castor oil expedition" since many believed "it would go straight through the rebellion and bring a speedy result."

Sherman too was excited; this was to be his first independent command.

By the nineteenth all Sherman's Memphis troops were embarked, seven thousand of his single division brought back from Oxford, plus two more divisions made up of fresh recruits from Halleck and McClernand's recruits. For not only was Sherman departing before McClernand's arrival, he was taking with him those troops the politician-soldier had sent down from Ohio for his own use.

Those transports leaving Memphis rendezvoused with the transports sent to pick up the extra eleven thousand troops from Helena, and on December 25, the expedition had reached Milliken's Bend, a long curving stretch of the river twenty miles above Vicksburg. While one brigade was sent off to cut the Vicksburg, Shreveport, and Texas railroad on the Louisiana side of the river, others were free to celebrate Christmas Day.

After a fine lunch, invited officers of army and navy adjourned to the stateroom of Porter's flagship *Black Hawk*, where Jesse sang carols to the gentle accompaniment of an upright piano wheeled in for the occasion. For a few hours at least, these men, filled with esprit de corps, courtesy of Porter's strong punch, could forget that war and all its accompanying miseries were waiting beyond these creaking timbers to engulf them.

By the following morning, they were at the mouth of the Yazoo River, where it drains into the Mississippi five miles just north of Vicksburg. Sherman went out looking for a suitable place from which his troops could assault the enemy. Judging by the way Jesse's horse sank into the mud every time he tried to get past a slow trot as she followed the commander on his quest, there wasn't much to choose from.

However, two days later, his troops were disembarked on what could only have been described as a swamp, or as Sherman himself described it, "Mississippi alluvion," an island four miles wide and twelve miles long, bounded on the south by the strongly flowing Mississippi. Along the eastern side of this island was Chickasaw Bayou and, rising above that, Sherman's immediate objective, Chickasaw Bluffs. If his infantry could survive the barrier of trees, felled by the enemy, a levee in the form of a parapet, artillery, and marksmen, they would then reach the bluffs themselves, defended by more Rebels, well protected behind their gun emplacements. The assault would be uphill all the way, his men exposed to pitiless, enfilading crossfire from batteries and rifle pits that commanded every inch of this hazardous terrain. The weather didn't help much either. It rained almost constantly.

Sherman and Grant had arranged to coordinate their attacks, but there was no sign from Grant that he was ready. As the Ohioan told Porter, "Grant would never let me down, unless dead or taken prisoner, but if I delay any longer we will lose any chance that we still have for surprise."

At noon the following day, the twenty-ninth, Sherman gave that signal and the main attack began.

By late evening, wild-eyed and breathless, the Ohioan was back on board the *Black Hawk*, soaked through to the bone and covered in mud, where Porter was awaiting him.

"The assault was a disaster. I've lost seventeen hundred men—" Sherman declared.

"Bear up, Sherman," answered the admiral, taking him to the warmth of his stateroom and sending Jesse for rum from his steward. "Seventeen hundred is simply an episode in the war! You'll lose seventeen *thousand* before this war is over and think nothing of it. We'll have Vicksburg yet, before we die. Drink your rum and we'll see what needs to be done."

The wounded and the dead lay scattered among the trees and bushes, while those who were able dragged themselves to the place where they had started, and awaited the medical orderlies and surgeons who now moved among them in biting, icy rain. Others, too badly injured to extricate themselves, lay half-buried in the mud, the thick brown waters of the Yazoo oozing into their open wounds as they cried for help, their cries sounding louder and more pitiful than ever in the rainy night.

Men of the Sixth Missouri, who had managed to cross the bayou and been pinned down beneath the steep bank, had used their bare hands to scoop out holes in the earth to shield themselves; now enemy soldiers were holding their muskets outside of the parapets in a vertical position and firing down directly upon their heads. Southern farm boys using their countrymen instead of squirrels for target practice.

Jesse on the deck of the *Black Hawk* listened to the cries of the wounded and heard the occasional shot ring out, a crack, a brief flash that illuminated the darkness, followed immediately by a cry of surprise and pain, then silence. Dr. Cartwright and Jacob were out there somewhere, moving about in the mists, tending the wounded, comforting the dying. How could she sleep?

As dawn broke on January 1, 1863, celebrating New Year was the last thing on anyone's mind. Overnight, the mists had turned to a fog that had settled thick and impenetrable on the river. It was still raining, a cold icy rain that seemed to penetrate to the very bone, leaving the men on the riverbanks shivering and cursing as they waited to hear if they would be facing the enemy, as well as the elements, that day.

Sherman, as always unwilling to trust to subordinates, rode out personally to reconnoiter the situation. He was glad that he had, for immediately he saw that the trees lining the banks bore watermarks ten feet above his head. His conclusion was unavoidable. If they remained there, his entire army risked being swallowed up and drowned. The second attack was postponed.

By midnight, hospital ships had hastily gathered in all their sick and wounded, their staff, and their tents. Stores, artillery, and troops were once more herded onto the boats. As Jesse brought a dejected Sherman a mug of coffee laced with rum they could both hear the whistle of enemy troop trains bringing reinforcements into Vicksburg. Reports had been coming to Sherman all that day of battalions of uniformed men marching up toward the Rebel fortifications at Synder's Bluff, a dozen miles up the Yazoo, and into Yazoo City forty-five miles away. Jesse looked at Sherman's drawn features, the bony nose over the forbidding mouth, the haunted look in the eyes, and the hands that shook ever so slightly. Clearly, Grant had not kept Pemberton busy. Something had gone badly wrong.

As the *Forest Queen* steamed slowly away from the half-drowned valley of the Yazoo the following morning, the dead from the assault of the twenty-ninth buried along the shifting riverbanks, bayous, and channels were already sinking into the mud, along with their crude wooden headboards. Soon nothing would remain.

For Sherman matters were about to get worse.

On January 2 the steamboat *Tigress* came down from Memphis to the mouth of the Yazoo River to Sherman's headquarters at Young's Point, Louisiana. Onboard was Major General John McClernand, and with him he carried an order from Abraham Lincoln to take over the Ohioan's command.

McClernand's first act was to divide the Thirteenth Corps into two, renaming it the "Army of the Mississippi," which the politician himself would lead. He then gave Sherman more bad news. Grant wouldn't be coming up to join them. There would be no movement on Vicksburg in the near future, he announced with relish, at least by Grant. On December 20 Earl Van Dorn's men had raided Grant's enormous supply depot at Holly Springs, rampaging through the town and destroying what they could not carry away. There had been sufficient troops to defend the place but they had surrendered without a fight. Grant had lost fifteen hundred men as prisoners and a million dollars in foodstuffs, munitions, and forage. He'd tried to warn Sherman through General Dodge at Corinth, but Nathan Bedford Forrest, raiding in western Tennessee, had cut the telegraph lines.

Grant's army, without supplies or a supply line, had been immobilized. He was unable to keep Pemberton busy at Grenada, and consequently Pemberton had been able to send reinforcements to Vicksburg to meet Sherman's attack at Chickasaw.

Sherman issued a message to be read to his men:

A new commander is here to lead you—I know that all good officers and soldiers will give him the same hearty support and cheerful obedience they have hitherto given me. There are honors enough in reserve for all and work enough too. Let each do his appropriate part, and our nation must in the end emerge from this dire conflict purified and ennobled by the fires which now test its strength and purity.

"Why do you stare at me that way?" he demanded of Jesse, as she waited by his desk to take the message to his clerks for copying. "Do you suppose I enjoy having a man like McClernand as my superior? But if I believe in anything, I believe in the right of our government to *govern*! If I abide merely by the decisions I think equitable and right and *rebel* against those I deem to be unjust and wrongheaded I shall be no better than those traitors in Richmond who seek to destroy our nation."

A week later, on January 9, Porter's ironclads demolished Fort Hindman, also known as Arkansas Post, fifty miles up the Arkansas River, while Sherman's infantry attacked from the land side. It wasn't Vicksburg, but it was something to boost the men's morale and McClernand, who had remained safely onboard the *Tigress*, made the most of it to a pack of toadying reporters scribbling down his every self-serving word.

As the old year died, so did more Americans, this time at Stone's River, a mile north of Murfreesboro, Tennessee, where Rosecran's blue-clad army had met Bragg's gray forces at dawn of December 31. Despite achieving an apparent tactical victory in the first stages of the battle, by the third day of January, Bragg had unexpectedly withdrawn his forces toward Tullahoma.

Though Negroes and abolitionists celebrated freedom on New Year's Eve, not even the "glory of his *Emancipation Proclamation*," or the sight of free Negroes and former slaves testifying, lamented a New York newspaper, had eased Abe's suffering. Peace Democrats were calling for an armistice and a repeal of the Proclamation while soldiers from Ohio, Michigan, Iowa, and especially Indiana and Illinois were threatening to desert, angry at being ordered to fight and die *just* to free niggers.

As for the news from the east. "The Army of the Potomac, is still at Fredericksburg, and so am I," Jack Coppersmith had written Seth Cartwright, "encamped on the northern bank of the frozen Rappahannock in thick snow, fighting battles on behalf of my patients, against scurvy, typhoid, dysentery, diphtheria and pneumonia, and oh yes, homesickness," for which, Cartwright's best friend had written him, "there was but one cure—*home*."

Meanwhile, back in his camp on the narrow levee, at Young's Point, five miles from Vicksburg on the Louisiana side of the Mississippi, where the Rebel guns could not reach them, Sherman was, according to the *New York World*, "subject to fits of insanity, hates reporters, and foams at the mouth when he sees them, sure signs of a deep seated mania." He was also, stated several newspapers, about to court-martial a reporter. That part was true.

Since the regular arrival of the newspapers, the Ohioan had given himself over to a depressed state of mind. Jesse watched him pace in his tent, smoking one cigar after another, while everyone else slept. It seemed inconceivable to her and to his staff that following the courage and strong leadership he had displayed at Shiloh and the hard work and dedication he had invested in his role as military governor of Memphis, he should once again find himself the victim of an insulting and vicious press campaign to discredit his command abilities and slander his reputation. Just how many times did a man have to prove himself?

The volatile and sensitive Sherman was threatening to retire before he was forced to join the miserable ranks of McClellan, Buell, McDowell, and Burnside, in his words "all killed by the press."

However, Jesse was not overconcerned, for this was a different Sherman from the man who had sunk into dangerous melancholy in those early dark days. This was a far stronger Sherman, and though he had suffered badly from the failure at Chickasaw, he had come through and knew his value to Grant. He knew also that he occupied a significant position in an army of brave veterans.

There was something to celebrate. On January 18, despite McClernand's confident assertion that Grant would not be coming up to join them, he appeared. He immediately assumed overall command, dividing the "Mississippi Army" into three corps. Sherman got the Fifteenth Corps. McClernand got the Thirteenth, and McPherson, the Seventeenth.

As the first glimmerings of spring appeared on the banks of the Mississippi, the Ohioan decided against resigning. Instead, he settled for that court-martial.

Thomas Knox, of the *New York Herald*, a civilian reporter, stood before a military court accused of revealing information to the enemy, of being a spy, and of disobeying Sherman's order barring reporters from the Chickasaw Expedition. Knox admitted that the article he had written about Sherman was "malicious and based upon false information received from parties interested in defaming Sherman and his command" and that he had "brought up the old story of Sherman's insanity merely for the purpose of gratifying personal revenge." He further confessed, "Of course, General Sherman, I had no feeling against you personally, but you are regarded as the enemy of our set, and we must in self-defense write you down."

After four days of deliberation, the board acquitted the reporter of the first two charges, but found him guilty of the third. He was expelled from the lines of the Army of the Tennessee and would be arrested if he ever returned. Colleagues from two other New York newspapers pleaded Knox's cause with Mr. Lincoln, who agreed to revoke the banishment if Grant agreed. Grant would agree only if Sherman consented. Sherman would not consent.

As Jesse sat in the rear of "the courtroom," in reality a large tent, and listened, the affair shook her hitherto unshakable faith in "Honest Abe's" integrity. If such a great and good man was prepared to bow to the influence of the press, what chance was there for lesser mortals?

As for Sherman, he felt that he had won a major victory over these "sneaking, croaking scoundrels" but still he felt cheated, he had wanted Knox put in front of a firing squad and shot as a spy.

One thing was certain: All toadying reporters of *every* shade of yellow would now think twice before they ever again "wrote him down," whether in self-defense or otherwise!

As for Sherman's first independent command, no one could have been as brutally frank as he was. "I reached Vicksburg at the appointed time," he had written Ellen, "landed, assaulted, and failed. I assume all responsibility and attach fault to no one—"

During February and March there followed a series of frustrating and abortive attempts at diverting the course of the Father of Rivers, searching for passages through clogged inlets, cutting levees that overflowed, trying to redirect lakes that did not wish to be redirected, while his men grew sick and ragged. A pure waste of human labor was how Sherman described it.

The men of Sherman's beloved Fifteenth Corps, in their flood-plagued camps, were dying by the hundreds, falling victim to dysentery, diarrhea, typhoid, malaria, and various fevers. That wasn't all. Cart-wright told Jesse that homesickness was so prevalent there in the mud and the swamps, where they shared their blankets with snakes and frogs and crawfish, that men were literally losing the will to survive. Those that succumbed to disease or melancholy were buried on the levees, the only dry land deep enough for graves, and even then, after a particularly persistent rainstorm, arms and heads could be seen protruding from the mud, and headboards simply washed away.

Grant was not immune to the muttering of his unhappy men, and he read the newspapers, who wrote that he was holding onto his command by the skin of his teeth. He was getting desperate.

In mid-March, he and Porter came up with a new idea. With five ironclads and three tugs the admiral was to go up the Yazoo River to Steele's Bayou, and after traversing a series of waterways he would reen-ter the Yazoo on solid ground far above Haines Bluff.

However, the Rebels sniffed out these plans and Porter sent an elo-quent plea to his friend via a Negro: "Help! We are trapped."

Sherman threw himself and his men into the admiral's rescue with his usual frenetic energy. He'd received the message on the evening of the nineteenth; by midnight he had loaded three small regiments on a trans-port, reached firm ground and disembarked his men. If not for Sherman, Porter and his boats would have been in enemy hands.

For Jesse it was a breathless, candlelit adventure through flooded bay-ous, snake-infested swamps and thick mud, in heavy rain, beneath a pitch-black night to rescue the general's desperate but profoundly grate-ful friend.

For Grant it was yet another of his schemes that had come to noth-ing. His army was still on the wrong side of the river.

Finally, with the press and his enemies in the North urged on by the constantly intriguing McClernand, a disheartened nation, where volunteering for military service had all but ceased, and an election-bruised president badly in need of a victory to celebrate, Grant was forced to make a momentous decision.

Besides, there was another piece of intelligence to consider. Joseph E. Johnston, a general that both Sherman and Grant respected, was now in overall command of the Rebel troops in Mississippi and Tennessee.

When Sherman returned to his headquarters that evening from Grant's headquarters onboard the *Magnolia* he was spitting nails.

"Grant wants Porter to run the Vicksburg batteries!" he exploded, rummaging around in his footlocker for a bottle of whiskey he had there. Before every item in the locker had been thrown into the air, Jesse took over the search and finally located the bottle. She poured him a full glass, half of which he downed before he continued. "He says he will then use those transports, if indeed any remained afloat after the Rebels have finished bombarding the flotilla, to pick up his army, which would meanwhile have marched down the Louisiana side of the Mississippi." He moved to the map spread out on his table, and jabbed at the river, which separated them from their adversary. "Then the army will embark on Porter's ships and he will cross them over to the Mississippi side at Grand Gulf, twenty-five miles below Vicksburg at the mouth of Big Black River. From there he will march inland and attack Vicksburg from the rear, in other words from the landward side."

Jesse studied the map for a moment. "Why can't we just cross to the other side and march toward Vicksburg?"

Her question brought forth a torrent of sarcasm. "Because, *General* Davis, there is an obstacle in the way, a small obstacle, called the Mississippi River. Have you been sleep-walking during our time here? Do you propose our men swim across? It's a mile wide. Do you know what the ground is like west of the river? Exactly like it is here only more so. Directly to the north," he pointed on the map, "is the vast Yazoo Delta, impassable to any large body of troops. Swampy, cut up with watercourses. Too wet for men to march and not deep enough to float a ship. You saw what happened to the men and horses. The locals say this is one of the wettest seasons they can recall. That makes the bayous and swamps protecting Vicksburg all the more impregnable. The army cannot march and it cannot cross the river without transports and we have no transports below Vicksburg."

"Then why can't Admiral Porter's gunboats and mortar boats bombard the enemy artillery overlooking the river? Admiral Farragut tried it."

"Yes, and failed, and no one would call him a coward and a slouch! We can bombard Vicksburg from the river 'til kingdom come but it doesn't mean a damn if the army cannot land along the waterfront and take the city by storm. Have you any idea the level of casualties there would be if we ordered a river assault with troops coming ashore on the town's waterfront, escalading the bluffs and storming the enemy's positions? From the west, the riverfront, Vicksburg is impregnable. But Grant is now *determined* to risk Porter's entire flotilla and Porter, being the brave and loyal man he is, even knowing the terrible risks, will comply, I know it." He started to pace, his loud sighs punctuating his words. "I do not favor the scheme at all, not at all. It is hazardous in the extreme. I fear it is one of the most dangerous moves of the war. I *must* talk Grant out of it."

Jesse, perhaps unwisely, persisted. "If the army cannot march and it cannot cross the river without transports, and we have no transports below Vicksburg, then surely General Grant's idea to move the transports to a place where the men can embark and cross is a good one?"

Sherman walked to the opening and stared out at the rain. "If I can't persuade Grant against this insanity, I'll resign," he stated as if Jesse hadn't spoken. "I'll quit and go where no one has heard of me."

Jesse joined him at the tent fly and asked reasonably, "May I know if you intend to go to a hot climate or a cold one?"

"What the hell difference does that make?" Sherman slanted his eyes to stare at her as if he would eat her alive.

She shivered against the damp. "I need to know whether or not to pack my flannel underclothes."

The first anniversary of Shiloh, a battle charged forever with meaning for those who had fought it in early April of '61, came and went. Sherman chose to mark the somber occasion by giving Jesse the compass he had bought for himself on his way up to West Point in his seventeenth year.

"What is it?" she asked examining the watchlike object with letters.

"What is it? What is it? Why you ignorant wretch. It's for telling direction. Now you'll never again lose your way."

As for Grant's decision to run the gauntlet of Vicksburg's batteries, despite Sherman's four-page letter arguing articulately and passionately against it, his mind was made up. Even the straight-talking Porter could not persuade him otherwise. "You must understand," he told Grant, "that once my ships pass the batteries, assuming they do, they will be past the point of no return. If we try to come back upstream my vessels' progress against the current will be so slow that the batteries will pound my transports to firewood and sink my ironclads."

Even though Sherman thought the plan sheer madness, he would, as always, do everything in his power to ensure the success of the plan.

If Grant lost the fleet and his army, McClernand would be back in command. Then Sherman would certainly, ". . . quit, and go to Saint Louis."

20

In mud that's many fathoms deep

★ ★ ★ ★

Grant is honest and does his best. I will do as ordered.

—GENERAL W. T. SHERMAN to Senator John Sherman, April 3, 1863

On the night of April 16, under a cloudless sky, unfortunately bright with stars, Admiral David Dixon Porter, aboard his flagship *Benton*, steamed out into the darkness to lead off the flotilla of eleven vessels from the mouth of the Yazoo, across the dark, murky surface of the Mississippi. Except for the dim signal lights, hooded to prevent them from being spotted by the Rebels along the eastern shoreline, all vessels moved under blackout conditions.

They proceeded in single file at fifty-yard intervals into the first stretch of the mile-wide river, whose bend would swing them south, beyond which the giant bluff itself, holding the city aloft, disdainful in its apparent invincibility, rose up beneath the moonless heavens.

Federal soldiers, straining to see the flotilla's progress from their camps at Milliken's Bend on the Louisiana side of the river, held their breath in frustration, for they could see nothing but the lights of Vicksburg itself, slowly snuffed out, one by one, as the residents went to their beds, unaware of what was unfolding below.

While the author of this daring drama waited aboard the *Magnolia* with Mrs. Grant and their two sons, who were visiting, Sherman had given himself a more practical and active role. Practical and realistic as ever, "anticipating a scene," as he explained to his protesting staff, he had ordered four large rowing boats hauled across the swamp to the river below Vicksburg. He had manned them with strong, willing sailors and struck off, with the intention of picking up any survivors from the disabled wrecks that he expected to be floating by, as soon as the Rebels realized what was happening. Positioning himself and the boats in the center of the straight stretch of the river below Vicksburg, Sherman waited.

Jesse waited too. With Sherman's warning still echoing in her ears, that dire consequences would result from her attempt to follow him, she had bribed one of Porter's young ratings. Two dollars and a penny whistle had got her the loan of his naval jacket and a cap. A cap into which she had crammed every telltale red hair and pulled it so far down over her reddish brows that here on the surface of the dark water she could hardly see a darn thing. But with the cap pulled down and the coat collar pulled up there was no chance that even the eagle-eyed Sherman would spot her manning a pair of oars in his brave little flotilla.

No matter how dire the consequences, she would not have missed being at Sherman's side for this adventure, or at the least in one of his boats.

An hour went by as they sat there in self-imposed silence, muffled up against the cold, with nothing much to see, but plenty to think about as they stared into the blackness of the invisible shore. Then a low buzzing of voices started up, a rumor that the flagship *Benton*, with Porter onboard, leading the seven armored gunboats with coal barges lashed to their sides and three army transports loaded with supplies instead of soldiers, their boilers protected by water-soaked bales of hay, had cleared the mouth of the Yazoo.

"They're passing Young's Point!" announced someone in another boat, but was quickly silenced by his companions. How could he know? They couldn't see a hand in front of their face.

Then Jesse, like her companions, watched in open-mouthed awe as a massive shadow seemed to drift out of the night and come slowly down-river toward them around the hairpin bend that led past Vicksburg's dark, impenetrable bluffs.

It *was* the *Benton*, and everyone cheered, at least in their hearts, for even a murmur now might alert the Rebels manning the cannons on the riverfront. Then secrecy no longer mattered. As the *Benton* reached the first of the batteries, all hell broke loose.

A dazzling light suddenly illuminated the scene, followed by muzzle-flashing thunder and lightning. The sailor in front of Jesse shouted excit-edly that Vicksburg itself was on fire and his companions took up the call. But they were wrong, it was not the city that had set the riverbanks ablaze, back-lighting Porter's ships for Rebel cannoneers, but vigilant enemy pickets who had torched the abandoned De Soto railroad station midway up the point, and set fire to prepared tar barrels and pitch-soaked wood, turning black-night into bright day, as soon as they saw Porter's ship and realized what the Yankees planned to do.

Sherman had been right to anticipate a scene, and what a scene!

Jesse heard the dreaded heavy artillery pieces of Vicksburg's mighty defenses open up on targets lit up by the flames now leaping along the riverfront. The houses on both sides were engulfed in fire that threw its lurid colors across the water, making it seem as if the river itself were ablaze. Smoke billowed from ship and shore, flames leapt into the night sky, obliterating the stars while Rebel cannons sent out a deafening boom-boom.

There was an advantage however: Now with all pretense of secrecy stripped away, Porter's ships could defend themselves, and Jesse joined in the cheers as the admiral's vessels answered the Rebel broadsides by sending cannonades of their own into the city, the gunboats returning fire as they passed, trying to protect the transports desperately hugging the Louisiana shoreline. The noise was so deafening, as Rebel shot and shell rattled against the ironclads like hailstones, that many of the sailors in Sherman's little convoy were forced to put their hands over their ears. But no one could drag their eyes from this fearful yet exciting scene as the *Lafayette*, with the captured Rebel ship *General Price* lashed to her starboard side, was penetrated by artillery fire. Jesse tried to count the hits on the *Price*, but lost count at ten when the *Lafayette* and *Louisville* became tangled in midstream, escaping destruction only through the courageous actions of the sailors aboard who cut loose the attached coal barges, setting both vessels free.

Next to feel the wrath of the enemy's guns was the transport *Henry Clay*, set ablaze by cannon fire that knocked out her engines. The transport appeared to stagger, bringing full-throated cheers from the Rebel gunners on the Vicksburg heights.

As the now unmanageable steamer ran erratically past the gauntlet of Rebel artillery pandemonium broke out on her decks, a blinding flash, as though a bolt of lightning had struck the vast river, was instantly followed by an explosion that blinded those in the nearest rowboats. Jesse averted her gaze and, when she could look again, the *Henry Clay* was a blazing inferno, engulfed in swirls of black smoke.

The bowels of hell could not have been more hot and fierce, more deafening with fury and thunder, or more shrouded with choking, sulfurous clouds.

Sherman now ordered his boats to row toward the stricken *Clay* as members of her crew, some of them with their clothing on fire, jumped overboard. Some found a piece of flotsam to cling to, and floated downstream, others were picked up by the nearest of Sherman's rowing boats.

As Jesse's boat got closer she readied herself to help haul in the survivors, but one particular survivor, struggling desperately to maintain his slipping hold on a small piece of wood, caught her attention and all but drove the breath from her lungs.

It was Seth Cartwright.

In the next second, Jesse discarded her heavy jacket and hat and went over the side of the boat. With her breath snatched from her throat by the shock of the cold water, she struck out with strong strokes toward the dark-haired figure. She reached him just as his fingers had slipped from the splintered wood. He had gone under. She dived down and held him about the waist, breaking through the surface with his head so he could quickly gasp for air. But why did the surgeon seem so heavy? She grabbed another hunk of deck as it floated by, urging Cartwright to hold on with all his strength. Then she dived once more beneath the surface.

She saw immediately what was wrong. His father's medical bag was tied to one end of a length of rope, while the other end was tied around his waist. The bag was a dead weight, an anchor dragging him down. She fumbled with the knot, her fingers stiff from the cold, finally untying it. She rejoined him on the surface.

The sailors in the nearest rowboat had spotted them and were heading in their direction.

She saw Sherman stand up in the yawl, tear off his shapeless hat, and heard his hoarse voice shouting, "Jesse Davis?" with unmistakable shock, straining for a better look at the two heads bobbing about in the water. "Hang on, hang on, Sherman is here! Sherman is coming! Have courage, we are coming for you."

She was so close to the burning ship, that even in the water she could feel the heat of the flames searing her skin, singeing her eyebrows. She heard Sherman shout to his oarsmen, "Take us in as close as you can! Take us in closer. Closer!" as he crouched in the boat and leaned out so far that these exhausted men, muscles straining to obey Sherman's orders, feared he would fall in, held fast to his field coat. "Jesse, reach out for my hand? Can you stretch out to me? Try, you must try!"

"I can't sir—if I lose the float—we will both—go under." She was fighting to keep from swallowing the water that swept repeatedly over her head. "The doctor can't swim, sir, and he's been injured." Saying this she took in a mouthful of the river and choked, coughing until her face was red.

"Jesse!" Sherman bellowed.

"I'm all right," she shouted, gulping for air, "you must take up the doctor first. He's near unconscious."

With water washing over the blood from cuts to his forehead and cheeks, spectacles gone, Cartwright barely had the strength to grasp the hands stretched out to him. "My bag—" he said with failing breath, "—my bag—"

"I have it, sir—I have your bag," Jesse reassured him as the soldiers finally hauled him into the boat, where he lay, still mumbling about his bag.

As Jesse jettisoned the wooden float, willing hands, above all Sherman's, grabbed at her waterlogged clothing. The water rose in a sudden swell and completely covered the top of her head. She was choking. Her lungs were bursting. Her eyes were on fire. She was floating downstream, and away from Sherman's boat. She struggled to get back, to swim against the current, but her arms and legs were aching and would no longer obey her commands. Some of the men were rowing toward her, while others reached out to her, their fingertips touching hers, Sherman's arms stretching the farthest. But it was useless, Jesse's strength and fortitude had finally given out. The last thing she saw as she disappeared beneath the churning swell was the look of horrified disbelief on Sherman's face. She heard him, as if in a dream, shout her name and tried to respond, but her voice had been silenced. All was a watery darkness. She closed her eyes and felt a strange kind of peace.

To the whimsical among the sailors, it might have seemed as if the mighty Mississippi had tried to swallow the boy. Then disgusted with such a scrawny catch had spit him out along with an old black leather bag that hung from a length of rope around his waist, for that boy rose from the depths of the river as though hurled to the surface by an unseen hand.

Now when several pairs of strong arms reached out, Jesse found herself lifted to safety and a blanket placed around her shoulders.

Her first concern was for the doctor, but he looked comfortable enough with a folded blanket beneath his head and one to cover him. They had come well prepared.

Even with the muddy waters of the Mississippi still flowing from her ears, Jesse had little trouble hearing a voice bellow, "Jesse Davis, you are in grave trouble!"

"Sir!" she cried in breathless alarm, ignoring Sherman's warning as water dripped into her eyes. She was holding up the end of the rope that had held Cartwright's medical case. "The bag—where is the doctor's bag?"

"I got it here, lad," said the sailor who had cut the rope.

"Thank you. Thank you—" she told him. "You don't know how much it means to him."

"Does it mean more to him than a young lad's life?" he asked, handing over the surgeon's heritage with a rueful smile and a shake of his venerable head.

His beard and face all coated in gunpowder, his eyebrows scorched, his bloodshot eyes encircled in soot, Sherman boarded the *Benton* to be greeted by an exuberant but weary admiral. He struck the sailor on the back with a force that would have felled a less robust man.

"Do you have many injured?"

"A few cuts and some broken bones, there's been a deal of damage from what I can see, but only the *Henry Clay* lost. But, bravo, Sherman, I saw what you and your men did, sir, I saw what you did. You were magnificent!"

"One of my surgeons was injured doing his duty. Can we bring him aboard?"

"Not dead, I hope, Sherman?"

"He was breathing last time I looked."

A litter was lowered over the side and doctor *and* bag were strapped to the canvas and passed up carefully by the sailors who had rescued them. Jesse checked his pulse, wiped his wet, bloodied face with the corner of the blanket. He was in good hands, Porter's own surgeon was in attendance as they carried him below.

"Forshaw—*who is* this drowned rat?" Porter inquired cheerfully of Jesse shivering in her blanket. He then asked her the question Jesse had heard him ask of many a subordinate as he passed along the deck of his ship, "Do you have your underflannels on, my boy?"

Jesse tried to answer but her teeth were chattering so much only a strange whirring noise emerged.

Porter laughed heartily as he said, "Later, lad, you can tell us all about your adventure, later!" The robust seafarer beamed at her, he beamed at her a lot these days, a strange kind of knowing, winking smile and a slight inclination of the head, as though they shared a secret and he was reassuring her that it was quite safe with him.

————

Porter's flotilla, knocked about, with the exception of the *Henry Clay*, which had sunk without the loss of one single hand, was now at anchorage at New Carthage, on the west bank of the river.

Seven days later, under cover of darkness, it was the turn of Porter's remaining vessels to run the batteries; twelve more barges and six more transports, packed to the rafters with forage and rations and ammunition. All made it but for the *Tigress*, whose cargo had been even more important than bullets and food and hay. She'd been carrying the medical and surgical supplies. The *Tigress*, which was holed below the waterline and sank, had served as Grant's headquarters at Pittsburg Landing and had brought McClernand up from Memphis to take over Sherman's command in December. Jesse mourned for the fact that McClernand was no longer aboard when she sunk.

The New Carthage area opposite Grand Gulf turned out to be unsuitable to make the crossing to the east bank and put troops ashore; the Rebels had fortified Grand Gulf since Grant had chosen it for his crossing point. So by the time the *Tigress* had sunk to the bottom of the Mississippi two of Grant's corps, one led by McPherson and the other by McClernand, were marching down the west side of the Mississippi to Hard Times, a plantation twenty-odd miles farther south. Porter ran his ships past the Grand Gulf fort at night and came down to Hard Times to pick up the cheering men waiting on the west bank.

The following day, McPherson's Seventeenth and McClernand's Thirteenth Corps crossed the Mississippi and set foot on the east side of the river at Bruinsburg Landing, guided by a contraband. This was further cause for cheering as the men suddenly realized they were now on the same side of the river as the enemy. All that was between them and Vicksburg's back door were two Rebel armies and they would be dealt with in due course.

On April 20, Grant issued Special Orders No. 110. The purpose of this last move, he wrote, was "to obtain a foothold on the east bank of the Mississippi River, from which Vicksburg can be approached by practicable roads." They'd done it.

However, Sherman was to remain behind for a special purpose. Grant had asked him to complete yet another difficult task before he and his corps could join the rest of the army. Grant wanted something to distract Pemberton's attention from the original crossing point at Grand Gulf.

So Sherman, the theater lover, predictably put on a fine show for his audience, the Rebels manning the fortifications at Snyder's Bluff, on the Yazoo River, not far from the December assault at Chickasaw.

Jesse, watching with Captain Jackson from the bridge of a transport, thought this serious exercise the most comical sight she'd ever seen. Sherman disembarked the men from the steamers and marched them up the east side of the Yazoo, where they waited. Then the steamers would go upriver, and take onboard the very same men, and repeat the pantomime several times at four different locations, with much clattering of equipment and shouting of orders, presenting the very opposite of a secret landing. Small groups even found time for foraging expeditions, scaring the wits out of the local plantation owners, stealing cattle and pigs from nearby farms, and herding them aboard their steamers with exultations that would have gladdened the heart of any buckaroo.

The following morning, as a grand finale, the navy's guns opened fire on the already panicked men in their fortifications, adding even more weight to the impression that *this* was a full-scale Yankee assault.

This "display of strength" continued until Grant finally wrote to Sherman from Bruinsburg, "I am on dry ground on the same side of the river with the enemy. Come up and join me."

Meanwhile Grant left Bruinsburg and headed east twenty miles, to Port Gibson, where his men fought a day-long battle, taking control of the roads leading to Grand Gulf, Vicksburg, and Jackson, the state capital.

By May 1 the Rebels had fled Grand Gulf and retired across Big Black River, north through Bayou Pierre, where they hung around awaiting reinforcements from Pemberton that never came. Grant made his new supply base at Grand Gulf. Here he halted his army and waited for Sherman, who was marching his corps eighty-three miles through the muddy bayous and down the Louisiana side of the Mississippi.

On May 7, when Sherman arrived, his friend David Dixon Porter was waiting to ferry him and his troops across to the east side of the river.

There was still the vital question of a supply line, of feeding his men. Napoleon had said, "An army marches on its stomach," and American soldiers seemed to get hungrier than most.

The farther they marched into the interior of the state the more stretched would become their supply line, making it vulnerable to Rebel attack.

Grant decided to move without a supply line. His men would subsist almost exclusively from what they found in the countryside, they would eat off the civilian population. Each regiment would take along the army staple of hardtack, coffee and sugar and salt. Meat—poultry, bacon, beef—and vegetables could all be found aplenty in this rich agricultural area. Southern farmers would feed Northern soldiers as they marched.

The prospect of the army in hostile territory depending for sustenance on what the men could steal from the locals filled Sherman with foreboding, but, as always, he put his full weight behind Grant's decision.

On May 8 the Army of the Tennessee cut loose from its supply base and resumed its overland advance, all three columns moving in a northwesterly direction, McPherson on the right toward Raymond, McClernand on the left covering Big Black River crossing points, and Sherman's corps in the center, closing in on Auburn, all heading toward Jackson. Grant's immediate goal, as the railroad that ran from Vicksburg to Jackson, was Vicksburg's only connection with the rest of the Confederacy. If Grant's army could break this link and destroy the supplies already at Jackson, Pemberton's army and Vicksburg itself would be cut off. Pemberton, realizing this at the same time as Grant, had at last come out of Vicksburg to face Grant's army. He was marching east toward Raymond.

At sundown on May 12, Sherman was with Grant at Auburn, on Dillon's Plantation, off the Old Port Gibson Road, when news arrived that McPherson had, in his first independent field command, clashed with Rebels in a two-hour battle at Raymond, six miles southwest of their position. McPherson had driven the enemy out of town, no doubt with

Grant's urgent inducement still ringing in his ears: "We must fight the enemy before our rations fail."

Grant and Sherman conferred. Both men agreed that a wrong move now and their troops would be trapped, caught between two enemy armies, Pemberton now reported to be at Edward's Station, on the Mississippi Southern Railroad, in their front, and Joseph Johnston rumored to be gathering a large force at Jackson, in their rear. Spies had told Grant that Pemberton was expecting Grant to attack Edward's Station directly from his present position at Auburn, before continuing his march to Vicksburg, and no doubt Johnston was readying himself to move out of Jackson and attack Grant's rear. Raymond was just fourteen miles west of Jackson. Therefore, Grant would do the unexpected. Instead of continuing to Vicksburg via Edward's he would turn his columns and head directly for Jackson. He would send McPherson forward to attack Johnston, to soften him up, then follow with Sherman's corps to finish the job and push the Virginian out of the capital, preventing him from achieving his immediate ambition—joining his army with Pemberton's.

This accomplished, they could catch Pemberton while he was still wondering where Grant's army had gone and force him out into open battle. It was common knowledge that the two Rebel generals had been feuding. Pemberton's first thought was of defending Vicksburg, and he wished to return to the town to command his divisions from behind the safety of his defenses. Joe Johnston, on the other hand, wanted Pemberton to stop worrying about Vicksburg, and defeat Grant before he managed to reach the city.

By 11:00 A.M. on the fourteenth, Sherman and Grant had reached the outskirts of Jackson in pouring rain to hear that McPherson had already attacked the town.

Shells were still exploding on all sides. A clean-up movement was underway by Sherman's infantry.

Grant followed Sherman across the bridge over a stream, where their party emerged from the woods to see the line of entrenchments, from behind which the enemy was keeping up a brisk artillery fire, enfilading the road ahead.

Raising his voice to be heard above the exploding shells that came ever closer to finding their mark, Sherman turned his mount to find Jesse following closely in his wake, a tiny figure all but hidden inside an overlarge oilskin.

"Go to the rear!" his hoarse voice called, while a series of shells exploded in the woods behind them.

Jesse saw Grant watching her, as one small branch plonked onto her hat, then another and another, before turning his introspective gaze onto Sherman, who was bellowing at the girl,

"Did you hear me? I said go to the rear!" He shortened up his horse's reins as the nervous animal tossed her handsome head restively. He had chosen to give Dolly, his "cowardly" sorrel mare, another chance to redeem herself in battle conditions. Her response was not promising.

Jesse frowned and cupped a hand over her ear as though she couldn't hear above the angry roar of shot and shell which shook the earth, and the zip-zip-zip of musket fire as it cut the leaves. Her horse suddenly defied those that had added the epiphyte "Old" before his name, and leapt into the air, a veritable colt once more, causing Sherman's high-strung mount to break and run, carrying the commander some distance away before he could sufficiently quieten the anxious animal.

In the next moment, there was one tremendous explosion and a shower of debris, clods of dried mud, bits of shattered foliage, broken branches and all that was human and equine rained down through the smoke-filled air. On the spot where Sherman had only moments before been sitting his horse, issuing a whole flurry of commands, an exploding shell had scooped a crater out of the innocent earth, leaving a lieutenant of artillery, two orderlies and their mounts, writhing on the ground in mortal agony.

If Jesse pretended not to hear Sherman, after he galloped back across the field to rejoin them, Grant clearly did. He stared in amazement as the Ohioan, tears streaming from his smarting eyes, removed his battered hat, used it to strike Jesse hard across the head, not once but twice, and spat out, through a cloud of dust and gunsmoke, "*Damn you*, I am sick and tired of giving you orders you do not obey."

Jesse fell back, out of sight and out of mind, to where Captain Jackson sat calmly upon his calm horse, watching.

"Well," he said philosophically, with a sniff, "you ain't never gonna make old bones, and that's the gall darn truth." Maybe this thought consoled him, for he was smiling.

Ten minutes later the loud cheers from the men in the front line confirmed that the Rebels had fled. Joe Johnston and his army were retreating along the Jackson and Great Northern railroad, in the opposite direction to Vicksburg. Johnston's decision to abandon Jackson had separated the two Rebel armies.

The Army of the Tennessee could now march on the ineffectual Pemberton and Vicksburg.

21

Lords, knights, and gentlemen

★ ★ ★ ★

Sherman was right behind us with an army, an army that was no respecter of ducks, chickens, pigs, or turkeys, for they used to say of one particular regiment in Sherman's corps that it could catch, scrape, and skin a hog without a soldier leaving the ranks.

—Admiral David Dixon Porter,
Incidents and Anecdotes of the Civil War, 1885

So sudden had been the Federal attack on Jackson and so complete the Rebels' retreat, that many of the inhabitants did not realize what had taken place. Now as they came out of shops, saloons, and eateries, and from their homes, they stood around as if punch-drunk, as if too shocked to be afraid of the blue bellies rapidly filling their streets.

In and around the town looters were on the rampage, fired up by barrels of bad rum found in the cellars and given out before the battle had ended.

When Sherman was told, he threatened severe punishment for soldiers caught drunk on the streets. But it wasn't just blue bellies.

There were also contrabands to deal with, men, women, and children who had swarmed into the Union lines over the last few days, and who were now milling about the town, many of the males being plied with rum by their liberators.

Jesse, watching from the sidewalk outside the hotel, could just wonder at the sight. They came on foot, on aged mules or horses, in farm carts, some driving masser's best barouche now that he had fled, fairly loaded up with whatever they could take from the houses of their old tormentors. Small children and babies shared space with grandparents, an old painting, a musical instrument, a bookcase, an antique blunderbuss, but nothing of any real value to the hungry or the homeless. Why hadn't they taken food or blankets or even cooking utensils? Had these downtrodden people been so enthralled by this abstract idea known as "freedom" that they'd cleaned out the plantation attic, instead of the kitchen larder?

By early afternoon, the only Rebel soldiers in the area were prisoners. While the Union surgeons attended the wounded, the rest were rounded up and herded into a cattle pen alongside the railroad tracks. Once there, they were given canteens of water and hard bread and excitedly questioned, as if they, the Yankees, were invaders from a foreign land, eager to learn about a strange race of people called Southerners.

As daylight was fading, Sherman, charged with policing the town, and never one to take provost duties lightly, had already dealt uncompromisingly with the skulkers, stragglers, and deserters of all persuasions and colors.

Satisfied that order had been restored, Sherman met McPherson and Grant at the Bowman House, principal hotel of the town, to discuss the unfolding developments over a good bottle of wine and a very decent meal, which, much to McPherson's surprise, Corporal Davis shared. At least the food, if not the wine. Grant, on the other hand, did not seem at all surprised to hear Sherman order the young corporal to sit at the table with them, "like a civilized person."

After dinner, Jesse took up her favorite position, curled up on the armchair in a corner of the large dining room from where she gazed longingly at the brandy decanter, not for herself, of course, but for a thirsty surgeon of her acquaintance. She had already appropriated three large green pears and handfuls of figs the size of a man's thumb from the fruit bowl, and concealed them inside her baggy shirt. However, the cut-glass decanter stood there like a challenge; how to find a way to transfer the French brandy within to her canteen, under the eyes of these men.

Sherman was now at the map spread out on the polished oak dining table, the symbols of civilized living—decanter, fruit bowl, silver cut-lery—pushed aside to make room for the practicalities of war.

"When Mac and I leave Jackson in the morning I want you to remain behind for one day to tear up the railroad tracks, burn the arsenal, the factory, the foundry, and all other public property that could be of use to the Rebels," Grant told Sherman, joining him at the map. "We've rid ourselves of Johnston, for now, but we mustn't allow Pemberton to cross the Big Black. I want to smash Pemberton's army before he gets back to Vicksburg. We can settle this campaign at the Big Black, and then march on Vicksburg."

There was a brisk knock on the door and Charles Dana walked in, briskly, squinting. Erstwhile newspaperman and now assistant secretary of war, whom everyone knew had been sent here by Stanton to spy on Grant and report on his drinking, had crossed with Grant at Bruinsburg. After greeting each man in turn, he handed Grant a dispatch.

"I rode my rear end off to get you that, General Grant, kindly read it aloud, sir, no doubt General Sherman and General McPherson will want to congratulate you and each other!" With that, the nearsighted Dana made unhesitatingly, instinctively for the brandy decanter, without bumping into anything that stood between him and it.

Watching him, Jesse screwed up her face. While Grant, reading the dispatch, let out what was for him a hoot of pleasure.

"It's from Mr. Stanton," he announced. He passed it to Sherman, say-ing, "Read it aloud, will you, Sherman?"

" 'General Grant has full and absolute authority to enforce his own commands, to remove any person who, by ignorance, inaction, or any cause, interferes with or delays his operations. He has the full confidence of the Government, is expected to enforce his authority, and will be firmly and heartily supported; but he will be responsible for any failure to exert his powers. You may communicate this to him.' "

Sherman was beaming around his cigar as he slapped Grant on the back and congratulated him. This dispatch was a not-so-veiled reference to McClernand and his attempts at causing trouble with his communiqués directly to Mr. Lincoln. This was total support, and support for Grant was support for his best subordinates. No longer did Sherman have to worry about losing Grant and coming under McClernand's self-serving command.

"Thank you for this—" Grant was effusive, for Grant, as he shook Dana's hand before the bearer of good tidings used it to relieve Sherman of his plate of roast beef with a cheerful, "Are you going to finish that, General? No, then allow me to finish it for you." He tucked the beef inside a chunk of freshly baked bread and devoured it hungrily with the brandy.

Jesse watched him with resentful gaze. The crusty bread and the rare beef were also earmarked for that surgeon and his equally deserving steward. As for the brandy, if she didn't act soon there would be nothing left to steal. Fate, however, was about to take a hand.

"Where's that smoke coming from?" McPherson interrupted the celebrations to ask, pointing out the window, where black plumes were indeed billowing into the sky beyond the capitol building.

Sherman went to the door, opened it, and was almost knocked over by Colonel Wilson, rushing through to announce in his excited, reedy voice: "The convicts in the penitentiary have been released by their own people; they've set the prison buildings on fire."

Sherman had long since gone to the front of the hotel to see what was happening. Grant now followed, with Wilson and McPherson bringing up the rear. Jesse stared at Dana, who was staring squint-eyed at the brandy decanter. He reached out for it; his hand hovered there, and then withdrew. He shook his head and hurried after the generals. The brandy could wait. He wanted to have something exciting, if not scandalous, to report to his master in Washington.

Jesse wasted no time. She drained the decanter to the last drop and rammed home the stopper. Then she put the canteen over her shoulder.

An hour later Jesse returned to the hotel dining room to steal the remaining fruit in the bowl. She was just fastening the strap on her groaning saddlebags when Cartwright's head appeared around the door.

"Captain Van Allen said I'd find you in here. Got any booze?"

"Schhh—" she told him, and gestured for him to come in. "Close the door." They were like two schoolchildren plundering the school larder at midnight.

She gave him the canteen. He sniffed the contents appreciatively and grinned. "Good girl. What else you got?" She showed him the fruit, some of which he took for Jacob, who was suffering a rare bout of constipation. "How 'bout tobacco?" There was a knock on the door. They both fell silent.

"Jesse?" It was Thomas Ransom's distinctive voice.

"Chrissake!" Cartwright exploded. "I thought he'd be in Vicksburg by now waving Old Glory from the courthouse."

Jesse looked at her companion uncertainly. Ransom opened the door and came in.

"Can't turn 'round without bumpin' into you," the surgeon told him. He took the canteen and threw himself lengthways on the couch.

"We *are* going in the same direction," Ransom pointed out good-naturedly, wincing slightly as he put the gunnysack he was carrying on the armchair. He produced three apples, a small jar of honey, some cornbread, a hunk of brittle-looking toffee, and a small pouch of tobacco. "It's not much, but you can share it with the doctor, and Jacob, of course," he told Jesse.

Poor Ransom, his generosity was admirable, but misplaced. Jesse was turning into an expert forager. The occasional still-warm egg snatched from under a protesting hen, a wedge of freshly baked fruitcake disappearing off a window ledge where it had foolishly been left to cool. Some dried bacon stolen from a smokehouse that parched the throat but filled an empty stomach, cold, hard sweet potatoes, and a handful of overripe corn supplemented the petrified bread and coffee still untouched in her saddlebags after three days. Five days' rations, Jesse could proudly boast, was easily stretched to ten if need be, for she was already learning, like so many other "veterans" of this rough and toughened army, "to live off the country."

"The provisions came from my own mess table," Ransom was saying, "the tobacco from a prisoner, an artillery captain, in exchange for a pair of my dry socks." His smile was rueful as he placed the tobacco pouch in the doctor's lap. "I hope you will appreciate my sacrifice and think charitably of me in my one pair of wet socks while you smoke it," he said laughingly.

Cartwright took the tobacco as he took everything, with a resentful grunt. He looked at the Vermonter's suddenly tight features as he winced again, passing a hand across his stomach.

"What's the matter, got the Tennessee trots?" He knew the signs, the pale skin, the drawn look about the eyes. "Or is it 'Mississippi mudslide' in this state?"

"I'm fine." Ransom was quick, too quick, to respond. "I don't believe you have noticed?" He turned back to the girl, and made a slight forward motion of his shoulder, before grinning broadly.

"You've got your stars, sir," Jesse said.

"Yes, it's official, at last." Ransom smiled at her hesitantly. "Won't you congratulate me, Doctor?" he asked the surgeon who was watching them from the couch.

"Yer—congratulations." The surgeon took a swig from the canteen.

The Vermonter brought something from his coat. "Jesse, I would like you to have these." He put his eagle straps in her hands. "Take care of them for me."

"I'd rather not."

"I want you to have them." Ransom stared at her, a pained expression on his handsome features and Cartwright stared at him.

"I wouldn't know what to do with them." Jesse put them on the table. "Send them to your mother."

"But I want you to have them."

"I said no." There was a moment of strained silence before Jesse said in a calmer voice, "I can't be responsible for them—after. They'll be lost." She put the eagles onto the empty gunnysack and pushed the sack toward him. Their eyes met for an instant and Ransom said, "All right. But if you change your mind—"

"I won't."

"I have something else for you," the Vermonter said with an attempt at forced cheerfulness, "to celebrate my promotion." He took a necklace from his pocket. "Some of the men were making them from the iridescent shells we found at Lake Providence. I thought of you—"

"General Ransom—" she began and then looked at Cartwright, who was lying on the couch grinning at her maliciously. "Thank you, sir."

"Shall I tie it for you?" Ransom asked.

"I'll put it on later."

He looked so disappointed that she said, "Yes, tie it for me." She lifted her hair, turned her back, and waited. Cartwright noted that Ransom took some time fixing the string. His hands were shaking, and unch…aracteristically clumsy. The surgeon didn't blame him. The girl had tiny red curls on her neck that would have driven any man wild. She looked as if she was being tortured, not loved.

"Here. I'll do it," he said, pushing the new brigadier aside. "You can't beat a surgeon for skillful fingers. There." He had made a neat little bow with the string.

The girl fingered the shells at her throat. "Thank you," she said softly, trying to avoid contact with Ransom's eyes.

"You remember the letter I got from Jack," Cartwright said, "the one telling about syringes being issued to surgeons in the Army of the Potomac to administer morphine. Well, he sent me this." He brought a rolled-up medical journal from inside his frock coat and held it up in front of her face. "According to this article, this one here, they've discovered the drug works more effectively and quicker injected *subcutaneously* with an endemic syringe directly into the tissue." He looked at Ransom. "This should interest you, you're one of our best customers. *Subcutaneously* means *under the skin*, rather than administered orally or dusted into the wound. Jack says they're gonna issue them to surgeons in the Potomac Army. I wish to hell they'd let us have some out here." He showed Ransom the illustration. "What do you think? Wood's syringe.

Listen to this: 'By use of this little instrument, a new and extensive field for doing good is open to the humane military surgeon, and he who is the fortunate possessor of this talisman, will receive daily the thanks and blessings of his suffering patients.' "

"Last time a patient called *you* humane you ran screaming from the tent," Jesse reminded him tartly.

"You cut me to the quick, Jesse Davis, you know that don't you? *To the quick.*"

Ransom read the advertisement carefully. "Why don't you purchase a syringe through the catalog, Doctor? Look, there's an order form, already printed, all you have to do is fill in your details and send off the money with a return address."

Cartwright's finger traced the crude drawing lovingly, as though it were a woman's curvaceous body. "Yer—but I don't think the package would ever reach me. The way we move around it might take months," he said in that ingratiating tone Jesse knew so well, and followed it up with a heartfelt sigh, his expression turning winsome and ingenuous.

"The longer you wait, Doctor, the longer it'll be before you get the syringe. Why not set the wheels in motion?" Ransom was as determined in this as he was in anything he set his mind to.

"You do it," Cartwright suggested, "my writing's like a drunken spider. Order two, one for me, one for Jacob."

Unhesitatingly, Ransom sat at the desk. He dipped the pen in the inkwell, scraped off the excess ink, and filled in the form. Cartwright stood beside his chair as the sound of the nib scratched across the paper, filling the silence. He glanced across at Jesse, winked, and grinned. She narrowed her eyes and shook her head in disapproval. She knew what was coming. Finished, Ransom announced, "Do you have the money, Doctor?"

"Money?"

"For the syringes. Four dollars and twenty cents plus postage and packing, to be included in the envelope."

"Ah—" The surgeon looked crestfallen. "Of course, the money." He turned the pockets of his pants inside out. "That might be a slight problem right now. Unless—?" He looked at the girl, held out his hand and wiggled his fingers. Jesse brought forth all the money she had in the world. Without formality, the surgeon scooped every cent, paper and coin, from the small palms, quickly calculating. "We need six more cents."

"*Doctor*," Ransom's tone was sharp, "must you take all Jesse's money? Leave her something. Here, I've got five dollars and some coins, take that."

"No, no, I couldn't possibly, I hardly know you—" Cartwright took the money and placed it with Jesse's on the table.

"No," Ransom declared. "Return what you took from Jesse, or you'll not get a cent from me."

"Well, since you put it like that—" Reluctantly, he returned two dollar bills to the girl.

"*All of it*," Ransom insisted, that discomforted expression passing over his features again.

Cartwright gave back the money. "You and your goddamn principles," he said. He finished counting the money Ransom had given him. "Nearly six dollars. What do they pay a general these days? More than a surgeon, that's for certain. Doesn't it strike you as kinda immoral to get paid more for taking life than saving it?" Cartwright went back to the couch.

"Comfortable. Grant likes the good life, they say. Too much of the other kind before the war started, I guess. You commanders live well."

"My bivouac is a small wall tent, Doctor," Ransom said. "I'll get an envelope from reception."

While he was out of the room, Cartwright said, "Now do you believe me? The necklace, his rank insignia. I don't know much about these matters. But I'd say a man doesn't give his shoulder straps to just any passing female." Cartwright put the pipe stem between his teeth and bared them in a fatuous grin.

The Vermonter came back into the room. "There you are, Doctor." He held out the stamped, addressed envelope. "All you have to do is mail it."

The surgeon sniffed, shook his untidy head. "With all my duties, takin' care of the sick and injured, I'm likely to forget. Would you mind?"

Ransom put the envelope in his pocket. "Of course not."

"He's done everything else," Jesse muttered.

"I have to return to my brigade," Ransom said, "I just wanted to make sure you were safe and had enough to eat. Some of the commissary wagons have been trapped on the road and the men didn't get their suppers."

"I got mine," Jesse said.

"Yes. I should have realized, you'd not go hungry with Sherman. Walk me to the stable?" the Vermonter added softly.

"You've got a new horse." She stroked the broad, handsome face of the large bay that Ransom had led from the stall to the water trough. "What's his name?"

"Barney." Ransom lifted the stirrup over the saddle and tightened the girth strap.

"Barney," she repeated, laughing. "Hi there, Old Barney boy, how handsome and brave you are, just like your master." She stopped abruptly and looked at the brigade commander, who was watching her with a gaze so soft it seemed to stroke her freckled cheek.

"He's three, hardly an *old* boy."

"He's *my* old boy, my old Barney boy." Jesse cuddled up close to the animal's head and stroked his face. "Next time we meet I'll have some sugar for my new friend or maybe a juicy carrot. Look, he likes me."

"*Everyone* likes you, Jesse."

"You must stop giving me presents. I won't know what to do with them."

"Keep them with you forever. If I were wealthy I'd buy you anything you wanted."

"I don't want anything. I shall call him *Old* Barney because it makes me think of Old Bob," Jesse said, stroking the animal's head.

"Barney here is steady as a rock, aren't you, boy?" He looked at Jesse. "*Old* boy!"

She laughed as Barney nuzzled up against his master, who was combing the animal's mane with his long fingers.

"Would you have another photograph taken, just you alone?" Ransom asked her.

Jesse looked up. The surgeon was coming toward the corral. As he reached Ransom, he passed something into his hand.

"Four times a day," he said quietly. "Regular. We don't want you caught with your pants around your ankles when you take Vicksburg, do we?"

"Thank you, Doctor," the other man said, offering his free hand.

Cartwright ignored it. He thought, *I hate him.* The way he hated all men of Ransom's type, with their easy friendship, their abundance of boyish charm and nobility of spirit. He hated him, for despite all resistance, all protest, all objections, you finally found yourself giving in, and grudgingly admitting you might be in the presence a good man. "Keep yer head down," he said.

The colonel swung effortlessly into the saddle, his long, slender frame ramrod straight. He gazed down sympathetically at the surgeon. "You look tired, Doctor, you should turn in."

"Don't worry about me. I've got Jesse to take care of me."

The next time Jesse saw Thomas Ransom was three days later at Big Black River. There, the Rebels, reeling from their defeat by McPherson's corps at Champion Hill, four and a half miles southwest of Bolton, the previous day, fought with their backs to the river, only to be beaten again, by Union forces under the Irish general Mike Lawler. Retreating, many of the Rebels had been drowned, and eighteen hundred captured. Last seen, Pemberton and what remained of his army were staggering back to Vicksburg in disarray, after burning the bridge at Big Black. A lack of bridges and vessels would never discourage the men of Grant's army. They merely built their own.

A bridge-building competition was in progress. The southernmost bridge, a strong raft affair, had been erected by the Thirteenth Engineer Corps. Next, about two and a half miles downriver could be found a bridge of cotton bale pontoons, lashed together with rope. No one doubted this would be an excellent effort, since General McPherson, first in the class of '53 at West Point, graduating with a commission in the elite Corps of Engineers, was supervising, in person. However, it was the most northerly bridge that interested Jesse, the one being built by Thomas Ransom. Beside this bridge sat Sherman and Grant, on a log, smoking segars and talking, like two weatherbeaten old farmers discussing the price of corn.

Jesse hid behind one of the huge oaks that bordered the riverbank. The darkness was falling fast and the men who had been working in the dense tangle of underbrush had lit torches of pitch pine, driven into the earth along the banks, to illuminate the scene. All afternoon gangs of strong, clean-limbed men, stripped to the waist, torsos and necks glistening with sweat, had swung axes and hammers, while their comrades carried timber from the wagons, passing it across to others, up to their waists in the dark, impenetrable waters. Their commander had joined them. Standing naked to the waist in the stagnant water, his chest, shoulders, and face streaked with dirt and sweat, his skin scratched from the branches, Ransom had not only supervised the building but pitched in. Sherman and Grant had called it "an impressive and remarkable construction."

Ransom had given orders for six trees to be cut down on this side of the river, and six on the other, personally selecting those that grew closest together. He had then explained to his men how only *one* side of the trunks were to be chopped, the side that allowed them to fall toward the water. The trees had to remain attached to the stumps, giving the structure extra support and strength. The branches that protruded from the surface were then cut away to make a smooth surface, while those beneath the water had sunk into the soft riverbed, interlacing and underpinning the eventual roadway across which a portion of the army would pass. Finally Jesse had watched as they laid the lumber across the trunks and fastened it with strong rope, to produce the result she now saw, a bridge that looked as though it would last as long as the river itself.

Many of the exhausted men were making their way back to their bivouacs, thinking, no doubt, of a hot meal, a pipe of tobacco, and their blankets. Only a handful of officers remained, among them, Ransom himself, who fought off several staunch attempts to persuade him to return to his headquarters and rest. He had promised to follow, after one more check of the struts and ropes, and the officers reluctantly departed, leaving only the pickets of the Ninety-fifth Illinois to guard the brigade's proud handiwork.

Jesse watched him walk the few feet to a large oak tree and sink down, unbuckling his gun belt and placing his holstered Colt by his side, with the safety catch off. He rested his head against the trunk and closed his eyes with a sigh of weariness that tore at her heart.

She started back to the commanders' camp and then stopped. She waited a moment, staring up into the moonlit sky, and then turned around again.

She moved quietly to the tree and stood there studying Ransom's sharp, elegant profile, as sweat ran slowly down his neck. The almost identical wound scars on his shoulders looked particularly livid in the unreal light of the pine torches. His damp hair, normally combed severely to the crown of his head, fell forward over his furrowed brow, the features beneath strained with the intensity of a man who has given himself and his brigade over with total commitment to the work they have been assigned. The hot, sultry evening was alive with the sounds of maddened insects. A small gossamer-winged creature landed on his bruised shoulder, and fluttered against his pale skin as he slept. How strange it was to see this always-immaculate young man looking so disheveled, so dirty, a two-day stubble on his strong chin, strange and so *human*. She had almost made up her mind to walk away when his eyes opened. He stared in astonishment at the small uniformed figure standing over him in the shadowy darkness.

"Jesse?" His pleasure at seeing her was so palpable as he jumped to his feet that tears started to her eyes. "What are you doing here?" He reached for his shirt on the grass but Jesse took it from his hand.

"You're bleeding," she said, touching one of the grazes with tender fingers.

"I . . . I was working in the water—"

"Yes, I know. I watched you. It's a wonderful bridge."

He smiled. "I've tried to be worthy of my engineering degree."

"Sit down against the tree."

He obeyed and she knelt beside him, took the stopper from her canteen and held it out. He murmured thank you and drank thirstily, the canteen trembling against his lips. Jesse steadied it as the young general's deep-set eyes remained on her face.

"I didn't know you had an engineering degree."

"We don't know much about each other. Your letters, when you did send them, were always full of what Sherman or the doctor was doing."

"Yes, I'm sorry." She opened her haversack, took out a piece of clean cloth, dampened it with fresh water from the canteen, and started to bathe his bloodied and scratched torso. "Lie back and relax. Close your eyes."

He rested his head against the trunk of the tree. "I want to look at your face. That feels so good, so soothing. You have the gentlest touch."

She started to work on his face, lowering her gaze when he smiled so tenderly at her.

"Norwich," he said, "Norwich University. That's where I got my engineering degree."

"The doctor attended Rush Medical in Chicago."

"Chicago? I know it well. My uncle George and I went into partnership in Chicago."

"Is Norwich University in Chicago?"

"No. Northfield, in Vermont."

"Do they have picnics in Vermont?"

"Picnics?" He laughed at the strangeness of the question. "Yes. Picnics are an American institution. We have extra-fine ones in Vermont."

"I've never been to a picnic."

"I'll take you one day, when the war is over. I'll take you on a picnic every Sunday," he murmured, sleepily. He leaned back, his blue eyes focused steadily on her face as she painstakingly cleaned the blood and dirt from every cut and graze on his brow and cheek, from his arms and chest and shoulders. When her face came close to his she could hear his shallow breathing. She pressed the damp cloth carefully against his forehead and cheeks. His eyes dropped from her face to the shell necklace around her throat. He put his hand on her face. She removed it, with an almost imperceptible shake of her head. Then, immediately, she grasped his hand and put it back on her cheek. She stared at him and then as he stroked her freckled cheek with his thumb she closed her eyes and swallowed thickly. He leaned forward and lightly touched her lips with his own. A shiver passed through her slender frame. He moved a little closer and kissed her brow, her nose, and then her lips again. He heard the breath catch in her throat. She remained perfectly still, her lips slightly parted, moist and full, and her brow drawn into a frown, as if she were experiencing something that awed her completely, that could not be understood unless she gave it her absolute attention. She was so still that she seemed like a statue, except that he could hear her breathing.

"Jesse—" he said after a moment.

"I want to . . . remember everything—" she whispered. "I don't think it's possible—after I am no longer . . . in this existence—but I want to try."

This time when Ransom touched her lips with his own she put her arm about his neck and returned the pressure, so much so that he pulled away. Her eyes opened, questioning, confused, his intense gaze was on her face and she shivered. She kissed his cheek, the corner of his mouth, ran her hands over his hair.

"It hurts—" she said, "—when you kiss me—it hurts with a pain that is so exquisitely beautiful that I feel as if I will pass out. Breathing, eating and seeing, walking and hearing, is not living, is it?" she asked him earnestly. "It's not truly being alive, is it? You have to *feel* to be truly alive. Feeling is living. At this moment"—she put his trembling hand to her cheek—"I feel truly alive." She put her fingertips to his sculptured lips. "You've breathed life into me. My lips are burning, though the fire is down here." She touched just below her stomach. "Why are you looking at me that way? Did I say something wrong?"

"I want to do the right thing by you."

She moved her fingers across his naked chest, up to his shoulders, and then rested at his throat. "I like to watch the pulse beating in the hollow of your throat. I feel as if I have a pulse beating—down there." She touched the place.

Ransom got to his feet. He helped the girl up.

"What is it? What have I done wrong?" she asked pleadingly.

"Nothing at all. You are alone in the world. No parents, no guardian.

I will not take advantage of your innocence. If we were back North now I would ask permission to call upon you and we'd talk in your parents' drawing room—"

"But we're not back North. I have no parents and therefore no drawing room. If you knew how I felt right now—"

"If you care for me, then do as I say." He bent down to get his shirt. "When the war is over—"

She backed away from him. "That's not what I want, or need. I want *now*. I want to love and feel *now*. I want to go on a picnic now." She scooped up her haversack. "You started this feeling in me. It was as if I was asleep. A sleepwalker. You woke me. You opened my eyes and my heart. Please don't put me to sleep again—I couldn't bear it."

There was now nothing to prevent the Army of the Tennessee from marching right up to the back door of Vicksburg itself and they did just that.

On May 18, Grant ordered his triumphant army to surround the city.

During this nineteen-day campaign, starting with the Bruinsburg landing and ending with the investment of Vicksburg, Grant's armies had fought and won five battles; captured five thousand prisoners; burned Jackson and destroyed its rail network; and hurled Pemberton's army back inside the fortress city. No wonder Sherman had turned to Grant and said, "I want to congratulate you on the success of your plan. And it's your plan too, by heaven, and nobody else's. For nobody else believed in it. Until this moment, I never thought your expedition a success. I never could see the end clearly 'til now. But this is a campaign, this is a success if we never take the town."

By midday, Grant had made up his mind. He believed, he told Sherman and McPherson in his headquarters, that the Rebel army had been demoralized by their recent clutch of defeats, and persuaded that his own army, in contrast, was confident enough, he ordered a general assault to take place at two o'clock that same day. He was convinced that an immediate hard push, while the Rebels were still licking their wounds, would capture the city, sooner rather than later. "Besides," he added, the trapdoor mouth and deceptively sad eyes bringing forth the hint of an embarrassed smile, "I don't think our boys will have it any other way."

At the appointed hour Jesse stood to Sherman's rear and heard the three salvos that signaled the start of the assault. By 4:00 P.M. the assault was over, called off by the more than usually stoical Grant.

The Federals had attacked with almost blind confidence and been repulsed with a vicious ferocity.

In this hurriedly prepared movement Sherman's only regular battalion, the Thirteenth Regulars of the U.S. Army, had lost forty-three percent of their brave number as they attacked. So determined were these men to uphold the reputation of the United States Regular Army that five standard-bearers fell trying to get their shot-torn flag to their objective, before Sherman's own brother-in-law planted it on the exterior slope of the Stockade Redan where it hung, shredded but proud, holed fifty-five times.

While the dead rotted in the Mississippi sun and before the casualties were hardly back inside their lines, Grant had already issued orders for another assault to take place on the twenty-second.

22

The women who went to the field

Forward men, we must and will go into that fort! Who will follow me?

—Brigadier General Thomas E. G. Ransom, May 22, 1863

Jesse Davis opened her eyes. The sun was high overhead. The Mississippi sun. She was lying on her back on the bare ground. She was stiff
and every part of her body ached. Sweat was rolling down her face, down
her back inside her coat, and her hair was damp. She shivered. Hot and
then cold. She heard a low groan, which surprised her, because she was
not the type to groan, at least not aloud. Then she realized that the groan
had come from someone else. With a considerable effort, she rose into a
sitting position and stared at her bare feet. That someone had stolen her
shoes came as no surprise. Wherever she was, it was not at Sherman's
headquarters, and she was not alone. She was at the end of a long row of
soldiers, sitting, lying, and stretched out, all wearing blue. The soldier
beside her was the one moaning. He was begging for water now. She felt
for her canteen. It wasn't there. She too was thirsty. Her throat was
parched. Her lips felt cracked. Her medical haversack was gone. She felt

with sudden panic at her waist. The Bowie knife that Thomas had given her was also gone. She squinted up at the sun and tried to remember.

The morning of May 22, the dawn's silence had been broken by the crash of thunder and the glare of lightning from a hundred Federal field guns. In a while the sharpshooters, who by now had acquired a feel for the ground, joined the artillery fire, the whizzing of the balls lost in the unceasing shriek, hiss, and scream of bursting, swooping shells that made the soldiers in their holes wonder if the whole world was exploding about them. As Grant's infantry assaulted the Rebel breastworks from the land side, Admiral Porter's gunships had supported their army comrades with a coordinating bombardment on Vicksburg from the river on the western side.

Four hours of nonstop barrage, of deafening, discordant explosions that had filled the sky with palls of smoke, smoke that rose up from the sandy yellow clay of the hillsides, turning the air yellow-black above the Federal parapets and Rebel breastworks, making their occupants cough and choke, and bringing burning tears to eyes already bloodshot and strained.

To the soldiers who awaited their turn to move forward, it seemed not like a pall of smoke at all, but a giant, sulfurous cloud of doom, ready to envelop and carry them off to the nether region.

During the bombardment, General Sherman and his staff had taken up a position within two hundred yards of the Rebel parapet in their front, on a sloping grassy spur of ground, from where the commander could watch the proceedings through field glasses. Most of those present agreed they had never see anything to compare with what happened next, and most prayed they would never witness anything like it again.

A simultaneous attack had been launched by all three corps along the three miles of the Federal front.

Hundreds of columns of cheering men and boys, veterans all, led by officers wielding swords above their heads, seemed to rise up out of the very bowels of the earth and rush forward, a solid mass of blue, as though neither shot nor shell, nor musket ball, could break their ranks. Almost at the same moment, blood-chilling, heart-stopping, and with equal suddenness, equal determination, a wall of gray rose up behind the works and poured the most fearful fire into this charging, reeling, shouting, agonized mass.

Repeatedly the Federals tried to advance under a relentless hail of lead, repeatedly was it thrown back and cut down as it fought to overwhelm the Rebel fortifications. From behind every protective head-log, every fort and embrasure, every lunette, ditch and cavern, every hole and rampart, clearly visible against a now mockingly blue sky along the high, irregular bluffs, rifles, siege guns, and cannons exploded into the faces and bodies of the crumbling Union advance. Down went officers and men who had been with Grant since Belmont and Donelson and Shiloh, their lives ending here on the broken ground before Hill City, crying as they fell, "*Vicksburg or hell!*"

Leading the way were the color bearers, proud to be so honored, brave to the point of recklessness, as they carried their regiment's flag into battle.

Jesse had watched, tears rolling down her cheeks, tears of sorrow and anger, as one after another, first the color sergeants, then the corporals, and finally any soldier with courage enough to lift the precious flag and run forward, only to be mown down. Some managed to advance as far as the earthworks, but could get no farther, and planted their colors on a forward slope, before succumbing. Others used the shot-torn emblem to encourage the failing, crumbling columns, waving it back and forth to rally men caught up in the gathering darkness of defeat, in the raging storm of death and injury.

A glimpse of the flag brought new strength.

A frightened soldier, seeing his regimental colors swirling defiantly in the wind, might forget that all around him, beneath his stumbling, ill-measured steps, lay a carpet of blue stained with blood. He would no longer see headless bodies, bloody torsos, and dismembered limbs. He would go deaf to the shocked cry of a comrade struck by minié ball or shell. Perhaps now *he* could go on, this frightened soldier, less conscience of his own fears, seeing less and less, hearing only the loud beating of his heart in his heaving chest through the leaden storm.

Eight good men were lost trying to plant the emerald-green flag of the Seventh Missouri on the parapet of the Great Redoubt. Sherman's men.

Turning to look at the staff officers, Jesse saw their impassioned faces, heard their fervent pleas as they cheered these men on, willed them to succeed, or merely to survive.

"Ammunition, for God's sake! Send up ammunition! We must have more ammunition!"

It was a hellish place. Infantrymen lying upon their fallen comrades, piled high in the ditches outside the enemy earthworks, a hellish place from which, without covering support, they could not crawl back nor go forward. She knew for she had been one of them.

"Ammunition, for God's sake! Send up ammunition!" had shouted the courier who spurred his horse up to Sherman's side, and Jesse had responded to his plea.

"Water . . . water . . . oh Lord . . . please give me water."

Jesse blinked and turned her gaze upon the wounded boy, as if coming out of a trance.

He was crying like a child. His right leg was gone below the knee. The wound was open, raw, exposed, and smelled just awful. Blood was dripping into the earth beneath. Her own jacket was torn away at the right shoulder. There was some dried blood on the sleeve, but if it was hers she felt no pain. Some determined pulling with her left hand and the sleeve came away. She used it to bind up the boy's knee.

"I'll get you some water," she told him.

He clutched at her coat, blood was coming from his mouth as he said, "I'm dyin' . . . dyin' . . . and ma folks won't . . . even know. They . . . they don't bury us . . . Yankees—they let us rot . . . in the sun—"

Jesse frowned. What was he talking about? She looked around her. Her wits were gradually returning. Now she saw that the injured were lying everywhere. She had seen enough of these places to know she was in some kind of makeshift dressing station. But this one was different. Most of the soldiers here were wearing gray. This was a Rebel dressing station. She looked at the heavily bearded gray-clad soldier leaning against a tree to her left, a musket cradled in his arms, smoking a corn-cob pipe. He too seemed in a daze until he saw her stand up, shakily, like an uncertain drunk swaying on the sidewalk, and then he stirred.

"Don't you try nuthin' now, yer hear?" he called lazily, as if it would have involved a great effort on his part to even raise his musket, never mind sight it and pull the trigger. "I can see just as fine outa one good eye, than some so-called markses-men shoot outa two."

"Water," she said, holding out her hand. The guard, for that was what he was, had a canteen hanging around his shoulder. *"Please."*

"Sit down," the Rebel said with a little more energy.

"Just a mouthful for this soldier." Jesse pointed to the soldier with the leg wound.

Some of the others in the line joined their plea to hers.

"I said ter sit down," the guard insisted. He was angry now that his peace had been disturbed by this squirt of a Yankee boy, getting all the others riled up and vocal. There was always one. You shot him and you didn't get a peep out of the others.

Jesse sat back down. Now she was the one in the daze. What had the insane urgings of her limitless pride led her into this time? Shock distorted her features. She brought a trembling hand to her brow. She was a prisoner of war.

She had moved along the parapets and ridges, crouching low, she and another, a large man who did not move with her agility; they had filled their shirts and hats with ammunition taken from the dead and wounded, passing it out to the men whose rifles were silenced by a lack of cartridges.

Her companion, even as he bent low between the ravines, was too large a target and was cut down almost immediately in his work, clutching his head, before tumbling down the steeply sloping Rebel works. She had carried on, small and swift, a tiny figure gathering up ammunition with a furious energy matched only by the desperation of the men to load their weapons.

She stumbled over the uneven ground as a hail of musket balls sent up clods of hard dry earth that struck her a blow at every part of her body. Her hat was gone. But she held something else in her hand. A flag, regimental colors for which so many men had paid dearly trying to plant it on the Rebel works. She had run with but a few brave souls to keep her straight and true, soldiers who rallied to that beacon of light in the gathering darkness. Jesse and her small escort made it to the front of the Great Redoubt. Beside her a soldier fell. Hands reached out to help her, and together they planted the flag beneath the enemy's muskets and cannons. How easy it had seemed. How easy to grab up a flag and run. As she had been reflecting on this there had been an explosion, followed by an overwhelming hush that fell over the forward slopes.

"Jesse is missing." Sherman, being Sherman, came straight to the point, speaking three words that made Cartwright's chest constrict and brought beads of fresh sweat to his already damp brow.

"*Missing?* What do you mean missing? How can she be missing?" the surgeon heard himself ask as though from a far-off place, and as if he had lost control of his mouth. If Seth Cartwright asked once through that long and bloody day as he worked on shattered limbs, he must have asked a hundred times. "Has anyone seen Jesse? Where the hell is Jesse?" Now he had his answer. It was late evening and Sherman was standing before him outside the operating tent, both men surrounded by the injured and dying of that day's madness. The surgeon jerked his aching shoulders. He blinked out from under his damp fringe, frowned, blinked, twitched. Sweat ran into his bloodshot eyes and stung like hell.

Jacob, at his side, stared at the surgeon's drawn, sweaty, blood-besmirched face, the soft lips grown thin and hard as he demanded to know, "Missing where? Missing in what way?"

"Missing out there." Sherman waved his cigar toward the parapets. "Corporal Davis fell in the assault. I knew how much Jesse meant to you. I wanted to tell you myself before you heard it from someone else."

"What are you talking about?" Cartwright uncurled the wire earpieces and held his blood-spattered spectacles with shaking hands. He looked at Captain Jackson and at Marcus Van Allen, who flanked their commander. "How can she be missing? How can she have fallen in the assault? She was with you. She's *always* with you."

"There were calls for ammunition, Doc," Andy said. "Jesse answered those calls—darn it, she even planted a regimental flag on one of the Reb forts—there was a big explosion, then we couldn't see her no more."

Cartwright stared at Captain Jackson. The aide's words made no sense to him. How could a girl, barely sixteen, with her whole beautiful life ahead of her, be missing in the assault? He had a newspaper article in his pocket, all about Lincoln's Homestead Act. He and Jesse were going to California after the war and get some land to work for their kids. She didn't know that yet, he was going to tell her when the time was right. He was going to be one of those doctors who worked their land. That way your family never went hungry. He knew how hard a doctor had to work to put food on the table and a roof over his family's head. If your patients paid you in chickens, how could you pay the rent?

So how in the name of all that was holy could she have planted a flag on the Rebel fort?

This was utter madness. The world was spinning; *his* world was spinning. Then far down, buried deep, almost out of reach in its own shadowy darkness, he located a hope, crouching there like a fearful animal, something to cling onto in this madly spinning universe.

"You saw her fall, but you don't know if she's wounded—right?" He searched Sherman's grizzled features for a sign of encouragement, then looked at Van Allen's handsome face, swallowed hard and thick. "Am I right?" He looked from Marcus to Sherman to Andy and back again.

"Corporal Davis fell almost upon the enemy lines," Sherman informed him.

"What does *that* mean, exactly? Almost upon the enemy lines? Explain it to this nonmilitary man."

Jacob was standing very close to him now as if to catch him when he fell, calm him if he lost his temper.

"If Jesse *is* alive she would have been taken to a Rebel hospital. If she's closer to our lines, sir," Sherman continued, "she'll be brought in to a hospital the same as all the wounded."

"Is that all? *Is that it?*"

"Doctor—" Jacob began; tears had formed in his eyes. Oh, he had known, God help him, he had known all along—for *nothing* would have kept Jesse from the hospital this terrible day. He tried to take the surgeon's arm, steady him, preempt the force of one of Cartwright's often unreasonable outbursts, and perhaps even a trip to the stockade, but the surgeon shook himself free with an angry, "Stop mothering me—*for God's sake*—I've got a goddamn mother, what I need is a steward. Go back in there and help . . . I don't need you . . . I don't need anyone— leave me alone—goddamn you—"

The Dutchman stood his ground.

"I can't organize a search party for one single soldier, Doctor," Sherman was saying, "even if that soldier is . . . is someone we shall all have cause to miss."

"*Cause to miss?*" Cartwright's mouth twisted the words and then spat them out.

"We need you, Doc," called one of the orderlies, coming to the entrance of the tent.

"Yes . . . yes—I'm coming—I'll—" Cartwright drove a trembling hand through hair already standing on end and seemed unable to get the wire hooks of his spectacles around his ears. He turned away from Sherman and then back again. He spoke four words, more a plea than a demand, before his voice broke. "*Find her—I beg—*"

While Sherman and Andy returned to the horses, Marcus went after the surgeon. The soldier on the table was bleeding from a chest wound. There was blood everywhere. Marcus had never seen so much blood. How could a human lose that much blood and live? The answer was they didn't. Small wonder the surgeons drank. Small wonder Dr. Cartwright often appeared quite crazy. He watched as the surgeon cleaned his spectacle lenses with an almost manic energy. There was blood on his begrimed handkerchief and on the lenses. He was merely smearing one lens from the other, until the lens came away in his fingers. Cartwright didn't seem to notice. He curled the wires over his ears.

"Doctor," Marcus said anxiously, "you've dislodged the lens."

Cartwright looked down at the circle of glass in the center of his palm. "It's all right, it happens all the time—Jesse fixes it—Jesse fixes it good as new."

The New Englander squeezed the surgeon's arm and went after his commander.

The Dutchman placed the anesthetizing cone over the patient's nose and mouth, ignoring the tears that were running down his face into his beard.

Cartwright looked at him distractedly, then went to work.

Night had fallen. She was aware of a dull ache in her upper arm and she felt sick. She was hungry and thirsty. She and the other wounded soldier had been left to sit here in the boiling sun without shelter or a drop of water. Beside her the boy with the leg wound was quiet and still, staring into space at a vision only he could see. She knew about the prison camps. Those run by the Federals as well as the Rebels. Hadn't Thomas's own young brother been captured at Fort Donelson and exchanged with a hundred others, six months later, a mere shell of the sweet boy he had once been? The bearded guard had been replaced by another, far more dedicated to his duty. The older one had obviously mentioned her as a troublemaker, for this one kept his beady eyes on her even while he ate his evening meal and when she tried to ask for water for the wounded boy and a crust of bread he'd done nothing more than toss his own food aside, clamber to his feet, and point his musket at her stomach, as though he was good and ready for her nonsense.

The other Yankees in the line had also tried to get water. One had earned a blow to his stomach from the Rebel's musket stock, and that had discouraged any further attempts to solicit mercy from their captors. There were more guards now, anyway, and more Yankee prisoners. Jesse looked at the boy lying beside her. She passed a hand over his sightless gaze. Felt for a pulse at his throat. He was dead. She closed his eyes. Covered his face with her bloody neckerchief. Her fingers touched the necklace Thomas Ransom had given her. The neckerchief had been covering it. That's why it was still there. She buttoned her coat and put up her collar. She felt hopeless and, worse, helpless and indescribably stupid. She had to try to get some sleep. If she could sleep, tomorrow she might be able to think straight. The temperature had fallen. Her bare feet were cold. She hunkered down, curled up, and closed her eyes. She couldn't even pray. She wasn't worth saving.

The pain in her arm had somehow transferred itself to her ankle. Dawn's light was trying to squeeze under her aching lids. Then she realized someone was kicking her. She opened her eyes and sat up slowly. Two gray-clad men, one an officer, the other a private, were standing there. The young officer was staring down at her, quizzically, blinking as if the misty morning light hurt his eyes. The dead boy was still lying beside her. For the first time she noticed that he had red hair. His jacket had been removed and the enlisted man was rifling through the inside pockets.

"Ain't nuthin' 'ceptin' this photo," he said, tossing it aside.

"You, boy," said the officer to Jesse, "what's your name?"

"Corporal . . . Davis," Jesse managed, moistening her lips.

The private and the officer exchanged glances.

"May I . . . have some water . . . please?"

"Po-lite, ain't he?"

"Shut up," the officer told the enlisted man. Then to Jesse, "Get to your feet."

Jesse tried, oh, she tried, and on the fourth attempt the officer ordered the enlisted man to drag her up and there she stood swaying, the earth where the sky should be and the sky beneath her feet. She was stiff as a board. She couldn't feel her feet. Then, to her surprise, the officer handed her the canteen he was holding. When she'd drunk her fill she went to pass the canteen down the line to those of her companions who were sitting up. The private brought his musket up and used it to strike her hand. The canteen fell to the ground and the water spilled out. Jesse grabbed up the canteen and gave it to the nearest soldier, putting herself between him and the private, who raised his musket.

"No," the officer told the private.

When the soldier was finished, Jesse passed the canteen along to the next man, and so on, until the canteen was empty. Then she turned to the officer and held it out.

"Sir," she said, and arched her red brows.

The officer stared at her, small and defiant, with a strange pair of blue eyes. "Fill it," he told the private, who muttered a string of oaths but obeyed. He filled the canteen from the barrel and then thrust it at Jesse's chest so hard it drove the breath from her lungs.

"Thank you," she managed with an ironic smile.

She and the other men helped those too weak to take a drink, while the officer watched with a curious gaze and the private a hostile one. When Jesse had handed the canteen off to one of the men, she turned to face the major.

"Some of these men need medical assistance," she said. "They *all* need something to eat."

"We do not have enough food for our own men, Corporal, damned if we are going to feed the enemy."

"Then you'll starve them?" Jesse demanded to know.

"It makes very little difference if they starve here or in the prison camp."

The private looked shocked that his major would deign even to answer this scrawny Yankee boy. He raised his musket, stock toward Jesse as if to club her. Three of the other prisoners got to their feet.

"Goddamn you, I said no!" the major shouted at his subordinate. "Bring the boy," he said and then walked off.

"Git gon'," the private told her, using his musket to enforce the order and shoving her forward with his arm.

"Where are you taking me? Why did you want to know my name? What will happen to the others?" She gazed at the prisoners as she was led away.

A glimmer of purple light had begun to creep stealthily under the tent flap when Captain Van Allen raised his commander from the fitful slumber into which he had just fallen at his desk, after spending the previous night walking the camps, even more restless than usual.

"Sir." Marcus shook him roughly. "General Sherman, wake up, sir, you must come at once, sir, at once."

Sherman stood below the Federal parapet and aimed Marcus's field glasses at three figures, two in gray and a third, much smaller, in dust-covered blue, coming slowly toward them under a flag of truce.

When they stopped on the narrow belt of neutral ground between the lines the Ohioan shouted, "*My God!*" Sherman brought forth his grimy handkerchief. Both men looked at it and laughed.

"Damn it, Marcus, give me your handkerchief, sir, quickly!"

The aide shook out an immaculate white linen square and, borrowing a rifle from a nearby soldier, tied it around the bayonet. Sherman snatched it from his hands and mounted to the parapet, followed by the New Englander.

"For pity's sake, sir, be careful."

"Nonsense . . . don't you see . . . they're returning her to us . . . my vagabond . . . after one night they're eager to return her to us. I may refuse, sir, I may refuse."

Nevertheless, since the commander was already walking briskly across the distance to meet them, Van Allen simply shook his head.

The Rebel officer, young, clean-shaven, with arrogant blue eyes, was now gripping Jesse by the arm as if he thought she would make a run for it. The other, the tall, lanky private, was looking around him, wary and scared as if he mistrusted this momentary cease-fire and no longer cared about any Yankee prisoner.

Sherman nodded jerkily at the officer, then looked at Jesse. Her feet were naked and dirty. She was hatless and the leather belt with the shiny U.S. buckle that Grant had given her at Jackson was gone, as was her most treasured possession, the Bowie knife. But she was defiant as ever as she wrenched her arm free of the lieutenant's grip, demanding of him,

"One of your thieving men stole my Bowie knife. I want it returned."

"Sir," said the Rebel officer and saluted Sherman. "Major Ormsby, at your service. We have complied with your request, sir, owing to the special circumstances. But General Pemberton wishes you to know that no further return of prisoners will be considered."

"Thank you, Major Ormsby, and please convey my compliments to General Pemberton. Tell him General Grant will be suitably grateful, as will be the boy's widowed mother, General Grant's sister. You will appreciate the reasons for General Grant not coming in person to thank you?"

Ormsby nodded. "Corporal Davis," Sherman's voice was abrupt, almost harsh. "Welcome back, welcome back."

"Thank you, sir," Jesse said. "They took my knife," she added viciously. "Tell them to return the Bowie knife that Thomas gave me—"

Ormsby looked uncomfortable "I can assure you, suh, our men are not thieves."

Jesse laughed contemptuously. "You're a liar—" she said through clenched teeth. "Ask him if he intends to feed any of those Federal soldiers he has up there?"

"Again, Major, thank you," Sherman said as if she hadn't spoken.

"Sir." Ormsby saluted and turned back toward the Rebel defenses.

The private peered one last time over his shoulder. "See-en that'en weeth the reed hair, hees Ole Shermin his-self."

"Don't be ridiculous. *Shut up!*"

"General Grant's sister, sir?" Van Allen inquired when they were out of earshot.

"So, you have come back to us, Corporal Davis?"

"Sir, they've got dozens of our men, they haven't eaten or drunk for two days. Some of them need a surgeon."

Suddenly, ahead of them and with no connection whatsoever, regimental brasses had struck up "The Star Spangled Banner" in morning band practice. Jesse raised her eyes to Sherman's face.

"Did our assault succeed, sir?"

"The men fought bravely and well. Yours was not the only regimental flag placed upon the exterior slope of the fort." He did not think it necessary to tell her that despite acts of bravery similar to hers all along the Union lines the assault had been a costly, bloody failure. A complete disaster. He did not tell her that theirs had been a fifty percent mortality rate, or repeat what he had written Mrs. Sherman after the battle that the Federal soldiers had been ". . . swept away as chaff thrown from the hand in a windy day."

Jesse smiled wanly. "I knew it wouldn't fail. Please, sir, can we go home now, I'm *so* very tired."

"First we will show young Cartwright that you are back with us. He'll want to clean up that wound on your arm."

Jesse looked at her left arm, at the dried blood. She nodded. Sherman nodded.

It was nearly midnight. Cartwright came out of Jesse's tent to the rear of Sherman's headquarters. In the light of the campfire he blinked myopically at the tall, slender officer dismounting in something of a hurry and handing his reins to the orderly. It was Thomas Ransom and he spoke to Cartwright as he approached. "Why didn't you send word to me? Where's Jesse? Is she badly injured?" He glanced toward the tent and tried to bypass the surgeon, who gripped the tent flap. "For God's sake, Cartwright, tell me."

"It's not a bad wound. If she keeps it clean it'll be healed in a few days."

"Thank God—" The Vermonter removed his hat and seemed to breathe for the first time. "Can I see her?"

"She's sleeping. She was exhausted."

Ransom nodded, nodded again, and then stared at the surgeon, his handsome face distorted with anger. "Why didn't you send me word, as soon as it happened?"

"Because she was back before we knew she was gone," Cartwright answered facetiously.

"Two days?"

"Was it that long? Even the Rebs got sick of her. They sent her back."

Ransom bowed his head. The surgeon watched him trying to steady his breathing. He saw him squeeze the corners of his eyes and saw that moisture stood out on his lashes.

After a moment Ransom said, "You should have sent me word."

"You were busy with your five regiments. I didn't want to bother you."

The Vermonter looked up at him. A nerve was beating in his left cheek; his hands were clasping and unclasping, making fists. Every muscle in his lean body seemed tensed to strike. The surgeon swallowed and glanced, as if against his will, at the saber in its scabbard at the other man's waist. He wondered if this murderous expression was the one he'd been wearing when slicing off the top of that unfortunate soldier's head in Jones Field. He also wondered if this noble officer would ever strike a man in eyeglasses.

"Who told you she was missing, anyway?" Cartwright said. *"Jacob!"* He answered his own question, venomously. "Why that lousy . . . good-for-nothing Dutch Judas—" Cartwright stopped and backed up because Ransom had taken a menacing step toward him.

"I know you care deeply for Jesse," he said, "I know the anxiety of the last few days has added to your already heavy burden, but if you utter one more derogatory word against Sergeant De Groot I will knock you down, Doctor, I swear it."

Cartwright took another step backward because Ransom's hands had balled into fists which did not unclasp. "He's my steward, and I'll say what I damn well please."

"No, sir, not in my presence, or you will prepare to defend yourself."

Cartwright laughed. It was a nervous laugh and it carried a nervous question with it. "Are you challenging me to a duel?"

"I can only say that any miserable bullying attempt on your part to cast a shadow over Sergeant De Groot's exemplary character will be promptly resented by me in a most appropriate way. In other words, sir, I'll punch you on your damn nose."

There was a second's tense silence and then the surgeon shrugged his shoulders.

"If you put it like that—" he said. He took out his pipe and played with it as he spoke. "I've been meaning to talk to you." He walked off toward the trees, lest Jesse hear their voices. Ransom followed. "I think somewhere along the line you've gotten the wrong idea about Jesse and me. Don't let the fact that we fight like a couple of wildcats fool you. We've got a special relationship."

"Doctor, please, there's no need to—"

"Well, clearly there is a need," Cartwright broke in emphatically, looking at his rival sideways. He put his pipe into his mouth and made sucking noises through the stem, then said, "Girls as young as Jesse have a tendency to be very impressionable. They can so easily have their heads turned by someone like you."

"Like me?"

"A brass-mounted general, always in the front line, leading your men. You cut a *dashing* figure in that uniform, from a well-respected New England family. You've paid Jesse a lot of attention and she admires you, maybe she's even infatuated by you, but infatuation ain't love."

"You underestimate Jesse's intelligence if you believe she's impressed by rank or brass buttons."

"I may not cut so dashing a figure as you but I've looked after her since Pittsburg Landing."

"I know that, Doctor," Ransom said earnestly.

"Yes, but what you don't know, or don't want to know, is that Jesse and I have an understanding. When the war is over we're gonna get married. We've talked it over a dozen times. She knows I'll make a good husband. I'll take good care of her. You know about the Homestead Act? Jesse and I are gonna buy some land." He took the newspaper article from inside his frock coat and held it out to the other man as though it was concrete evidence of all he had said. As though the headline did not say "Homestead Act Passed," but "Jesse Davis Has Agreed to Marry Seth Cartwright." Official. "Read it, go on. I cut it from the newspaper back in May last year. Any adult citizen who has never borne arms against the U.S. government can claim 160 acres of surveyed government land. Claimants are required to 'improve' the plot by building a dwelling and cultivating the land. After five years on the land, the original filer is entitled to the property, free and clear, except for a small registration fee."

Ransom looked at Cartwright's desperate face and then at the article in the surgeon's hand, a hand trembling slightly.

"Go on—read it—" Cartwright urged, thrusting it at the other man's chest. That he take the time to read it seemed so profoundly important to the surgeon that the young general lifted the article and pretended to read. It had been taken out, read, and folded so many times in the past months that the paper was disintegrating at the folds, but he already knew about the act. He handed the paper back and nodded.

Cartwright gave an answering jerk of his head, moved his gaze across the Vermonter's calm countenance. Only his eyes showed something. Not anger, not envy, not even suspicion, or disbelief. Cartwright did not recognize it as compassion and sympathy. He thought, so he has decided to take the bad news on that well-bred chin? And said, "I thought you deserved to know."

"Yes." Ransom moistened his lips. "Thank . . . you . . . for . . . for your frankness." His voice wavered now; but the steady eyes did not even flicker, though they were full of pain for both of them.

"I'm telling you for your own good. Duty comes first with you. Now you know about me and Jesse you can stop worrying about her and dedicate all your time to promotion and winning the war."

23

Our hearts, our hopes, our prayers, our tears

O I see now that life cannot exhibit all to me—as the day cannot,
I see that I am to wait for what will be exhibited by death.

—Walt Whitman, "Night on the Prairies," *Leaves of Grass*

The Army of the Tennessee settled in for a siege.

The noise of Federal rifle fire along the picket line was constant and the Federal siege guns relentless as they pounded the city from sunrise to sunset. The returning fire from the Rebel defenders, musket and artillery, was more sporadic, and becoming less every day, constrained as it was by the lack of ammunition.

The blue-clad soldiers dug and advanced, dug and advanced, at over thirty feet per day, constructing breaching batteries at point-blank range now, without too much fear of being blown up or shot.

Trenches were extended forward toward enemy positions, and hundreds of artillery shells were fired with devastating accuracy and regularity at their fortifications. The bombardment of both the city and the Rebels behind their barricades was savage. Admiral Porter, with the heavy guns brought from his vessels and hauled ashore, and more rifled cannons being added all the time, now controlled the waterfront, holding the Mississippi River both above and below the city. Grant had drawn more troops from Memphis, and received from the North the Ninth Corps, which he posted at Snyder's Bluff, the sight of Sherman's presiege pantomime, so as to prolong the line to the left, completely closing off the land side.

Of course, there were casualties, from sharpshooters' bullets, grenades, and an occasional artillery burst, but as always sickness was the biggest problem. Sunstroke was rife, treatment simple but effective. Cold water compresses to bring down temperature, water to drink, and shade. The last easier said than done. While snake bite, insects, chills and fevers, diarrhea and constipation, boredom, ticks and lice and fleas, were all a way of life for these citizen-soldiers.

However, there was plenty of grub. No more did Grant hear the cry of "*Hardtack! Hardtack!*" from hungry Federals as he rode the lines.

While Vicksburg's civilians and soldiers were forced to count each grain of corn, eat their horses and mules, their rodents and pets, good roads had been constructed to bring provisions of all kinds up to supply the Union forces, likewise medical supplies. In the Rebel hospital the basic needs of any surgeon, clean bandages and chloroform, morphine and quinine, were almost gone. But Grant was inexorable. Unyielding. Hoist the white flag over what remained of your rooftops, or cling to the rubble and see the entire city razed to the ground. Surrender or starve. The time for mercy was past. Though the tanner's son had lost the momentum that had driven them on from Grand Gulf to here, he would have Vicksburg, whatever the price, and the desperate frontal assaults of May 19 and 22 had proved he was willing to pay that price, when the coinage was the lives of his brave, eager, and mostly uncomplaining veterans.

Vicksburg may have been crumbling, but another city, constructed entirely of canvas, had now sprung up on the hills beneath the bluffs. A tent city of field hospitals, mortuaries, post offices, photographers' studios, embalming establishments (much in demand), and of course row upon row of "thievin'" sutlers' tents, where copies of *Harper's Weekly*, with Grant's picture on the cover, changed hands for up to seven dollars. That the engraving looked nothing like the western commander mattered not a jot. This "souvenir" of the siege was more highly prized by his veterans than a ten-day furlough.

The lines were now so close together that Yank and Reb could pass letters back and forth, messages for a brother or a friend in the opposing army, converse about politics with the sensible conclusion that the war would end tomorrow if it were left to them. When discussions got too heated, they threw insults and clods of earth, a written jibe or insult, wrapped around a piece of candy to lessen the sting, as well as the odd hand grenade. They stood up in the trenches, and exchanged tobacco for coffee, and other sundry items. Since the Rebs had little to exchange but what they stood up in, the fun was more often in the exchange than the exchanged.

Most nights they sang, first one side and then the other, and then both at the same time, until the result was no more than a contest to see who could outshout the other with the bawdiest of songs. But mostly when night fell they simply lay in their trenches under the stars, and thought of home and loved ones far away.

Once, Dr. Cartwright, paying a "house call," and not remotely inebriated, climbed upon the parapet and ordered these jawing men to shake hands, to admit they were fighting for the "glorification of generals, politicians, and planters," and go home. Persuaded only by Jacob's impassioned prediction that he would be shot by Sherman for preaching mutiny in the ranks or by an enemy sharpshooter, but either way he would be dead, the surgeon climbed down. He feared neither Rebel shot nor shell, and Sherman could go to hell, but he would have no man say he preached.

When not with Sherman, Jesse spent her time at the hospital.

The Mississippi sun had sunk over the Rebel entrenchments. It was cooler, but only by a degree, cooler around suppertime before it got even hotter around the time the men tried to sleep. The birds had quieted down, now was the time of day for all insects, those that squatted, stung, crawled, or simply irritated, to rally in regiments, and assault anything that moved. You couldn't shoot an insect with a Henry but that didn't stop some of the men, maddened by the heat and these assaults on their flesh, trying. If the men hated Southerners before entering this deadly region, now they hated the very land itself, from out of which seemed to come the disease and the bugs and all that crawled on God's earth and the heat that tormented man and beast, day and night.

Jesse came out of the operating tent and breathed in the fresh air. She was emptying a gourd full of water over her head when a young corporal thrust a piece of paper into her hand. It was, surprisingly, a message from Sherman. Terse and pithy, like its author: "No hospital duties tonight. Report to my headquarters at nine. Without fail."

"—So, gentlemen, General Joseph Johnston is thirty-seven miles northeast of Vicksburg, collecting the shattered forces we whipped at Champion Hill and Jackson. Spies tell us he is also expecting reinforcements from Bragg at Tennessee, and when they arrive, he plans to attack our rear between the Yazoo and the Big Black." He interrupted himself to puff at his cigar, now no more than a stub, and looked at it in surprise, as if he could not recall smoking it down that far. He tossed it aside, smoke emerging with his next words. "But we're going to stop him by establishing a defense line between those two points." As always the Ohioan had his extensive maps, well thumbed, well marked out, spread upon the table before them so that they could push forward and see where that bony finger was going. "Haines Bluff to the railroad bridge over the Big Black, from there we'll counteract any movement on Johnston's part to relieve Vicksburg or reinforce Pemberton's position."

Jesse slipped into the tent, crowded with brigade and division commanders and waited in the rear as they filed out, talking among themselves.

Sherman was still standing behind his desk, doing what he always did before and after such meetings, studying his maps as though he had never seen them before, always searching for the unexpected, leaving nothing to chance, his red head encircled by clouds of blue-gray smoke. He knew she was standing there, all right, but he chose to ignore her. In time, she moved to the front of his desk.

"Good evening, sir."

He sat down, drew a well-thumbed copy of the *New York Herald* toward him, and growled before tossing it aside again in disgust. "Grant's movements from Grand Gulf to here have been the most successful and hazardous of the war. He is entitled to all the credit for its completion, for *I* would not have advised it." He hooked his thumbs over the arm-holes in his ash-stained vest and leaned back in his chair. "He is now deservedly the hero, belabored with praise by those who a month ago accused him of all the vices in the calendar, and who next week will turn against him if so blows the popular breeze. Vox populi—vox humbug!" He passed his disdainful gaze over the assortment of garments she was wearing. "You look like a tramp," he finally declared. "Did you have nothing clean to change into? Every night at the hospital. I don't believe I've seen you for more than five minutes these past two weeks." He smacked at something that had been crawling up his neck. "Goddamn mosquitoes. Bring the whiskey bottle from my trunk."

Jesse obeyed. She filled the tin cup and Sherman immediately swallowed half the contents. His narrow eyelids reddened. He wiped his bearded mouth on the back of his hand and stared hard at her. "So, you suffered no lasting effects from your brief stay with the enemy?"

"I'm healthy as a horse," she said so quickly that he gave a burst of rasping laughter.

"Look at you; you are all skin and bone. If you *were* a horse I'd have you shot to put you out of your misery. Why my son Willy could wrestle you to the ground with one arm tied behind his back."

"I do all right." She drew her red brows together in a mean old frown. "Maybe Willy *could* wrestle me to the ground, but I couldn't easily be kept there, I reckon I proved that on May twenty-second!"

"Your behavior on May twenty-second impressed no one, least of all me." He started to pace once more, fiddling all the while with the tarnished buttons on his coat, plucking at his short, wiry beard. During the past five months, from December '62 until now, the first days of June, from Chickasaw Bayou and Fort Hindman, through Grand Gulf and Jackson, and here to Vicksburg, it seemed that he never relaxed for a moment, was forever alert, to the point where he did not sleep, but lay in his blanket, either on the ground or on his cot, fully clothed, dozing restlessly during the predawn hours, ready and waiting to carry out Grant's orders or to respond to the enemy's next move. Vicksburg was under siege but neither Sherman nor Grant possessed a siege mentality. They were men of action. Both had different ways of coping with boredom. It was being whispered that Grant was ready to give in, not to Pemberton, but to the melancholy he felt at being stuck here, and to the lure of the whiskey bottle. Sherman's nature, on the other hand, gave him no rest, no opportunity to stare vacantly into space. He filled every waking moment with letter writing, reading, poring over his maps, questioning deserters, and riding his siege lines. He fixed her with those hypnotic eyes beneath their lowering sandy brows. Her hair was a tangle of short red curls and her clefted chin and lower lip thrust out defiantly. She looked no more than fifteen, yet in the very depths of those strange eyes was an expression as old as time itself.

"General Grant personally went to a great deal of trouble to get you back after your misguided heroism. He was forced to tell a whole parcel of untruths about you." He poked her in the shoulder, but very gently, in fact it was more a tickle than a poke. "Do you know *why* he went to so much trouble?" Sherman asked as he circled her. "For some misguided reason he likes you, has done since Pittsburg Landing. He believes you are brave and spirited and noble-hearted and can't understand why I haven't raised you to the rank of brigadier general and given you a whole regiment of cavalry since he says you love horses." Jesse blinked as his breath, hot and pungent from cigars and whiskey, seared her features, then he was off again and pacing, as restless as any disembodied spirit. "Well, you've been wounded and captured by the enemy and survived, that should be enough excitement and adventure for one lifetime." Sherman stopped suddenly and remained motionless, studying her, the cigar stub twitching at the left-hand corner of his mouth. There were still faint dark shadows beneath her eyes, but what eyes, they were afire with a determination that would not be ignored or thwarted, a fire that matched and equaled his own. A fierce little flame. "—Are you now ready to forget all this perfidious and absurd nonsense about becoming a soldier?" His face was thrust close to hers and challenging.

Jesse hitched herself up to her full five foot three inches and drew back her narrow shoulders. Then she said boldly, "No sir, I am not, and I never shall be, not until the war is over."

"I thought not." He straightened and jammed the cigar between his teeth. "This will be positively the last time I ask you. Now you will face the consequences of your recklessness and see if I give a damn!"

The following evening outside Fifteenth Corps headquarters, in sight of the Vicksburg ramparts, freshly minted Second Lieutenant Jesse Davis, junior aide de camp to General William T. Sherman, sang for the commander of the Army of the Tennessee.

Grant, who appeared none the worse for his well-concealed recent drunken binge, now sat conscientiously whittling with a small pocketknife, cutting a small stick into smaller sticks, as different from the beautifully crafted wooden images that sprang from similar pieces in Jacob's creative hands as Jeff Davis was from Mr. Lincoln. To Grant's left sat the inevitable Rawlins, and behind him Colonel James Harrison Wilson, a man even more treacherous than the tubercular Rawlins.

On Grant's right sat Sherman, long legs crossed, frock coat open, smoking compulsively, still unable to relax, and looking to all the world as if he would suddenly leap from his chair. Beside him sat Admiral Porter, far more at ease, despite suffering the effects of sunstroke.

Accompanied by three enthusiastic musicians on fiddle, harmonica, and banjo, Jesse opened her performance with "The Star Spangled Banner," a perennial favorite, even though no one appeared to know the words of Key's poem to their revolutionary forefathers. Then, as instructed by Rawlins earlier, she approached Grant and asked him if he had a special favorite she might sing for him. He sat hunched forward in his chair, the trapdoor mouth closed over his cigar, the pocketknife in his hand, a mound of tiny chippings between his feet and admitted, in that gravelly monotone, to the sycophantic amusement of his staff, and without a trace of shame or pride, "I only know two songs, Lieutenant. One is 'Yankee Doodle' and the other isn't."

"Lieutenant Davis, why don't *you* choose a song for General Grant?" Rawlins suggested as though this scene had not been previously rehearsed. Jesse obliged.

"The Union forever, hurrah! Boys, hurrah!
Down with the traitor, up with the star,
While we rally round the flag, boys
Rally once again."

By the time she had reached the chorus for the second time most of those sitting, standing, and milling around the fire were all "Shouting the Battle Cry of Freedom."

While Sherman clapped his bony hands in time to the music, Porter stamped his foot, his natural geniality increased by periodic imbibing of his own smooth Kentucky bourbon.

Presumably, Grant enjoyed the song and the voice, it was almost impossible to judge, since the tanner's son sat with his brown head bowed, chewing on a cigar stub, just whittling away stubbornly at the stick as though it was the very embodiment of Pemberton and his equally stubborn refusal to surrender.

From every nearby bivouac they came, eager enlisted men and young officers. Had Jesse not possessed so stirring a voice, her sheer energy alone would have lifted every heart and distracted every mind. The passionate gestures that animated the slender young body and strong features attested to the depth of feeling that went into every word issuing from those full lips.

Together, the voice of spun gold, the glowing face, and the earnestness were irresistible, even to Seth Cartwright, who now stood in the shadows by the large wall tent, trying desperately to resist, as he twisted his battered old kepi nervously in his hands, like a teenager come acalling on his sweetheart for the first time and didn't that sweetheart look breathtaking tonight. His eyes moved slowly, in disbelief, over her slender boyish figure in the uniform of a cavalry officer. So Sherman in all his wisdom had commissioned her. Well, that was a turn-up for the books. How well the tight-fitting single-breasted Union-blue shell jacket, the light blue pants with the white stripe, the crisp white shirt, the polished riding boots, suited her, together with the stiff-brimmed hat with the crossed saber insignia and the brass-tipped cord. His eyes came eventually to rest not on her handsome flushed face or burning eyes, but on the leather holster at her narrow waist, before moving slowly to the saber in its plain sheath, hanging by her slender leg. However, Cartwright had come prepared to match such sartorial elegance. Well, he wouldn't go quite that far, but he had brushed his frock coat, had a close shave, washed and combed his hair, and polished his boots. He was even wearing a clean shirt. He had almost made up his mind to be a little more social, to step forward, and to suggest that perhaps Captain Van Allen, his one true ally at headquarters, might pour him a glass of that fine whiskey when the arrival of several officers drove him even farther back into the concealment of the shadows. He watched with a sinking heart as they dismounted, handing their reins to an orderly. He saw Sherman get to his feet and welcome the commander of the Seventeenth Corps with a warmth that was both sincere and grateful, for perhaps the Ohioan craved the company of someone whose mind required more stimulation than stick whittling. Accompanying General McPherson were members of his staff, and Thomas Ransom.

Cartwright turned his gaze onto Jesse. As soon as she saw the Vermonter move into the firelight, her voice, if it were possible, took on an even greater vigor and pride. She attacked the third verse of "Grant's request" with such gusto that an elderly black cook from Sherman's own mess ran forward to dance and prance with total abandon, still wearing his overlarge apron, as he threw his white-palmed hands into the air and rallied 'round the flag, an enormous skillet clutched in his hand. Everyone laughed. Everyone applauded the wrinkled "monkey on a stick," as one enlisted man called him.

The surgeon watched Ransom on the periphery of the circle staring at the girl, who without hesitation began her next song, as though she had merely been awaiting his arrival.

"As the blackbird in the Spring, on the willow tree
Sat and piped, I heard him sing; singing Aura Lea
Aura Lea, Aura Lea, Maid of golden hair
Sunshine came along with thee
and swallows in the air."

There was silence now except for the crackling of the flames and Jesse's strong, affecting contralto, quivering slightly with emotion. Ransom stood tall and erect, his hat in his hands, his deep-set eyes riveted on the young girl in the blue uniform whose curls had turned to a halo of burnished gold in the firelight.

When Captain Van Allen approached Cartwright with a tin cup and a bottle, the surgeon looked like a man standing at the very edge of a cliff trying to decide whether to jump.

After a second the New Englander said, "Doctor?"

Cartwright drew in a deep breath, called himself back from the edge with an effort and looked into the aide's handsome face as he held up the tin cup.

"Drink, sir?"

He gave a jerk of his head; it was all he could manage. He took the cup and without ceremony drank almost half the contents in one gulp.

"Thirstier than usual," Van Allen observed with an indulgent smile, then he said, "Are you quite well, sir?"

"Will be in a tick." His voice was almost normal now, if a degree constricted by the alcohol. "Wooo—" He released his breath. "—Hits—the spot. Thanks."

"For the relief you bring to our wounded and sick, sir, you deserve an *entire* distillery."

"If I was in the Rebel army I'd have one by now. Did you know that the Rebels are opening several more distilleries in the Confederacy? They have at last realized the abundant restorative powers of alcohol to the sick and injured, not to mention those who *doctor* the sick and injured." Van Allen laughed and placed a hand on the surgeon's shoulder. The surgeon didn't mind. He liked Van Allen. "It's true. I was reading in the paper how doctors in a Virginia hospital kept a seventeen-year-old soldier alive by feeding him forty ounces of brandy a day. Now *that's* the kind of army *I'd* like to serve in. Water and molasses, that's all it takes. Mix one barrel of water with three gallons of molasses, add vinegar for bite and ginger for flavor, and you've got quite a passable substitute. Molasses gives it color and enough sugar to set your heart going a mite faster."

Van Allen was studying his companion. "You really are, underneath all that hair, a passably good-looking fellow." The New Englander tweaked his mustache reflectively.

Cartwright rubbed a hand over his smooth chin and managed a bleak smile that conveyed everything and nothing. The aide glanced across at Jesse and a wave of sadness came over him. As an incurable romantic himself, he wondered if there was anything quite as sorrowful as unrequited love.

"General Ransom appears to be most moved by Jesse's singing." Van Allen indicated the officer with his cup. The Vermonter seemed to be transfixed, as though every living thing upon this earth had disappeared, leaving only himself and the girl at the center of the universe. "Whereas you, sir, are made of far sterner stuff." He lightly punched the surgeon's upper arm.

"Me and old U.S." The two men looked at Sam Grant, still whittling away, the only man in their entire gathering, apart from the zealous John Rawlins, who was *dry*. "They say Grant gets drunk when his wife isn't around. You notice how it's always a woman that turns a man to strong liquor? Grant's a strange bird all right, he drinks because he misses his wife, most men drink to forget they've got one." He laughed at his own pertinent observation.

"Why don't you request that Jesse sing a song for you, Doctor? That would cheer you up, sir. Jesse's voice could cheer the dying."

"I don't have a favorite song, 'cept maybe 'Think of Your Head in the Morning.' "

Van Allen laughed.

Cartwright finished his drink. "Thanks for the whiskey *and* the conversation. I've had a long day, I think I'll turn in with *Medical Illustrated*." He slipped the handle of the cup over Van Allen's finger and walked off into the darkness.

"May God protect us all," Van Allen murmured. He raised his cup and drank the solitary toast.

By the time Jesse had reached the last verse of "Lorena" there wasn't a dry eye in the camps, except perhaps one. She looked across at General Sherman; his eyes were dry but they remained intensely focused upon her face while she sang, as though the song, about love found and denied, had taken him to a time and place far beyond this one. To his youth perhaps, or into a future he did not care to see or acknowledge. Admiral Porter winked at her—or did he?

General McPherson sat unashamed of his tears, thinking no doubt of his beloved Emily now at home with her disapproving parents in that seething cauldron of confused loyalties at Baltimore. Any day now, according to the newspapers, "the thunder of cannon and the cries of the wounded might be heard in that State as the armies of Hooker and Lee clashed on the outskirts of the Federal capital in a battle that could well decide the fate of the nation."

There were so many shouted requests and so much cheering and clapping that Sherman got to his feet, his glittering eyes staring at the faces of the enlisted men and low-ranking officers, all drawn to Grant's bivouac by the singing and the music.

"Damn you!" he said with pretend anger. "Is anyone *left* out there to guard our entrenchments?" He jammed his cigar into the corner of his mouth. "I tell you boys, this would be a fine time for Joe Johnston to sneak into Vicksburg, but I swear he would pause at the Jackson Road and on hearing Lieutenant Davis's glorious voice be so damned enthralled he would forget what he came for, and surrender!" The cheers turned to riotous laughter. "A little whiskey to keep your vocal cords loose, Lieutenant Davis." He offered his own cup.

"Thank you, sir." She raised the cup to him in a silent toast and then drank.

Admiral Porter topped up her cup. "Drink up, my boy," he instructed, "how about a cigar?" He put one of the tobacco batons into her mouth, and he said, "Like father, like son." Or maybe he didn't, the cheering and laughter and applause was so deafening that it was impossible to tell.

Four more musical interpretations later and with the audience enthralled by Corporal Buford Crabtree's "dancing fiddle," Jesse was able to escape. She walked around the outside of the circle, toward Thomas Ransom standing alone at the edge of the festivities. He saw her, but instead of coming to meet her, he turned around and would have made good his escape, had two young officers not stopped him. Jesse waited as they talked with him about the siege, their voices and eyes filled with respect and admiration for the young general. When they walked away toward the fire, Jesse came forward.

"Good evening, sir," she said.

"Good evening," he said formally.

"You once accused me of hiding from you. Now I think you're trying to avoid me."

"Forgive me. I'm not feeling particularly sociable this evening."

"Yet you came?"

"General McPherson told me you would be singing." He laughed shortly. "I'm only human."

Jesse looked at the rigid back and ramrod-straight shoulders, the determinedly steely profile under the stiff-brimmed hat, and murmured, "Sometimes I wonder."

If Ransom heard it, he let it pass. "Congratulations on your promotion."

"Do you mean that?" She looked for irony in his tone or expression and found none.

"It's a queer situation," he said quietly. "I am surprised that Sherman approves."

"It was General Rawlins's idea, and General Grant's decision."

He nodded. "The other evening I heard an officer of Grant's staff say if you knocked Grant on the head Rawlins's brain would fall out." A small group of officers to their left turned their heads to look at Jesse as she laughed. "Our conversation may appear suspicious," Ransom said. "A general and a lieutenant."

"Can you walk with me?"

"I don't think that would be wise, Jesse."

"Why wouldn't it be wise? At Big Black, you kissed me and I felt so alive. Why didn't you come and see me? I sent you three notes. Why didn't you answer them? I was wary of coming to your headquarters without your permission." She waited and then said, "I sang your song."

He glanced across at a small group of young officers who were watching them with curiosity. "Perhaps we *should* walk."

They walked in silence until they'd left the headquarters guards in their rear and had not yet reached the picket guards in their front. When they came level with the cluster of a half-dozen closely standing oak trees, Ransom stepped into the shadows where they could not be seen or heard. Ever the gentleman, he removed his hat.

They blended into the darkness, invisible, except to each other. Now he could kiss her. Jesse was trembling a little with anticipation; now would be a good time to kiss her. The feeling she'd had at the Big Black when he kissed her had almost driven her mad. She removed her hat, held her breath. The branches rustled overhead. The stars were hard points of glittering light.

"How is your arm?" he asked.

"Healed, thank you. It was nothing. Jakob told me that you sent word every day asking how I was. But I don't understand why you couldn't come yourself, at least once. Were you so busy with your duties?"

"It wasn't—" he began with a pained expression, and then stopped. "Yes, my duties must come first."

"But I wanted so much to see you." She touched his hand and he moved it out of her reach. He stared off into the darkness, unable to look her in the eye. "Thomas, what's the matter with you? Why have you grown so cold toward me?" She gazed up at the handsome face framed by those distinctive sideburns. The moonlit shadows accentuated the lean manly beauty of his features, yet it was a touchingly boyish face.

"When you see Dr. Cartwright please say I shall look forward to play-ing that game of chess with him in Vicksburg. I doubt I'll see him before General Sherman moves out to the Big Black."

"But you're going with us?" Jesse's heart made a leaping motion in her chest. "General Sherman said part of his force will be made up of General McArthur's division."

"All but my brigade, which will remain here. We are in the process of digging a massive redoubt deep into the Rebel lines near the Third Louisiana Redan. General Grant is planning a third assault. We will place two thousand pounds of gunpowder beneath the Redan and deto-nate it as a prelude to the attack, in that way we may establish a foothold inside the enemy fort." He stared into her blue eyes for a long moment and then seemed to come back to himself with a great effort and moved slightly away from her. The distant sound of a brass band now wafted on the light breeze filling the night with the stirring strains of "Colonel Meeker's Quickstep." Above them, the branches gently swayed their ghostly dance against the pale moonlight in the warm night air. His eyes traveled over the top of her head. He had a way of looking at her, as though she alone filled his world. Yet he would not kiss her, would not touch her in a way that would make her feel *alive*. "You've cut your hair." She nodded. "I like it."

"Did you always prefer long hair before you met me?"

He thought for a minute. "I have no preference."

"Most men like long hair," Jesse said.

"I like your hair the way it is." He brought his hand halfway to her head and then dropped it. He tried again and this time he touched her hair, felt the texture, stooped a little to let the aroma drift into his nostrils, before letting his hand drop. He would remember this when he was alone in his tent late at night. This much he could take unselfishly for himself. "The uniform suits you too."

She laughed softly, a girlish laughter, coy, yet bold. "Better than a dress?"

"I've never seen you in a dress. I'd like to see you one day," he added, almost dreamily.

"What color?" Her voice was a croak.

"Red gold. The same color as your hair. I'd also like to see your wings, just once." He smiled to show he was joking, but the look of longing, of sorrow, in his eyes made Jesse gasp.

"I loved it when you kissed me—" She came closer. "Please, kiss me now?"

He held off with one hand. "May I walk you back to the encampment?" he said.

"Oh Thomas—"

He put on his hat. She said,

"No—no—I'll wait here just a moment longer."

He nodded. "Good-bye, Jesse. God bless you."

"Not good-bye!" she called into the darkness. "Not good-bye! How can you give us up easily?"

So the hot, rank, fly- and mosquito-infested month of May had long faded and the hotter rank, fly- and mosquito-infested month of June had taken its place.

On the morning of June 18, news went through the camps like wild-fire. John McClernand, the politician-general who had been a thorn in Grant's side since Fort Donelson, was relieved of his command. McClernand had caused to be printed in the *Memphis Evening Bulletin* a congratulatory order to his troops after the assault of the twenty-second, praising them and casting aspersions upon the loyalty, courage, and leadership of the other two corps. Sherman read the story and had shown Grant a War Department order of the previous year, which forbade the publication of all official letters and reports on pain of dismissal, by the president himself. Grant sent McClernand packing and General Edward O. C. Ord, a recently arrived sober-looking Catholic with impressive gray whiskers, and lifelong friend of Sherman, got the Thirteenth Corps.

"It remains to be seen if McClernand will continue his lies and treacherous ways against Grant and myself with his supporters in Washington," Sherman said, "but for now and hopefully *forever* he is where he cannot harm this army or its most loyal officers."

On Saturday, June 20, by virtue of a presidential proclamation, West Virginia officially took its place as the thirty-fifth state of the Union. As though to mark this event there was an especially loud bombardment of Vicksburg by the Federal navy and army in perfect concert, which lasted six hours and left most occupants on both sides temporarily deaf. When the chorus of heavy siege guns ceased, the roar of the mortars took up the repetitive warrior chant, interposed with the occasional but regular crack of those much-loved solo performers on both sides—the sharpshooters. There were always those who thought they could outwit a bullet. Anything, even the risk of death or serious injury, was sought to alleviate the soldier's worst enemy—*boredom*.

William T. Sherman was never bored.

Among his many other skills and accomplishments he was an engineer. When not riding up and down the siege lines checking the entrenchments, talking to his men in the rifle pits, he supervised the digging and breastworks as they extended ever farther toward the Rebels. He spent the nights writing letters, or reading Gibbon's second volume of *The Decline and Fall of the Roman Empire*, a treasure that Jesse had exchanged with a Rebel artilleryman for the gold tassel around her new stiff-brimmed hat. That he would live to finish this large tome was a matter for conjecture considering his recent habit of riding along his lines atop the steadfast Sam, in full and unconcerned view of the Rebel marksmen. By now the familiar red-bearded commander had become a favored target. One could imagine sharp-eyed, tousle-haired farm boys eagerly striking wagers against their skill and expertise as to who could finally shoot the scowling Yankee off his horse. Musket balls whizzed past his head with such determined regularity that a story actually appeared in the newspaper reporting the serious wounding, if not death, of Major General William T. Sherman, commander of the Fifteenth Corps. It was a report so convincing that it had apparently caused Old Abe much apprehension and dismay, until it was proved to be, like most newspaper reports, complete humbug.

The general's stubbornness in ignoring all pleas from his staff to exercise a little more caution in his daily inspection tours, and the direct admonition from Mrs. Sherman "to keep his head down," had brought the following retort from her husband:

> As to my exposing myself unnecessarily, you need not be concerned. I know where danger lies and where I should be. Soldiers have a right to see and know that the man who guides them is near enough to see with his own eyes, and that he cannot see without being seen.

As for Jesse, she was uncharacteristically and increasingly preoccupied these days.

Since the night of the concert, she had written a barrage of notes to Thomas Ransom. They had begun as reasonable requests to meet with him so they could talk. But with no response the wording of the notes had grown to desperate pleas, begging for an explanation as to why he no longer sought her company. If you do not reply, her last note had said, I will visit your headquarters.

Finally, he had responded, but not in a manner she had expected. His severity had shocked her. He had written,

"Please cease your correspondence. It is both dangerous and inappropriate under the circumstances. I have replied. Do not visit my headquarters. There is nothing to be gained by our meeting or talking."

Of course, it was like a flashing cape to an already maddened bull.

24

And all the gods go with you

Most men make the voyage of life as if they carried sealed orders which they were not to open till they were fairly in mid-ocean.

—James Russell Lowell, *Among My Books*

As Jesse rode into Ransom's camp that morning the ever-amiable Captain Dickey, Ransom's best friend, came to meet her.

"Congratulations on your promotion, Jesse."

"Yes sir, thank you." She had neither the time nor patience for niceties. "Is Thom—is General Ransom here? Would you tell him it's me."

"You seem agitated, is everything all right?"

"I'm not agitated." Jesse could not keep the insistent irritation from her voice. "Only I must speak with the general."

"Yes, of course."

An orderly took Jesse's horse and in a few seconds Dickey emerged from the brigade commander's tent with a very confused and discomforted expression on his face.

"I'm sorry, Jesse, General Ransom extends his apologies. He is just about to begin an inspection tour of the parapets."

"I'll wait."

Dickey watched in surprise as Jesse walked with decisive step to the campfire and sat down. He went back into Ransom's tent and a moment later joined the girl.

"Lieutenant Davis, I spoke to the general again and he says he has a few moments to spare." The words were barely out of his mouth before Jesse had sprung up and was going toward the Vermonter's tent. Dickey's frown deepened as he watched her.

The Vermonter was standing behind his desk, perhaps to keep something solid between her and him, and his thickly veined hand gripped the top as if to steady himself.

"What do you think you're doing?" he demanded of her, his handsome face pale and his eyes flashing with anger. "Didn't you get my note? I told you not to come here."

"I got your note." Jesse could hardly breathe. She tore the paper from her pocket and flung it on the desk. "I got it, and I'm trying to understand it. I'm trying to understand *you*."

"I don't know what you're talking about. There's nothing to understand."

"I'm confused. I feel as if all light has gone out in the entire world. I can't eat and I can't sleep. What are you doing?" she said hopelessly. "This isn't you. I refuse to believe this is you. Why are you treating me this way? What's happened to you? To us?"

"I've come to my senses, that's what's happened." He stared at her stricken face and lowered his intense gaze to his hand on the desk. He tried, and failed to stop the hand from trembling. "I simply cannot have any relationship with a young woman who has attached herself to a general during a war, as you have done."

"It never bothered you before."

"How would you know, you've never asked me. How can it not bother me to hear that you've been captured by the enemy? How can it not bother me to know that you are riding around the country dressed as a boy, exposed to all manner of pain and suffering, in danger every second that you remain here?"

"I assumed—" She stopped and frowned.

"Yes. You assume too much."

"Did I assume you had special feelings for me?"

"Dr. Cartwright—" he began.

Jesse waited. "What about him?" she said. "What did he tell?"

"Nothing I didn't already know. Nothing I can't see with my own eyes. I'm not blind, Jesse."

"Oh, but you are, blind and deaf."

"He needs you," Ransom declared forcefully.

"And all *you need* is another star on your shoulder, is that it?"

"It's for the best."

"How can it be for the best when we're both so unhappy? Why are you doing this? I'm begging you—"

"Don't beg. I've made up my mind." Suddenly he became composed. The tremor in his hand subsided. He stood erect as if to emphasize the strength of will that had gone into his decision. "You really will have to go, Jesse. I have an inspection tour to make."

She gazed up into his eyes that, despite his declared intent, were swimming. She tried to take his hand but he shook her off. "Is it because I was too forward, too brazen with you? Because I can be demure, like the sweetest of females. You wanted to see me in a dress—I can find one and have my likeness taken all on my own. Tell me what I've done wrong and I'll put it right—only don't send me back to sleep again—I couldn't bear it." She was crying now, tears were streaming down her face.

"Jesse, for God's sake stop it. You've done nothing wrong, please believe me, you've done nothing wrong."

"Then why won't you love me anymore?"

"I told you!" He glanced toward the entrance and then lowered his voice to say again, "I told you."

"You haven't told me anything. After we leave here I'll write to you every day. I don't care if you tear up my letters and never reply. I don't care if they send you halfway across the country. I'll keep writing until you change your mind. I can't sleep—I can't concentrate—if you only knew how I—" Suddenly she raised a trembling hand to her brow and seemed to stagger. "Oh no—" she murmured as Ransom reached for her elbow.

"Jesse—what is it? Are you sick?"

"Sick? No—" She tried to focus on his anxious face. "The general—"

"What general?"

"What have I done?" She stared at him distractedly before walking unsteadily out of his tent.

He followed her to the corral and watched her climb aboard her horse, saying, "Jesse, what in heaven's name—?"

She rode out of his camp without a word of explanation.

"Jesse—I've been . . . waiting for you," Sherman said in his hoarse voice, now slightly faltering, and unmistakably relieved. He was sitting on the edge of his cot, his blouse outside his pants, his usually red face as drained of color as she had ever seen it, his raw features pinched.

"I'm sorry, I'm so sorry—can you ever forgive me?" She placed her medical haversack on the floor by the cot. She had come prepared.

"Forgive you? Why, it wasn't your fault." He laughed and grimaced with pain. "A lucky shot, a well-aimed Rebel ball. They were flying everywhere this morning. They were waiting for me. They've had old Sherman in their sights for days now. You know that. It's nothing."

Jesse knelt down on the floor and carefully drew his blouse aside. There was a rip in the red woolen long johns just above his narrow waist under his right arm and the area was stained with fresh blood. It was still bleeding. She helped him off with his blouse and ripped the upper part of the long johns around the wound. Then she made him lie down on the cot and hold a wad of lint there while she went for fresh water, telling him, "Please don't move."

"Jesse—" He gripped her arm. "Tell no one. Not even Captain Jackson. I hid it well. My staff scattered as the firing began. No one noticed. I don't want them to say I told you so."

She nodded.

Her hands would not remain steady as she cleaned the edges of the wound. It wasn't so bad, no, not so bad. He'd lost some blood, but it had stopped now and persistent, if painful prodding had convinced her there was nothing left in the wound to inflame it, not metal nor pieces of clothing. The ball had taken a small piece of flesh with it as it went by, but it would heal well if she kept it clean. She had already had him swallow some morphine with several glasses of water.

"Why are you so nervous?" Sherman asked from his prone position, a cigar wedged into the corner of his mouth. She was being uncharacteristically clumsy. "It would require something far more serious than this to kill off old Sherman."

"You said you would be postponing your daily ride along the siege lines until after your meeting with General Grant."

"I said I would be going directly from the siege lines to General Grant's headquarters," Sherman declared irritably. "What damn difference does it make, anyhow?"

"I should have seen this was going to happen—I was distracted," she said, placing a gauze dressing against the wound, which fell to the floor. Even her doctoring skills were failing. She tossed the gauze aside, cut a fresh one and held it there with strips of sticky plaster. "It will never happen again."

"That's most comforting, or at least it would be if I thought you had any control over such matters." His hiccuping laughter seemed to assault her ears, to add to her guilt and shame.

She stood up abruptly and glared at him. "Do you think this is a subject for laughter? Do you think what happened to you today, because of me, because I allowed myself to become obsessed by matters that should not even have been on my *mind*, let alone totally occupying it, is somehow *amusing*?"

"Jesse, what in the devil has gotten into you? You will get ahold of yourself. It's a scratch, nothing more."

"It's *not* serious, because I came to my senses just in time—if I had taken a moment longer the entire course of the war would have been changed."

"Stop jabbering!"

She gave him a glass of whiskey. "For the shock. When the morphine wears off you'll have pain. This will ease it."

He drained the glass thirstily and held it out. "We cannot know how quickly the morphine will wear off, or how bad the pain will be," he said wiggling the glass.

She started to laugh then, and could not stop, could not restrain herself, and in the midst of all the hysterical laughter came the tears and she found herself laughing and crying at the same time as Sherman lay there with his empty glass extended, his cigar drooping, staring at her as though she had finally, inevitably, gone stark raving mad.

By June 16, speculation had ended as to whether or not Lee was going to invade Pennsylvania. His Army of Northern Virginia had continued to move north into Maryland and crossed the Potomac. To meet this threat Mr. Lincoln had called for militia from Ohio, Maryland, West Virginia, and Pennsylvania itself, where families were departing in droves, crowding onto the cars, with all they could carry. In Washington, Mr. Lincoln was offering Hooker advice on how to fight Lee. Rumors of Fightin' Joe's death had been exaggerated. He was moving northward but couldn't *find* the Rebel army. He had then announced to the papers and to his president, "Now is the time to march to Richmond." Mr. Lincoln had replied, "I think *Lee's* Army, and not *Richmond* is your true objective point. Fight him when opportunity offers. If he stays where he is, fret him, and fret him." In the event, it was Mr. Lincoln who fretted.

Hooker meanwhile, instead of girding his loins for the coming battle, had told the president, "It is not in my power to prevent invasion." A statement that must have cheered Mr. Lincoln and the loyal citizens of Baltimore, Maryland, and Pennsylvania, waiting in trepidation for the enemy to pour over their borders.

In Louisiana, Banks too wasn't having much luck. He had called once more upon Port Hudson to surrender. They'd refused and at dawn on June 14 he ordered an assault. This, his second assault, failed as miserably as the first. The shocking disparity between Federal and Rebel casualties, 1,792 blue-clad and 47 gray-clad, seemed to prove conclusively that attacks against entrenched enemy positions brought only slaughter for the attackers. Now two Rebel strongholds were under siege along the Mississippi.

On the morning of June 18, exactly one month to the day since the army invested Vicksburg, General William T. Sherman led his Expeditionary Army out of the Federal encampment around the Walnut Hills to an encampment on the Big Black, twenty miles to the northwest of the city. Here he would keep an eye on Joe Johnston, and if the Rebel general moved to help Pemberton, the Ohioan would be there to stop him.

From his headquarters at Bear Creek, Sherman daily rode the circuit of his command, visiting outposts and pickets, questioning spies and deserters and civilian informers, constantly on the lookout for news of Joe Johnston's anticipated move to reinforce Pemberton.

Although small groups of gray-clad horsemen and infantry could be seen camped on the east side of Big Black, openly facing their blue-clad opponents, there was no sign of the large force that was rumored to be gathering at Canton, twenty miles to the northwest. This did not surprise Sherman, as he told his commanders, "However important Vicksburg might be to the Rebels, Joe Johnston is too intelligent a commander to throw his men onto fortified entrenchments and risk losing one army to save another, and possibly lose both."

While Sherman kept Grant up to date with his movements, Grant sent word of Vicksburg. On the twenty-fifth over two thousand pounds of gunpowder buried under the Rebel positions at the Third Louisiana Redan was detonated. Logan's division went plunging forward with fixed bayonets. The fighting was desperate, hand to hand, the worst kind. The two-pound howitzers in "Fort Ransom" that the Vermonter himself had personally helped to drag into position did their duty, blazing away as Logan's men went forward. All in all the assault was another failure. At four in the afternoon of the following day, Logan's men retreated from the Rebel fort and all fell quiet once more.

News was sporadic from other areas of the war. Rosecrans had pushed Bragg across the Tennessee River in the direction of Chattanooga. Hooker was groping around in the dark for Lee's army. Then on the twenty-seventh, President Lincoln relieved him of his command. Contrary to popular belief, it was not John Reynolds who was to replace him, but Major General George Meade. It seemed that Meade would have little time to get over the shock of being made commander. It was said every Rebel in the area was converging on Gettysburg.

The booming of the Federal cannons bombarding Vicksburg could be heard at Bear Creek. But at midday on July 3, the booming suddenly ceased and the telegraph lines between Sherman and Grant hummed like a swarm of maddened bees. The reason? Unconditional Surrender Grant had sent Pemberton a letter proposing an armistice, a copy of which Grant sent to Sherman, who replied,

> I have your despatch. Telegraph me the moment you have Vicksburg in possession and I will secure all the crossings of Big Black and move to Jackson or Canton—If you are in Vicksburg Glory Hallelujah the best fourth of July since 1776. Of course we must not rest idle only don't let us brag too soon. Will order my troops at once to occupy the forks of Big Black and await with anxiety your further answer.

Sherman paced outside his tent and in due course Grant responded.

> I want Johnston broken up as effectually as possible, and roads destroyed—When we go in I want you to drive Johnston from the Mississippi Central railroad; destroy bridges as far as Grenada with your cavalry, and do the enemy all the harm possible. You can make your own arrangements and have all the troops of my command except one corps—McPherson's say. I must have some troops to send to Banks, to use against Port Hudson.

It wasn't until seven the following evening that the eagerly anticipated news came through. Jesse, sent to the telegraph wagon to wait, ran back to Sherman as fast as she could. Pemberton had accepted Grant's terms. Men leapt out of their trenches at Vicksburg. Sherman's men, there on Big Black, cheered also, but it was a terrible shame, after all, they, like their commander, had contributed so much to the final fall of the city, yet were unable to be there to enjoy it.

Sherman wrote to Grant,

My Dear General: The telegraph has just announced to me that Vicksburg is ours; its garrison will march out, stack arms, and return within their lines as prisoners of war, and that you will occupy the city only with such troops as you have designated in orders. I can hardly contain myself.

He would now go after Johnston.

The pursuit of Joseph Johnston, who had rushed his army back into the Mississippi capital on hearing of Pemberton's surrender, was a nightmare, and well described as such, since the daytime heat was so intense that Sherman ordered his men to march at night and rest during the day. Water was scarce, men had only what they carried in their canteens. Johnston had ordered kerosene poured into wells, pumps broken, and horses, dogs, mules, driven into the streams and shot, to be left there polluting the water. The rancid smell followed Sherman's men all the way to Jackson over dusty roads toward a powerful enemy.

By the tenth of the month, Sherman had reached the Mississippi capital. For the next two days, he ordered the city bombarded. As the Ohioan observed, listening to his twenty-pounder Parrott guns, "I can make the town pretty hot to live in!" and he did. Cannons roared at five-minute intervals from four different batteries, night and day. In a forty-eight-hour period it was estimated that Sherman's artillery had discharged three thousand shells into the city, now all but engulfed in a pall of choking black smoke that hung there, a giant cloud of doom, presaging the inevitable outcome.

Meanwhile his cavalry was not idle. They broke up railroads, burned locomotives, destroyed the telegraphs, bridges, and ferries. They ripped up railroads, brought destruction to farms and plantations, to fields and smokehouses. Cattle and hogs, sheep and poultry, anything that grew and ate, bleated or snorted or clucked, was descended upon by willing hands, and either strangled on the spot and stuffed into gunnysacks or led away to be slaughtered later. Before the new corn was a foot high, it was "harvested" and thrown into wagons to be fed to mules and horses.

On the third day of the siege, news reached them that Port Hudson had finally fallen.

This made Sherman even more impatient. "If Johnston breaks and runs," he told his commanders, "pursuit would be impossible in this unbearable heat, men and horses would perish in days. If he moves across Pearl River, and makes good speed, I will let him go."

On the sixteenth, in the dead of night, Johnston did retreat across the Pearl River. Sherman's men captured all of his guns and five hundred prisoners. Then they poured into Jackson, and for the second time in three months, they set about punishing the town, plundering, burning, and stealing. When a group of soldiers broke into a tobacco warehouse Jesse was unashamedly and aggressively in the front rank. Small and swift, like a rabbit, she tore through the aromatic-smelling building ahead of her fellow looters, filled her hat to the brim with the precious leaf, stuffed it inside her jacket and vanished before the provost guard arrived to round up the culprits.

Occupied twice by Johnston's men in retreat and twice by Sherman's in pursuit, Jackson's was a sad fate, but one brought about not by Sherman, but her erstwhile defenders. Four days after this last occupation by his men the Ohioan was able to write Grant, "Jackson is one mass of charred ruins, terrible to contemplate. We have desolated the land for 30 miles."

Ever a man of profound contradiction, he then set about feeding the inhabitants.

Their last evening at Jackson brought dispatches from Grant. James McPherson was to be military governor of Vicksburg. Sherman's earlier mood of "high feather" was replaced by one of gloom, bordering on self-pity. He had expected that job. He had wanted to do there what he had done at Memphis, bring the citizens back into the Union.

"Sherman is always in the wrong place at the wrong time," he said as

Jesse cleared away his untouched supper. "Vicksburg capitulates and I am nowhere near. Let someone else follow Johnston. I've written to Brooks Brothers of New York to send me two coats and two pants, sweat and dust have made my clothes shabby." He stuck out his long leg to show her. "And the bushes have made me ragged below the knee. I took the opportunity of ordering you one jacket and one pair of pants. You may pay me out of your next poker winnings and don't bother denying that you gamble."

"Thank you, sir. May I say something?"

"If I say no will it stop you?"

"Without you Vicksburg would never have been captured. Grant knows it. You gave every ounce of energy, strength, and determination to making the seemingly impossible possible. Without you and brigade commanders like Thomas Ransom, without loyal and brave men like Admiral Porter, Grant would still be digging ditches on the wrong side of the river."

Satisfied with his work, Sherman started his troops back to Big Black, troops who were anticipating nothing more than a short furlough and a long look at loved ones they hadn't seen for years.

"Wonderful news—" The surgeon was leaning against the tree in shirt and pants, one leg crossed over the other, his forage cap with the broken visor sunk low over his brow, his thumbs hooked around his frayed suspenders. He was watching Jesse groom her horse. "—Vicksburg, Port Hudson, Gettysburg—surely it'll all be over soon?" There was more hope than certainty in his voice.

After so many disasters, under so many incompetent commanders, it was almost impossible to believe that the Army of the Potomac had met and beaten Lee's army at Gettysburg, Pennsylvania. Lee retreated from Gettysburg on July 4, the day after the conclusion of the fierce fighting. Then after Mr. Lincoln had announced it to the country as "a great success to the cause of the Union," Meade had gone and spoiled it by not pursuing Lee, trapped on the wrong side of the Potomac by swollen waters, finally destroying that army and, in conjunction with Vicksburg and Port Hudson, bringing about the end of the rebellion. For Sherman the battle had brought a personal sorrow. His good friend John Reynolds had been killed on the first day by a sharpshooter.

"Meade should have gone after Lee," Jesse said.

"The way Sherman went after Johnston?"

She shifted the curry comb from right to left hand and went on brushing the animal's flanks. "You're the one usually voting for us all to stay home and knit. Maybe you didn't notice how the men were collapsing with heatstroke? They've been marching and fighting for seven months. They're exhausted."

"That's a hell of a thing to say to a surgeon. Yes, the men are exhausted, all right. It must be all that destruction they heaped on Jackson."

Jesse gave him that look.

"I'm entitled to my opinion," he said defensively. Then he remembered he was here to get closer to her, not to alienate her even further. He frowned suddenly. "Hey, where have I seen that horse before? Goddamn it—can't be—it looks just like the horse you rode that day at Pittsburg Landing."

That was just what Sherman had said. But it was the very same horse, Quicksand by name and shifting sands by nature. One morning Sherman had told her she needed a horse to match her rank. Before Shiloh, he had promised that this palomino would be hers when she became an officer. Now the promise was fulfilled. Only no one believed it.

"Have you had any letters from Major Coopersmith?" Jesse stopped to ask this, leaning on the saddle.

"No—" the surgeon said quietly, shaking his head. "He's too busy with the wounded, I guess."

"I'm sure that's true." She went back to grooming her horse.

"Have you heard from Sir Ransom?"

She came around to the front of the horse, rinsed the cloth in the cool water, squeezed out the excess moisture, and used it to wash the horse's face and eyes.

"Is it true what the newspaper reporters are saying, that Sherman's going to march on Chattanooga or Atlanta?"

Sherman's new fear was that Washington would send either him or

Grant east. He had predicted they would be in Mobile in October and Georgia by Christmas and they were now his favored moves. Cartwright watched her using her currycomb on the horse's flanks. Her new uniform was already beginning to look shabby, though it fitted better. There was something so inexpressibly attractive and touching about her boyish form and short red hair, the sculptured jaw, and of course, that cleft in the thrusting chin. Evidently, she was in a less talkative mood this morning.

"I've been thinking about my father," he said into the summer afternoon silence, swatting a fly from his face. "About what you once told me—about him being proud of me. I just don't believe the dead watch us, that's all."

"The dead that we have loved are inside of us, all around us, in our hearts and thoughts, in our memories, they share our joys and pain." She stopped brushing. "Your father is with you."

"Did you say you haven't heard from Ransom?"

"Look," Jesse rounded on him, fire in her eyes. "If you're trying to find out what's going on between General Ransom and me you can stop worrying. I have neither seen nor heard from him since we left Vicksburg. I lost my way. I made a mistake. Now it's over with." She tossed the wet rag into the bucket. "However, if you think it makes any difference to our relationship, you'd best think again. You and I are true friends, but if you want to keep my friendship you'll have to give up this . . . this—" she made a dismissive gesture with her hand—"ridiculous dream of us sitting on the back porch of your house after the war. Because that's just what it is, *a dream*! Your dream, not mine. You have to accept that, otherwise you can find yourself another whiskey supplier."

"Is that all you think you mean to me?"

"I know what I mean to you. I've tried to avoid meaning that to you since the moment we met. But I tell you now, Doctor, make your choice, friendship or nothing."

"Everyone's got a dream, Jesse, even you. What's the point of living if you can't have a dream?" Cartwright was staring at her as if she was someone he'd never seen before. All trace of emotion had vanished from her face. He'd heard it all before, the threats to cease their association, but this time he couldn't help fearing she really meant it. He felt as if he had been kicked in the stomach by that crazy horse of hers. "If that's the way you want it," he said quietly, after a moment's strained silence.

"*I do*," she said emphatically.

Something died inside of him. He sunk down onto the ground. "Okay," he murmured.

"Okay," she echoed with a jerk of her head, as if putting her voice to a verbal contract.

"Am I allowed to know why you and Ransom—?" He ceased because her expression told him to drop the subject—permanently.

She caught up the canteen from where it hung on the branch of the tree, removed the stopper, and handed it to him. Then she sat down beside him.

"Thanks," he said and drank. His mouth was dry and his hands were sweating. "Can I tell you something?" Jesse nodded. "I can diagnose erysipelas with my eyes closed; perform the most completed amputation with one hand tied behind my back. At medical school I could relate by heart the properties of a thousand drugs and dissect a frog so exactly you would think his guts were a work of art—Jesus, I ranked so high in my surgical anatomy class they marked me separate to the other students so they wouldn't get disheartened—but try as I might I can't understand human nature."

"Taking a minié ball out of a man's skull has nothing to do with understanding what goes on inside his mind."

"Why did you do it, Jesse?" he asked suddenly as though he had been busting to ask this question since May 22. "Why did you join the assault that day?"

She got that look in her eyes. The one he hated; the one that seemed to cut her off from him, from all humanity, like the blind eyes of a stone angel in a cemetery. Benign and yet detached. The look that made her an outsider, a watcher, a witness, instead of a participant in this crazy business of living. That look made him feel lonely and disappointed. Somehow, since the day he'd met her, he believed she'd hold the answers to all those questions of living.

"Death," she said softly.

"You wanted to die?" Cartwright was incredulous, horrified.

Jesse turned that introverted gaze onto his face. "No, I don't think so, I don't think I wanted to die."

"You don't think so?" Cartwright had started the conversation, asked the question, now he was sorry he had. Most times what the girl said made no sense to him, frightened him, even.

She released her breath as a sigh. "You were born, you live, you feel, you're *allowed* to feel, to grow old and die. For you it's a natural progression. You take it for granted. Being given life, having a life to do with what you will, is a most wondrous thing."

Cartwright blinked and stared at her. "Maybe you grew up too quickly," he said, groping toward some understanding of her words. "With no family that can happen. Looking out for yourself. You're old before your time."

She laughed ironically. Then she admitted, "What I did, joining the assault, was dangerous. Not only for me."

"It didn't do my nerves much good."

"Wanting to experience life, love, death—"

"For chrissake, haven't you experienced enough death in the operating tents?" the surgeon interrupted with venom.

"I envy you, your anger, your vast capacity for love and hate. Your passion. You couldn't hold back if you tried and you'd never want to try. In a way, Thomas and I are alike. Single-minded. At least I will be from now on."

"Just once, Jesse, I'd like to figure just what the hell you're talking about. Just once."

Jesse drank from the canteen and then rammed home the stopper with such violence that he said, "It's okay. I'm not going to spend the rest of my life chasing after you like a cat in heat. There's just so much rejection a boy can take before he howls, enough!"

"That's not it. I was just informed by the general that Mrs. Sherman and four of his children are coming to stay." As if this wasn't bad enough, Sherman had named his family's temporary home, nestled there in a grove of oaks, "Polliwoggle Retreat" in honor of the horse pond, very convenient to their camp, and, in his words, "full of songster frogs."

"It's not forever." Cartwright was genuinely trying to make her feel better. He grinned suddenly. "Know what I'd wish for now out of everything? A pitcher of cold milk and a plate of my mother's gingerbread." He sounded like a child.

Jesse laughed.

"Friends?" the surgeon said with a sad, hesitant smile.

"Friends." She handed him the canteen.

Three days later, after supper, Jesse turned up at Cartwright's hospital, with her horse and all her worldly goods. The surgeon was sitting on a tree stump trying to sew a button onto his frock coat. "Ouch! Goddamn it! How come I can sew a man's guts back into his stomach but can't sew a goddamn button on a goddamn coat?" He squinted at her and at her saddlebags. "What's up?"

She saluted and said, "Mrs. Sherman has just arrived, sir. While the general's family remain I'm transferred to your hospital." She compressed her full lips and her clefted chin quivered. Her next words came out jerkily, as though there was an obstruction in her throat. "Will you . . . show me where . . . I'm to bivouac during my . . . reassignment, and tell me my duties."

Cartwright broke the cotton thread and swore roundly. "I'll tell you your first duty, it's to stitch this goddamn button on my goddamn coat."

Jesse looked at the button. "Don't you have another one, this one's all twisted."

"Like everything else in this goddamn army."

In mid-July, there was a riot in New York, a mostly Irish mob, precipitated by the new Northern draft laws. Any man who could find a substitute to fight in his place for a small bounty or raise $300 to pay to the government as a "commutation fee" was exempt. Jacob's brother-in-law had written to tell him of a professional bounty jumper who signed up, pocketed his "reward" for enlisting, then deserted his regiment to repeat the process twenty-six times.

Grant was, as Sherman observed, "the hero whom all worship—" including Mr. Lincoln. He had been rewarded with the rank of major general in the Regular Army. If the war finished tomorrow, he would never again have to sell cordwood on the streets of Saint Louis.

For Sherman there was also a reward. On Grant's recommendation, he was made a brigadier general in the Regular Army, together with James McPherson. Their country had acknowledged the debt it owed these men who had captured a large army and brought free navigation back to the Mississippi.

Though all praised Sherman and to a lesser degree McPherson, and called Grant "the hero of the hour," it was "Gettysburg" that Washington spoke with hallowed tones. The Rebels must have seemed too close for comfort, and the Army of the Potomac had saved their bacon, whereas Vicksburg was thousands of miles away, deep in enemy territory. Only those who had fought and commanded in that mosquito-plagued, alligator-infested, mud-encrusted, dust-caked, thirst-inducing, health-destroying, diarrhea-ridden, hot, wet, dry, sun-baked hell that Rebels called home understood just what miracles had been achieved in so short a time. Maybe only the veterans themselves knew that because of their hard-fighting, hard-marching Army of the Tennessee, in Mr. Lincoln's words, "The Father of Waters now flowed unvexed to the sea—"

One morning in early August, Jesse and Cartwright met the general and his eldest son as they crossed the oak grove. Jesse saluted and Willy responded in kind, a smiling sunburned child with glowing freckles, all decked out in his sergeant's uniform.

"You haven't met my son, have you, Doctor," Sherman said with unconcealed pride, as though this was his only son. "Dr. Cartwright, Sergeant William T. Sherman Jr., of the First Battalion, the Thirteenth United States Regulars." Nine years old that past June, so much did this redheaded, light-skinned, bright-eyed boy resemble his father that John Rawlins had told Sherman that on the cars coming down to Vicksburg he had been able to identify Mrs. Sherman, simply by looking at Willy. Tall for his age and strong, with an alert intelligent gaze, and a more restrained manner than his younger brother, as if he realized his importance as the oldest male, heir to the name, and, if Sherman had his way, the military mantle. Judging by Willy's behavior the father had no fears on that score, for no sooner had Willy arrived than he was taking from the corps commander's locker dress sword, major general's sash and dress and epaulets, which he placed about his sturdy person like a child who knew he was born to be a soldier. He lunged and parried, cried blood-curdling warnings to traitorous Rebels, and slipped the sword beneath the sash only to study intently, like a commander receiving his battle orders, the maps spread out upon the trestle table under the tent fly.

"I'm honored to meet you, sir," Willy said, looking up directly into Cartwright's amused, bespectacled eyes. His was the manner of a gentle, polite, and reflective little boy, completely at odds with his father's attempts to portray him as a rough and tumble rascal who had once ter-rorized his sisters.

"I hope you're enjoying your stay here in our encampment on the beautiful Big Black River?" Cartwright tried and failed to keep his usual cynicism at bay.

"Very much so, sir, thank you. Yesterday Father and I went for a ride to see the colored pickets out at Bald Ground Creek. There is a very funny-looking Negro with a terrible meat cleaver hanging from his belt and a large ostrich feather in his hat. He sits a horse that is even older than he is." Willy laughed the same skipping laughter as his father, only his was youthful and ingenuous. Cartwright and Sherman laughed right along with him. "He told Father very seriously that he need not be alarmed for his army while he was on guard duty." Willy puffed up his chest in imitation of the brave Negro.

"No doubt General Sherman was relieved to hear that?" the surgeon said.

"Oh he was, sir. He was the only one of our group not to laugh at that funny-looking Negro. Last week Father took us all to see his old camps outside Vicksburg. I found some minié balls and pieces of shell." Willy brought them from his pockets to show Cartwright, who examined them carefully, with interest, not like a man who had been removing them from human flesh for the past thirty-one months. Maybe there was hope for him yet. Maybe he just needed a dose of fatherhood to soften the cynicism. "We went to see General McPherson in Vicksburg so that Father could advise him how to deal with the Rebels of that city."

Sherman rubbed a hand over the boy's red hair. Like Sherman's hair it was straight and not easily tamed without a lick.

"I don't believe General McPherson needs my advice, Willy, but thank you, sir, for that vote of confidence. General McPherson has his headquarters on one floor of Dr. Balfour's house, corner of Cherry and Crawford streets," Sherman continued conversationally, speaking directly to Cartwright. "There are some very interesting young ladies in the house."

"Really?" Cartwright made a great fuss of straightening the frayed collar on his shirt. "I don't suppose you could arrange an introduction to one of them, could you?"

"What could I possibly say to recommend you to *any* young lady, sir?" Sherman tapped the top of the whiskey bottle sticking out of the surgeon's pocket. "Especially the refined young ladies residing at Dr. Balfour's house."

"You could call attention to my profession, that always goes down well with the ladies." Cartwright raised and lowered his eyebrows.

"Have you heard from General Ransom?" Sherman asked Jesse, bringing up the subject, Cartwright suspected, to annoy him. "He's in Natchez. General Grant sent him there to capture and bring up to Vicksburg beef cattle that the Rebs had been collecting to feed Joe Johnston's army. General Grant stopped to see him on his way to New Orleans. He says Natchez was full of bitter Secesh women."

Females, especially the Southern variety, seemed to be a subject very much on Sherman's mind that morning, Cartwright reflected. Perhaps it was the proximity of *Mrs.* Sherman. "I don't mind 'em bitter," he said with a grin, rubbing his hands together.

Sherman ignored him. "Are you making the most of your free time, as I advised you, reading and broadening your mind?" he asked Jesse.

"I'm teaching the lieutenant to fish," Cartwright said.

"Fine sturdy rods, sir." Sherman examined Jesse's rod, using it as a switch across the palm of his hand.

"There's nothing to teach," Jesse wrinkled her pug nose, "you just sit on the edge of the bank and let the string dangle in the water until some poor fish swims along and takes the bait and that's it. He never catches anything anyway." She threw a disdainful look in Cartwright's direction.

"No, because you talk too much," Cartwright said, "you never stop your yammering. It scares the fish away. They're not stupid, they know there's someone up there waiting to catch 'em. The whole point of fishing is to lie there quietly, dozing, not talk the hind legs off a donkey."

"You can lie there quietly, dozing, *without* a fishing rod," Jesse pointed out. "I prefer to read."

"Then read, no one's stopping you, but you don't read, you yammer. You read and then you yammer. You have to talk about everything you read, book or newspaper."

"I can't help it if you'd rather lie there with a vacant smile on your face than discuss important topics."

"Important topics—you call politics and poetry important topics?"

"Willy, did you know that Benjamin Franklin organized the first library in America?" Sherman told his son, leaving the girl and surgeon standing there arguing with each other. "Your grandfather Mr. Ewing once walked forty miles as a youth to borrow a book. You, Willy, have only to reach up and take one from the shelf."

25

Times that try men's souls

Child of mine, you fill me with anguish;
To be that pennant would be too fearful;
Little you know what it is this day, and after this day, forever;
It is to gain nothing, but risk and defy everything;
Forward to stand in front of wars—and O, such wars!—
  what have you to do with them?
With passions of demons, slaughter, premature death?

—Walt Whitman, "Sing of the Banner at Day-Break"

The talk in the camps at Big Black those latter days of September was of the Federal troops in Tennessee. The Army of the Cumberland, bottled up at Chattanooga by Bragg, was literally starving to death. Washington was in a panic. They had sent troops from the east but Grant was ordered to send a division. He sent Sherman's First Division. The day after they departed Sherman went to see Grant at Vicksburg. On his return, a galvanized Sherman gave the immediate order for his tents to be struck. Grant wanted not only *Sherman's divisions* in Chattanooga; he wanted *Sherman*.

The idyllic days in the grove of oaks, known as "Polliwoggle Retreat," were over and no one who saw Sherman could doubt that he was elated to be once more a man with a mission.

Jesse dismounted and tied Quicksand's lead rein to the back of a folding chair that had been brought from Mrs. Sherman's tents, now spread across the ground in the haste to dismantle the camp and load everything onto the wagons. All was confusion, ordered confusion it was true, but confusion, nonetheless. After being knocked aside several times, abused and scolded and cussed at, Jesse finally managed to get to Major Jackson, who was bad-temperedly supervising the loading of Mrs. Sherman's baggage into the wagons.

His small, sharp eyes glared at her as he was forced to start counting trunks all over again.

Finally he said, "Now what's so gall-darned important it can't wait 'til I'm finished?"

"I can't find the general anywhere, sir."

"That's 'cos he *ain't* here."

"I need to be reassigned, sir."

"Reassigned? From where to where?"

"Why, sir, from the medical department *back* to the general's headquarters. The general said I could return immediately Mrs. Sherman departed, sir."

"I don't know nuthin' 'bout that. Now get out from under my feet before I have you horse-whipped."

Jesse found Major Van Allen. The New Englander told her patiently that General Sherman had taken his family into Vicksburg. He had booked passage for them on the *Atlantic*.

"The general and his staff will go with them as far as Memphis, then his family will continue on to the north and we'll head for Chattanooga."

"He left without me?" Jesse was horrified.

Van Allen's smile became laughter. "Well, Lieutenant Davis, I wouldn't be too offended. He had a lot on his mind. Will you take my advice? Remain with Dr. Cartwright until I have a chance to speak with the general at Memphis. I'm sure that when he recalls having lost one of his most trusted aides he'll right this terrible wrong and you'll be back in the bosom of your army family."

"But sir—why can't I just stay with you? I have all my belongings in my saddlebags." She indicated Quicksand, who stopped chewing the canvas chair long enough to lift his handsome head and nod lazily.

"I cannot give the order for you to be reassigned to headquarters. You have to wait for General Sherman. Away you go, before Major Jackson has the both of us marched off by the provost guard."

Jesse looked across at Jackson, who was watching them with those small, gray, suspicious eyes, the same small, gray, suspicious eyes that had watched her since Pittsburg Landing. She collected her horse before the animal had completely chewed off the canvas seat and hurriedly joined the columns of marching men heading for Vicksburg.

The wharf at Vicksburg was a writhing mass of blue-clad soldiers. The excited men of Sherman's corps talked and laughed and sang as they waited impatiently to file onto the transports for the first leg of their trip downriver to Memphis. The Army of the Cumberland needed rescuing and these veterans of Shiloh and Vicksburg were the right ones to do the job.

Moving among this noisy gathering was one diminutive lieutenant, hat squashed under her arm, a look of gritty determination on her sunburned face. She pushed past cussing teamsters and their stubborn mules, elbowed cooks and clerks aside, endured the threats of bad-tempered officers, slid between the wheels of the wagons lining the quayside, clambered over artillery pieces and caissons stacked high with ammunition, and ran up the gangway, finally reaching her goal, Major Van Allen on the deck of the *Atlantic*.

"Sir, did you manage to speak with General Sherman about having me reassigned?"

"No, Jesse, I'm afraid not."

"Do you think you will have an opportunity to speak with the general at Memphis, sir?"

"I doubt that—look around you. You know the general; he takes personal responsibility for everything and everybody under his command. He also has to make certain his family is safely on their way back North."

"Then I might not be reassigned until we reach Chattanooga?" Her voice and expression were becoming ever more desperate.

"That's possible."

"And even then, sir, the general will be busy relieving General Rosecrans, I might not get reassigned until after the campaign?"

The kindly New Englander looked at her anxious face. He took a second to think and then against his better judgment suggested that she take passage with them on the *Atlantic*. "We have room for an extra lieutenant. I cannot see why you should not join us for the trip to Memphis. No doubt between here and there we'll find an opportunity to talk to General Sherman about having you reassigned."

"Oh thank you, sir!" Jesse called out. She was already running down the gangway.

"But if Major Jackson asks—it *was not* my idea—" the aide murmured under his breath.

Cartwright stared at her. Jesse wanted his permission to travel to Memphis on the *Atlantic*—after all, he was her commanding officer. It wasn't New Year, but he'd made two resolutions, one of which, it was true, had been thrust upon him; the other made good sense if he didn't want to end up like his father. But it wasn't going to be easy—after all these weeks of having her to himself, it was a wrench now to let her go.

"We'll meet up at Memphis, right?" he said at last.

"I hope I shall have been reassigned to the general's headquarters by then," the girl said, smiling at him and saluting. "But we'll certainly see each other in Chattanooga. Thank you, sir."

He returned her salute uncertainly, not a real salute, a kind of limp flick of his wrist, but then he'd had very little practice. He stood there as the girl took her affectionate leave of Jacob. She led her horse up the gangway onto the side-wheel steamer. He looked at the Dutchman, who was watching him with a sympathetic, indulgent smile.

"I'm trying," he said. He held out his hands that were trembling ever so slightly. "Rock steady."

The older man embraced him. "You are a paragon, an example to us all."

"I wouldn't go that far," the surgeon murmured.

Ten minutes after the steamer was due to depart, it was still at the quayside, the gangway still in place. Jesse stood on the deck, out of sight, but within earshot of the general and his wife as they made the discovery that Willy was missing. The general sent an officer of the Thirteenth Regulars to the Balfour House. In a little while he returned with Willy in tow, a little sergeant, red-faced and sheepish, aware that he deserved a good drubbing for being absent without leave. No doubt relieved at having him returned safely, Sherman thanked the captain for his diligence and teased the boy about the small double-barreled shotgun he was toting.

"What do you have there, Sergeant? Carrying off captured property, sir?"

"No, Father," the boy replied in an unusually subdued tone. "Uncle James gave it to me as a gift."

"Very well." Sherman tenderly smoothed the child's disheveled hair.

The whistle blew for a second time. The waters were churned up by the paddle wheel. Jesse waved to Cartwright and Jacob from the deck and they waved back.

By midafternoon, the steamer had made up lost time. Sherman and his family returned from their after-dinner sojourn to stand by the guardrail. Jesse hung about on deck, biding her time, and when Sherman moved some way from his family to light his cigar Jesse saw her chance.

"Sir, I'm sorry to disturb you, but may I remind you that I've not yet been reassigned to your headquarters?"

Sherman looked at her over the top of the match flame as he puffed. "Not now," he said dismissively. "I have my family." He turned back to Willy, careful to keep the cigar smoke from the boy's eyes.

Sherman showed his son the places of interest on the great river and received what was for Willy an uncharacteristically lethargic response. When they reached Young's Point, the Ohioan became particularly excited. As he explained in great detail how his men had spent months digging canals, fighting Mississippi mud and all manner of diseases, as well as the Rebels, the boy leaned against his father's leg as though he did not have the energy to stand on his own two feet. For the first time Sherman, up until that moment lost in the enthusiasm of relating his story, appeared to notice that the child was not himself. The father questioned his son, and then took him below.

It was late afternoon before Jesse could speak with Major Van Allen to ask him, "Sir, what's wrong with Willy?" There had been much commotion outside the child's cabin, and Dr. Roler of the Fifty-fifth Illinois, who happened to be onboard, had been called. He had remained with the child for several hours.

The New Englander looked distraught. He knew what Sherman's eldest son meant to him.

"Dr. Roler believes it may be typhoid. He wants to get Willy to Memphis as soon as possible."

The *Atlantic* finally arrived in Memphis on October 2.

Jesse stood at the guardrail as Sherman carried his sick child carefully down the gangway wrapped in a blanket, the beloved red head just visible against the father's arm. She could not take her eyes off the Ohioan's face, half-hidden by his slouch hat. The hard-bitten features looked to have been set in gray molding clay, which, in a moment of fury, the sculptor had slashed with a knife.

Behind him came a weeping Mrs. Sherman and the other children.

Jesse rode directly to the Gayoso Hotel. She made it as far as the second floor, where she'd heard Willy was being examined by all the best physicians in Memphis, before Major Jackson spotted her.

"Stop yer sneekin' around and get back to camp," he told her. "There's nothing you can do here."

Jesse went down to the foyer and found a space in a corner behind some potted plants. Perhaps they would need someone to run an errand; she was quick and bright, the general always said that about her.

Daylight was trying to creep under the shutters in the now-empty foyer when Jesse, awake all night, saw Major Jackson striding across the carpet to the front doors. She jumped up and called him. He turned and stared at her, then he took off his hat and scratched his head.

"Well, I'll be a lop-eared—I was just comin' to get you. The gen'al wants to see you." He manhandled her around and gave her an unnecessary shove toward the elevator. This was one time that the scrupulously truthful and plain-speaking Hoosier appeared unable to bring those small gray eyes into contact with Jesse's earnest, questioning gaze.

In a room on the second floor, where twelve months ago Sherman had held ruthless but benign sway over the wavering citizens of this Secesh city, Jesse now found him awaiting her arrival. He was standing at the window, staring out at the emerging dawn, his back to the door, smoking a cigar. He was one of those restless creatures who cannot be closed up without a glimpse of sky, open fields, a horizon beyond which the naked eye can see, as an unhappy animal will pace the floor of his cage, stare longingly through the bars at some image in his own imagination, memory, vision, of a time when freedom was his. Sherman was like one of those caged animals. In any room or tent, he would be drawn automatically to the window or flaps where the open road beckoned like a siren song.

Without turning around he said, "Thank you for coming."

"You have no need to thank me." When he remained silent she said, "How is Willy?"

"The doctors say there is nothing more to be done. My son lies there dying, so brave, though he realizes that he is breathing his last hours on earth."

"I'm . . . so . . . sorry—" Her eyes had filled with tears, but Sherman's next words were destined to fill them with consternation.

"I asked you to come here because even before the Shiloh Battle, I had heard the men talking about you, about your . . . your powers of healing." As the Ohioan turned from the window and looked at her for the first time, she saw that the past few days had taken their toll, more than all the marching and fighting, fighting not only with the Rebels, but with political generals and newspapers. The lines in that molded-clay face had deepened almost to scars, the mouth was straight and turning bitter, only the eyes revealed the pain of a father struggling to come to terms with the knowledge that his dearest child, the one who was the extension of his own life and ambitions, might soon be taken from him.

Jesse briefly shook her head, her big sad eyes on the lined map of sorrow that was his face.

"All who have spoken about you to me, even the rational Major Jackson, a man who would doubt the evidence of his own eyes—" He paused to lift a trembling hand to his furrowed brow. Sherman the realist was evidently very uncomfortable with what he was about to say. "At Chewalla, while we were salvaging the cars from the swamps, I was stricken with malarial fever. You nursed me."

"Dr. Cartwright brought you back to health, sir, Doctor Cartwright and quinine."

"*No.* That is not the whole story. Major Jackson told me." His tone and his eyes were hardening a degree with every word. "He told me you reduced my fever by merely placing your hand on my burning brow. He told me how you spoke in the voice of my Minnie and thereby comforted me when I might have sent you away from me, when you *knew* I *would* have sent you away from me."

Jesse was staring at him, at last understanding. She moistened her lips before she said finally, and with finality, "I *cannot* help your son."

Sherman came near and placed a hand on her shoulder. He spoke inexorably, as if his ears were closed to her protestations. "We both know that you are different. Do you recall you once told me, you are anything we wish you to be? I have at times suspected that might be true—the idealistic Cartwright, the compassionate Dutchman, the moral young Ransom, my own aides, the roughest, wildest men of my Fifteenth Corps. Can you deny that you affect all who touch or are touched by you?"

"I too have been profoundly touched by those I have known here—"

Sherman gave a dismissive shake of his head as if her feelings did not count at this moment. "Jesse, I would not ask for me, *believe me,* if it were not for my poor wife—"

"Sir." She looked him directly in his deep-set piercing eyes. "I cannot help the boy. I cannot save Willy's life any more than—"

"I care little for my own future and will care even less without my precious son." He leaned forward and spoke into her face in that rasping voice. He seemed not to have heard her, or wasn't listening, except to the grief in his own heart. "Willy is my namesake. The child on whose future I have based all the ambition I ever had, the child who will follow me into the army. Willy *is* my future! I am not a religious man, though, as you know, I believe in God. I ask this of you not for myself, but for Mrs. Sherman, who blames herself for not realizing sooner that our child was so ill. Yet I know I am the guilty one for bringing Willy to this sickly region in the summertime, but I truly believed my camps were clean and free of fever, and I have ever put my duty to my country, to the lawful government before all else. If this is God's punishment for my devotion to country above family, then let him punish me and not Willy."

"Please, sir, I beg you, believe me when I say I have no power to help your son. So much do I love you and know how deeply you love your son that I would forfeit my own precious existence now if it would save him. But it would not. I've seen so many brave men breathe their last on the battlefield, in the hospital tents, if I could have given even one of them an extra hour, an extra day of life—would I not have done so? I can offer comfort, hope—"

"He has plenty of comfort and hope from his mother, his brother and sisters," Sherman cut in harshly. "They believe unwaveringly in an everlasting life. They believe that his soul will live forever in heaven. I only know that he is the pride and hope of my life here on earth. I can only believe in the beautiful child with whom I can converse and laugh and hug to my chest. The child that I will lose because I brought him here to this accursed place."

Jesse tried to touch his hand but he shook her off. As the tears overflowed her lashes and ran down her face, he said in a frighteningly composed voice, a voice far more menacing for that. "I ask you once more—" Jesse gazed up at him in silence. "I beg you—" After a second of composing himself, he said, "Get out—you are dismissed."

She left him as she had found him, staring out the window at the blue-gray dawn.

At seven that evening, with his family all around him, with Father Carrier administering last rites and several nuns from Sister Angela's old convent in attendance, William T. Sherman Junior, five months past his ninth birthday, passed away.

His father spent the night searching all of Memphis for a small lead casket.

The following morning the child's mortal remains, dressed in his beloved sergeant's uniform, sealed in that lead casket, was escorted from the Gayoso House with full military honors by the Thirteenth Regulars, weeping bare-headed men of Sergeant Willy's own battalion, to the steamship *Gray Eagle*, for burial in the North.

The regulars gently removed the small coffin from the gun carriage and carried it with deep respect up the gangway, Sherman remaining on the quayside, watching. Among the crowds of mourning soldiers were Seth Cartwright, Jacob De Groot, and Jesse Davis.

Mrs. Sherman, face and eyes red and swollen with weeping, and three of her children boarded the ship for their last journey with their brother.

The *Gray Eagle* steamed slowly out of the harbor and the general, a terrible suffering burned into his brow, turned to the grizzled, hardened veterans, none of whom hid their tears. As he murmured his appreciation, his tragic gaze came to rest, by accident it seemed, upon Jesse. With a tightening of his features, he looked away.

Cartwright put an arm around her shoulders and stared at her sorrowful profile. Under different circumstances, there were reasons he might feel pleased that morning. Ransom was out of his hair, sent off, according to Jacob, who'd had a brief note from him, to Texas as part of Banks' Army of the Gulf, and far away from Jesse, who didn't seem to care about that fact. Somehow Cartwright couldn't rejoice. There was no letup to the slaughter and death.

"That little boy was just as much a victim of this lousy stinking war as if he had been struck down by shot or shell," he said suddenly, bitterly.

An enlisted man, standing near, the veteran of a hundred skirmishes and a dozen battles, from Donelson to Vicksburg, spoke up, as he wiped his damp eyes.

"Yer right there, Doc, and I wouldn't wanna be in the boots a any damn Rebel that crosses Billy Sherman's path from this time on."

The war would not stop because William Tecumseh Sherman had lost his son.

Sons were dying every day. There was little time to grieve.

Charged with moving his twenty thousand men, their horses, artillery, and equipment, a distance of three hundred miles over steep rolling hills through hostile country and across the Tennessee River, urged by Henry Halleck in Washington to "act with all possible promptness," Sherman's duty was clear to him.

His special orders were to make all haste to Chattanooga, using the Memphis and Charleston Railroad, repairing it as he went, and to draw supplies on that route so that no further burden should be put on the already overtaxed roads back to Nashville, upon which Rosecrans's besieged forces in Chattanooga were dependent for their meager rations.

On October 2, 1863, as Sherman and his family had arrived at Memphis with their mortally sick child, the Ohioan had learned the movements of his divisions. General Osterhaus had already taken his by rail as far as Corinth. The Second Division was ready to start for that place by the same means after reaching Memphis in tandem with their corps commander. The Fourth Division, led by General John Corse, had arrived two days later.

The railroad as far as Corinth, already two-thirds destroyed and running across territory wide open to Rebel guerrillas and cavalry, was being repaired daily, but cars to carry the troops and locomotives to pull them were in short supply. Therefore it wasn't until the ninth that the Second Division got off, followed by the Fourth, who gave new meaning to the phrase "foot soldiers." Because of the lack of rolling stock and Sherman's worries for the safety of a railroad, they were set off overland, with artillery and horses, to march the ninety-six miles to Corinth.

Sherman was forced to wait three more days for a special train. But during the time of Mrs. Sherman's departure and his own, he had thrown himself into making his usual detailed and meticulous arrangements. A welcome diversion for a man who could not sleep, nor even close his eyes, without seeing the sweet face of his lost child.

Every day Jesse appeared at his headquarters, and every day Captain Jackson told her, "Get yerself back to the hospital. If the gen'al wants yer, he'll send for yer."

On Sunday the eleventh, while most of Memphis was still abed, Sherman and his entire headquarters staff, along with clerks, orderlies, and horses, boarded the cars.

On the roof were the faithful battalion of the Thirteenth United States Regulars, *Willy's own.*

Jesse Davis tied Quicksand's lead rope to the tailboard of a nearby wagon and quickly approached Major Van Allen as he was heading toward Sherman and a group of officers.

"Sir." She touched his arm, in her eyes such a desperation that he said, "Wait here a moment, Lieutenant."

She watched him speak to Sherman, and saw the Ohioan give a downward jerk of his head. She held her breath until the New Englander's return.

"You may travel on the cars with the horses, Jesse." He saw her face. Her eyes. "I'm sorry, it's the best I can do."

"No—no sir, that's . . . wonderful—at least I'll be on the same train as the general." The journey between Memphis and Chattanooga was a long one, over the roughest, most difficult terrain; anything could happen.

He touched her arm, his brief smile reassuring.

Jesse traveled in one of the horseboxes with Quicksand. There were worse places to be, but with the heat, and the flies, and the steaming horse manure it would have been difficult to think of one. There was an air of melancholy about the horses this morning. Jesse knew how they felt. Dear old Sam, their leader, so beloved of Sergeant Willy as he rode in reviews by his father's side, had been left with Captain Lewis, the quartermaster at Memphis, to be sent on to Lancaster. Sam's war was over. His master wished him kept safe for Willy's sake. He had earned an honorable discharge and comfortable retirement, but he would be sorely missed, by his fellow mounts and by a commander who had grown to respect his courage and fortitude.

Jesse pressed her face to the wooden slats. They were passing through Germantown, eight miles out of Memphis. She had dropped off, but not completely, and a noise had brought her back to wakefulness. Now she could hear shouting, but it wasn't the Rebels, it was the men of the Thirteenth Regulars crowded onto the roof of the train, jeering and laughing at their less fortunate comrades, Corse's division marching beside the track. Several well-aimed missiles were traded, among them tin cups and plates that clattered against the boxcars, as well as a battery of equally bruising insults. Soon however Corse's footsore soldiers and their loud cursing were left far behind.

Around noon Jesse squinted once more through the slats as the sun's rays slanted across the dusty boxcar. They were coming into Colliersville station, where soldiers from the small garrison guarding the depot waved at their comrades and exchanged the usual bantering. The train went right on through without stopping.

Another half-mile down the line the train suddenly jolted, throwing several of the horses against the sides of the car, then shunted back and forth and slowed down. Jesse spent the next few minutes trying to calm the nervous animals as they moved restlessly about in the stiflingly hot, confined space, before the train finally came to a shuddering halt. She stared through the slats. All she could see were Sherman's men running up and down the platform. While she stood there trying to decide what to do next there were several bursts of sporadic gunfire, followed by shouting. A blue-clad soldier paused outside the boxcar, a single shot rang out and he fell clutching his stomach. There was the chatter of musketry and a terrific roar and crash that she recognized as cannon firing, a roar and crash that was quickly answered.

The Rebels were attacking the train.

In another moment she heard horses pounding down the embankment, saw the gray uniforms of Rebel cavalry, shouted orders, the flash of gunpowder. She snatched up her carbine and checked the chamber. It was fully loaded, but as she stood beside the door, it was abruptly and violently thrown open. She just managed to jump aside as a lighted torch was tossed onto the hay by a heavily bearded lieutenant. She had never acted so quickly in her life. She grabbed Dolly's head rein, led her to the entrance, and found herself face to face with the Rebel lieutenant and two others, all wearing self-satisfied grins.

"Too hot in thar, Yankee boy?" one demanded to know, waving his pistol in the air.

They had already put down a ramp. The lieutenant leapt up onto the car, snatched Dolly's reins from Jesse's hands, and shoved her aside as though she was no more nuisance than a fly. He then sent the heaving, sweating, and overexcited animal down the ramp to his fellow soldiers. Then he stared around him with wild eyes, eyes that alighted on the handsome palomino, which was a terrible mistake. Jesse got to her feet and held onto the Rebel's arm. He tried to shake her off, but with Quicksand bucking and kicking and the straw on fire around his feet, this time she was not so easy to dislodge. He released Quicksand and brought his hand around, striking Jesse across the right ear. Staggering, lights flashing inside her head, she fell back against the side of the car and sank down, stunned by the violence of the blow and bleeding from her ear. She was conscious, barely, watching as though through a trembling mist as Quicksand, rolling his eyes until the red had completely filled the outer corners of the sockets, reared up on his hind legs and brought his front near foot down upon the Rebel lieutenant's head, crushing the skull with the ease of a sledgehammer crushing an egg, and with quite as messy a result. There was more firing, shouting, cursing; a shot pierced the wooden slats just above her head. Blue-clad men were leading the horses gently down the ramp as the flames licked up the side of the boxcar. Thank God the horses would be safe. Jesse's eyelids drooped.

"Sir, those godforsaken Reb bastards, if you'll excuse me, have made a bloody mess a the rear of this train, sir—got their filthy hands on five of our best horses, sir, and it would have been more but for the lad—he tried his damnedest to stop 'em, sir, and got a goddamn box on the ears for his trouble, sir." Sergeant O'Connor, head teamster, was in full flow. "Sir—those thievin' bastards tried to have it away with the lad's own beloved animal, sir—but that dee-vil of a beast went berserk, sir, I ain't never seen nuthin' to compare—crushed that Reb's skull to a gray pulp right after he laid his fists upon the young lieutenant. He's deader than a turkey at Thanksgivin'."

Andy and Marcus exchanged looks. Andy lifted his hat and was scratching his head as he looked at the mess of bone, blood, and brains spread across the damp straw.

Jesse opened her eyes. For a moment, she had trouble remembering where she was and what had happened, but a sharp pain in her ear and the smell of burned straw quickly reminded her. She looked dazedly over to where the teamster was pointing, as if General Sherman couldn't see for himself the Rebel officer with a crushed gray pulp where his brains had once been. Sherman waited for the last of the horses to be led down the ramp, then, without a word, he tossed his cigar stub aside and walked up the ramp. He stood there a moment, unable to take his piercing eyes off Jesse's face as she stared up at him. Her cheeks were smeared with soot and sweat and her beautiful eyes made red by the smoke. That strong jaw already bore the promise of dark bruising, but it was the thin trickle of blood, which came from inside her right ear and ran down her neck into the grimy collar of her shirt that held him fascinated. He knelt down, held her chin, and turning it aside, asked in an emotionally thickened voice, "What have they done to you, Lieutenant Davis?" He took the clean handkerchief that Van Allen held out to him and dabbed at her bleeding ear.

"They got your favorite mare, sir. I tried to stop them, but there were too many of them and the flames made the horses crazy. More than anything, sir, horses hate fire. Though I stopped them getting Duke, they badly wanted Duke and Quicksand, but Dolly has gone."

"I appreciate your grand efforts on my behalf, Lieutenant." He drew in a deep breath. "I regret the loss of my favorite mare, but it affords me great satisfaction to know that she'll break the neck of the first guerrilla that fires a pistol from her back. Can you stand, Lieutenant, if I assist you?" He held her about the waist and she got groggily to her feet. Even when she became more steady he gave her his arm to lean on as they walked slowly down the ramp.

"Quicksand saved my life, sir," she said. "The Rebel struck me across the ear and would have done worse if not for Quicksand."

At that moment an orderly came running up, saluted, and blurted out nervously to Sherman, "Sir, they got your second-best uniform."

"Goddamn those wretches," Sherman cried. "Did they victimize only General Sherman?"

"Oh no, sir," the orderly said, smiling suddenly, relieved that he could report the tale of another officer's woe. "The Rebs used Colonel Auden-reid's fine shirts to kindle the blaze."

"That makes *me* feel better, but I am damned sure the news will bring no relief whatsoever to Colonel Audenreid."

It was indeed a fine greeting for a new member of the commander's staff.

Sherman was staring out of the train window into a darkness studded with the crackling bivouac fires of his Thirteenth Regulars as they cooked their evening meal. Jesse placed the tin plate and coffee cup on the wooden seat beside him. He looked at her reflection in the window.

"Did you see my surgeon about your ear?" he inquired tersely.

"Yes sir." The hearing seemed to have lessened on that side, but the surgeon had assured her it was only a temporary condition. "Will you eat something?"

He glanced with disinterest at the plate of food and then out of the window at the shimmering campfires. The sight somehow comforted him. "I confess, I am somewhat ashamed—I should not have asked you to help my son. My grief and that of Mrs. Sherman combined was more than I could bear."

"Please, you don't have—"

"Let me finish. As I told you before, I do not believe in spectral visions, unearthly phantoms, or any such nonsense, but that night I was not myself. You were right to refuse my request."

"Sir"—Jesse's frown deepened to show the extent of her almost physical pain—"I did not refuse. I spoke the truth; I had no power to help your son."

"I can see my little boy now stumbling over the sand hills on Harrison Street in San Francisco, where he was born, eating his supper at the table in Leavenworth, running to meet me with open arms at Black River. Will my son ever understand and forgive me—with so many officers requesting furloughs I felt it my duty to remain with my command and bring my family to me."

"They wanted to come here; Mrs. Sherman and the children were excited to see you."

"*I know that*," he flared up, "but they came at my bidding. *I* told them that my camps were free of fever."

"How do you know Willy became ill at our camp? He went to Vicksburg often, he rode about Big Black. It wasn't your fault, you acted in good faith."

"Good faith—what is good faith when the life of my beloved child has ebbed away—tell me, why should my son be taken from us? Would that I could subside into some quiet corner and live the remainder of my life in peace—but how can I? I will go on to the end but the chief stay to my faltering heart is now gone."

"Willy thought himself a sergeant of the Thirteenth; he showed the same courage in death as he had shown in life. If you falter now other fathers will weep as you weep now, as they *have* wept in the past two years and there will be no end to their tears. The war will not cease, even for a moment, to listen to the sound of one father weeping for a lost son. You, sir, know the truth of this better than anyone, for would you not tell a mourning father to dry his tears and go on and do his duty for his country as you have done these past few days?"

"Let me alone, Jesse," he said in a voice devoid of emotion, "I wish to be alone with my memories, with my grief."

The following morning, with the locomotive and railroad repaired, the train was ready to continue on to Corinth. Jesse approached Sherman on the platform as he was about to climb aboard. He stopped, looked at her, and waited.

"Sir, I realize you have much on your mind and I hesitate to ask, but in our camp on the Big Black you had me transferred to the medical department and I have remained there for four months. May I now know my duties and my fate?"

"Your fate, Lieutenant Davis, is known only to Almighty God; your duties, however, are well known to yourself, as you have on many occasions demonstrated to the complete satisfaction of your commander. Now hasten aboard, sir, hasten aboard, we have a long way to go."

Jesse stood on the platform car at the rear of the train. She felt as if she was saying good-bye to something. Something was ending and another thing taking its place. However, the ending and the beginning were not yet complete. She needed to perform some kind of ceremony. She brought a sheet of folded paper from inside her shirt. She dropped her saddened gaze to the final lines of Thomas Ransom's year-old letter.

"—But most of all I think of you, your compassion and courage, your love of country, my darling Jesse, a bright and constant light, guiding us all through the dark days to come—"

With a deep breath and setting her face determinedly, she screwed up the letter and tossed it onto the tracks. In a moment, it was out of sight, left behind, a painful if sobering memory.

They were on their way to Chattanooga, where the Army of the Cumberland was besieged in the shadow of Lookout Mountain and, after that, it could be Mobile, Alabama, or Atlanta, Georgia, or even Virginia. Already there had been rumors that Sherman would be given the Army of the Potomac. He would resist any efforts on the part of Washington to send him east, to the Virginia battlefields. His mission, as he saw it, was to protect the newly liberated Mississippi.

As for her, she also knew her mission. She had lost sight of it for a while there, but that was to be expected. Romantic love was the most powerful of all human emotions. Stronger even than fear and greed, vanity and man's desire to go to war—why, it had even been known to stand up to death itself. More than once she'd heard Seth liken it to a fever that no amount of quinine could dispel. It has to run its course, he had said. In her it had run its course and now, thankfully, she'd come to her senses again. The fever was passed. She had woken up with a clear head.

She went into the car. Across the aisle Sherman's harsh voice was raised in bitterness:

"I was wrong, gentlemen, two years have passed and the Rebel flag still haunts our nation's capital. I see no end—or even the beginning of the end. Jeff Davis is as defiant as ever, and will not stop until the South is on her knees, begging for mercy. We cannot change the hearts of these people of the South, but we can make war so terrible and make them so sick of war that generations will pass before they again appeal to it. War is the remedy our enemies have chosen and I say let us give them all they want, not a word of argument, not a sign of letup, no cave in, till we are whipped—or they are!"

Oh yes, she knew her mission. She clutched at the compass Sherman had given her. He was right; she would never again lose her way.

Acknowledgments

★ ★ ★ ★

I would like to begin by acknowledging my unquantifiable debt to Major General William Tecumseh Sherman—to his incomparable *Memoirs*, his published letters, his unforgettable quotes, his inexhaustible opinions on every subject under the sun, and his indefatigable energy in conveying them to posterity. It is on these that I have based my humble portrait of this great American patriot and the story of his war. The characters who surround him, with obvious exceptions, are of course fictional, the better to tell his story, and theirs.

I also acknowledge a debt to all Sherman biographers and to the best histories of that war.

If an author is fortunate, the most important person on the list of those to thank will be his or her editor. I am one of the most fortunate. My editor is Robert D. Loomis. He does not lead a horse to water—he simply points out the well. Sometimes he just tells me it exists. That is his genius.

My gratitude goes to the following people:

Mark J. Schaadt, M.D., chairman of the Department of Emergency Medicine at Blessing Hospital in Quincy, Illinois, and one of the country's foremost experts on Civil War medicine and surgery. He became my guide and mentor through the blood and horror of a Civil War operating tent.

My research on Thomas E. G. Ransom would have come to a frustrating halt if not for James Huffstodt, author of *Hard Dying Men*, the story of General T.E.G. Ransom, and his Eleventh Illinois. Jim's great-grandfather Martin Baker served under Ransom as a private soldier.

Mary Carpenter, support services manager at Council Bluffs Public Library, Iowa, tracked down much of the information available on Thomas Ransom.

A very personal thank-you goes to my dear friend Marvin Terban—scholar, educator, author. His wit, wisdom, and encouragement never faltered. He helped in ways he understands.

About the Author

S. C. GYLANDERS was born in London and lives there with her husband, Jed. After leaving school at fifteen and struggling through a succession of dead-end jobs, she finally found her vocation. Her first novel was published in 1981. *The Better Angels of Our Nature* is her fourth novel, and the American Civil War is her passion. In 2001 she was responsible for the dedication of a historical marker outside Rome, Georgia, to honor Major General Thomas E. G. Ransom, U.S.A.

About the Type

The text of this book was set in Janson, a misnamed typeface designed in about 1690 by Nicholas Kis, a Hungarian in Amsterdam. In 1919 the matrices became the property of the Stempel Foundry in Frankfurt. It is an old-style book face of excellent clarity and sharpness. Janson serifs are concave and splayed; the contrast between thick and thin strokes is marked.